A Chain of Lakes Series Novel

Dance of Grace

Stacy Monson

Blessings—
Stacy

His Image Publications
Plymouth, Minnesota

Copyright © 2015 Stacy Monson
All rights reserved.

Scripture is taken from the New International Version of the Bible.

ISBN: 978-0-9861245-2-6 (print)
ISBN: 978-0-9861245-3-2 (ebook)

No part of this publication may be reproduced or transmitted in any form or by any means, electronic or mechanical, including photography, recording, or any information storage and retrieval system without the prior written consent from the publisher and author, except in the instance of quotes for reviews. No part of this book may be uploaded without the permission of the publisher and author, nor be otherwise circulated in any form of binding or cover other than that in which it is originally published.

This is a work of fiction and any resemblance to persons, living or dead, or places, actual events or locales is purely coincidental. The characters and names are products of the author's imagination and used fictitiously.

The publisher and author acknowledge the trademark status and trademark ownership of all trademarks, service marks and word marks mentioned in this book.

To those who believe all is lost. The Creator of the Universe knows your name. He created you, loves you, upholds you, and goes before you. He will never leave you.

The Lord is gracious and righteous; our God is full of compassion. The Lord protects the simplehearted; when I was in great need, He saved me. Be at rest once more, O my soul, for the Lord has been good to you. For you, O Lord, have delivered my soul from death, my eyes from tears, my feet from stumbling, that I may walk before the Lord in the land of the living.

Psalm 116:5–9

1

In that moment, Vanessa Jordan was glad her mother was dead.

"I'm going to lose the studio." She tightened her grip on the canes and met Stephen's reluctant gaze squarely.

"I'm afraid I've run out of options, my dear. The last of the potential buyers said there wasn't enough equity in the business to justify the purchase. With the accident more than three months ago, most of the clientele have moved on."

"Not the seniors. There were twenty in the gentle-dance class I started after Christmas. We were building wonderful relationships in the neighborhood." She couldn't let go of her mother's legacy without a fight. "And how about the children? There were so many, we had to add a third class."

He slowly shook his head, concern evident in the pinch of his wiry gray eyebrows. "The studio has been empty since January. Refunds for the cancelled classes put you in the red. No one is making inquiries about the spring schedule anymore." He sighed. "I'm sorry to say, there's no business left to sell."

His words, though spoken kindly, knocked the air from her lungs. Her gaze drifted around the familiar room. The dance studio had been in this corner of the Minneapolis Uptown area for decades. These walls couldn't be finished whispering encouragement to young ballerinas with Sugar Plum Fairy dreams or welcoming nervous beginners, reflecting warmth and love to all who spent time here. She owed it to her family to keep the studio running.

"What if I found some high school students to teach afternoon classes? I'm sure they'd do it in exchange for a free advanced ballet class."

But who would teach the advanced class? She couldn't now. "I don't need much of a salary anymore. Just enough for the mortgage payment and a few groceries. I'll think of some more ideas—"

"Vanessa." Stephen's gentle voice stopped the rush of words. "There's no money to even pay the missed lease payments."

"But Roger has been so kind in the past. I'm sure he'd be willing to wait a little longer until I get on my feet, so to speak, to get caught up. I'll go talk to him right now."

"The space is leased to someone else."

A stinging charge shot through her. "What?"

He removed his glasses and wiped his face with a wrinkled hanky. "The Minneapolis Neighborhood Coalition moves in next week. Roger said he's willing to forgive the missed payments. He sent his condolences and wanted me to tell you how much he admired your family."

The tightness in her throat strangled any words of gratitude. If he meant it, he wouldn't let them all fade into a memory. She turned away and ran her fingers along the wooden barre. At one time she'd had to reach up to it—when she was young and full of dreams.

"So." Her voice echoed in the emptiness. She looked at the reflection of the man who'd been her mother's friend and attorney for all of Vanessa's twenty-four years. He'd always been kind to her and her siblings, like she imagined a favorite uncle might have been. This had to be hard on him too.

"So," she said again, facing him with shoulders set. "Do I need to sign something?"

"Yes." He moved to the counter to retrieve the envelope he'd brought. Pulling out a handful of papers, he sorted through them. "This one is from the bank. This one is from Roger. And this one too."

As she scribbled her name on each, he considered the nearly empty room. "There isn't much for inventory. Shall I try to sell the mirrors and the barres? You can take the coffee pot home. What would you like to do with the coat rack? And this desk..."

His voice faded as decades of memories rushed over her. The wood floor was worn from years of pointe and tap shoes, the paneled walls faded in places where the morning sun had lingered. In the floor-to-ceiling mirrors, she could see the children making faces at each other, chattering as they waited for class to start. How many times had she wiped small handprints off the glass?

"Vanessa?"

She blinked. "I don't want any of it. Sell it, donate it. Leave it for the Coalition." Chin quivering, she pressed her lips together. Failure added an acidic bite to the bitterness of defeat. "If you get any money, give it to Roger for back pay."

Stephen grasped her shoulders, frowning down at her. "My dear, this isn't your fault. You know the studio was in financial trouble before your mother died."

"But the accident—"

"Was an accident." His fingers squeezed gently. "I know you blame yourself, but no one else does. Life is just really unfair sometimes."

"Thank you," she whispered. He was a kind man. Wrong but kind.

He released her with a sigh. "I'll get these papers delivered. And I'll drop you at home on the way."

"I think I'll stick around for a few minutes and then walk home."

"You can walk that far now?"

"I'll manage." She put a hand on his arm. "Stephen, thank you for everything. My mother treasured your friendship and your counsel. So do I."

He hugged her gently. "You've all been family to me. I miss them too." Leaning back, he pressed a kiss to her forehead, his moustache prickly against her skin. "Call me if you need anything."

"I will."

He cast a doubtful glance at her canes then his footsteps faded into silence. Vanessa stood still in the middle of the room and breathed deeply, finding the familiar scent of rosin under the stuffiness. Eyes closed, she rose onto the toes of her good foot. Lifting her face, she tried to remember the magic of an arabesque, the freedom of spinning en pointe, the joy of a final bow.

The canes wobbled and she lowered with a thump. That was all she had now—fragile images of dancing, of her mother and Angie and Matt. Of life as she knew it. She found a scrap of paper in the wastebasket and a lone pen. She wrote the simple words slowly, wedged the sign in the window of the door and turned off the lights. The door shut with a final click and she pressed her fingertips to the glass, the letters blurring as she read the words that spelled the end of her dream. *Thanks for the memories.*

Kurt Wagner stopped at the busy intersection, enjoying a deep breath of spring air and car exhaust. On this bright April morning with the sidewalks of Uptown filled with chatter and activity, who could find anything wrong with life?

He glanced at the clock on the bank sign. Just enough time for his Saturday morning espresso before the meeting started at ten. He might actually be early. Grinning, he turned his attention to the young woman waiting beside him. White-blonde hair gleaming under the sun, she stared down at the ground, leaning heavily on two metal canes. She was way too serious for a Saturday.

"Beautiful morning," he said.

She started and glanced up.

"Sorry. Didn't mean to startle you."

She returned her gaze to the ground. A moment later, as she dug in her coat pocket, one of her canes toppled onto the asphalt.

Kurt retrieved it. "Here you go."

"Thank you."

His smile faded. The heavy coat, more suitable for January than April, dwarfed her small frame; the top of her head barely reached his chin. She couldn't be more than twenty. And the canes...

He tried again. "Are you out running errands?"

She rolled her eyes. "Do I look like I can run anywhere?"

Nice choice of words, Wagner. "Sorry. I meant, you know, just out getting things done."

She deflated with a sigh. "It's all done."

Before he could think of a reply, the walk sign lit and she stepped gingerly off the curb. He watched her slow, measured progress, then shrugged off his curiosity and shifted his backpack over his shoulder. Drawn to the enticing aromas of The Java Depot just ahead, he passed her quickly.

"Look out!"

He was nearly across when a shouted warning jerked his head up. From the left, a black sedan raced through the red light, bass pulsing behind tinted windows. Spinning on his heel, he sprinted back and threw an arm toward the girl. He crashed against her and sent them sprawling as the car roared through the intersection, passing so close a current of air swept over them. Several people shouted expletives at the driver.

For a stunned moment, Kurt struggled for air. When the girl squirmed beneath him, he rolled over and sat up, pulling one of her canes from under his legs. She rose on an elbow and put a hand to the back of her head, pale face scrunched in pain. People gathered around and helped them to their feet.

"Whoa, man. You almost got nailed." A young boy stood beside him, shirttails flapping, a battered skateboard under his arm.

An older woman hovered near the blonde. "Are you all right, dear?"

Kurt rubbed his arm that had taken the brunt of the impact then accepted his backpack from the boy. He slung it over his shoulder and flinched. He was going to be sore tomorrow. Several people slapped him on the back.

"Nice footwork there, buddy."

"You're a hero."

He bit back a laugh. He'd been called a lot of things over the years but never that. Shoving his hands into his pockets, he nodded his thanks and turned toward the girl. She leaned heavily on a cane with one hand, straightening her coat with the other. Her right leg jutted at a slight angle, as if disconnected from her body.

His breath stuck in his throat. Had *he* done that? "Are you okay?"

She pushed the tangle of long hair from her face. "I'm fine." Accepting the second cane from the older woman with murmured thanks, she thrust her arm into the support.

"But your leg—"

"I said I'm *fine*." Her head lifted and frowning blue eyes challenged him, a striking contrast to her frail appearance. "I can take care of myself."

Seriously?

She yanked the errant leg into place. "It doesn't matter, anyway." She turned, wobbled a moment then pressed through the silent onlookers.

"Wait!" Should he follow her? Leave her alone? "Can I at least..."

She crossed the street with an awkward step-hop. Kurt stared after her, fists clenched. It didn't seem right to let her go off by herself, but she clearly didn't want his help.

A long breath escaped. No matter how hard he tried, he always messed something up. Even being a "hero" had managed to hurt a complete stranger. What a loser.

Don't go there. That's the old Kurt.

"Wow," the boy said, still at his side. "She'd be, like, dead meat if you hadn't pushed her. You'd think she'd say thank you or sumpthin'."

"I think she was pretty shook up. Thanks for your help, man." He reached a fist toward the boy who bumped it with his own.

"No problem." He hopped on his skateboard and pushed off in the direction of the young woman, slowing to look her up and down before speeding ahead.

Kurt remained rooted to the sidewalk, his gaze following the girl. The click of the canes reminded him of his former cellmate, Petey, who'd used something similar. Sturdy, with forearm supports and extra padding around the handles, he'd needed them to maneuver the long hallways and, on occasion, to protect himself.

He shoved the memory away. The girl had disappeared into the bustle of activity filling the sidewalk. As the light turned yellow, he jogged across the street to follow her. A glance at the clock changed his mind. Even skipping the espresso, he was going to be late.

A deep, calming breath eased the tension in his shoulders. *It was a good thing to do. Shake it off.* Another cleansing breath unclenched his jaw.

"Watch over her, Lord. I have a feeling she needs it." He turned at the corner. "We both do."

2

The Sunday evening worship service at Faith Community Church released a horde of teens and young adults into the foyer. Kurt pressed back against the cool cement wall to avoid being trampled by an assortment of dirty sneakers, colorful flip-flops, and three-inch heels.

Many in the crowd greeted him as they surged past, offering high fives and throwing out one-liners. They jostled each other, laughing and chatting, checking their phones. Within minutes, the hum of activity and the aroma of fruity perfume and sweaty adolescents faded as the building emptied.

Retrieving the vacuum, he headed to the lobby. He gave thanks often for the growing number of kids attending the Sunday evening service as well as the Wednesday night activities. But it was the kids who'd never go near a church that he worried about and prayed over. Kids who didn't dress or talk like these but who ached with the need for God, for hope, for grace in their hurting lives. He'd been one of them. He still was, at twenty-seven.

He finished vacuuming and stretched, his back and arm still sore from yesterday's near hit-and-run. The wall clock showed thirty minutes until tip-off. Enough time to get something to eat before settling in to watch the Celtics beat the Knicks.

Stepping inside the quiet, spacious sanctuary, he dropped onto the cushioned back pew. The scent of candle wax drifted past where he sat in the fading sunlight. He enjoyed ending his workday in peacefulness like this.

Eyes closed, he offered the simple, familiar prayer. *God, thanks for saving me from me. I don't know why you didn't just let me rot in prison but since you didn't, I'll do whatever I can to show you it wasn't a mistake. I don't know what that is, outside of cleaning this church and trying to help these kids, so I'll just keep at it until you tell me different.*

A hand landed on his shoulder and he jerked away. Nearly three years out of the joint but still on the defensive. "Hey, Joel."

"Sorry. I thought you heard me coming." The senior pastor dropped down beside him. "Boy, this was a long day."

"Yup."

Joel Barten, a man in his mid-forties who looked ten years younger, turned his head and offered a tired smile. "Good work with the senior high kids last Wednesday. I don't think I told you how impressed I was."

Kurt shrugged. "No problem." It wasn't work. He loved hanging out with the kids, talking about God stuff, trying to help them grasp the height and breadth and depth of a God who was beyond understanding. A God who could redeem a broken, useless life in the time it took to put knees to a prison cell floor. "It seemed to go okay."

"It was more than okay, my friend. I heard from several leaders what an outstanding job you did pinch-hitting for Mike. Most people can't keep a hundred junior and senior high kids focused for ten minutes, let alone forty-five." He chuckled. "I know I can't. You shared some pretty powerful stuff that impacted both the kids and the leaders."

Kurt nodded and rubbed the back of his neck, the unexpected praise a sweet surprise. He was beyond grateful for this patient man who had led him to faith inside the prison walls, then offered friendship and a job when he got out. "Thanks for letting me do it."

Joel stood and stretched. "I'm beat. You gonna watch the Celtics?"

He grinned. "Of course."

"No surprise there. See you Tuesday at the all-staff."

Ten minutes later, Kurt locked up the church and headed out to the back parking lot. He pulled in a deep breath of freshly tilled garden dirt, enjoying the chirp of sparrows nested above the light fixture.

The sound of shuffling feet stopped him mid-breath. He turned sharply, every muscle tensed as he scanned the grounds. A lone figure sat on a bench in the center of the garden area, hair pulled into a disheveled ponytail, hands deep in her coat pockets.

People from the neighborhood often came to enjoy the peaceful solitude of the gardens, but not usually this late. He hesitated. He should at least make sure she was okay before heading home.

The scuff of his footsteps was magnified in the stillness, and he had the sudden, ridiculous urge to tiptoe. He stopped a few feet from the bench and cleared his throat. The harsh sound broke the quiet of the evening. "Hi."

Her head turned and their eyes connected. His widened, jumping to the canes resting beside her. It was the girl from the corner! He'd prayed for God to watch over her, to take care of whatever her issue was. Apparently He had—by dropping her back into Kurt's lap. *Now what?*

Vanessa lifted her head. The guy looked familiar. She narrowed her gaze. "I know you."

He settled onto the bench opposite her. "I'm the guy who pushed you away from that car."

"Yeah. The superhero guy."

A frown touched his face.

She bit her lip. *That was uncalled for.* "I'm sorry. I was...rude yesterday." She dropped her gaze to the sidewalk between them. "I appreciate what you did."

"Well, it was probably a shock when I came at you outta nowhere. Are you okay? I was worried."

"I'm fine. Thanks."

He relaxed into a smile. "Good. We sure had a close call. So, I never got your name."

"Vanessa."

"Vanessa. That's pretty. I'm Kurt. Have you been here long?"

She glanced around. Had she? It was almost dark. Time had become unmeasurable since the accident. Minutes blurred into hours, days into weeks. "I'm not sure. I was walking and saw the garden back here. What is this place?"

"Faith Community Church."

She swiveled sharply to look at the building behind her. Where was the steeple? The forbidding cross perched on the rooftop? The solid doors that kept people like her out? "It doesn't look like a church."

"I don't think so either. It's a renovated warehouse."

"I can't believe this is where I ended up." It was the last place in the world she wanted to be.

"Why?"

She met his question with a challenging stare. "Because I hate God."

He didn't flinch. "Why do you hate Him?"

"He's a lousy God." She retrieved the canes and pushed to her feet. "I can't stay here."

"Wait." He stood to face her. "Can't we talk some more? I can see something's wrong."

Her fingers tightened around the handles. "Are you the pastor?"

"No. Just the janitor. But I'd still like to help you."

The fire in her veins faded into numbing grief and her shoulders drooped. "There's nothing you can do." She released a slow breath. "There's nothing anyone can do."

"Maybe if we talked a little..."

She opened her mouth to argue but nothing came out. He'd never understand.

He sank back down on the bench, his expression hopeful. "Can we sit just for another minute?"

She'd run away if she could. But really, did it matter where she was? The pain would follow, wearing her down. It was like being flattened again and again by a steamroller—waves of grief sweeping over her, then rolling back even harder after she managed to grab a breath.

She lowered to the bench and set the canes beside her. Fading sunlight bathed the gardens in golden light. Sparrows resumed their gentle twittering.

The church guy pushed dark hair out of his eyes, tucking it behind his ears. He leaned forward and rested his elbows on his knees. "What happened to make you hate God?"

"He..." She swallowed. "He took the kids." The words had a metallic taste.

"He took the kids," he repeated, then sat up straight. "Are they—did they...die?"

She folded her arms across her stomach. "Yes." The whispered word was a shout that echoed in her empty heart. She fought to hold her ground against the steamroller. *How can they be gone? I did the best I could.*

"Oh. Wow." He ran a hand through wavy hair, releasing a whistling breath. "Do you, maybe, wanna tell me about them?"

Did she? Could she? A light breeze ruffled her hair; overhead lights flickered to life, chasing back the encroaching darkness.

He waited, frowning.

"Angie was...almost fourteen. Matt was sixteen. I promised..." A memory surfaced—sitting at their mother's bedside, clinging to her cold, thin hand. She had promised to watch over the kids, to carry on as best she could. She'd have promised the world at that moment.

"What did you promise?" His gentle question severed the memory.

Their gazes met before she looked away. "To take care of them. I told my mother I would keep them safe."

"Ohhh." He nodded slowly. "They were your sister and brother. Your mom's gone too?"

She managed a nod. Why had she been left to figure out how to live, how to breathe without them? She focused on her hands clenched in her lap. "It was my—" *My fault. It was my fault.* She couldn't say the words out loud.

"I'm really sorry, Vanessa. How's your dad holding up?"

"My parents divorced when I was young. He moved to California and we haven't heard from him since."

His mouth formed a silent "O." It was a moment before he spoke. "So you have friends that help you?"

She shrugged. "I never had much time for friends. When my mom got sick, I helped care for the kids and the house. When she died, I quit college to work full time at her dance studio, but it closed after...after the..." She bit her lip and blinked quickly.

"Man, I can't imagine how hard this is for you."

In the days and weeks after the accident, before people stopped coming by, she'd heard pity like that, seen helpless shock on their faces. It only magnified her loss, made the ache burn hotter. It had been a relief when they left her alone.

"If I could just breathe without feeling like my heart will shatter." Pressing a fist against the constant ache in her chest, her voice was hoarse. "If I could sleep without dreaming about them."

She welcomed the anger that straightened her spine. "You want to know why I hate God? Because He took everything—my family, my future. Even my—" She stopped and closed her eyes, clutching trembling hands together. *Everything that mattered.*

Signing the papers for Stephen yesterday had signed away the only work she knew how to do. The house was all she had left, but soon He would take that as well. "When I go to bed, I hope I won't wake up. But then I do, and I have to face another day alone. Thanks to Him."

The church guy tapped his foot quietly. "I'd be mad at God too," he said finally.

He would? The visiting church people had told her God had a plan, a reason for everything that happened. Not one had commiserated with her, understood the suffocating fear and anger and shock.

"I wish I had a good answer for you, Vanessa. I think, maybe, sometimes just putting one foot in front of the other is all we can do."

Yeah. If I had two feet. "I suppose." The anger slid away, leaving her exhausted and battered, hands limp in her lap. "I miss them every minute of every day. They were great kids, and I messed everything up."

"How?"

Her gaze clung to his kind face. Dark eyebrows angled over the sad questioning in his eyes, inviting her to tell him the whole sordid story. She looked away. "I broke my promise."

"But you're young. No one would expect you to be able to do that."

"I'm old enough to know better."

"Better than what?"

The longing returned but she clamped her lips and looked away with a shrug. "It doesn't matter. I can't change anything now." She rose, the canes wobbling under the effort. "I should go. I'm sorry you had to stay so late."

"I'm not. I'm glad we talked." He stood. "I'll give you a ride home."

"I can walk."

"It's too dark. Nobody should be out walking at this time of night. I promise I'm not a serial killer or anything."

She shrugged. "It wouldn't matter if you were."

"It should." His response was firm. "Everyone should be careful, especially in the city." He directed her across the empty parking lot to a small car that had seen better days. Once she was settled, he jogged around to the driver side. As the engine rattled to life, he raised an eyebrow. "Which way?"

She looked around then back at him. "I'm not sure. I live at 33rd and Dupont, near Lake Calhoun. Does that help? It can't be too far."

"Not far at all."

Minutes later they were parked at the curb. The shadowy two-story seemed to shrink away from its light-filled neighbors. Four broad wooden steps led up to the front porch, which spread across the front of the house. An empty swing at one end swayed in the evening breeze. For an instant she saw Angie settled on it, blonde head bent over an ever-present book. A blink and the image vanished.

"Why do I have to stay?" Tears made the words sting. "I did the best I could. What does God have against me?"

"I wish there was an answer for everything that's happened."

"Me too." She glanced at him then pushed the car door open. "Thanks for the ride."

"Not a problem." He climbed out and came around the car, then matched his pace to hers along the front sidewalk.

Her slow progress up the porch steps brought a burn to her cheeks. Her easy stride had been reduced to a painful Frankenstein kind of walk. She pulled open the screen door then turned to face him.

He held out a business card. "I'm happy to listen, Vanessa. Anytime. Here's my number at the church. Call me if you need anything, okay?"

She accepted the card automatically and lifted her gaze to his. What she needed, he couldn't offer. "Thanks..." She glanced at the card. "Kurt." The tightness in her face softened. "I appreciate it."

Once inside, she stood at the window and watched his taillights disappear around the corner. She stared into the darkness, the faint flicker in her heart fading with the lights. Silence and pain swept over her again and she drew back from the glass. For one brief moment she hadn't felt so completely, utterly alone.

Kurt pulled away from the curb, an odd flutter in his chest as if the significance of what had just happened was far bigger than his ribs could contain. He was glad she'd come to the church, glad he hadn't hurried past her to get home. He had a growing suspicion God had something to do with both.

The blue eyes that had locked on his were shadowed and red-rimmed, huge in her pale face. He'd had no answer for the tragedies that rocked her life, no great words of wisdom to give her peace.

Pastor Joel would have said all the right things, had the right answers. Made her feel better somehow. But it wasn't Joel who had pushed her from the path of the car, and it wasn't Joel who found her in the garden tonight.

Resolve swept through him, tightening his fingers around the steering wheel. *Okay, God. I'm ready for whatever this is. Bring it on.*

3

The staccato ring of the doorbell broke the silence, and Vanessa bolted upright on the couch, sending Merton to the floor with an offended meow. She rubbed her face, trying to clear her mind.

The dream about Matt and Angie had been a montage of picnics and school events, dance recitals and band concerts. Happier times when they'd all been together—laughing, talking, dancing. Pushing her hair from her face, she leaned against the back of the couch and swallowed over a lump of disappointment.

The bell rang again and she tossed the tattered afghan aside, grimacing as she swung her feet to the floor. She knew better than to nap with the artificial leg still attached. It always got tangled in the blanket and never wanted to cooperate when she tried to get up. She couldn't get the hang of living with it, and it hurt like crazy when she put weight on it. There were times when it even ached where there was no leg to rub the pain away. She probably should have continued physical therapy.

With a muttered curse, she pushed herself up and straightened her sweatpants before limping to the door with the canes. The wood floor creaked beneath her uneven gait. Merton jumped up on the rocking chair and settled onto the cushion with his back to her, ears flat.

"Sorry, Mertie."

Through the window she saw the guy from the church waiting on the porch and her heart jumped. *He's back?* She'd been mortified at how pathetic she acted two nights ago. Should she apologize? Or maybe pretend she hadn't heard the bell.

She pulled the front door open and squinted against the sunlight.

"Hi." He grinned at her through the screen door.

She pushed it open. "Hi."

Propping the door with his shoulder, he stuck his hands in his pockets. "I was in the neighborhood and wanted to see how you're doing. And I'm dog-sitting. I thought you might like to meet my friend." He swept his arm back toward the golden retriever sitting at the bottom of the stairs. "This is Fred."

"Fred?"

"I know." He rolled his eyes. "No self-respecting retriever should be named Fred. Duke or Prince, maybe. But not Fred."

The dog stood and gazed up at her, his long feathery tail swinging back and forth. Stepping onto the porch, she wrestled with the sudden desire to bury her face in his coat and cry. Biting her lip, she shoved the feeling down.

She managed a weak smile instead. "He looks like a nice dog."

"He is, but he sheds like crazy. I've got dog hair all over my house, on my clothes. Even in my food. But still, if I had more time, I'd get one just like him. They sure don't come any nicer."

She nodded. "My neighbors have one. The kids loved him."

Kurt's eyebrows tilted upward and he bobbed his head. With dark hair pushed behind his ears, a tiny earring glinting in the light, and holes in his worn jeans, he hardly looked like a guy from the church. But there was something about him, something peaceful and unhurried that spoke to her aching heart.

You've been alone too long. You are definitely losing it.

"So." He lifted his shoulders. "How're you doing?"

"I'm okay." She smoothed her hair then waved a hand toward the living room. "I was just...lying down for a few minutes."

"I slept a lot after my mom died. It was hard just getting dressed some days."

"Yeah." Some days she didn't bother. Luckily she had today.

They stood in stilted silence, studying their feet. The afternoon air, fresh and warm, was a sharp contrast to the chill in the house.

He pulled a slip of paper from his pocket. "I thought of something after I dropped you off the other night that might help. I know this really amazing grief counselor. She helped me a lot after my mom passed. She's easy to talk to, and she's got good ideas on how to get through this. I think you'd like her."

Vanessa took the paper he held out. Talk to a counselor? She didn't have the energy to butter toast. "I'll...think about it."

"My cell and work numbers are on there too. Call me anytime."

She frowned. After months of being alone, it was bizarre that someone was interested in her welfare. "Look. I appreciate you saving me from the car and giving me a ride home the other night, but I can take care of myself."

Shoving his hands in his pockets, he rocked back on his heels and shrugged. Guilt poked her and she dropped her gaze. Her ever-gracious mother would be appalled. He'd come back, after all.

"Really." She softened her tone. "You don't have to worry about me."

"I'm not worried." He didn't look offended. A little uncertain, maybe. "I just thought—people say I'm a pretty good listener. And I dunno...it seems like you could use a friend."

That was an understatement. She needed a friend. And her family...money...health. Pretty much everything. She pulled her right leg back a fraction and glanced down to make sure her pant leg covered her fake foot. "I'm sorry. I didn't used to be so cranky. I was actually pretty friendly before." She lifted a shoulder. "I know that's hard to believe now."

"Not hard to believe at all." He looked sincere. "Well, before I go, is there anything you need? Any errands I could run for you? I've got some free time."

Something flickered inside her at the offer. He had a nice smile. "No, but thanks for stopping by." *Please come back again. It's so quiet with only Mertie to talk to.*

"Sure. Well, see you around."

As he and Fred headed out to the street, she closed the inside door and leaned against it. If only he weren't part of the church.

Hobbling toward the kitchen, she paused to read the slip of paper. Jenny Meyer, Christian Counselor; one phone number. Kurt Wagner, Faith Church; two phone numbers. With a snort, she let the paper flutter to the dining room table as she passed.

No one would change her mind about God. Ever. While He'd knocked her down hard, she'd pulled herself back up. She was still standing—on only one leg, but she was standing. There was nothing He could do to her now that would be worse than what He'd already done. She'd beaten Him at His own game when she refused to stay down.

She filled the teakettle and set it on the stove, then turned to stare past the faded ruffled curtains into the backyard. Familiar despair clutched at her, squeezing the breath from her chest. She folded her arms tightly.

The credit card company had called yet again with a less-than-friendly message. She was almost a year behind in mortgage payments. The disability checks weren't enough to cover payments on all the debt. Her mother's meager life insurance had been eaten up providing for Matt and Angie.

She was slowly coming to grips with losing the dance studio, but it would be unbearable to lose the house. Though the old place was in desperate need of repair, it was filled with memories and love.

The teakettle whistled and she turned back to the stove. She needed a job, but doing what? The only job she'd ever had was teaching at the studio. She couldn't stand on the artificial leg for long. Until she learned how to drive again, she'd need a job on the bus line. And the accident had totaled the car anyway.

Making yet another cup of tea, she wondered how many more times she could get knocked down before she didn't have the strength to get back up.

4

A performance review was hardly the ideal way to end the week. Kurt pushed his hair behind his ears, wishing he'd remembered to get a haircut, and stopped in the doorway of the senior pastor's office. "Hey, Joel."

"Kurt!" Joel's enthusiastic greeting was reassuring. "Come in. I've been looking forward to our meeting."

"Well, that makes one of us." Forcing his shoulders down, Kurt stepped in and closed the door behind him. For a moment he couldn't breathe. Would he ever get past that initial feeling of being closed into a cell?

Joel came around the desk to shake his hand, chuckling. "My friend, this meeting is all about the great work you've been doing around here."

"So why do I feel like I got called into the principal's office?"

"Good question." He raised an eyebrow. "Need to do any confessing?"

"Not that I know of."

"Okay, then. Let's get to the good stuff. Have a seat at the table."

For the next twenty minutes, Joel shared comments from the church staff, youth ministry volunteers, and even some kids from his small group. Then he added his own observations.

While the last two reviews had been good, this one was hard to believe. Kurt focused out the window on the budding tree branches, gnawing the inside of his cheek and nodding occasionally. The glowing report left him speechless.

"And after you spent a couple days fixing last summer's Vacation Bible School scenery, the directors gave me a letter raving about how reliable you are, how great you are with even the littlest kids, and how calm you were amidst the chaos of three hundred kids filling every corner of the building."

A half-smile touched Kurt's mouth. It had been a wild week, but who could complain when it involved so many kids from the neighborhood who otherwise might not hear about Jesus?

"So." Joel leaned back in his chair, hands behind his head. "What do you think?"

What do I think? I'm just a custodian who puts his head down and gets the work done. Not the cheerful, encouraging, faith-filled man Joel had described. Just a plain guy who screwed up his life and was getting it back on track, one day at a time.

He shrugged. "I don't know what to think. It sounds like they're talking about someone else."

Joel leaned forward, leveling a serious gaze on him. "In your mind, you're just an ex-con. To us, you're a man with a heart for God who relates to people on a level that meets them where they are. There's no pretense in you, Kurt. What we see is what we get, and the staff appreciates that more than you know. So do the kids."

Kurt scratched the bridge of his nose. "I'm glad. It's a great staff."

"We are truly blessed here at Faith." His bearded face lifted into a smile. "So now we're at the part where *you* get to say something."

Kurt's shoulders released. He had a list of stuff that needed attention before he could head home. Slapping his hands on his thighs, he pushed to his feet. "Okay. Well, I guess just...tell everybody thanks."

Joel stopped him with a laugh. "Hang on. That's not what I meant."

Heat blazed across his face and he sank back into the chair. *Idiot.* "Oh." He slid his hands under his thighs and tried not to squirm under Joel's smiling gaze. One knee bounced in the silence.

"What I want to hear about are the dreams you have for yourself, what you'd like to see happening at Faith, what you want your life to look like a year from now."

Kurt rubbed the back of his neck and blew out a slow breath. Before coming to Faith, life had been far too random. He'd never planned anything. He enjoyed the predictability of this job, his new life. "If my life looks like it does now, I'll be happy." *Thrilled, actually.*

"Really?" Disbelief colored Joel's words. "There's nothing you'd like to see happening that isn't right now? No dreams for the kids you work with on Wednesday nights?"

"Well…" There was one idea that just wouldn't leave him alone. "I guess I'd like to see us develop a program to reach the kids who don't show up here on Wednesday nights or come to the Sunday evening youth service."

"Go on."

Go on? That was pretty much it. Well, he'd thought of a few more details but saying them out loud was a lot different from thinking them. He shifted in the chair and ran a finger inside his collar. "Like a drop-in center, maybe. A place where kids could hang out and hear about God."

He met Joel's gaze. "I wouldn't have fit in here when I was younger, but I needed God bad. So a place where kids like me could go to check out faith and God and stuff."

"Interesting. Tell me more."

Leaning his elbows on the table, excitement ballooned in his chest. Maybe if he explained his idea good enough, Mike Reed and his youth ministry team could get it up and running. His toes tingled inside his work boots.

"Well, I'm thinking a house, a fixer-upper where the kids could learn skills and help with repair work. Like carpentry for dummies, only for teenagers."

Joel's chuckle released the tension in his neck. The tingle raced up his legs, straightening his spine. This was his chance to give his dream wings. Then Mike could make it fly.

"In between work sessions you could have, like, a Bible study about Jesus being a carpenter. You know, to show 'em it's cool to work with their hands. Maybe some kids could help with the design so there'd be places for them to hang out, like a game room or something, and maybe a couple of meeting rooms where they could get help with their homework."

Joel settled back in his chair, nodding. "I like this. Tell me more."

The secret ideas burst into color. Maybe this could make amends for some of the ways he'd screwed up in the past.

"We could offer programs on certain nights—like Bible study on Mondays and group stuff on Tuesdays. And I think we should have tutoring every day after school." He lifted his shoulders. "I still wish I'd graduated, so I think it'd be cool if we could help them stay in school."

Words tumbled over each other. "There'd have to be house rules, of course." He gave a lopsided grin. "Not that I ever liked rules. But if we get the kids to help make 'em up, I think they'd be more willing to follow them. Oh, and I was thinking if we could get some people from Faith to be mentors, that would help the church be involved and show the kids that adults are okay."

Finally he sat back and crossed his arms, embarrassed that he'd spewed ideas at a guy who ran a church of more than two thousand people. *God, if this is a good idea, can you help Joel see that? And Mike too?*

"This is great stuff." Joel nodded. "How do you want to get started?"

Hope did a crazy dance in his chest. "Well, for starters, Mike can get some people together—"

Joel held up a hand. "No, I asked how *you* want to get started."

Kurt frowned.

There was a glint in the senior pastor's eye. "It's a fantastic idea, Kurt, and I want *you* to run with it."

Panic flattened the excitement. "Me? I can't run it!"

"Why not?"

Hello? "I'm an ex-con, remember?" The words threw cold water in the face of the dreams that had escaped his carefully built filter.

"Who better to show these kids how to do it?"

"Do what? Be a failure?" *I'm an expert at that.*

"Get back on your feet and make your dreams come true."

Kurt rubbed a hand over his face. The earlier thrill drained into a puddle at his feet. "I'm not exactly a role model, Joel, unless it's for what *not* to do with your life. These kids need someone they can look up to."

Joel's steady gaze seemed to expose the dreams he'd kept locked in a corner of his heart. He clenched his fists under the table. Joel didn't know how long he'd prayed about this, how badly he wanted to see it come true. But for that to happen, it had to be run by someone with brains and connections.

The silence pounded at his temples. He wiped clammy hands on his jeans and got to his feet. "I really appreciate all the great things people said about me. Thanks for asking for my ideas. But now you need to take it to someone who can make it happen. *If* you think it's worth trying."

"I do." Joel stood to look him in the eye. "*You* are that person, Kurt. We've seen you at work for nearly three years. We see how you relate to the kids. I think we know who you are better than you do."

Kurt shoved his fists into his pockets and pressed his lips together against an explosion of frustration. He knew exactly who he was—and who he wasn't. He opened his mouth, but Joel spoke first.

"I know this is hard for you to hear, but I believe in you. Mike believes in you. The kids believe in you." The intensity on his face eased into a smile. "And most importantly, God believes in you. Now it's your turn."

Kurt stared at the man he loved and respected, fear and excitement pounding an erratic rhythm in his chest. "I don't know what to say."

Joel set his hands firmly on Kurt's shoulders. "Say you'll think about it, my friend. I want you to go home right now and spend the weekend listening. Find out if this is what God is calling you to do. And if you think so, come back Monday morning and hand in your resignation."

His eyebrows shot up.

"You won't have time to be the custodian if you're the new Director of Youth Outreach."

Joel was offering him a new job? Based on what—some half-baked dream? This whole conversation didn't make sense. He shook his head. "You need a vacation."

"Probably. But I still want you to do what I asked. I've prayed about this for some time now, about what God's been preparing you to do next and what Faith can do to help. I think this is it. We'll talk on Monday. And the only answer I want is whether you think God is calling you to this new ministry. Not if you're qualified or if there's someone better, but if He's calling *you*, Kurt Wagner. Got it?"

He held out his hand and Kurt took it automatically. "Got it," he choked out.

Moments later, Kurt was standing outside the front doors of Faith Community Church, squinting against the afternoon sun. *What just happened?*

Vanessa made her way out into the sunshine, determined to keep the budding flowers alive. Her mother had loved the gardens. During her chemo treatments, she'd said it was good therapy to keep her from dwelling on the disease. Vanessa needed some of that therapy. It was time to stop dwelling on the mess that was her life.

She turned on the hose and dragged it across the front yard, leaning heavily on one cane. The grass was pretty hairy. Maybe she should try mowing again. Her first attempt had been a failure, but she felt a little stronger now so maybe she could manage.

Spraying the wildflowers in the corner garden, she lifted her face to the late afternoon sun, enjoying the warmth on her cheeks.

"Miss Jordan?"

Elwood Hauge, the elderly man from across the street, waited on the sidewalk. He spoke to her of his own volition? She could count on one hand the number of times he'd bothered. "Hello, Mr. Hauge. How are you?"

"Fine. Thank you for asking." He cleared his throat and fingered his bowtie. "I'm wondering when you plan to mow your lawn. It's a mite shabby."

She stared at his wrinkled face, wrestling back the urge to turn the hose on him. Couldn't he see the cane? Maybe if she whacked him with it—

"It's important to keep our yards in good shape, you know. Good for property values. Good for keeping undesirables from moving in." His eyes wandered across her lawn then returned to the garden she was watering. Determined weeds stood proudly beside sunny daffodils.

His nasal voice droned on. "There are lawn services in the phone book, or I'd be happy to give you the name of ours. Must keep our properties looking the best they can, wouldn't you agree?"

Unable to form a response that wouldn't singe his bushy white eyebrows off, she nodded.

"Good, good. I'm sure you'll have it taken care of promptly." He tottered across the street.

She stomp-hopped back to the house, dragging the hose and muttering. How dare he march over here and order her to mow her lawn! The old codger had never had time for the "divorcée and her offspring" unless he had a complaint about something. She'd let the grass grow another foot before she'd mow. Maybe she'd never mow again. She yanked the hose closer. It bounced against the edge of the porch and swung around like a snake, spraying cold water across the front of her before dropping at her feet.

For a long moment she stood perfectly still, eyes closed, fists clenched. Water dripped from her chin. She didn't need a reminder from that hateful old man about how inept she'd become.

She shut off the water, bitter tears mixing with the cool wetness on her cheeks, then limped up the front steps and locked herself in the house.

5

Vanessa opened the front door Saturday morning to find the church guy grinning at her, no dog in sight. After several days without a visit from him, she'd stopped waiting, hoping. But here he stood, hands in his back pockets, looking ridiculously happy to see her.

"Hey, Vanessa."

His bright-eyed cheerfulness lifted the corners of her mouth. "Hi."

"I really need to burn off some energy. I've already mowed my lawn and my neighbor's, so I'm wondering if I could mow yours."

Her tiny smile dropped into a frown. "You want to mow my lawn?"

"Yeah." He nodded, eyebrows raised. Dressed in worn jeans and a black T-shirt, a navy bandana over his dark hair, he looked the part of a yard worker.

She glanced across the street, expecting to see Elwood Hauge standing on his front step. His house was closed up as usual.

Her chin lifted. "No, thanks. I can take care of it myself." Or not. It was her decision, not theirs.

"I'm sure you can." He glanced back at the shaggy lawn. "But do you *want* to?"

He had a point, but she wasn't about to become a church project. Then again...her yard wouldn't be a blight on the neighborhood. This week anyway. "How much would you charge?"

"Nothing. You'd be doing me a favor. I'm sure you think this is a little weird." He lifted his shoulders. "I just feel like maybe I can help make life a little easier for you. The way people helped me when I needed it. And I really do need to burn off some energy.

"I work fast. I could have your yard cut in an hour and then, if you want, I'll go home and leave you alone."

His request seemed so genuine, his expression so hopeful she didn't have the heart to resist. She waved her hand toward the garage. "Knock yourself out. The mower's in the garage. I have no clue if it'll start."

She went back into the house and plopped onto a living room chair. Arms folded, she glared at her right leg. She'd been perfectly capable of caring for the house, the studio and the kids all on her own before the accident. Now she couldn't even mow her own lawn. She blinked against the burn in her eyes.

The mower sputtered into action. With a grunt, she got to her feet and limped to the kitchen where she'd been about to make lemonade when he arrived. She added water to the frozen yellow lump in the pitcher and stirred. The physical therapist had warned her it would take a while to get used to her new leg, that some activities would be harder than others.

"Pretty much everything is harder," she told the lemonade, watching it swirl around the wooden spoon. For a moment she wondered what it would be like to be sucked down into the vortex created by the spinning liquid, to disappear into that hole at the bottom...

The lawn mower roared past the window. She let the spoon clatter into the sink. Her mother had never complained after the diagnosis, not once as cancer ravaged her body. She would honor her by not complaining, which might mean she never opened her mouth again. But she could at least try.

She filled a glass, watching Kurt pass by again. He paused at the side of the yard to wipe his forehead and she reached for another glass.

Relying on only one cane, it took several trips from the kitchen to the back deck to set the table with the pitcher and two plastic glasses. It was a pathetic offering. She went back in and returned with a plate of chocolate chip cookies and a few cheerful summer napkins. There. Her mother would be proud.

She retrieved two of the chair cushions Matt had stored in the garage last fall. Several strong whacks with the cane sent the dust flying. She paused to admire the neatly trimmed lawn. Her mother had spent countless hours creating a wonderland of flowers and ornamental shrubs. Since her death, it had become wild and overgrown. Like her heart.

The mower faded into silence and she heard him wheel it into the garage. He'd given her a cheerful wave while she retrieved the cushions and now joined her on the deck.

His eyes lit up at the festive table. "Wow. Is this for me?"

Warmth crept up her neck and she shrugged. "I thought you might like some lemonade after—" She looked around the yard again. "After doing such a nice job."

He wiped his hands on his jeans and nodded. "I sure would. Thanks for going to the trouble."

They settled into the chairs and she watched him drain his glass. With a hopeful lift to his brow, he held the empty glass out. "This is really good. Could I have a little more?"

Vanessa refilled his glass, unable to meet his gaze now that they sat together at the table. It felt a little too intimate. Maybe she shouldn't have added the napkins.

He finished two cookies and settled back in his chair. "This hits the spot. Thanks."

"You're welcome."

She breathed in the sweet smell of fresh-cut grass. The laughter of boys on bikes zigzagging down the alley mixed with the muffled sound of other lawn mowers.

Kurt cleared his throat. "Vanessa, this might be kinda nosy, but is there anything else you need help with? House payments, maybe? Or food? The church can help, if you do."

Defenses shot up like iron bars around her heart. Did she look as helpless as she felt? She straightened and leveled her gaze on him. "No, I don't need help. I can take care of myself, not that it's the church's business."

His eyebrows pinched together. "Wait. I didn't mean... I just thought you might, you know..." He dropped his gaze like a chastised child. "Sorry. Never mind."

Vanessa closed her eyes, cheeks flaming. She was the one acting like a child. What was wrong with her? She swallowed over the shame of her outburst. "No, *I'm* sorry. That was rude. Again. It was nice of you to ask. But really, I'm doing okay." *No, I'm not. I'm not okay at all.*

He offered a crooked smile and rolled his eyes. "Well, I'm a pretty big idiot sometimes, so there was probably a better way to offer." He turned his attention to the yards on either side of hers. "This is a real nice neighborhood. How long have you lived here?"

She released a silent breath, grateful for the change of subject. "We moved here after the divorce, so about fourteen years."

As they chatted, the afternoon sun warmed the top of her head, seeping down over her shoulders and along her bare arms. It was wonderful sitting in the peacefulness, chatting with someone. She refilled her glass and took another cookie.

He was pleasant company, keeping up a light conversation, eagerly accepting a third refill. He told her about the house he was renting less than a mile from hers and the work that needed to be done. He'd learned a ton about drywall, painting, and woodworking through trial and error.

"Lots of error," he added with a grin. "But the more work I do on the place, the more they cut my rent. Can't argue with that." He shared his dream of owning a home someday, saving as much as he could for a down payment. "So what do you dream about, Vanessa?"

The question was like a blanket thrown over the sunny afternoon. The future stretched before her in black and white, silent and empty. What was there to dream about when your own actions had caused the deaths of those you loved most? The napkin in her hands ripped in two.

"My dream was always to run the dance studio." Her tone was flat, the ache in her chest suffocating. "I danced from the time I could walk. It never occurred to me it wouldn't always be part of my life."

"So why isn't it?"

Because handicapped people don't dance! And they certainly don't teach other people how. Her gaze fell to the shredded napkin. Even if she still had her leg, she didn't deserve to be happy.

She set her jaw. "Things happen. Dreams change. It just isn't part of my life anymore."

Silence stretched between them. "I've lost some dreams too," he said quietly. "I think you should know something. I'm a convicted felon. I served two years in prison. Not the workhouse, either—the real thing."

She stared at him, mouth open. So she wasn't the only one with issues. But he'd at least served his time. It would take the rest of her life. "I...I didn't know."

"I can go, if you want. It usually makes people uncomfortable being around an ex-con."

The sadness and defeat in his voice touched her heart. She'd never known anyone who had been in prison. Ex-cons always seemed big and mean and scary, at least on TV. He was thin and not too tall and rather sweet. "How long have you been out?"

"Thirty-one months, thirteen days." He offered a pained smile. "But who's counting? I'm still amazed sometimes how clean the air smells out here, and how much I enjoy my freedom and my friendships and the chance to do what I want when I want."

"Those are good things to value."

"Yeah. There's so much that we take for granted. So many little things we don't appreciate until they're gone."

She couldn't imagine being in prison. "Like what?"

With his gaze directed past her, she wasn't sure he'd heard. Finally he said, "Birds."

"Birds?"

A twinkle lit his brown eyes. Cheerfulness replaced the wariness. "Yup. There aren't many hanging around the prison yard. Not pretty ones anyway. Like bright red cardinals that whistle, or blue jays with their pointed heads. Yellow finches and orioles."

It was hardly what she expected to hear from an ex-con.

"Hummingbirds," she added, "that hover in midair. And those adorable sparrows."

Dimples appeared on both sides of his mouth as his grin deepened. "And butterflies. Monarchs. Swallowtails. Longwings."

They shared a chuckle, then she sat quietly studying him. He was cute when he smiled.

"Can I tell you what happened to me at work yesterday?" he asked. "It's the reason I've had enough energy to mow three lawns in two days."

She nodded and sipped her lemonade.

"So yesterday was my annual review."

"Ooo."

He grinned. "Yeah, that's what I thought. I hate reviews, but this one...could change my life." He pulled the bandana off and ran a hand through his wavy hair. The gaze he turned on her was serious. "They want me to start an outreach program for kids on the fringe, kids who probably won't ever step foot in the church. Kids like I used to be."

"Sounds like a great opportunity."

"For someone else. What do I know about starting something like that?" He picked at a hole in his jeans. "I never went to college. I'm not smart like Mike."

"Who's Mike?"

"Mike Reed. The youth director. He's my best friend and eight hundred times smarter than me. I think *he* should be doing this, but my boss thinks it should be me."

"Did he say why?"

He shrugged. "He said I've done a really good job working with the kids and they can relate to me. It was just an idea I had."

He was far more complex than she would have guessed. "I suppose if you're the one who saw the need and thought of a way to meet it, then that's why he wants you to run with it."

Kurt released a sharp breath. "I'm an ex-con custodian who never went to college. What do I know?"

"I would think you know life in a way few people do. Prison taught you to appreciate the little things that the rest of us miss. And you've learned how to start over."

"I'm not exactly someone they can look up to."

"Why not?"

"Because I'm an ex-con!"

"So what? Did you kill someone? Rob a bank? Have you kidnapped children?"

"Of course not."

"Then what's your point?"

He bit his lip and looked away. His leg bounced so hard she thought he'd fall backwards. "I was arrested making a drug drop."

"Oh." That might change things. "Are you a drug dealer?"

"No way!" He jumped to his feet and the chair skittered and fell. Arms folded tightly, he stared across the yard. After a long moment, a deep sigh made his shoulders droop. "I was stupid. I said I'd drop a package off for some guy."

He shook his head. "I knew what it was but I needed the couple hundred bucks he said he'd pay me. I was in the wrong crowd. I had a drinking problem. I was pretty messed up."

"I see."

"Yeah." He turned and leaned back against the railing. "You see why I'm not the person to do this."

"No, I see you made a stupid decision." She folded her arms to mirror him. "How long ago was that?"

"Almost five years."

"Do you do drugs now?"

"Never did."

"Do you drink?"

"Sober since I went to jail. And I'm gonna stay that way."

"Well, if you learned something from the whole experience, and you want to share that with kids who might be headed down the same path, why *wouldn't* you be the right person?"

Kurt frowned down at her, his eyes dark and focused. She fidgeted under his stare, wrapping her fingers around the handle of the cane. *Maybe it's a bad idea to argue with an ex-con.*

"Did Joel call and tell you what to say?"

She raised an eyebrow. "Joel?"

"My boss. The senior pastor."

"Oh. Well, since we've never met it's safe to say we aren't in cahoots." The very idea made her shiver.

"Yeah, I know." He pushed the chair back to the table and plopped into it. "You just sound like a secret agent he sent to work me over."

The image of being a one-legged secret agent was amusing. She released the cane. "So what have you got to lose if you go for it?"

In the silence that followed, she heard his foot tapping beneath the table. "Yeah," he said finally. "What have I got to lose?"

A grin slowly erased his frown. She definitely preferred the ex-con smiling.

6

Monday morning, Kurt paused in the church lobby to see if the carpet had been cleaned last night. Satisfied, he headed for the main office. If he didn't meet with Joel first thing, he'd lose his nerve.

As he neared the pastor's office, his legs wobbled and he stopped just short of the door. He clenched his teeth against the nerves that threatened to send him running for home and swallowed hard.

Okay, Lord. I'm gonna make a mess of this if you don't take the lead.

Vanessa's question floated to mind and he latched onto it. What's the worst that could happen? A very public failure. But he would have tried. Her parting words on Saturday had stayed with him the rest of the weekend. "At least give it a try—for the kids."

Joel was on the phone, glasses perched on the end of his nose, writing in his calendar. He glanced up and motioned Kurt in as he finished the conversation. When he hung up, he stood with a welcoming smile. "Come in, come in. I've been looking forward to hearing your decision."

"You have?"

"I have." Joel gave him a pat on the back as he moved past him to shut the door, then gestured toward the table. He took the opposite seat. "We're onto something that's going to have a great impact on the community."

Great. Raise the stakes before I even get started. In slow motion he handed Joel the slightly crumpled sheet of paper.

As Joel read the brief note, a wide grin filled his face. He looked up and stuck out a hand. "Welcome to the youth ministry staff, Mr. Wagner. It's going to be a pleasure working with you on this new venture."

Kurt nodded, his head bouncing like a bobblehead. "Thanks. I hope I can pull this off as good as you're expecting."

Joel's grasp tightened. "This isn't about how well *you'll* do. This is about what God's going to do *through* you. He gave you the idea in the first place, right?"

Kurt held his gaze, the panic slowly dissipating. He was good at following orders and getting things done. He nodded. "Yeah. It's about God."

"Always." Joel left the office for a moment, returning with several notepads and pens. He slid one of each in front of Kurt. "Okay, let's get to work."

At six-foot-five, Mike Reed looked goofy dancing around the Youth Room. He let out a whoop that echoed off the colorful walls. With an extra six inches and sixty pounds, the joyful wallop he gave Kurt sent him staggering.

"This is the best news I've had in a long time, buddy. I've been praying about this, wondering what else we could be doing, and the answer was right under my nose."

"Literally." After two hours in Joel's office, Kurt's notepad was half full, and his head ached with ideas and questions and quaking excitement. He'd headed straight for the Youth Room when Joel left for another meeting.

Mike dropped into an overstuffed chair and propped his size fifteen shoes on an ottoman. "Sit down and tell me the whole story. You said you were wrestling with an idea, but it was weird that you wouldn't tell me what it was."

Kurt settled on the couch and offered an apologetic shrug. "I didn't want you to sway me either way."

His friend looked mildly offended. "Would I do that?"

Kurt raised an eyebrow.

Mike lifted his hands. "Hey, I just want you to hear God's call in your life."

"Working with you is gonna be great, but I didn't want that to be why I said yes. I wanted to be sure I was doing this because God's calling me to it, not because Joel thought I should or it would be cool to have a new job."

"So what swayed you?"

"Vanessa."

"What's a Vanessa?"

Kurt laughed. "Someone God dropped into my life a few weeks ago."

"Very interesting." Mike leaned back and folded his hands across his impressive girth. "Okay, let's hear it—from the beginning."

After a dinner of cold pizza, root beer, and a handful of cookies, Kurt plopped onto the couch to stare at the TV, hoping to drown out the voices that insisted he wasn't good enough, smart enough, or in any way suited to his new job. Halfway through a sitcom, he realized he hadn't heard a single word.

He pulled on his running shoes and left the oppressive house. Running was the one thing that calmed him when his thoughts went nuts or he wasn't sure what to do. It was the best time to talk to God, to think and listen.

Thirty minutes later he slowed his determined pace and stopped, hands on his knees to catch his breath.

"So what did you decide?" The familiar voice snapped his head up.

Vanessa stood at the edge of her yard, hose in hand. He looked at her house then back at her to get his bearings. He hadn't had a destination in mind when he set out, but it made sense he would end up here. She was the one who had talked him into the crazy idea.

"To go for it."

"And now you're wondering why."

"Maybe."

She turned her attention back to her watering. "I would imagine it's a scary idea."

Kurt wiped the sweat from his forehead and then folded his arms, watching her. "Are you really only twenty-four?"

She glanced sideways at him. "Want to see my driver's license?"

He chuckled, the mental exhaustion of the day fading. There was something about her simple, direct responses that intrigued him. She wasn't coy or silly like some girls he knew. She seemed wise beyond her years. "You look younger but you seem older."

"A dichotomy, apparently."

Whatever that meant. "Apparently."

She limped toward the house and turned off the water, letting the hose drop to the grass. When he remained on the sidewalk, she motioned with her head for him to join her on the porch steps. As he settled beside her, she adjusted her pants, which were always dragging on the ground. Probably because she was so short.

"So you told them you'd do it but now you want to back out."

He shrugged. Put that way he sounded like a chicken. He didn't like the image.

"You're not in prison anymore, Kurt. You're free to walk away."

Ouch. "I know. And I'm not going to. It's just a little...overwhelming. I sure didn't see it coming."

"Now that you're in it, you'll need a plan."

He offered a one-sided grin. "Got one in your pocket?"

"I'm hardly the person to ask."

When he raised an eyebrow, she pursed her lips and looked away. "I don't have a plan for my *own* life, so I don't think you want me creating one for you."

Her quiet words were a slap upside his head. *Since when is it all about you, Wagner?* "Maybe we can help each other then."

She was silent for a long moment before she shrugged. "I don't think I'll be much help beyond being a front yard therapist."

"As long as you don't mind doing it for free, I'd be happy to hire you as that."

The perpetual crease between her eyebrows eased. Someday he was going to get a real smile out of her. His heart did a funny jig. Maybe even make her laugh.

"Fine. No charge." She met his gaze. "For now."

7

Vanessa fingered the official-looking envelope, dreading its contents. Another mailing from the bank, reiterating the earlier warnings or issuing a new one. The fact that it was the third envelope this month screaming *Foreclosure Notice* in red letters was yet another punch to her stomach.

She gazed out the kitchen window at the setting sun. There were no more options. Most of the jobs she'd seen in the paper required her to be on her feet at least part of the time. She could handle the office manager positions, but without a college degree she wasn't even invited to apply. She had anyway. It didn't seem to matter that she'd run the dance studio on her own for three years.

Bankruptcy had been an option until she learned it wouldn't save her from foreclosure. Being bankrupt *and* losing her house was a double whammy.

"What am I supposed to do now?" The whisper swirled around her in the silent kitchen as she dropped her head into her hands. She was trying so hard to stay afloat, but for what? Who even cared? Her heart beat sluggishly against her ribs. It was just too hard to do this alone.

When she lifted her head, she sucked in a breath. "Oh!"

Across the dusky sky, the clouds were streaked with pink and purple. Angie's favorite colors. She watched in fascination as the pink intensified into streaks of fuchsia, then deepened to purple and mauve. It was breathtaking.

The fear in her chest eased; a smile softened the despair. Angie cared, wherever she was. And Matt would care, if he ever stopped playing his guitar long enough to realize there were other people in the world. Whatever world he was in now.

The colors faded and she straightened, heart pounding. "Wait!" *Don't go!* Tears splashed onto the envelope in her lap. *Don't leave me here.*

My child.

She spun in the chair, looking around the empty kitchen. "Who's there?"

There was no creak of floorboards, no sense of someone else in the house. Instead of danger, she felt an odd calm. Maybe even relief. She sat still, trying to capture the feelings. Two simple words as warm as her mother's embrace, filled with comfort.

She relaxed and shook her head. "I am definitely losing my mind."

A buzzing sound made her jump. Her cell phone vibrated on the table. The number was unfamiliar. Maybe that voice was calling. "Hello?"

"Vanessa? It's Kurt Wagner. I hope it's okay to call."

Kurt? "Of course it is."

"Good. I want to show you something, but since it's after nine, maybe it's too late?"

"C'mon over." *Where'd I leave my leg?*

She wiped her face, set the teakettle boiling then hopped toward the living room. The less-than-realistic prosthesis was lying on the couch, Merton curled up next to it. She plopped down, making the cat bounce on the cushion. He shot her a serious cat frown.

"Sorry, Mert. I have to get Leggy on before Kurt gets here." She pulled her pant leg above her knee and slid the first elastic sock on, chatting as she worked. "I probably should have told him right away, but I didn't know how. It'd be a bit of a shock if I answered the door minus a leg now, don't you think?"

The large tomcat stood and stretched. He rubbed against her and she ran a hand over his silky back before she snapped the limb into place, flexing her leg.

When the doorbell rang a moment later, she gave him a stern look. "Let's keep this between us, okay? I'll tell him someday, I promise.

Just not tonight."

Kurt was waiting on the front porch with a silly grin on his face.

She couldn't help smiling in return. "You look pretty cheerful for this time of night."

"I'm a night person," he said, following her into the entryway. "I'm just getting warmed up." He looked around the spacious living room. "Nice place."

"Thanks. It's old and needs a ton of repair, but it's home." The cat strolled toward them, studying Kurt. "This is Merton. He's been my buddy since I was nine."

"Hi, Merton." Kurt squatted down to offer his fingers for the cat's approval, then scratched his head. "How are ya, old boy? You've been around quite a while. You seem like a good ol' guy."

"I don't know what I'd do without him. It's way too quiet around here now."

Kurt stood and nodded. He had kind eyes. Sympathetic, curious, caring. "Yeah, I'll bet it gets quiet by yourself here. It's a big house."

"Let's sit in there." She pointed toward the kitchen. "I think I have some root beer. And the teakettle is whistling like crazy so there's hot tea."

"Root beer would be great." He followed her toward the back of the house. "Sorry to barge in so late. I had to show this to someone and you're the first person who popped into my head."

"Wow. Thank you."

He chuckled, accepting the can she took from the refrigerator. "Wait till you see what it is before getting too excited." He settled into a chair and examined the want ads spread across the table. "Looking for a job?"

Turning sharply, she sloshed steaming water across the counter. The envelope from the bank sat right on top of the newspaper. "I am."

She hobbled over clumsily and shoved the papers into a pile. His gaze had landed on the envelope and she tensed, waiting for a remark. He remained quiet and she dumped the pile on a chair. Filling her travel mug, she returned to the table. "So what do we have for show-and-tell?"

He laughed. She liked his laugh.

"Hey, you smiled!"

His delight sent heat up her neck. "I do that on occasion. Well, I used to, anyway."

Eyes narrowed, he nodded. "I like it. You have a pretty smile."

The heat crept into her cheeks and she bit her lip. "Thanks. So let me see what you brought."

He slid a flat metal rectangle out of his coat pocket and handed it to her reverently.

It was an office nameplate. She read it aloud. "Kurt Wagner. Director of Youth Outreach." The excitement shining on his face made her heart do a tiny dance. "Wow. It's real. You've got a new job. Congratulations."

"I can't believe how fast they had this made. It's only been a week."

"So how does this make you feel?"

"Excited and scared outta my head. Crazy happy. I just wish I had a clue what I'm supposed to do."

Just as she had no clue how to keep from losing the house. She handed the plate back. "I'm sure you'll figure it out." Hopefully she would too.

Vanessa stared at the phone, waiting for the ringing to stop. Yet another call from the bank. When the answering machine finally kicked in, the air left her lungs and she dropped back against the couch, staring at the living room ceiling that needed paint. She couldn't avoid the calls forever. They were up to at least ten a day now.

"What am I going to do?" The whisper pulsed in the silence.

Frustration pushed her off the couch and she hopped toward the stairs. With a deep breath, she jumped onto the first step. It was easier going down than up. Ten minutes later, breathing hard, she reached the second floor. Instead of heading to her bedroom, she turned left and went into Angie's room.

The bed was unmade. Sleeping in it sometimes made the nights seem not quite so lonely. Angie's clothes still sat in the laundry basket, her slippers next to her nightstand. Textbooks remained balanced on the desk.

Sinking down on the desk chair, Vanessa looked at the photos taped to the wall. Pictures of life and fun and teenage silliness. She could hear the laughter as Angie and her friends mugged for the camera. Her sister's white-blonde hair and blue eyes were every bit as striking as their mother's.

Another memory flashed before her—Angie sulking in the backseat, arms folded tightly, staring out the window. Matt brooding in the front passenger seat. Ugly words filling the car. Exhaustion and frustration exploding from Vanessa moments before the world spun out of control. In the silence that followed, she'd stared up at the black sky, wondering what was lying on top of her.

She squeezed her eyes shut against the horror and put a shaking hand at her temple to rub the pain away.

"Why didn't you stop it?" she demanded. She'd asked the question countless times since the accident. "Why not take me and let them grow up? You could have, you know. Obviously you're punishing me for not paying attention."

She got to her feet, trembling under suffocating anger and shame. "Fine. I can take it." Turning off the light, she sighed. "I deserve it."

She paused in Matt's doorway and leaned against the door frame. His love of music was imprinted in every corner, from last fall's Battle of the Band trophy proudly displayed on his desk to the sheet music on the floor. Posters of current and former rock stars were plastered on the walls. One, created by his bandmates, had a cutout of his face taped over the original. He'd loved it.

His guitar rested in the stand, waiting for the budding rock star who would never touch its strings again.

The soft body rubbing against her leg made her jump. She leaned down and hoisted Merton into her arms. "Hi, little buddy. You miss them too, don't you? I can't be much fun to live with." His motor vibrated as they cuddled in the doorway and Vanessa drew comfort from his warmth. At least she wasn't completely alone.

"What are we going to do, Mert? How can we hold onto this house and keep their memory alive? I can't let it go. There's got to be a job for me somewhere." She rested her head against his.

"But we're running out of time."

Two days later, Vanessa sat stiffly on the hard chair, hands clenched in her lap as she listened to the mortgage banker. His monotone voice suggested he'd already delivered similar bad news today.

Until she had a job, there wasn't much he could do to prevent the foreclosure. If she had no income, how could she make the mortgage payments? They'd been patient up to this point, but once the process started there were only a few options to stop it.

"What would those be?"

He pulled his glasses off and leaned forward on his gleaming mahogany desk. "One would be, of course, you finding employment to prove you can meet your financial obligations."

"I'm working on that." She lifted her chin and forced her voice to sound firm and confident. "I'm sure I'll find something in the next month. I'd hoped selling the studio would make up some payments but... What other options are there?"

"Sell the house. You won't make any money but you also won't have a foreclosure on your financial record."

"So unless I find a job very soon, I'm going to lose the house one way or another."

He pursed his lips.

She got to her feet and wrapped shaking fingers around the cane handles. "Thank you for your time and for these few extra weeks. I'm really doing my best, and I hope I can call you soon with good news."

He stood and extended his hand. "I'll be looking forward to the call."

Feeling his eyes on her as she left his office, she straightened her back and tried to walk normally. If playing up her injury would get her more time, she'd give the performance of her miserable life. But it wouldn't. Her eyes burned as she pushed through the front door.

The cab she'd requested for the return trip waited at the curb. The driver hurried around to help her, and she climbed into the backseat. *Do not cry. You can cry when you get home but not here.* Lips pressed together, she listened to his cheerful, accented chatter, grateful for the distraction.

It wasn't until she'd hung up her sweater at home and set the teakettle on the stove that she allowed the tears to come. Sinking down at the table, she dropped her head on her arms and cried. With great heaving sobs, she grieved for her family and the studio and her home. For the dreams and potential that had died with them. For her own helpless, hopeless, angry, lonely self.

When the flood finally ended, she turned the burner off under the teakettle and shuffled into the living room, collapsing on the couch. With any luck, this time she wouldn't wake up.

8

The sanctuary of Faith Community Church buzzed with energy. Sitting alone in the front row, Kurt wondered for the hundredth time just what he'd gotten himself into. *Why did I think this was a good idea?*

He focused on the large white cross at the front of the room while Joel started the first part of their joint message. They would give this same talk at all three services—two this morning and again at the youth service that evening. He prayed he would be coherent through all of them. Actually he'd settle for being able to breathe normally. There seemed to be a vise around his chest.

Joel's voice sliced into his fear. "So with that thought in mind, I'd like to invite someone up here to share the details of this new venture. Mr. Wagner, would you join me?"

A murmur ran through the congregation followed by a smattering of applause. With his heart threatening to leap from his throat, Kurt left the safety of anonymity to climb the four steps and settle on the stool beside Joel.

A mosaic of faces spread before him. Hundreds of them, friendly and curious. There would be no going back once Joel made the announcement.

"Good to see you," Joel said.

Kurt nodded, his mouth too dry to form words.

"First, I want to remind you all of Kurt's journey, and then fill you in on the changes being planned for our youth ministry." Joel put a solid hand on Kurt's shoulder and started the story.

"Most of you know that Kurt has been on staff here at Faith for about three years. In that time, we've come to know him as an exceptional worker and a broad thinker, a man of deep faith. He's willing to go the extra mile or put in the extra hour whenever it's needed. But there's so much more to who he is, more layers than most of us would guess."

Tell your story.

Kurt frowned as the directive rang through his mind. No way. He wasn't that kind of public speaker. The idea became more insistent, with a sense of urgency.

Tell your story.

Before he could censor the move, he turned to Joel. "I'll take it from here." He had an immediate urge to snatch the words back.

Joel's brow lifted, but he smiled as he handed over the microphone. "Who better to tell your story?"

"Probably a lot of people." Kurt's reply sent laughter rippling through the audience. Holding the mic in a death grip, he swiveled on the stool to face the crowd. "Okay. Well, I don't have a lot of practice at this like Joel, so hopefully my mutterings won't be too painful."

"You rock, Wagner!" a young man bellowed from the balcony.

He knew that voice from his Wednesday night small group. That's what he'd do, pretend he was talking to the guys. He grinned up toward the crowded rows. "Thanks, Johnson. Okay, well, most of you know my story, but I think it's important to put all my cards on the table so you know where I'm coming from and where we want to go with this idea."

Calm settled over him and he strolled across the stage as he talked, even drawing a few laughs from the crowd. The words flowed as he shared his painful journey into adulthood, the missteps, the prison time.

"I didn't know Jesus until he showed up in my cell looking a whole lot like Pastor Joel. When we prayed together, my sorry mess of a life started on a new path. And I had something I hadn't had for a long time—hope. There's no future without hope, no reason to make good choices. No reason to try to make a better life. So that brings us to what we want to share with you today."

He turned back to Joel who motioned for him to continue, and he stifled a laugh at the absurdity of the situation. The articulate pastor sitting behind the babbling custodian.

"There are lots of teens who make lousy choices. Having someone offer the hope of Jesus could totally change their lives. That's what we want River House to be about."

River House? Where had that name come from?

"It'll be a place where kids who don't think they belong in church can come and hear the Gospel taught in a way that speaks to where they are in life. So they can see how God can make a difference in their world, no matter what kind of mess it's in. If He did it for me, He'll do it for anyone."

He outlined their plans to look at houses in the neighborhood then apologetically mentioned the need to raise funds to get the ministry started. It was easier to describe the need for volunteers to teach trade skills, to mentor the kids and just be Jesus with skin on to teens who might never otherwise experience it.

Finally he turned back to Joel with a lopsided grin. "Sorry. I guess I'm more of a ham than I thought."

"You're a man on a mission from God." At Joel's smiling correction, the congregation burst into applause. He stood and gave Kurt a hearty, backslapping guy hug. Then they turned to find every person on their feet as the ovation rang through the sanctuary.

His throat tight, Kurt pressed his lips together and nodded. That he'd just spoken coherently for twenty minutes was amazing and humbling. Whatever he'd gotten himself into, he was sure now it was a God project.

Thirty minutes later he stood in the foyer in a sea of well-wishers, shaking hands, receiving hugs, and waiting for someone to dump the ceremonial jug of Gatorade over his head. People acted like he'd just won a championship.

A group of teens offered to help get the new ministry off the ground, suggesting kids they thought might come to River House. Adults offered to help with the renovation. Three mentioned they were realtors and would watch for foreclosures. Too many to count told him he was exactly what Faith needed to reach out to the kids on the fringe and thanked him for sharing his story.

Wow, Lord. It was all his heart could say before he was swept back into the sanctuary for a repeat performance. *Wow.*

Vanessa glanced at the clock, the rumble in her stomach pulling her attention from the book she'd been engrossed in. Five-thirty already? She slid the bookmark in place and stretched her arms overhead.

Time for her usual dinner of peanut butter toast and coffee. Maybe she'd go all out and make an egg. Even use an actual plate, rather than just a napkin. She tossed the afghan aside and pushed off the couch, grimacing at the pain stinging her right thigh. Wobbling on her good leg, she rubbed the cramping muscle.

The doorbell rang before she managed to hobble all the way to the kitchen. She scolded her heart for its sudden leap of hope.

Kurt stood with hands in his pockets, an apologetic lift to his shoulders. "Hey."

"Hi. This is a surprise." A good one. She stepped back to let him into the entry. "Don't you have church Sunday evenings?"

"Not until seven. Am I interrupting anything?"

"Nope. What's up?"

"Nothing. Everything. I don't know." He lifted his shoulders. "I guess I just needed to talk to my front yard therapist."

"Well, this is good timing. She was about to make breakfast."

His eyebrows jumped up. "At five-thirty?"

"Haven't you ever had bacon and eggs for dinner? The kids used to call it 'binner.' Care to join me?"

When he shrugged and looked down at his feet, heat filled her face. Normal people probably didn't eat bacon and eggs for dinner. Maybe it was a stupid idea. Maybe the floor should open up and swallow her.

"I didn't show up so you'd have to feed me." There was little conviction in his response.

"But since I won't eat in front of you and I'm really, really hungry…"

He grinned. "Okay, if you put it that way. I make amazing scrambled eggs."

As they stood side by side preparing the meal, he shared stories about the youth at his church, the depth of their faith, the struggles they encountered. With her canes set to the side, Vanessa pretended they were just two normal friends cooking dinner. The thought warmed her deep inside as she flipped bacon slices and listened to his chatter.

Once they were seated, Kurt described the overwhelming response during the morning services.

She nibbled a slice of bacon. "But?"

Glass halfway to his mouth, he raised an eyebrow. "But?"

"It sounds like there's a 'but' coming."

He finished the juice, then pushed his plate away and leaned his elbows on the table. "No buts. It was just such an amazing morning I figured my therapist, who got me into this in the first place, should know about it."

"I'm glad you came by to tell me." She stacked their plates. Relying on only one cane, she carried the dishes to the sink. "Boy, this therapy job is pretty easy."

Kurt cleared the table and joined her at the counter. "I think I'm getting the better deal here. Not only do you provide free counseling, you feed me too."

She turned and angled her face to look at him. Standing so close, his presence made her feel small. And safe. "I miss cooking for people." For this brief time, she hadn't thought about her leg or the kids or how quiet the house would be when he left. She'd simply enjoyed sharing a meal with someone. With him.

"Well, it still feels like I barged in. I'll return the favor one of these days. Thanks for listening. I guess I needed to think through the morning out loud."

"Kurt, you're going to do great. The fact that you're so concerned tells me you'll give it everything you've got. That's the best place to start."

A smile touched his face and he nodded. "If nothing else, River House will make it on grit and determination."

"River House?"

His shoulders lifted. "The name just came to me during the first service. I call that a God thing. Like it?"

"It sounds inviting. You could have a couple of those small tabletop fountains in the house and maybe put up pictures of some cool rivers and waterfalls. And I like that the name is River House, not River Center or River Place. The idea that it's a house should be a draw for the kids."

Kurt's eyes widened. "Wow. I hadn't thought of any of that. I figured I was doing good just having a name for it."

Vanessa took her canes in hand, shaking her head. "Men."

He followed her from the kitchen, hands lifted. "What?"

They stopped at the front door. "River House is great because it creates an image of a hideaway," she said. "And the kids you want to pull in are going to need that kind of sanctuary from their everyday lives."

"Huh." Mouth quirked, he considered her words. "Can I hire you to be my think tank?"

She pushed him gently out the door. "You're doing fine. Apparently that God of yours has already given you the right name for the house and the right words to explain it to the church. Now go back there and do it again."

At the bottom of the steps, he paused to look back at her. "You're a wise old soul, you know that, Vanessa Jordan?"

Her mother had said that once. "That's one way to describe me," she said and closed the door, a smile tugging at her mouth.

9

Vanessa dumped the steaming tea into the sink, unable to drink one more cup. She hobbled into the living room and dropped onto the couch. The silence of her life had become oppressive. As desperately as she missed the kids and her mother, she wanted to live, to laugh and talk and dance again. Kurt's visits cast a spark of light into the darkness that shrouded her.

Merton rubbed against her shins and she reached down to scratch his lifted chin. "But Kurt's so busy, Mertie, I can't expect him to keep coming by." She sighed. "I'll sure miss him when that time comes. I think you will too."

She sat up. "It's you and me, big guy. So how do we start living again?"

Choose life.

The nearly audible words didn't frighten her this time. If she were going crazy, at least she had the voice to keep her company.

Her gaze wandered the room and stopped on the dining room table. Kurt had given her a slip of paper on his first visit. She'd rejected his suggestion of talking to a counselor at the time, but now... Her heart picked up speed. The paper was still there, the corners curled. The choice between life and mere existence was scrawled in black ink.

Three days later, Vanessa followed Jenny Meyer to a room at the back of the red brick rambler. Nestled in a neighborhood not far from her house, it didn't look like at all like a counseling center.

Jenny paused to let Vanessa enter her office first. Cheerful sunlight greeted her in the spacious room, warmth and serenity were reflected in the photos of smiling faces and peaceful mountain scenes. Wild pink roses and lavender spilled their gentle fragrance into the air.

The tranquil gurgle of a small stone fountain slowed the frantic beat of her heart. Vanessa drew a steadying breath.

"Please, make yourself comfortable." Jenny shut the door gently behind her. "Can I get you some water or a soda?"

"Water, please." Vanessa sank onto the overstuffed floral couch where a needlepoint pillow proclaimed, "Life is good." *For some people.* She propped the canes against the cushion and adjusted her pant legs over her shoes.

Jenny took two bottles of water from a small refrigerator behind her desk. Handing one to Vanessa, she settled into the leather chair on the other side of the coffee table.

Vanessa studied her from under her lowered brow. Jenny's round face was relaxed and friendly, green eyes meeting hers. A tortoiseshell clip held back kinky brown hair graying at the temples; unruly bangs danced across her forehead. She might be about the age her mother would have been now.

"So tell me why you're here," Jenny said after a moment of silence.

"I don't really know." Vanessa released a short breath and shook her head. "That's not true. Of course I know."

Jenny's eyes crinkled at the corners.

"I just...I've never been to a counselor. I don't know what to say."

"It can be awkward at first. Let's start at the beginning. Did someone refer you to me?"

"Kurt Wagner."

Jenny's smile deepened. "Ah. One of my favorite people. How do you know him?"

Vanessa pursed her lips, searching for an answer. "We met at his church."

"You were attending the service?"

"No. I don't go to church. We met outside in the garden area." When Jenny raised an eyebrow, she added, "I'd been out walking and I got tired."

Vanessa pulled herself out of the vague memory and turned her gaze back to the older woman. "Actually we met the morning before on a street corner where he kept me from getting hit by a car. Then we met again in the church garden."

That simple explanation broke the ice and her shoulders lowered, like warm hands pressing down with gentle reassurance. As the soothing aroma of a vanilla candle wrapped around her, she suddenly wanted—*needed*—to tell Jenny the whole story.

She began with her parents' divorce when she was ten and then her mother's illness, how much she missed her and the wonderful talks they'd had. "When she died, I was so scared. I was in college, barely twenty-one. What did I know about raising kids?"

She described how she'd had to fight for custody of her brother and sister, leaving her senior year at college to raise them as best she could while working full time. She'd tried so hard to make a good life for them.

"I think they were pretty normal," she said with a slow nod. "They were involved in so many things. Matt played guitar and Angie danced. Not at the same time, of course."

Jenny chuckled.

"They had tons of friends. I think life was okay. We were still a family, the three of us. Until..."

Pain hammered against her ribs as it had the day they'd told her the kids were gone. Then she was standing alone in the cold cemetery, alone in a silent life. Without a leg or a family or a future.

Finally she sank back into the couch, exhausted. Unexpected release washed over her, as if whatever had kept her from drawing a full breath had loosened.

She glanced at the desk clock. "Wow. I'm sorry. I can't believe I talked for over half an hour."

Jenny smiled. "That's what you're here for."

The compassion on Jenny's face was a balm to her aching heart. "I just—I don't normally talk that much."

"You've been alone for months after an enormous trauma. I would be surprised if you hadn't wanted to talk. I'm glad you came in."

"I am too." Relief made her light-headed. "Thank you for listening."

"It's an amazing, heartbreaking story. I can't imagine the pain you've experienced over the past years." She studied Vanessa for a moment. "You are one tough cookie."

She blinked. *Tough?* "No, I'm not. All I do is cry. And I'm so angry all the time. I can't find a job because of my—the injury. I don't even go out in public for more than a few groceries once a week. That's not tough."

"Oh yes, it is." Jenny's tone was firm. "Vanessa, you've been through more since you were ten than most of us endure in a lifetime. And yet you still get up, get dressed and face the day. You're here. That tells me you want to live, you want to figure out how to deal with all this pain and go forward."

Vanessa stared at her as the steamroller returned at full speed, flattening her newfound breath. "I *want* to live," she choked, "but I don't...know...how."

She dropped her face into her hands. When Jenny's arms came around her, she leaned into the embrace, torrential sobs shaking her body.

"It's okay to cry, honey," Jenny said, rocking slightly. "Tears are the spigot God gave us to release the pain."

The embrace felt like her mother's—the gentle voice, the hand that stroked her hair. She cried until the storm passed. Drawing hiccuping breaths, she rested against this stranger she knew would become a friend. She wiped her face with trembling hands, then sat up and accepted the tissues Jenny held out.

"Grieving is the hardest thing you'll ever do, Vanessa. As you already know, this is going to be hard work that sometimes you won't want to do. But you've come this far. You have a new friend in Kurt to walk alongside you. You're not alone." The lift to her brow was encouraging. "You want to live and that's half the battle. You can do this."

"I can do this," she echoed, barely above a whisper. "I think."

Jenny patted her arm before returning to her chair. "We'll do it together."

Kurt placed his palms on the cool wood of his desk and sank into the office chair. One day he was the custodian, weeks later he was running an outreach program with the directive to reach the very kids he'd prayed about for years. Here he sat in his own office with windows and a laptop and a phone with too many buttons.

The fears of the past few weeks had dwindled to a dull throb. Instead, a growing thrill woke him in the middle of the night and made him smile at the dumbest times. God had to be getting sick of how often he said thank you. Determined not to take a step on his own, he prayed daily, hourly, for guidance and help as plans for River House began to take shape.

His morning devotions had become a powerful quiet time, amazing him with its intensity and growing desire for more. He hadn't known he could be this focused, this driven. He'd hardly eaten the past few days as toe-tapping energy lifted him out of bed each morning and made it hard to sleep at night.

"Knock, knock."

"Hey, Ash! C'mon in."

Ashley Pepper plopped into the chair in front of his desk. "Wow. Your own office. This is so cool I can hardly stand it."

He laughed. Just two years out of college, the middle school director was an entertaining bundle of ideas and energy. "You and me both. I still can't figure out how I got here."

Her auburn curls bounced as she shook her head. "Doesn't matter. You're in too deep to bail now. Anyway, you're the perfect guy for this job."

"And you're crazy."

"Crazy but honest." She got to her feet and wandered across the room to inspect the lone decoration in the office, a large framed photograph on the wall. "Great picture."

"Yeah. The Dekovics took it during their trip to Israel last year. They said it might help me remember who's actually in charge here."

Hands on her hips, she studied it. "If the Garden of Gethsemane doesn't remind you, nothing will. It's beautiful."

The phone rang and Kurt jumped. His first call on his office phone. When he made no move to answer it, Ashley bounded across the room and snatched up the receiver.

"Kurt Wagner's office," she chirped.

He rolled his eyes and chuckled.

"May I ask who's calling? Okay, can you hold a moment, please?" With a flourish, she pressed the Hold button and held the receiver toward him. "A Vanessa Jordan on the line for you, Mr. Wagner."

Vanessa? He accepted the phone. "I even get a personal assistant. It doesn't get any better than this. Thanks, Ash."

"You're welcome. We're on for lunch later, right?"

"Yup. Stop by when you're ready to go." He turned his attention to the phone and tentatively pressed the blinking light. "Vanessa?"

"Hi. Wow, you even have someone answering your phone."

The goofy flutter in his chest made him laugh. "Hardly. Everything okay?"

"Everything's fine. Is this a bad time?"

"Nope. I'm just surprised that you called. How did you get my number? *I* don't even have it."

"I just called the main office. You might want to ask them for it." There was a smile in her voice. "I wanted to wish you well on your new adventure. Are you all moved in?"

"It took about ten minutes. I didn't have much to move. But I do have a picture on the wall."

"Impressive."

He chuckled. "I think so. You'll have to come see it. It's a beauty."

Her hesitation was a heartbeat. "I'm sure you have plenty to do without me nosing around. I just wanted to say congratulations and good luck as you take another step on your amazing journey."

"Thanks for your support, Vanessa. It really means a lot."

"You're welcome. I'm excited for you, and for the kids who'll be part of River House. I have a feeling your work is going to impact a lot of people."

Her encouraging words settled over his heart. "I sure hope so. But for that to happen, we have to actually find a house."

"No luck with the realtors yet?"

He leaned back in the chair with a sigh. "We're gonna look at a few more houses this afternoon. One sounds like a good fit, so we'll see. The church will front the down payment, so I sure hope we can find something soon."

"Let me know how it goes. Good luck."

"Thanks, Vanessa. See you soon." He hung up and swiveled to look out over the Faith gardens. From his second floor office, he could see the bench where she'd sat alone that first night, looking so pathetically lost. She was less guarded now, not as serious. Her occasional laugh always lifted his spirits and made him try harder to bring it out again. It was like coaxing a timid creature out of hiding.

She was smart and wise and beautiful. Quick to challenge him to face his fears and accept his gifts. So why couldn't she see her own value? He longed to see God's healing love poured into her life. He closed his eyes and lifted her up to the only One who could help.

The tour of available houses yielded no results that afternoon or the next three days. Kurt dragged back to his office on Friday. Maybe the idea of a house was dumb. Maybe they should just start in somebody's basement. Maybe Joel was wrong about him.

Feet propped on the windowsill, he stared unseeing out the window. He was tired. No, he was falling-down-cross-eyed exhausted after the roller coaster of the last two weeks. "God, I'm outta gas. If you don't have a plan, then this is just a big waste of time. I told you I'm not smart enough to do this."

A long breath released as he dropped his head back and closed his eyes, wrestling back the wave of despair that swirled around him.

"Kurt?"

Two high school girls stood shoulder to shoulder in the doorway. He spun his chair around and beckoned them in. "Hey, Kelly. Hey, Brooke. C'mon in."

They edged their way in like Siamese twins. With their long, straight blonde hair, ratty jeans and striped sweaters, they looked like so many of the girls here.

"What's up?" he asked when they remained silent.

They glanced at each other. "We're sorry to interrupt but we need a favor."

"Ladies, you're never interrupting." He motioned to the two chairs before his desk but they remained standing, glued together. "Something wrong?"

"No. We just have a question."

"Okay, shoot."

They shared another glance. "Well, we have a friend. She's really cool but she won't come to church," Brooke said.

"Yeah. She wants to but she doesn't think she'll fit in here," Kelly added. "We're wondering if maybe you'd come see her?"

"Sure. Where is she?"

"In the car. In the parking lot."

He got to his feet. "Let's go."

They grinned at each other, and he heard Brooke whisper, "I told you."

Following them outside, he asked about homework, school, the latest drama. Their chatter reassured him it was the office, not him, that had made them shy. He'd have to get out of his office when the kids were around.

He could see a dark head inside the small black Jetta they were approaching and prayed for the right words. Large brown eyes met his from the backseat. With some coaxing from Brooke, a tall brunette unfolded herself from the two-door and Kurt saw the problem.

"Hi. I'm Kurt."

She gave his hand a brief shake then clasped hers below her extended stomach. "I'm Tiffani. With an i."

"Good to meet you, Tiffani-with-an-i. I'm Kurt-with-a-k. You hang out with these two a lot?" He motioned at the girls with his head. They giggled.

"Yeah. They've been my best friends all year." Tiffani dropped her eyes. "They've been asking me to come to church on Wednesdays but...I don't think..."

"When are you due?" he asked gently.

"Seven weeks." Her glossy pink lip gloss matched the stripe in her hair. "I'm giving it up. I can't take care of it on my own and my mom is screamin' mad at me. She don't want me to keep it."

"Where's the baby's father?"

"He's at college so he can't help much. But he's a really cool guy."

Kurt managed a nod. Cool enough to get his high school girlfriend pregnant and then let her figure out what to do about it. "You're always welcome at our senior high night. Being pregnant doesn't mean you can't come."

"Yeah, well...thanks. Maybe after."

Brooke spoke up. "We wanted her to meet you before you open River House. She said she'd go to a place like that."

His heart shimmied. "So you know about River House?"

Tiffani's face lit up. "They keep talking about it. It sounds so cool. I'd rather go there than come to the church, no offense or anything. When do you think it'll open?"

So there it was—the reassurance he'd needed. *Thank you.* "I'm still trying to find just the right house. I'm hoping we'll have that done in the next week. The plan is to open by July first. Would you come hang out with us then?"

Her bright teenager smile contrasted with the seriousness of her situation. "That would be amazing. I believe in God and all that," she assured him. "I'm just not, you know, comfortable in church. I think it would be way cool to go to a youth house though."

"Well, Tiffani-with-an-i, I think it's gonna be cool to have a youth house too. And I definitely want you to be there."

When he pulled into his driveway an hour later, he was still praising God for the swift assurance that he was on the right track. He would not lose faith again while searching for the right house. River House was out there, waiting to be discovered. He could feel that as sure as the steering wheel under his fingers.

Early Saturday evening Kurt knocked at Vanessa's door, needing some solid conversation and exercise. The thoughts and questions bouncing around his head had given him excess energy. Somehow this tiny blonde always seemed able to help him calm down and wrestle it all back under control.

The door swung open. Wearing gray sweatpants and a pink T-shirt, her hair pulled up high in a ponytail, she looked no older than Tiffani. Her cheerful greeting made his heart happy.

"It's a beautiful evening," he announced, "and I'd like to spend time with my front yard therapist. Would she be up for a walk and talk?"

She folded her arms, head cocked. "A walk. You do realize I don't move very fast?"

Idiot. Maybe she couldn't walk very far either. "Or we could just sit on the porch swing and talk. That'd be good too." Heat inched up his neck as he stumbled over his words. "Forget the walk. Let's just sit here."

She hesitated and he held his breath, hoping she wouldn't kick him out for being stupid. When her smile reappeared, his shoulders relaxed.

"The physical therapist told me I should walk a little every day so...okay. Let me get some shoes on."

Making their way down the sidewalk a few minutes later, he recounted his visit with the very pregnant Tiffani-with-an-i. Vanessa looked away but not before he saw her smug expression.

He rolled his eyes. "Go ahead. Say it."

She turned wide, innocent eyes to him, the canes clicking rhythmically as they walked. "Say what?"

He laughed and gave her shoulder a playful punch. Turning the corner, they squinted against the sunshine that danced off Lake Calhoun a block away. "Man, I guess going west isn't a good idea when the sun's setting. Let's turn at the next corner."

She paused to shade her eyes. "Provided we can find it."

Kurt hurried a few steps ahead then turned to walk backwards, blocking the glittering sun for her. Her eyebrows went up as she met his smile then she dropped her gaze shyly. "Thanks."

"Now neither of us has to squint." Aside from the sun, she seemed to be doing pretty well. "Do you think you can make it around the whole block? We can go back whenever you want so just tell me—"

"I'm fine," she interrupted. "I'll let you know when I'm getting tired."

"Okay, good. So tell me how your time with Jenny is going."

She shared pieces of their ongoing conversations. "Just having that scheduled time to talk every week makes life a little more bearable."

"She's great, isn't she? She helped me work through a lot of stuff."

Turning left at the next corner, he resumed his place beside her, asking questions, laughing over some of Jenny's comments. They were mid-block and mid-sentence when she stopped abruptly.

He shot a hand out, afraid she'd fall. "Are you tired? Maybe we should sit for a minute."

"Look." She pointed with a cane across the street.

He turned. A man was connecting something to the realty sign in the front yard of a faded blue house. A porch ran across the front of the two-story house, its white trim in desperate need of paint. Metal fencing ran along the side yard leading to a garage on the alley.

The man finished hanging a sign that read "Foreclosure" in thick black letters. For a moment Kurt couldn't breathe, his heart pounding an irregular rhythm.

"River House," he whispered.

A tall oak tree stood to the right of the cracked sidewalk leading to the front porch. Three stately pines lined the opposite side of the yard. The grass was thin, the bushes scraggly. But he could imagine the porch repaired, see kids tossing a football, sitting on the railing, and gathered on the wide steps.

He looked at Vanessa where she leaned on her canes. The light dawning on her face matched the hope filling his chest. When she turned her head their eyes met, energy dancing between them.

He raised his eyebrows. "Wanna check it out?"

She giggled and started across the street. "Well, hurry up!"

With a laugh, he caught up to her as they approached the man. Hardly able to contain his excitement, Kurt introduced the two of them, his words running together in a jumble.

"I'm Aaron Barry, the realtor," the man said, extending a hand to each of them. He invited them in for a tour and turned a friendly gaze on Vanessa as they climbed the front steps. "Is this your first house?"

The pink that filled her cheeks made her eyes even bluer. Kurt's heart skipped a beat and a silly grin spread across his face.

She shook her head. "No, I have a house. I'm just along for the ride. Or the walk, in this case."

"Sorry. That's what I get for making assumptions." Aaron held the door open for them and they stepped into a spacious, empty living room. "This house has a ton of potential. It's perfect for the person who likes remodeling and redecorating. It's structurally sound, but as you can see, the interior needs some help."

Dingy beige walls were marked from years of wear, faint outlines where décor had hung and furniture sat. The dark hardwood floor, scuffed and worn, creaked beneath their footsteps. Built-in shelves filled the walls on either side of the fireplace.

In the center of the living room, Kurt turned slowly. A couple of couches could go over there for kids to sit and talk or for him to lead a Bible study. Maybe a TV on the other side of the room. He could almost smell the fresh paint, see the sunshine pouring through the front window, hear the laughter and chatter of the teens. God would have to provide some furniture. And the TV. And the kids...

"This is an usually large living area." Aaron's words echoed in the room. "Lots of space for a big crowd. Let me show you the kitchen. It's a wonderful place for people to hang around to talk, like we all seem to do with family or friends over. And wait until you see the rec room here in back."

"It looks a lot like mine," Vanessa commented. "They must have been built about the same time."

Kurt shot a wink over his shoulder as they followed the agent to the kitchen. "But your decorating is a lot nicer."

She snorted and poked his back with a cane.

"As you can see," Aaron said, "there is lots of counter space and tons of cupboards."

Kurt looked around the room. If the price was in their range, he'd need to talk to Joel, get approval from the church council, raise more money, get bids on renovating... His heart lifted in wobbling flight as reality tempered his growing excitement. Could he actually pull this off?

By the following Saturday, Vanessa had happily made the trek with him three times to inspect the house from various angles, stroll along the alley, and watch the neighborhood in action. With each visit, Kurt's words came faster, ideas tumbling out of him. A smile seemed tattooed on his face.

That morning as they ambled back to her house, he shared his relief about the church council's approval to buy the house. He jumped onto a short retaining wall, balancing on the narrow bricks, hands gesturing to make a point.

A memory flashed to mind, crowding out his words. A time last fall when she and Angie had strolled through the neighborhood, sharing confidences and exclaiming over the fall colors. They'd stood on this same wall, balancing en pointe, doing pas de chat and arabesque penchée, laughing at their antics.

Kurt landed beside her with a thump, bringing her back to earth. She blinked against a sudden burn and focused on his sweet excitement.

"I'm working on a funding proposal." He snorted. "Whatever that is. Mike's helping me. The problem is, I keep getting distracted by ideas that pop into my head for the renovation. So I finally started a notebook. There's no way I'll remember everything."

"Idea overload."

"I wonder if my brain could actually burst into flames."

"Let's hope not. There's no time for a visit to the emergency room. You have too much to do."

A car rounded the corner and they waited for it to pass. Then he put a hand to her back as they crossed the street. She hid a smile. It was the second time he'd done it this week. Since their first encounter, he seemed intent on keeping her safe. It had been so long since someone cared.

"It's been crazy busy," he said. "I just hope nothing goes wrong with the sale. Aaron told me the family is still trying to buy it back."

If—when—she lost her home, she'd spend the rest of her life trying to buy it back. "Why isn't there help for families when finances get so tight? They shouldn't have lost their home in the first place."

He glanced at her, an eyebrow lifted. "But it's River House."

"Not yet." The words had an unintended edge. Pain for the family, anger at her own mess. "Right now it's their home, but they're being forced out. Who knows what the problem is. Maybe the husband lost his job or it's a single mom and one of her kids is sick so she spends her time at the hospital. Or—"

Kurt put a hand to her arm to stop her. Eyebrows lowered, he looked stunned. "You sound like you'd rather we let *them* have the house."

"Why not? We can find another house, but it'll be a lot harder for them to find another home."

"It seems pretty obvious they can't afford it."

She lifted her chin. "Maybe they were doing fine until something unexpected happened."

He rolled his eyes. "Maybe they shouldn't even be homeowners. From the looks of the house, they weren't even taking care of it."

His words stung. "And maybe we don't know their whole story so we shouldn't judge them." She turned away, jamming the canes into the sidewalk as she continued toward her house—the old, in-desperate-need-of-repair-but-well-loved home she was about to lose.

He fell into step beside her, silent. She pressed her lips together. No doubt her tirade seemed ridiculous to him.

"Vanessa—"

She stopped and turned to him. "People do the best they can with what they have, Kurt. We don't all have your carpentry skills or a landlord who will cut our payments based on the work we do. Some of us are just trying to get through another day."

They finished the walk in stilted silence. At the bottom of the porch steps she stopped, unable to look at him. "I'm sorry. I just...I feel bad for them."

As she stared at the ground, his black running shoes came into view and stopped in front of her. She had the ridiculous urge to throw herself into his arms and tell him the real reason for her rant. When he put a finger under her chin, she gritted her teeth before letting him tilt her face up.

A crooked smile touched his mouth. "You have an amazing heart, Vanessa Jordan." His finger was warm against her skin.

The unexpectedly gentle words made her chin tremble. How could an ex-con be such a sweet man?

"Thanks for keeping things in perspective for me," he added.

Her stomach flipped over as they stood close together in the quiet of the early evening. His smile widened, pulling one from her in response.

"I'll bet you didn't know you'd befriended a nutcase, did you?" she asked.

He laughed, giving her chin a light flick before he stepped back. "I was short on nutcase friends, so you fill that hole nicely."

She started up the steps. "I'll take that as a compliment," she said over her shoulder.

"You should. Goodnight, cute little nutcase."

At the front door she paused to watch him. He was strolling down the sidewalk, hands in his pockets, whistling. As she unlocked the door, her hand trembled. He thought she was cute?

Vanessa ended the call. It was the bomb she'd been dreading. Since their meeting in April, the mortgage banker had been able to push the foreclosure back a few weeks at a time but the grace period was over. The lender was calling in her loan. She would be evicted by the end of the week if she couldn't pay the mortgage in full. Four days, which he'd called a bonus grace period, and it would all be over.

She sat in the silent living room through the long hours of the night, Merton close by her side. She hadn't been called for any of the jobs she'd applied for. There was only a thousand dollars left in her emergency fund. God was going to take the house and leave her with nothing. Fear and anger wrestled with grief as her thoughts circled in bleak despair.

The rising sun streaming through the dining room windows pulled her from her stupor. There had been tears last night, but now she was dry. She couldn't cry anymore. She couldn't even summon anger.

Merton sat at her feet, his soulful eyes on hers. She glanced at the clock and realized he was waiting for breakfast. Was there a cheap apartment that would allow pets? It was doubtful she could take him to the homeless shelter, which was where she was going to end up.

"I'm so sorry, Mertie." She looked at his wise old face and sighed. "I couldn't save the kids and now I can't save you."

She limped after him to the kitchen, managing a smile at the proud lift to his tail. He'd been her solace in very black nights. He had made her laugh, let her cry. He was all she had left. Dumping food into his dish, she ran her hand along his wide back. "Maybe Kurt will take you. He thinks you're pretty cool, you know." There was a sliver of comfort in the thought.

The morning passed slowly as she puttered around the kitchen, opening and closing cupboards, looking in drawers. What could she take with her? Who would get all of this—her mother's cookware, the kids' clothes? She wandered the house, unable to pull in a full breath. It would all go to strangers who'd never know the significance of each item.

She was halfway up the stairs when the doorbell rang. She hesitated, hardly in the frame of mind for coherent conversation. Merton trotted from the kitchen and settled at the front door, looking up at her.

"Well, if you want to see him so bad, *you* open it. And you explain the mess I'm in."

He blinked at her. With a huff, she hopped back down the stairs, smoothing her hair and wiping her face. She slapped on what she hoped was a smile and pulled the door open.

A frown occupied the place of his usual cheerfulness. His face was pale, dark circles ringing his eyes.

Her own despair vanished in the face of his. "What's wrong?"

With a shrug, he stuffed his hands into his pockets, his shoulders slumped. "I need a little time with my front yard therapist. Is she available?"

"Let me check her calendar. Apparently she is. Come on in."

He bent down to rub Merton's head then went past her into the kitchen to drop into a chair. She settled across from him and waited.

"I...Well..." He released a short breath and propped his elbows on the table. "The family has raised enough money to get the house back."

The burst of joy for them was tempered by the desperation in his eyes.

"I know the right thing is to let them have it, but...it's River House." He said it with a reverence that touched her heart.

"The paperwork is done, we're ready for the auction next week. Everything's in place for us to buy it. I know we can find another one, it's just...I'm having a hard time letting go."

"It seems the right thing isn't always the easy thing."

"Yeah." He released a long breath, his gaze wandering around her kitchen.

She squirmed. The flowered wallpaper was peeling up at the chair rail that needed a coat of stain. The linoleum had yellowed. The countertop had more dings than she could count, though Matt and his friends had tried one night last winter.

"I can already see kids there, music playing, people singing and praying and wrestling with the tough stuff of life." His eyes misted before he turned to the window. "But I guess we'll just get back out there and find another perfect house. I'm sure the family's been through enough. If they want their house back, we shouldn't get in the way."

A nudging started in her chest to do something, say something. It was the same feeling she got when she heard the voice. The pounding in her heart grew more persistent, the impression stronger.

Sell him this house.

What? No way. I'd have to tell him... No. She shook her head. The stress of losing the house was making her nutty. Now she was arguing with the voice.

Kurt's hand covered hers and she jumped. He wore a pained smile. "Thanks, Nessa. Just saying it out loud to you makes all the difference."

His fingers were warm and secure around hers. A tingle danced up her arm. Nessa. She liked that. "But I haven't been any help."

"You had the answer I needed." He squeezed her fingers and released them. "You said the right way isn't always the easy way."

"That was a good answer?"

"It's what I needed to hear. I was looking for the easy way out—for them to go find another house." The pain in his eyes lessened into a real smile. "But it's their home. *We* need to find another one. And God'll lead us to it, just like He did this one. This is only a bump in the road."

The nudge grew stronger. He didn't need to look further than this very kitchen. Or the living room that could hold fifteen kids, like it had for Angie's last birthday. But she'd have to tell him how messed up her life had become.

The scrape of his chair as he got to his feet startled her. "Thanks, my favorite front yard therapist. Once again you saved the day."

Pushing the internal discussion to the back of her mind, she stood, hands on her hips. "Your *favorite* front yard therapist? Do you have others?" She lifted her chin, pretending insult.

"My one and only," he clarified with a grin, stopping in front of her.

She felt a little dizzy looking up at him standing so close. Or maybe she was just off-balance by the thought of making her house *his*. His dark eyes held hers and her heart did an unexpected pirouette.

She forced a nod. "Good. If I find out you have others, my rates are going up."

He laughed and brushed her bangs from her eyes. "No other front yard therapists. Honest."

Folding her arms tight against the strange dance in her chest, she tried to frown. "Okay. Keep it that way."

"Yes, ma'am."

The voice was relentless through the next two days as she packed her life into old boxes and raggedy bags. No matter who got her belongings, at least they'd be in some semblance of order. If only she could afford a storage unit. Even a small locker would be okay for the important things.

She looked at Merton, hunkered down in an empty box, eyes half-closed. "I just can't imagine telling him what a mess we're in, Mert. How did we get to this point? I tried to do everything right."

Wrapping another piece of her mother's china in newspaper, she paused to study the delicate floral pattern. Then she released a long sigh and finished wrapping. "I can't imagine explaining all this to him."

Her heart reverberated with a persistent thought.

All is well. This is River House. And as she sorted and tossed and sat awash in memories, she started to hope it was true.

That night she sank into welcome sleep. As dreams drifted in, she was standing at the top of the stairs, dressed in the jeans and hoodie she'd worn the night of the accident. This was her house yet...different—sparkling clean, glowing with soft light. Leaning over the banister, she watched teens stream in through the front door. They were singing and laughing, shaking snow from their hair, sharing high fives. Every time the door opened, a fresh blast of winter blew in.

She started down the stairs, then paused and looked at her feet—what? No missing leg? Searching the crowd for Matt and Angie, she recognized many of the young faces filling the house. Angie's best friend, Kelly, gave her a warm hug. Matt's bandmates surrounded her in song the way they had after every practice. A few girls from Angie's dance team raised glasses of steaming cider as Vanessa passed. Jarrod, Matt's best friend, put his baseball cap on her head.

Disappointed she couldn't find her siblings, she let more happy teens in. Their joy was contagious. Soon she was laughing and dancing and singing with them. Peace enveloped her, happiness filled her empty heart. Buoyed by a welcoming love that held her securely, she reveled in the wonder of it all.

When she awoke, she lay still, staring at the brightening sky through the half-closed blinds. The panic in her chest had disappeared sometime during the night. In its place was an unfamiliar calm, the peace she'd felt during the dream.

She knew what she had to do.

When the knock came at noon, Vanessa pulled in a steadying breath and released it slowly as she left the dining room table. Everything was ready. Now she needed the right words. She could only hope he wasn't too shocked.

She pulled open the door. "Hi."

"What's wrong? Are you okay?" Kurt's eyes swept over her, his face clouded with concern.

"I'm fine." She stepped back to let him in. "I'm sorry to have been so mysterious in my message, but there was no way to explain it over the phone."

Hands jammed in his pockets, he faced her. "If you tell me you don't want to be friends anymore, I'm telling you right now you're stuck with me. We've been through too much—"

She held up a hand, smiling at the declaration that warmed her heart. She couldn't imagine not having him in her life. "It has nothing to do with that. But it's a long story, so let's sit in here for a minute."

He took several steps then stopped abruptly, looking around. "What's going on?" He spun on his heel to face her. "Why are you packing?"

She glanced at the half-filled boxes. "That's what I need to explain."

They settled in chairs at either side of the cold fireplace. Kurt sat erect, watching her.

"So I want...I need to, um..." She straightened her pant legs and adjusted her T-shirt. "I had a really good childhood, you know? It was hard after my dad left—we never had much money—but life with my mom and Matt and Angie was still good.

"My mom had a small life insurance policy that she meant to increase, but then the cancer came and she couldn't. Anyway, that money went to make house payments and put food on the table. And all the other things kids need." She managed a weak smile. "Boy, kids are expensive."

He nodded.

"Anyway, my mother taught dance all the years I was growing up. We practically lived at the studio." It seemed a boulder rested on her chest, keeping her from pulling in a full breath. "As I got into high school, I started teaching the littlest kids. Ballet, jazz, tap. Even some hip-hop. When my mom died, I took over the studio. We were never going to be rich but it was a good life.

"But..." Warmth flooded her cheeks and she looked at her knotted hands, the knuckles white. *Spit it out.* "I got behind in house payments. And after the accident I couldn't keep the studio running. The morning you and I ran into each other, I was coming from a meeting about selling it."

"You looked so sad that day." His brow lowered. "But after I cut your grass, you said—"

"That I was okay." She met his gaze straight on. "I can't stand pity, Kurt. I don't want to be a charity case. For you or the church or anyone. I've always been able to stand on my own."

The sympathy in his dark eyes invited her to tell him the truth—she *couldn't* stand on her own anymore. No, one surprise was enough.

"The bank has been calling. And the credit card companies. And the utility companies. Actually, my phone's been ringing off the hook." Embarrassment prickled through her. "There's been a great guy at the bank who worked really hard to hold off the foreclosure until…tomorrow."

"Tomorrow?" His eyes went wide and his mouth fell open. "Vanessa, why didn't you come to me sooner?"

"Because this is really hard!" She clenched her jaw. Her heart pounded so hard she was sure he could hear it. "That's why I called this morning. I think I'm the solution to your dilemma."

His eyes narrowed. "Wait—what? *My* dilemma?"

"Come with me." She led him to the dining room table where she'd neatly arranged the foreclosure letters and the credit card bills. "This is my life today."

Kurt scanned a few of them, flipping through the pages. When he looked up, the anger on his face startled her. "We can't let this happen, Nessa. There are good lawyers at the church—"

"We don't need them." She leaned the canes against the table and faced him. The boulder shifted enough for her to draw a breath. "I want this to be River House."

13

"You *what*?"

Kurt stared at her as if she'd suggested they burn down the house. She held his gaze, determined to make him understand. "I want you to buy this and make it into River House."

He shook his head and blinked. "Where would you live?"

"Well...I'm working on that." The voice had forgotten that detail. "I'll figure that out later."

"Vanessa, this is your home. I don't—" He ran his hands through his hair. "If it's just going into foreclosure, can we even buy it?"

"I don't get it exactly, but I think you can make a low offer on the house before tomorrow and the bank will—"

"No way." He put his hands up. "I'm not letting you get the raw end of the deal."

Panic shifted the boulder back into place. She hadn't considered a no. "Kurt, I can't lose this last connection to my family." She clamped a hand on his arm. "Please. Don't let them take my house. You know what it means to me, to my family."

Humiliation tangled with the fear in her chest, suffocating her. She'd never begged for anything in her life, but this was the right answer for both of them. He had to see that. Eyes brimming, she curled her fingers around his forearm. "Please."

He stood silent, frowning.

She tried again. "We both saw how much the other house is like this one. I know this isn't as nice, and it needs a ton of work, but that's what you want, right? A fixer-upper? There isn't one in the neighborhood that needs more fixing. And I've got all the paperwork so you know what's been done in the past, what the utility costs are. You've seen the yard. It's perfect for barbeques and volleyball games."

The words picked up speed. "It's a nice neighborhood. It would be a safe place for the kids. There's a piano in the living room, and the basement could be renovated for meeting space or a workroom." Words and thoughts slammed together. "You can keep most of our stuff. Unless you don't like it. Then we can get rid of it." A tear burned down her cheek. "The living room is plenty big. And the kitchen is big enough for—"

He pulled her into his arms, cutting off the rising hysteria. She stood stiffly as he murmured, "Shh. It's okay. I get it, Nessa."

She buried her face against his chest. Even if he didn't agree to buy the house, he knew now. Someone else knew. When the tears slowed, she rested against him, drawing in short, choppy breaths. For that brief moment, wrapped in his strength, she felt safe, not so alone in the mess of her life.

His smile was warm and encouraging. "I can now add persuasive to your long list of amazing qualities."

A corner of her mouth lifted, then her breath caught as he wiped her cheeks with gentle fingers. There was something deeper than simple reassurance in his eyes, holding them frozen in the moment. He blinked, dropped his arms, and stepped back.

"Vanessa, I would love to make this River House, but you need to be a hundred percent, a *thousand* percent sure. You know what we want the house to look like, which is a lot different than it looks now." His gaze bore into hers. "You need to be able to live with that."

She nodded. "I've thought about that. This is going to sound weird, but I had the most amazing dream last night. It's what convinced me this is the direction we should go."

"Tell me about it."

She shared everything but the part where she had use of both legs. He didn't seem at all skeptical, as she'd expected.

When she finished, he smiled. "I had a dream like that when I was trying to figure out if I should start up this ministry. It was the coolest dream I've ever had, and when I woke up, I just knew what I was supposed to do."

Her legs wobbled and she reached for the edge of the table to steady herself. "That's how I felt this morning. I knew when I opened my eyes what was supposed to happen."

He set his hands on his hips and looked around the dining room. "I wouldn't have believed it if you'd suggested this last week, but you're right, Nessa." He released a short breath. "Wow. I ran over here thinking something was wrong and now look where we are."

She mimicked his stance and nodded. "Standing in the middle of River House."

Vanessa stared down into the lukewarm tea, chin in hand, listening to Kurt's voice. In the three hours since agreeing to buy her house, he'd talked with the mortgage banker twice, the church council president, and now his pastor friend. His determination to keep her house from foreclosure settled a layer of warmth over the grief that tightened her throat.

She was losing the house. Knowing it would be loved and cared for helped. But the stark truth was that she had failed. The house would be in good hands but it wouldn't be hers anymore.

The conversation showed no sign of ending so she wandered out to the living room. Leaning on one cane, she ran her fingers across the mantel and then along the top of the old piano that had stood silent since the accident.

She stopped at the fireplace and looked at the large photograph hanging above it. The kids were young, her mother looked healthy, and Vanessa had both legs. The full bloom of her mother's garden provided a riot of color in the background. They all looked happy.

She leaned forward to study her legs in the photo. The normal legs of a nineteen-year-old who had no clue what would hit her in the next handful of years. She closed her eyes, trying to remember what it felt like to stand on two feet, without pain. To stand en pointe and spin to her heart's content. To leap across the stage. To hold a perfectly balanced—

"How old were the kids?"

With a start, she glanced sideways. "Eleven and nine. My mom was in remission. Isn't she beautiful?" She crossed her arms over the ache in her chest, gazing at her mother's serene face.

"You look just like her."

Her cheeks warmed as she shook her head. "Angie looks like her. I have more of my dad." How she would love to be beautiful like her mother, to have the same sweet spirit and open heart.

"It's interesting that Matt doesn't have blonde hair like the rest of you, but he has the blue eyes."

She reached up to brush a fingertip across her brother's smile. He was almost twelve in the photograph, still more boy than young man. His mop of brownish hair, curling at his ears and collar, was a contrast to the white-blonde of the female Jordans. She closed her eyes against a searing pain that took her breath away, and clenched her jaw.

Kurt's arm came around her shoulders and she leaned against him, soaking in the strength and calm he offered. Her world was crumbling, but at least she had this kind, warmhearted friend to lean on.

He gave her a squeeze before turning to face her. "I hope it's okay that I ordered a pizza. I'm starving."

She nodded. "I am too. Thanks."

"Maybe after we eat you could give me a tour?"

"Sure. You should know what you're buying before you hand over the money."

"I know what I'm buying." He set his hands on her shoulders. "A well-loved house with tons of great memories. I couldn't ask for a better place to build River House."

The tender words soothed her heart. She wasn't losing her home. She was gaining the River House family.

An hour later, pizza devoured and the tour complete, they settled at the kitchen table. Kurt still felt like he was walking through a dream, but the girl sitting across from him, writing out a list of items to be stored during the renovation, was very real.

The strength hidden within her small frame astounded him. This had to be killing her but she moved forward with determination. He doubted he'd be as strong if he were in her spot. "Okay, enough of the list."

She looked up with eyebrows raised. "But you need to know—"

"We can get the details later." He reached over and slid the paper away from her. "We need to talk about where you're going to live."

"Oh. Well..." She leaned back and shrugged. "I'll find something."

"That's not good enough. If I'm buying your house out from under you, I'm going to help you find some new digs. Have you got enough money for an apartment?"

Her chin lowered, a frown darkening her eyes.

He held up a hand. "I don't need the details, Vanessa. I just need to know what we're working with here."

Their gazes locked. He prepared for an outburst then watched her shoulders sag.

"Not much. I just have my disability check and a tiny Social Security check. I haven't found anything cheap enough around here. How much are they closer to downtown?"

"I dunno." He pulled out his phone and got online, moving to the chair next to hers. "We can look, but I don't like the idea of you moving too far from here."

Side by side they looked at websites. Her posture deflated as they checked the fourth site.

"Well, okay then." She got abruptly to her feet and hobbled to the stove to retrieve the teakettle. Jaw set, she busied herself getting water boiling, pulling two mugs from the nearly empty cupboard.

His heart ached. *Lord, what do I do? How can I help her? It's all so expensive.* "Vanessa—"

She jumped and turned, knocking a mug to the floor. In the silence, she stared down at the pieces then squeezed her eyes shut.

"I'll get it." He tossed the larger pieces into the trash, then swept up the shards. "Any other mugs?"

The blue eyes that opened and latched onto his showed a flash of despair before she shook her head.

"I'll just have a root beer, if that's okay."

"Or we could take turns having tea."

He lifted an eyebrow. She offered a feeble smile; he grinned. "Okay, you go first. I'll have a root beer while I'm waiting for my turn."

"Very gallant of you," she said before turning back to the counter. "You probably don't spend a lot of time drinking tea at your house."

He didn't spend much time doing anything at his house. He was rarely ho— His eyes went wide. *That's it!* He glanced up to see if a light bulb had actually appeared over his head. "That's what we're gonna do, Nessa! You move into my place and learn to drink root beer. I'll move in with Mike until the renovations are done, then I'll move in here and learn to drink tea."

She stared at him over her shoulder, teabag in hand. "Are you serious?"

"Think about it. It's not far from here. I don't have much for furniture, so we can move a whole bunch of your stuff over there. Merton would have a whole new place to explore. Mike's roommate moved out last month so there's a bedroom I could use for a couple of months."

He nodded encouragingly. It was the perfect setup for everyone. Well, it would be once he let Mike know. "What do you think?"

"Well, I...It's not..." She turned to face him. "Maybe you should check with Mike before showing up with a suitcase in your hand?"

"He won't care. If he says okay, are you in?"

Her eyes narrowed as she bit her lip. "It would depend on how much the rent is. Maybe they won't let you sublet it."

"I'll call them when I get home tonight. As for rent, it doesn't matter to me—"

"It matters to me. I need to know how much first. If we can iron out the details then...I guess... Okay."

Wow. Thanks, Lord.

Sitting in the mortgage banker's office the following morning, Kurt watched Vanessa review and sign legal papers. With each new page, his stomach knotted a little tighter. He pulled his chair closer to her as she signed the final sheet, ready to reach for her hand. "How long of a process are we talking?" he asked the banker.

"It can move quickly if there's no lien against the property or other issue." He turned to Vanessa. "Since the deed to your house is clear and there's nothing outstanding that might cause issues, we should be able to close this transaction within two weeks."

She dipped her head then looked at Kurt. The sadness he'd seen in her eyes while they waited in the lobby had been replaced by determination. "Can you get everything ready on your end by then?" she asked.

"We'll be ready." *No matter what it takes.* "You're sure you want to go through with this?"

"Yes. I'm glad it can be done so quickly." She stood slowly as if her leg was hurting then extended her hand to the banker. "Thank you for your help all these months. I've appreciated everything you've done."

Emotions flickered across the man's face as he grasped her hand. His tone was gentle. "I wish the outcome could have been different for you."

"Thank you, but I'm grateful for how this worked out. I think it will be good for everyone."

He shook Kurt's hand and promised to call with the appointment time for the closing before ushering them out of his office. Outside in the warm late-May air, Vanessa paused to slip sunglasses on before starting down the sidewalk, away from the direction of her house.

Kurt fell into step beside her. "So where to now?"

"You'll see." A faint smile played across her pale face as they continued down the block. They walked in silence until she stopped in front of a red screen door. "Shall we?"

He glanced through the shop's large window then back at her. "Are you serious?"

"Don't we have something to celebrate?" Her steady gaze challenged him to say no.

"Well, it's...I mean..." She wanted to celebrate River House at the same time she was losing her home? She was the most confusing girl he'd ever known. *If this is what she wants, I'll buy her the biggest cone possible.* "Yes. We have a lot to celebrate."

He held the door wide and she smiled and stepped past him into the shop.

Over the weekend, Kurt helped Vanessa pack up the house. He wrestled with warring emotions—thrilled that River House was moving forward but saddened that it meant the loss of her home. Watching her pack her life into boxes kept a dull ache pulsing in his chest.

He sat with her in Angie's room Saturday morning as she sorted through the overflowing closet and dresser drawers. She handed him items which he carefully put in the bins he'd bought for her—pictures, awards, artwork, and other personal belongings. And the tears flowed unchecked as she shared stories about her sister, laughing over some, sitting quietly with eyes closed after others, an item clutched to her chest. He felt intrusive sitting like a lump as she grieved, but when he offered to leave, the panic in her eyes kept him seated.

They tackled Matt's room the following afternoon. She worked quietly, her jaw clenched so hard Kurt's hurt from watching her.

Gently removing the posters from the wall, he asked if he could keep a few for River House. Her grateful smile made him glad he'd asked.

"When they won the Battle of the Bands," she mused softly, "he was so excited he didn't sleep that whole night. The boys sat at the kitchen table until at least three o'clock, reliving the whole event." A smile lifted a corner of her mouth.

Kurt followed her gaze to the two-foot-tall, shiny gold trophy on the desk. He'd had one of those himself years ago. A lifetime ago...

He'd been careful to keep his back to Matt's guitar in the corner. When she picked it up, an intense longing made him nauseous. His fingers itched to hold it, to play a familiar melody, to crank out a tune he occasionally heard in his sleep.

She wrapped her arms around the guitar. "He never had a lesson. He just picked it up and started playing." In slow motion she set the instrument in its black case. "The house is so quiet now."

The snap of the locks cut into the silence. Kurt flinched. He and Matt would have hit it off. Their love of music and playing guitar would have been an instant bond. But it was too late—for him, for Matt, for buried dreams that were best forgotten.

When they finished the last room Vanessa was barely speaking, leaning heavily on her canes as she made her way around towers of boxes.

Kurt got her settled on the deck with a glass of lemonade and a plate of crackers and cheese, then fired up the grill and returned to the kitchen. Slapping the hamburger into patties, he watched her through the kitchen window. She looked young and lost, staring across the yard nibbling at a slice of cheese.

Even having known her for two months, he was no closer to understanding her than that first morning. She was serious so much of the time, but then she would make him laugh—hard. So fragile he was sure she would break, but more resilient than anyone he'd ever known. And with a killer smile and no-nonsense way of putting him in his place.

He shook his head, glancing down at Merton who sat at his feet. "Mert, I don't think I'll ever understand girls. Especially that one."

The cat responded with a soft meow and Kurt chuckled. "You don't get her either, hmm? I guess we'll just have to do what we can for her together. She's pretty tough on the outside but not so much on the inside. Take good care of her in your new home, okay?

Merton rubbed against his legs and Kurt offered a piece of cheese. "Okay. I'm holding you to it."

15

Moving day arrived far too quickly. Vanessa wandered the silent house in the early morning hours, reliving snippets of life in each room. The blank walls echoed back laughter, arguments, conversations, music. Life as it had been.

Standing in the living room with boxes stacked along the fireplace wall, Vanessa set the canes down and stood quietly, face lifted, drinking the memories into her parched soul. She raised her arms to embrace them, eyes closed.

Using the mantel for balance, she rose on her toes and stretched her right leg back into an arabesque, then leaned into a penchée. The familiar movement released the tears she'd held back. She was eighteen again, carefree, dancing in the living room. She swung her right leg in front and extended her arms. A smile curved her lips and she completed a wobbling fouette turn.

She was whole and graceful, moving into familiar poses that stretched tight muscles. A car door slammed, followed by two more, and she lowered into an awkward curtsy. When the doorbell rang a moment later, she was firmly planted in the present, the memories tucked into a corner of her heart. Pushing a smile to her face, she opened the door.

"Good morning." Kurt's greeting included a questioning lift to his brow.

"Good morning to you." His acknowledgment of this difficult moment filled her with warmth. "Are you ready to work?"

"Yes, ma'am. Let's get movin'."

He turned and beckoned the teens to join him. After a round of introductions, the group from Faith Church jumped into action. The yellow group would move the boxes with yellow dots into the moving truck that would head to the storage unit. Faith Church had purchased most of the extra furniture to use in River House once the renovations were complete.

The green dot group would move the other boxes to Kurt's house, Vanessa's new home. She hoped the items she'd opted to keep would be enough to allow memories of her family to stay alive in the new place.

Pizzas arrived at noon. The cheerful banter of the kids kept Vanessa from sinking into the sadness that lingered at the edge of her heart. Mid-afternoon, the last of the boxes were loaded onto the truck for the final run.

She stood in the empty living room, imprinting the picture on her mind. *Goodbye, house. I'll miss you. Wish me luck.*

Shoulders set, she pulled the front door closed behind her and went down the steps to where Kurt waited beside the open passenger door. She slid in and glanced at the cat carrier in the backseat. Merton glowered at her through the metal grate door, ears flat.

"It's only for a short ride," she assured him. His unblinking green eyes remained locked on hers. *I don't want to go either, Mertie. At least we're going together.*

Kurt started the car then looked at her. "Doing okay?"

Soaking in his concern, she held out the key ring. He looked at it then back at her, wrapping his fingers around hers to keep the keys in their clasped hands. They exchanged a smile before she settled back in her seat and turned her attention toward the new life that waited.

Throughout the noisy busyness of the day, Vanessa had pretended it was an adventure of her making, not a new reality thrust upon her. It had worked...until now, when everyone had gone home. She sat in the quiet, studying her surroundings with Merton on her lap.

It was a simple red brick rambler with two bedrooms, a patio out back, and a neat patch of yard Kurt had happily maintained in his three years there. The décor was neutral with little personality. It wouldn't take much to make it feel more homey.

Kurt had hung her family photograph over the couch, unpacked her dishes in the kitchen, and made up her bed. He'd helped her set up the second bedroom with items she'd brought from the kids' rooms—Matt's guitar in the corner with the Battle trophy beside it, Angie's desk under the window, a montage of photos lining the bottom of the window frame.

He'd worked tirelessly all day directing people, laughing with the kids, checking in with her often. He had apologized so many times for his lack of decorating that she finally ordered him to stop.

Looking around the small living room, she released a tiny sigh. This house held other people's memories. Her own home would soon be renovated to someone else's needs and tastes. She leaned her head back against the chair and closed her eyes, resting a hand on Merton's warm back.

A tear slid down her temple and into her ear. Kurt had become a good friend, but she was still without a family. Jenny was helping her rebuild her life one day at a time, but the future still loomed hollow and silent. There had to be a reason she'd been left behind, some purpose for her life.

The answer seemed far beyond her reach.

Kurt looked up at Vanessa's empty house a few evenings later, excitement blooming as he scanned every detail of its weather-beaten face. River House was about to become reality. He could hardly wait for renovations to begin, right after tomorrow's closing. He knew God would draw in the kids who needed Him. The house had to be ready when the first teen showed up.

"Hello there, young man."

An elderly couple approached from across the street. Vanessa had mentioned them when she gave him an overview of the neighborhood. "Hello!"

The gentleman was slightly stooped to the right, but with thick white hair, wire-rimmed glasses and a red bow-tie, he presented a dapper picture. His tiny wife clung to his arm, bright eyes smiling up at Kurt from beneath a mop of curly gray hair. The lace collar of her dress seemed as stiff as cardboard.

Kurt straightened. *I should have put on a clean shirt.*

"I saw the Jordan girl moving her things out this week. Did she sell the house?"

The Jordan girl? "Yes, sir. Vanessa sold her house to me. I'm Kurt Wagner."

They shook hands. "I'm Elwood Hauge and this is my lovely bride, Priscilla."

"Nice to meet you both. How long have you lived here?"

"Fifty-four years," they said together. Elwood patted her hand. "I married this beautiful girl and brought her to this house where we raised four children. It's been a wonderful neighborhood."

"Wow, fifty-four years. That's amazing."

They exchanged a glance, then Elwood was studying him, his pale eyes taking in Kurt's hair, T-shirt and jeans. Kurt fought the urge to push his hair back.

"So, are you bringing a family to the house? We need more young families in the neighborhood. The Jordan clan had too many cars lining the streets, people coming and going all hours of the day and night. We're hoping for a whole family this time, two parents with young children."

The corners of Kurt's smile stiffened. "There will be plenty of young people, definitely."

Priscilla looked hopeful. "Do you have children?"

"Not me personally." She looked disappointed. "This will be a house for kids to come and learn about God and study the Bible—"

Elwood's friendly expression vanished. "A house for thugs?"

"What? No! Just kids that might not normally go to church." He forced a smile as the pleasant vibes of his new neighbors cooled. "It's going to be called River House. The kids can come after school or on weekends for tutoring and—"

"Kids who need tutoring aren't trying hard enough. They shouldn't be here in our neighborhood hanging around causing trouble. They should be in school."

"Oh, they will be, sir." The conversation was quickly disintegrating. "During the school year, anyway. But they can come here to learn computers or get introduced to a trade, or they—"

"Those are troublemakers," Elwood declared. His hand tightened over Priscilla's as if protecting her from Kurt and the bad influence of the nonexistent kids. "We've had riffraff try to move into our neighborhood before, young man. No one stood for their wild behavior then and we won't stand for it now. This is a peaceful place to live. We don't want trouble here."

"Elwood, dear," Priscilla said, "this excitement isn't good for your heart."

"Having troublemakers move in across the street is what's not good for my heart." He glared at Kurt and the house behind him. "We had enough problems with the Jordan family. It's time for peace and quiet around here."

"It sounds to me like the Jordan family could have used some peace and quiet after everything they went through. As for River House, we won't cause any trouble, Mr. Hauge. We're part of Faith Community Church over on—"

"That's what they always say," the old man said sharply. "The last group, they bought the old Nelson house down the block. Said they were part of a church as well, and then there were fights, and the police were called countless times. That's not church the way I know it, young man. And we don't want that in this neighborhood again.

"Do you have a permit for such a thing? The city isn't going to allow you to bring a drug house into this area. No sir, they don't want that any more than we do."

A permit? Breath caught in his throat. Nobody had said anything about needing a permit. The future of River House seemed to be spinning out of his hands. "Mr. and Mrs. Hauge, I promise you we won't be calling the police unless *other* people cause trouble. We want this to be a safe place..." His words trailed off as Elwood turned away, leading his wife back to their house.

Kurt stood rooted to the sidewalk, watching them shuffle across the street. The solid bang of their front door made him flinch. For a long moment he couldn't feel his heart beating. Was River House going to collapse before he even got to sign the papers. *God?*

He spun on his heel and ran to his car, the excitement of only moments ago now in tatters. He turned the car toward Faith.

After several conversations with the realtor and city planner, Kurt was satisfied they were doing everything by the book. All the correct paperwork had been submitted, and River House was still a go. According to the city, anyway. In the neighborhood, it was a different story.

Elwood Hauge was apparently well connected, and in a few short days he had managed to sound an alarm in a three-block radius. Letters and calls flooded the church with questions, concerns, and fear that the quiet neighborhood was about to be overrun by the worst riffraff in the state. Rumors ran rampant. It was a front for a drug house. They would have prostitutes there. Kurt was moving in with ten kids. No, twenty.

Kurt fielded call after call, reassuring, explaining, sharing his dream. Most of the people seemed calmed after a thirty-minute conversation, a handful were still concerned, and a few said they would sign the petition that was circulating and even put their house on the market if the plans for River House went through.

Sitting with Vanessa in her new home two evenings later, feeling battered, bruised, and more discouraged than he'd felt since the start, Kurt stared into his coffee mug. His brain ached from trying to stay a step ahead of Elwood Hauge's hate campaign; his body felt like he'd been mugged and left for dead.

"Hello?"

His eyes lifted. "Hmm? Oh. Sorry. What did you say?"

Vanessa looked at him for a moment, a slender finger tapping her chin, then she nodded. "I think some brainstorming is in order." She left the kitchen and returned with a notepad and pen. Settling into the chair, she clicked the pen twice and looked at him expectantly.

He frowned back at her. "I'm the guy with the questions, remember?"

"You're also the guy with the answers. You just don't know it yet. So let's think of how you can get the neighborhood on your side."

"Sell River House."

She made a buzzer noise. "Try again."

"Paint River House pink?"

With a dramatic sigh, she thumped her chin onto her hand. "This is supposed to be a serious exercise. Work with me here."

"Okay, okay." He folded his arms and leaned back, trying to force ideas to come. "Well...I could go around and talk to every neighbor."

"Good." She wrote quickly. "Next idea. Come on, keep 'em coming."

Thirty minutes later he could breathe again. He'd never brainstormed, as she called it, and was amazed at the ideas that flowed once they got started. Going door-to-door would take too much time. A neighborhood meeting at the house would reach more people, allow everyone to air their fears and concerns collectively, and give Kurt a platform from which to address the questions and hopefully sidestep the rumor mill.

Vanessa grinned as she refilled their mugs. "Feel better?"

"A ton. Now I just need to pray for the right words and the right attitude."

"You'll do great. You always do."

Her confident words were a balm to his tired mind, muting some of the uncertainty. "I don't know about that. I just hope I don't make things worse." *Something I'm pretty good at.*

He straightened in the chair. "So that's enough about River House. Tell me what's going on around here. Merton getting used to the place?"

"He seems to be. For an old guy, he's been pretty amazing."

Kurt looked around the kitchen. He hadn't realized what a man cave he'd lived in until seeing her simple touches. "Your decorating is a lot better than mine. This place looks great."

She smiled. "Thanks. It's starting to feel a little bit like home."

"Good." He sat back in the chair, studying her. She looked rested, not as pale and sad as she'd been the last few weeks. The circles under her eyes had faded.

"I haven't missed climbing a flight of stairs every night to go to bed," she said. "A first-floor bedroom is quite the luxury."

"Mert probably doesn't miss it either."

She looked down at the faithful companion sitting at her feet. "We're just glad to be here together." She offered a shy smile. "Thank you."

"For what?"

"For suggesting this. For working out an arrangement with the owners that makes this affordable. And for being our friend."

He chuckled. "You're welcome on all counts. It's been cool watching it work out for everyone."

And it was real easy being her friend.

Believing in God would come in handy right about now. Vanessa threaded her way through the crowded yard to the large maple she and the kids had climbed years ago.

Less than a week after their brainstorming session, the neighborhood meeting was upon them. She was stunned by the number of people spreading out of the River House yard into the street. Leaning against the tree, she willed her heart to slow its anxious dance, wishing she could believe God would help Kurt face this restless mass of people. *How will anyone even hear him?*

She recognized many in the crowd but more were unfamiliar. Where had they come from? Some had even brought lawn chairs.

Right up front, just below the porch steps, stood Elwood Hauge. For all his bluster about how important his neighbors were, he'd had little time for the Jordan family. Her mother had held her head high whenever she'd encountered them, a warm smile on her face and often a plate of cookies in hand.

While Vanessa had admired her calm in the face of the Hauges' disdain, she hadn't inherited her sunny personality. When her mother died, she'd accepted the plate of bars Mrs. Hauge brought over with a stilted thank you, then quickly shut the door before angry words could escape.

Her gaze moved to where Kurt stood on the porch chatting with people she guessed were from the church. His laughter at something the larger man said was strained. His eyes drifted repeatedly over the yard as the crowd swelled.

He'd replaced his comfortable jeans and T-shirt with khakis and a navy polo shirt. With a new haircut that made him look several years older, Vanessa was surprised at how cute he really was. This young man looked professional and far more self-assured than the casual guy who'd knocked on her door in April. What a difference a few months had made for him. For both of them.

He scanned the crowd until their eyes met and his knotted brow loosened as he smiled. She gave a firm nod, willing him to stay calm and focused. He winked in reply before turning to the older man in their small group. They shared a few words and the man patted Kurt's shoulder. Kurt drew a deep breath and moved to the edge of the porch.

"Hey, everyone," he called. "Let's get started. I know you're all busy." The crowd quieted instantly and surprise flickered across his face. "Thanks for coming. Can you hear me in the back?"

"Louder," a voice called.

He stood straighter. "Okay. I'm Kurt Wagner and I'm the director of youth outreach for Faith Community Church. I'm also the director for the new program we're calling River House." He gestured to the house behind him. "This house belonged to the Jordan family for many years. Now it's about to become River House, a drop-in place for kids who want to learn some skills and get help so they can graduate from high school. But mainly it will be a place where they can learn about having a relationship with God."

"Those kinds of kids take drugs," someone shouted. People nodded grimly.

"We'll have zero tolerance when it comes to drugs, smoking, drinking, or any of that behavior." He glanced behind him. "Let me back up and introduce the people here from Faith Community Church, which is over on 28th and Bryant. First is Joel Barten, the senior pastor."

The older man Kurt had been talking to stepped forward and waved. Slightly taller than Kurt, he had a kind face and a relaxed stance. Talking to him after the kids died probably would have been better than the hospital chaplain who'd been as sterile as the room she'd recovered in.

"Mike Reed is the senior high director," Kurt continued. "He'll also be a major part of River House."

The big guy lifted his arms and pointed upward. Vanessa smiled. There was something mischievous about his expression. He was even bigger than Kurt had described, built like the tree she leaned against.

"And this is Ashley Pepper, the middle school director."

The pretty girl waved energetically, sending a strange zing into Vanessa's heart as she watched the girl and Kurt exchange warm smiles.

"We're all here to answer your concerns," he said, "either now or afterwards, so come talk to us anytime." He outlined his dream for River House, the plans being made to create a safe haven for kids, the adults who would be involved. And especially the faith that would be shared.

He stood taller when he talked about his God, about the need these kids had for a relationship with Him. What was it about his faith that gave him the courage to face an agitated crowd like this with a smile on his face? What would it be like to be that sure about something?

When he finished, he invited questions. Elwood stood and turned to address the crowd. Vanessa glared at him, anger swelling at the disgust on her former neighbor's wrinkled face. He seemed determined to undermine River House before it got started.

"This is a wonderful neighborhood. We have families with children here. We've never been on the news for murders or drugs or any of that kind of behavior. And that's because we care about this community. We don't want a bunch of punks running around at all hours, causing trouble. We don't want the police being called for the shenanigans of this house."

He droned on, obviously trying to work the crowd into an uproar. Kurt listened, hands behind his back, his expression neutral. The crowd became more agitated the longer Elwood spoke.

Kurt, stop him before there's a lynching!

"So, young man." He turned to look up at Kurt. "We want you to take your big ideas somewhere else. You are not welcome here."

A smattering of applause answered his words. Kurt nodded, his lips set in a firm line. For a moment he stood so still Vanessa feared he would give up the dream.

"Thank you, Mr. Hauge," he said finally, "for stating your views so clearly. I'll try to answer all the points you brought up. Those are the very same things I worry about where I live, not far from here. I wouldn't want River House to be located in a neighborhood that didn't care as much as you do."

He held up his index finger. "The first point I want to answer is about drugs. I won't tolerate drugs messing up the work we'll be doing. We'll have strict rules at River House. Can I guarantee there won't ever be a problem? No, obviously I can't. Neither can the churches or schools, or even parents in their own homes. But we'll do our best to make River House a great neighbor for all of you."

Vanessa smiled as she watched him calmly deal with the restless crowd before him. She relaxed against the tree as he continued, his voice strong and decisive.

"River House is our way of addressing the issues kids face today. We want to be a safe place, a welcoming place, where they can learn skills to help them become productive, compassionate leaders in the community. *Our* community. And over all of our plans will be the prayer that God leads us in the right direction to become an important part of this neighborhood."

He worked the crowd as easily as Elwood had, striding across the porch, pausing to look directly at people. Passion threaded through his words, ringing in his tone and in his rising enthusiasm. Elwood had no response, sitting ramrod straight in his front-row lawn chair, arms folded tight across his chest.

"What other questions do people have?" Kurt asked.

The crowd was quiet, the earlier mob mentality dissipating in the face of his thoughtful, passionate response to Elwood's attack. Neighbors exchanged nods, talking quietly amongst themselves. Vanessa traded smiles with Kurt, her heart spinning joyfully.

A man's voice from the back of the crowd thundered, "Hey, Wagner. When did you get out of prison?"

Vanessa's heart stopped dancing, stopped beating. People turned around, craning their necks to see where the voice came from, then looked at Kurt who remained motionless, staring toward the street.

Elwood sprang from the chair, his face glowing with triumph. "I knew there was something fishy," he declared. "You're a con *and* a con artist."

Kurt continued to stare at the man standing in the street dressed in black leather, a blue bandana on his head. His wide-legged stance mirrored Kurt's. With a scraggly beard, dirty blonde hair sticking out from beneath the scarf, and mirrored sunglasses, he was a forbidding figure.

Vanessa looked back at Kurt. The church people stood frozen behind him. The murmurings of the crowd grew as Elwood egged them on, demanding Kurt forgo the house and leave their neighborhood alone.

"What'sa matter, Wagner?" the man asked. "You were always a smart mouth in the joint. Tryin' to be somebody you ain't, now that you're out?"

His voice was deep and scratchy. It was clear by the smirk on his scarred face that he was enjoying the standoff. Her dislike for Elwood was magnified ten times over for this dirty, hostile man standing between Kurt and his dream. Where was Kurt's God now, when his future hung in the silence? Fury at Elwood, the stranger, and God snaked through her until she wanted to scream.

Kurt gave a single nod. "Wolf."

"So this is the type of person you associate with?" Elwood demanded. "*This* is what we can expect to be visiting your drug house?"

Kurt's eyes remained locked on the stranger. "Wolf isn't interested in River House, Mr. Hauge."

"Is it true that you were in prison? You're a convicted felon?"

The stillness of the crowd pressed in on Vanessa as they waited for his response. At his nod there was a collective gasp and voices rushed into chaos. Kurt's gaze found hers, his eyes narrowing as if looking for her reaction. Frowning fiercely, she put her hands on her hips and gave a nod. The uncertainty in his eyes faded. He moved to stand at the edge of the step.

"Yes," he said clearly and the crowd hushed. "Yes, I was in prison. For twenty-seven months. I served my sentence and have been out for three years, gainfully employed at Faith Community Church ever since. I learned my lesson, I found my future in my faith in God, and I'm not ashamed to tell my story. In fact, it's my story that's the foundation for River House."

His gaze returned to Vanessa's. "As someone pointed out, if I can use the lessons I learned the hard way to keep kids from making the same mistakes, then I'm grateful for what I went through."

The man moved from the street into the yard, the chains on his pants jangling. People sidled away, giving him space. "Tell 'em *why* you were in jail, Wagner."

Kurt stared back at him and Vanessa's heart dropped. She closed her eyes as he spoke.

"Drug possession."

Bedlam broke out in the yard. Elwood gleefully raised a crooked finger in the air as he crowed, "I knew it! I knew you were trouble! My instincts are always right."

Kurt's response was lost in the commotion that filled the yard. People shook their heads, glaring at him. Fighting the urge to take a cane to the vile man's head, Vanessa pushed away from the tree and maneuvered through the crowd toward the stairs.

Kurt moved down the steps to block her approach. "Vanessa, stay out of this."

"Move," she said, pushing past him.

His fingers closed around her arm. "Nessa, I appreciate it—"

"You're not the only one who gets to talk." She yanked her arm away and went up the remaining steps. She faced the crowd, put her fingers to her mouth and released a shrill whistle that brought instant silence to the chaos. "I have something to say."

Kurt stared at her, openmouthed. The faces looking up at her were a collage of mixed emotions—suspicion, anger, surprise. She drew a deep breath and hoped her story wouldn't make things worse.

"My name is Vanessa Jordan. As some of you know, I used to live in this house. Now I'm living just blocks from here. I'm not part of River House but I am part of this neighborhood, and I want to tell you my story."

She waited until people had settled back into their chairs or turned fully to face her. She glanced at the vile man who stared at her, beefy arms folded. "I've lived in this house most of my life with my mom, my brother and my sister. Three years ago my mother died of breast cancer, so I was raising the kids by myself. This past January we were in a car accident. I survived but they didn't."

In the answering silence, she swallowed hard, determined to get the whole story out. Kurt's vision hung in the balance.

"I met Kurt on a street corner near here in April when he literally saved my life." She looked at him, biting her lip. "I have to admit I wasn't very nice to him. I didn't want to live so it wouldn't have mattered to me if I were killed. But it mattered to him so he risked his life to make sure a disabled stranger was safe."

The faces throughout the yard were attentive and sympathetic. She focused on familiar ones—the young mom Angie had babysat for, the elderly couple two doors down who had relied on Matt's lawn mowing, the next-door neighbor with the dog they'd played with.

"As I got to know Kurt, I realized his action on that street corner wasn't a fluke. I discovered a good friend with a huge heart. He told me right away about being in prison, and he also shared his dream to keep other kids from repeating his mistakes."

Elwood Hauge kept his gaze averted, arms crossed, muttering to himself. She looked out over the yard, relieved to see the hateful man stalk back to his car.

"Kurt has been an enormous encouragement to me on my journey of learning to live again. I don't share his faith but I respect his beliefs, his passion to help kids, and his heart for this neighborhood. He's my friend, and he'll be yours if you stop judging him before getting to know him.

"All of us have things in our past we're not proud of, but

hopefully we learned from them and moved forward, better for the experience."

She looked at Kurt. Tears shimmered in his eyes. "I believe in him and what he wants to do through River House. I hope all of you, including you, Mr. Hauge, will give him the chance to show how he can make this neighborhood even better. Thank you."

The click of her canes was the only sound as she moved back down the steps and returned to her place under the tree, nodding at people who thanked her. She leaned against the trunk again and waited for her heart to slow its wild pounding.

Joel took her spot on the porch. "Thank you, Vanessa. We'll remain here in the yard for however long is necessary to meet each of you, answer your questions, and share more of our dream for the youth of this community. Faith Church wholeheartedly supports Kurt in his desire to give kids an opportunity to become productive, positive adults, and we hope you'll join us in that endeavor. Thank you for coming."

For a long moment no one moved or spoke. Elwood sat entrenched in his chair, staring forward. Then a hundred conversations broke out at once and Vanessa released the breath she'd been holding.

Kurt had been amazing. Now it was up to the neighborhood to render a verdict.

In the days following the neighborhood meeting, responses filtered in to Faith Church. Kurt focused on each call, taking time to hear their stories and concerns. Most supported the ministry idea; a few were still fearful of how the neighborhood would be affected.

"We'd love to have you be part of River House," Kurt assured the neighbor who lived three doors down. "The more adults we have mentoring and encouraging and teaching, the better."

There was a short silence. "I'm pretty good with automotive stuff. Maybe I could help them repair their cars."

Kurt offered a silent prayer of thanks. "Great idea. And maybe down the road we could offer inexpensive car repair for the neighborhood. A way for the kids to learn hands-on and give back to the community."

"I like that." The defensive tone had softened. "Everybody should know basic car maintenance."

They chatted a few minutes before the neighbor agreed to email Kurt with more ideas about how he and his artist wife might be able to help.

"And that little blonde that spoke up? She's a keeper."

A smile burst across Kurt's face. "She sure is."

When he hung up, he was still smiling. He looked at the photo he'd pinned to the wall of the two of them celebrating River House with ice cream cones. The more he got to know her, the more she surprised him. He'd been stunned by her gutsy courage in the face of Wolf's threats as she defended him and their friendship. *I thought you brought us together for me to help her, Lord. But she's helped me more. I'm going to owe her big time after all she's done for River House.*

He stood and grabbed his keys and phone, needing to see the House. He'd postponed the major renovations until the neighborhood settled down. While he responded to community concerns, the demolition crew was gutting the kitchen to create a work station for Sam Jensen, the general contractor, and his renovation team.

Parked at the curb, he watched tall, lanky Sam squat down to talk to several children. The kids pointed at the drill he held, asking questions. He answered with a smile then added something that made them back away.

Kurt grinned as he swung out of the car. Even Sam was building relationships. He glanced across the street. But it would take an act of God to build something with Elwood.

On Friday, Kurt set out to spread the word about River House, enjoying the early June evening that meant few mosquitoes and longer sunlight. He wandered the busy streets in Uptown, inhaling the comforting aroma of hazelnut from the steaming cup in his hands.

Deeply buried memories pushed to the surface as he strolled the familiar haunts of a former life. Aimless nights hanging out in dimly lit pool halls, street fights, drunken brawls. He stopped outside the bar that had been a frequent hangout and flashed back to a scene seven years ago.

The guy across the pool table had paused before his next shot, pinning Kurt with a piercing gaze. "You got a job yet, Wagner?"

"Nah." He'd been too busy writing songs to do any serious job hunting. The band was about to sign a contract for their first tour. They were on the verge of making it big—he'd felt it in his bones. "Why? Got one for me?"

Wolf's menacing grin should have sent him running. "Wolf" was Mack Hammer, an acquaintance from those bad boy days, that hazy time of drinking that had sent his life reeling out of control.

Agreeing to that one "job" for Wolf had sent Kurt to jail. In most respects he was thankful. Those years in the joint, where he'd met Joel through the prison ministry, had saved his life.

Wolf's neighborhood drug empire had been busted along with Kurt, and he'd made his anger painfully clear in prison. By the time Kurt was released, he'd had enough random beatings to last a lifetime. He'd thought the worst was over. Why had Wolf bothered to find out where he was now?

He shook his head to banish the sense of foreboding. He was on a new journey now, with a mission so removed from those early days that he felt like a different man. Couldn't he move forward without his past barking at his heels?

"Hey, Wagner."

The call came from a group of older teenage boys standing outside McDonald's. The tallest was a boy he'd seen at Faith a few times. He crossed the street to greet them. "Hey, Pauly."

The boy's eyes lit with surprise. "You remember me? Cool."

"'Course I do." Kurt sipped his coffee. "How you been?"

"Real good, man. Got me a job at the hardware store a month ago. The one on Emerson."

"Yeah, a real workin' stiff," the disheveled boy next to him said, giving him an elbow. "Now my man can't play cards every night."

"Life is full of trade-offs." Kurt winked. "Probably leaves more money for you to win."

The boy straightened. "Yeah, I'll be havin' me a winnin' streak anytime now."

The others broke into raucous laughter. "Man, you can't even beat your little sister at Go Fish." More jostling and laughter.

Kurt turned to Pauly. "Do you get a discount at the store?"

"Fifteen percent."

"Cool. Maybe I can get your help. I'm renovating a house and I'm gonna need a lot of equipment and materials. Think I can talk to your manager about that?"

"Sure. You got a house now?"

"Sort of. We bought a house but it's not for me. It's a place for kids to hang out after school. I need help with everything, like hanging drywall, painting, woodworking. All that stuff."

The smallest of the boys, in baggy jeans, a baseball cap on sideways, had listened with interest. "So it's like a club or sumpthin'?"

"A club for everyone. But I need help getting it ready. Any of you guys handy with tools?"

They shook their heads, shuffling their feet.

"No problem. I just need warm bodies. I'll teach anybody who wants to learn."

"Do we have to, like, pay for that?"

"Nope. I need the help and I figure there are lots of people around here that could learn a skill. So we all win." He pulled business cards from his back pocket and handed one to each boy. "This is the address of the house. Stop by to check it out. And if you wanna help with the work, that'd be great."

He turned back to Pauly. "I'll come by the store this week to talk to your manager."

"Sure, man. That's cool. I'm workin' on Tuesday and Wednesday."

They bumped fists and Kurt continued down the sidewalk, his heart ready to burst. He could do this—just hang out and talk about River House. God would do the rest.

Into the evening, he wandered a five-block area along Lake Street, stopping to talk to kids he knew and kids he didn't. Some were happy to talk, others leery about engaging. He walked, handed out burgers he bought at McDonald's, and talked until his throat was sore. When all one hundred of the business cards were gone, he headed back to River House, exhausted to his toes and thrilled to his core.

Alone in the quiet house amidst the chaos and debris, he dropped to his knees. Heart full, he lifted his hands to offer thanks and to pray for the kids God had put in his path tonight and for those who would fill River House in the coming days.

And in the silence and holiness of the moment, he realized that the fear that had ridden his back since the initial conversation with Joel was gone. Not fading or waiting in the wings. Gone. He still had no clue what he was doing, but he would go forward each day trusting the God who had called him to this adventure.

With his jacket bunched under his head, he slept on Vanessa's old couch in the disheveled living room, the contented sleep of a man at peace.

As Vanessa approached River House Tuesday morning, the buzz of activity coming from the open windows signaled that the ministry was off and running. She paused to wait for the throbbing in her leg to stop, listening to the laughter and conversation that carried over the sounds of pounding and sawing.

Her beloved old home was being given new life and purpose through Kurt's ministry. She didn't have to worry about it crumbling around her anymore. The day she moved out, she'd decided she wouldn't think of it in terms of *her* house anymore, only as River House. It would always hold the lifetime of memories etched permanently in her heart, but now new ones would form within its walls.

Kurt stood in the living room studying plans with an older man. As she stepped into the chaos, a smile lit his face. "Hey, Vanessa! Come in and meet this guy. Sam, this is Vanessa Jordan. Nessa, this is Sam Jensen. He's the general contractor for this whole amazing mess."

Sam's handshake was hearty, his large calloused hand dwarfing hers. Kurt continued, "This is where Vanessa grew up. It was her idea to turn it into River House."

"So this is the little gal we've heard so much about. This house is perfect for the work Kurt will be doing."

She glanced at Kurt. "I'm glad. It's been a great old house."

Sam's friendly face seemed creased into a permanent grin. "And it will continue to be. I'm happy to meet you, Vanessa. Now I need to get out back and see what's happening in the garage."

He rolled up the large sheet of paper and tucked it under his arm, gave her a wink, then wound his way around piles of tools toward the back of the house.

Kurt turned to Vanessa, folding his arms. "So what do you think?"

She took a moment to look around. Three young women were scraping wallpaper in the dining room; several men removed baseboard in the living room. Voices floated down the stairs to mingle with conversations around her.

"I think it looks different already. And I think you've got a whole lot of people who believe in what you're doing."

"Yeah. Pretty amazing." His gaze followed hers around the room. "We'll be ready to start the structural work early next week. That's like a full week ahead of schedule. Come on, I wanna show you what's been done so far."

A steady stream of volunteers were making quick work of tearing out the old and preparing for the new—yards of carpet ripped up and padding scraped from the hardwood floors, walls patched and sanded.

"Man, just staying ahead of this crew is going to kill me," he said with a laugh as they finished the tour and returned to the main living area. "So I was thinking, since this is going to be the place where we have meetings and stuff, I thought it should have a name. How about we call it the Gathering Place?"

She looked around and nodded. "That's perfect."

He grinned. "Okay, it's official."

A moment later he was called to the backyard, leaving Vanessa amidst the girls in the dining room.

From atop a step stool, the girl Vanessa recognized from the neighborhood meeting introduced herself and the others with a wave of her rubber-gloved hand. "I'm Ashley, and this is Steph and Annie. You're the girl who spoke up at the meeting, aren't you?"

She nodded. "I'm Vanessa. What can I do to help?"

Not wanting preferential treatment, she set her cane aside and eased up several steps of a ladder, putting her weight on her left leg as she started scraping wallpaper. The surprise on Kurt's face when he reappeared sent a tingle of accomplishment through her. Maybe one day he'd see her as capable as Ashley.

Over the next few hours she melted into the group—working, laughing, and sharing lunch. The stories they told about Kurt made her giggle despite the halfhearted frown he shot from where he patched holes in the living room walls.

A whirlwind of energy, Ashley was especially entertaining as she told youth group stories that kept them laughing, removed twice as much wallpaper as the rest, and never seemed to break a sweat.

Scraping at a stubborn patch of wallpaper glue, Vanessa listened to Kurt joke with his bubbly coworker. Their good-natured ribbing created a spark of energy that filled the room with laughter.

"Oh, yeah?" Ashley countered his story with one of her own. "I seem to remember you getting your arm stuck in a wall once."

"Trying to retrieve *your* shoe."

"Which *you* threw after you unfairly tackled me in the touch football game."

He gave Ashley a playful shove then glanced at Vanessa before turning back to his work. It seemed obvious that Ashley's feelings for Kurt went beyond those of a friend, but he was harder to read.

He never talked about dates or any particular girl. Even after several months of walks and talks, he'd shared few details of his personal life. Maybe he'd forgotten to mention he had a special someone in his life. The thought pricked her heart.

"Wagner," asked an unfamiliar male voice, "how much did you pay these people to do all your grunt work?"

"Nada." Kurt didn't look up, but Vanessa could see a smile on his profile.

The bearded young giant strode into the room, filling it with his stature and enthusiasm. She recognized him from the neighborhood meeting and from Kurt's countless stories.

He stopped when he caught sight of her, his smile broad and

curious. Arms folded across his chest, his green eyes sparkled at her from behind wire-rimmed glasses.

"Wait, I know you," he boomed. "You're Vanessa, the little gal with the big whistle. You snuck off after the meeting before I could meet you. That was you, right?"

From her new spot sitting on an upside-down bucket in the corner, she gave a cautious nod. "Maybe."

He threw back his head to release a deep laugh and Vanessa decided she liked him. He seemed full of life and fun.

"Kurt has good taste in friends," he said.

She smiled in return, a hand on the wall as she pushed to her feet. "I'd have to agree."

Kurt joined them, shaking his head as he met Vanessa's gaze. "If I don't introduce him, he's gonna make up something about being the King of England. Mike Reed, Faith Church senior high director, meet Vanessa Jordan. 'Nuff said."

Mike gave him a slap on the back and Vanessa giggled at Kurt's wide-eyed expression as he staggered forward. She pulled off her work gloves and extended her hand. "I've heard a lot about you, Mike. It's nice to finally meet you."

He ignored her proffered hand and engulfed her in a bear hug. "Wow, you're just a munchkin. I didn't know they made grownups so little."

She stepped back to look up at him—way up—and put her hands on her hips. "Watch out for the little ones," she warned with a smile. "We can be the sneakiest."

Kurt chuckled. "And the feistiest."

"Well, anyone who could convince Wagner that God put this amazing call on his life deserves special recognition. We'll have to make you a crown or something to recognize your part in starting River House. And to make sure people don't step on you."

With Mike's dynamic presence now part of the group, the last few hours of work passed quickly. Vanessa was sad to have it end. She'd enjoyed being swallowed into the work crew. The open and accepting friendship extended to her had obliterated the fact that they all believed in a God she despised.

Tired and content, she stood in the driveway and rubbed her arms lightly, savoring the lingering warmth of the girls' farewell hugs. She couldn't remember the last time she had been part of something that felt this good. The biggest surprise of the day was setting a coffee date with Steph and Annie, the girls she'd worked beside all afternoon. Friendships and normal life seemed like a distant dream, and she'd been thrilled when Annie suggested they meet on Friday. Joy took the edge off her aching leg as she headed home.

Moments later, a car pulled up beside her. "Hey lady. How about a ride? You've gotta be tired. I'm wiped out."

She hesitated, wanting to be tough enough to get home on her own, but the growing throb in her leg convinced her to accept. Kurt hopped out and opened the door for her. She settled in with a sigh. "What a great group you had helping today."

"Yeah. I was amazed at all the people who showed up. A few even took vacation days just to be here."

"That's how much they believe in what you're doing."

"In what *God's* doing," he corrected with a grin. "It was so cool to see you there too. Thanks for coming."

"Thanks for letting me stay to help."

His gaze swung over to hers, eyebrows raised. "*Letting* you stay? Vanessa, you're as much a part of River House as I am. It wouldn't exist if you hadn't knocked some sense into me in the beginning. And you're the one who provided the house. I'm going to put a plaque on the front door with your name on it. Or maybe I'll just change the name to Vanessa's House. Or Jordan House."

She laughed. "That's funny. Would it be okay if I helped again tomorrow?"

"Of course. What's that saying? A bunch of hands make speedy work or something."

"Something like that. So tell me about Ashley. She's very fun."

Kurt shared a number of amusing stories about his coworker and they arrived at Vanessa's in the middle of a tale that had them both chuckling. He ordered her to get comfortable in the porch swing, promising to return with lemonade.

She rubbed her aching thigh, then positioned her pant legs over both feet as she always did, hoping it made her right leg look normal. He reappeared with two tall glasses, ice clinking in the pink liquid.

Accepting one with a smile, she took a long sip. "Mmm. This is wonderful, thank you." The wooden swing creaked as he settled beside her. "So," she said with a nonchalant air, "are you two dating?"

He spewed out a mouthful of lemonade before looking at her, wide-eyed. "Me and Ash?"

"Dating usually involves two people."

"No." He frowned. "No dates."

"Have you thought about asking her?"

"No!" He turned to look out at the street and took a long drink.

Perhaps he'd asked and been turned down.

"She's like a kid sister, Nessa. I can't imagine taking her on a date. She's fun and nice and all, but..." He shrugged. "That'd just be too weird."

She was pleased with his answer. Too pleased. His private life was none of her business. She dropped her gaze to her shoes. It's not like he'd ever be interested in someone like her, anyway. Friends, sure. Anything more, no way.

The sip of lemonade suddenly tasted bitter.

After two weeks in her new home, Vanessa's world was coming into focus. The cold fog of grief had given way to the warm brilliance of summer. Flowers bloomed in a riot of color everywhere, waving at her in the gentle breeze.

Life had burst into song, as well—the cheerful chatter of birds as she walked in the neighborhood, the laughter of children at the park, the clatter of skateboards in the alley. Each morning it was just a little easier to get up and face her life.

Regular talks with Jenny allowed her to revisit memories of the kids and her mom without wallowing in the pain. She shared stories, raised issues, and wondered aloud where God was that terrible January evening, and where He was now in her struggles.

She continued to wrestle with the guilt that plagued her, the accusing thoughts that told her she had no right to move toward the future when she'd destroyed everything that mattered. But as she talked and laughed and cried, the sadness dissipated a little more, allowing her to take deeper breaths of her new life.

Kurt came every day for what he called a walk 'n talk. She was happy to have his company, to share a laugh and hear about his busy day. One early evening they strolled to Lake Calhoun where he bought chocolate shakes from the concession stand.

As they settled on a bench with a view of the sparkling water, Vanessa looked at him over her cup. "You don't talk much about your family."

He seemed suddenly intent on his ice cream. "There isn't much to tell. Dad left when I was about twelve. Then it was just me, my little brother Scott, and my mom. After a few years, my mom remarried." He swallowed hard. "She died a while ago."

"Oh, I'm sorry." She knew that pain so well.

He shrugged. "It's okay. I'm glad she didn't see how messed up I got."

"Yeah. I get that. It's good you still have your brother. How often do you get together?"

"He lives in Seattle, so not very often."

"You must talk on the phone a lot."

When he shrugged again, a chill ran through her that wasn't from the ice cream. She lowered her cup. "You don't talk?"

"We're both pretty busy. He's got a family—"

"That's even more reason."

Kurt shifted on the bench, looking out at the lake. "We just...there never seems—" He sighed and leaned his elbows on his knees. "It's hard to explain."

"You have a brother, Kurt." If she had a sibling left, they'd be burning up the phone lines. "You have the gift of *family*."

He winced. "I know." They sat silently for a minute. "I went out there when he and Hayley got married. And they came here for a visit after their little girl was born about a year and a half ago. But he's got a good job that makes it tough to get away so they haven't been back. And I haven't had the money for a plane ticket. We email once in a while."

Vanessa pressed her lips together, holding back the response that shot up her throat. She'd never had money either, but that hadn't stopped her from taking care of what mattered. And family mattered more than anything. She'd hitchhike out there, if she had to.

"He's a great guy. Hayley's perfect for him," he continued, still staring at the lake. His posture drooped. "They're happy out there, Nessa. He doesn't need me."

"Of course he does. You're brothers. Nobody outgrows their need for family."

"Maybe not, but you'll have to trust me on this. He's better off without me in his life."

"I don't believe that for a minute. You have so much to offer him. He's lucky to have you. He's *family*, Kurt."

Jaw clenched, he looked at his watch and got to his feet. "I have a meeting with Joel in half an hour so we should head back."

She stared at him for a long moment. He didn't meet her gaze. "That's okay. I'll walk home. You can go right to the church."

"Vanessa—"

"It's okay, Kurt. I can take care of myself." The earlier cheerfulness had dissolved into an aching void. "Walking is good for me, remember?"

As they faced each other, he sighed. "Maybe someday I can tell you the whole story. Then you might understand."

"You don't owe me an explanation." *Or more excuses.*

He grasped her shoulders, an intense light in his eyes. "I want you to understand. It's sort of—it's complicated. But I don't want you to think I don't care about my brother. I do."

"I'm sure you do. You're a good man."

"Yeah, well, I don't know about that." He dropped his arms and stepped back. "You're sure you don't want me to walk you home?"

"I'll be fine. Thanks for the ice cream." She walked away, tossing her half-eaten shake into a trash bin. Grief made it hard to breathe. She wanted a family with every fiber of her being. Kurt had one he barely talked to. Life was so unfair.

After an evening of meetings and phone calls and a struggle to finish what he called the "state of the ministry report" for the board of elders, Kurt lay in bed staring at the ceiling. The memories he'd refused to acknowledge all day now washed over him.

As a kid, Scott had followed him everywhere. Or sat quietly on his bed, watching while Kurt fumbled with chords on his guitar. Even then Kurt had known he didn't deserve the worship in his little brother's eyes.

Darker memories pinched his heart. Scotty cowering from their father's rage. Hugging Kurt hard at the jail after a visit.

Scotty was his kid brother. That should draw them together, but it made him want to run in shame instead. Vanessa had looked horrified at his lame excuses. She didn't know everything about his past. She would just have to think he was irresponsible or heartless or something. Maybe he was.

A tear slid into his ear as he closed his eyes. The silence of the room pressed him down into the mattress. His brother was a great kid who'd grown up to be a really cool guy. Scotty didn't need Kurt in his life anymore. He turned on his side and let the tears lull him to sleep.

But he needed Scott.

The next few days seemed out of focus. Concentration eluded him as he tried to put the finishing touches to his report. Friday's planning meeting was cut short when he and Mike were called to the hospital following a skateboarding accident involving Faith Community kids.

Several hours and many prayers later, he left Mike with the kids and their parents and wandered out into the evening air. Reaching his car, he stood for a long moment, eyes closed, enjoying the light breeze on his air-conditioned skin. He offered a prayer of thanks that the kids' recklessness hadn't resulted in more than a broken leg, a couple black eyes and some very frightened teens.

Gentle warmth blew across his heart, soothing the tangled emotions he'd been wrestling for days.

You are forgiven.

His eyes popped open and he stood very still, waiting. *Of course I am.* He'd clung to that promise since coming to faith. So what was that seemingly random statement about?

He shook his head as he climbed into the car. If he'd learned anything over the past few years, it was that nothing with God was random. He turned abruptly at the next corner and drove to his old house.

He needed to talk. About what, he wasn't even sure, but Vanessa had become his go-to person. His friend.

Everything had felt off-balance since their exchange by the lake. Hopefully she was still speaking to him. He jogged up the steps and knocked.

Her eyes widened in surprise. "Hi!"

"Hi." He shoved his hands into his pockets and rocked back on his heels, relieved she hadn't slammed the door on him. "I probably should have called. Sorry for coming by so late."

She quirked an eyebrow. "I'm usually still up at eight o'clock." Stepping back to let him in, her eyes narrowed. "Is something wrong?"

"No. Not really. I don't think so."

A smile played at the corners of her mouth. "Well, that clarifies things."

"Yeah." This was stupid. He didn't have anything to say. He'd just needed to see her. Merton strolled over and Kurt squatted to scratch his chin. "Hey Mert, old boy. You behaving?"

A rumble started in the cat's oversized belly.

"So," Vanessa said, "how about a glass of milk?"

He looked up. "For me or Merton?"

"Mertie prefers a bowl. A glass of milk always worked for the kids when they had an issue." He stood and she pushed him gently toward the kitchen. "Go on. We obviously need to talk about something, so let's do it over milk and cookies."

Settled at the table, Kurt wrapped his fingers around the glass, staring at the white foam. Just sitting here with her eased the tension in his neck. His shoulders dropped away from his ears, and he blinked when she slid a plate of Oreos in front of him. "Hey, my favorite!"

"According to the package, they're also milk's favorite."

He chuckled and then lifted his gaze to hers. "I want to tell you about Scott."

"Okay." She propped her elbows on the table and sipped her milk.

He launched into memories waiting just below the surface. Two years apart, he and Scott had been best friends through childhood. Scott was the natural athlete—Kurt had cheered him on at track meets and tennis matches. He rode his bike ahead of his little brother to encourage him to run faster and farther.

"There was this time when we went fishing. We weren't supposed to go near the Mississippi but I figured we'd be okay if we stayed along the edge. Somehow Scotty fell in. Man, I've never been so scared in my life."

He could still hear Scott's frightened cries over the rushing water, smell the dankness of the river. He'd scrambled along the bank, twigs and branches reaching for him, snagging his shirt as if trying to hold him back.

"The current pulled him downriver. I ran like crazy along the shore until I found a tree to hold onto and grabbed him as he went by. When I finally got him out, we sat in the sun to dry off and calm down. We never fished the river again."

He was vaguely aware of Vanessa refilling his glass. She asked a few questions but mostly sat listening, nodding, occasionally smiling.

Memories continued to pour out. They'd played catch for hours in the yard, built forts in the woods. He'd helped Scott with his homework until it was stuff he didn't understand. He was there for every band concert; Scott was crazy good on the trumpet. And when their dad went on a drinking binge and things got ugly, he made sure Scotty was tucked away safely until it was over.

The memories darkened and he slammed the door on the ugliness. Drawing a deep breath, he met Vanessa's encouraging smile. For one irrational moment, he nearly told her everything.

"So that's a little about Scott," he said instead.

"He sounds like a really great guy. And he obviously adored his big brother."

"Yeah."

"I'll bet he still does." The gentle words were soothing.

He dropped his gaze, swirling the milk in his glass. "Not so much. Big brothers can do really stupid things."

When Vanessa was quiet, he looked up. She waited, watching him with a steady gaze. Her silence unnerved him. He hadn't meant to talk so much. She pulled stuff out of him he didn't even know he wanted to talk about. Stuff he hadn't shared with anyone.

He glanced at the clock over the sink. "Wow. It's almost ten. I didn't mean to stay so long."

"I'm glad you came by." She took their glasses to the sink, then turned and leaned back against the counter. "Thanks for sharing your memories of Scott. I hope I can meet him someday."

He stood. "I hope so too. Thanks for letting me drop in and talk at you for two hours. I'd be happy to return the favor."

"It was my pleasure," she said with a smile.

His heart jiggled as he moved forward to tap her nose playfully. "Watch it, Nessa. Even white lies can get you in trouble."

She released a huff and set her hands on her hips. "I mean it, Kurt. I usually do most of the talking, and I've learned so little about you over these past months. It's nice to get a glimpse inside the real Kurt Wagner."

He chuckled. "The real Kurt Wagner. Makes me sound pretty mysterious."

"You are. I'm feeling quite privileged that you would share your brother with me."

He said goodnight and headed to his car. He didn't mean to be mysterious. Some things were just better left unsaid. And buried.

19

Early morning sunshine spilled across the front of the house, sparkling off new windows, dancing across a gleaming black roof. Kurt stood on the sidewalk and breathed in the smell of flowers and freshness, tingling with anticipation.

For the rest of the city, it was a normal Saturday morning in July, but here on Dupont Avenue, it was the official opening of River House. In a few hours, people would gather to surround the house with prayer as they dedicated this new ministry. Then the house would be open for the day so people could see the renovations.

He'd hardly slept the past few nights, tying up loose ends and praying nonstop for this journey that stretched before him. Excitement had chased away his appetite. He'd been living on caffeine and Twinkies since Thursday. Several Faith families were donating breakfast this morning for those who came to pray. The thought made his stomach rumble. He'd have to make sure he grabbed something before the day got away from him again.

Glancing over his shoulder, he sighed. The Hauges' curtains were drawn tight, but they would be watching, today and every day. He was determined to turn them into River House supporters. Only God knew how that would happen.

He stretched his arms overhead, hooking his fingers together to crack his knuckles. Dozing off last night, he'd had the distinct impression he needed to be here early to pray for the community, the neighbors, the kids God would bring to River House.

He set off slowly around the block, praying over each house, asking for God's protection and blessing in the coming months. When he returned an hour later, he was more at peace than he'd been in weeks.

The shine of Vanessa's blonde hair caught his attention where she was settled on the porch swing, two cups in a Java Depot container beside her. She was wearing her usual long black pants, with a pink sleeveless shirt that highlighted the new color in her face. The pale girl of their first meeting had been replaced by this vibrant young woman who brightened his days.

His heart jumped at her welcoming smile and he jogged the remaining distance. "Hey, good morning!"

"Good morning to you. I had a feeling you'd be here bright and early. Or didn't you go home last night?"

He settled next to her and accepted the cup she held out. "Thanks. I did, but I wanted to spend the morning praying before everybody got here. What has you up so early?"

"River House." She grinned. "I'm so excited for you I was awake with the sun."

They chatted quietly, enjoying their coffee and the warmth of the summer morning. He was thrilled she'd come. He couldn't imagine opening River House without her, but he'd figured the prayer service would keep her away.

As ingrained as she was in his daily life now, discussions about faith and God had been sporadic. He was careful not to dismiss her feelings, but he longed for her to let go of her defenses and open her heart to God's love. When the time seemed right, he'd invite her to a service at Faith.

As she talked about plans for the yard and suggested landscaping ideas, her words were quick and animated, her blue eyes sparkling. When she touched his arm to make a point, the funny staccato beat of his heart made him pause.

He'd prayed many times lately for control of the growing feelings that tangled his tongue. She'd never given any sign that she thought of him as more than a good friend, maybe her best friend. But he was an ex-con. That part of him would never go away. And if he wasn't careful, his overactive imagination could end up embarrassing both of them big time.

She deserved someone like Mike, who could offer a solid, rosy future, a nice home with a white picket fence. Or at least a decent yard. He could never compete with that. Beyond getting River House up and running, he had no clue what his future held.

Ashley pulled into the driveway with Mike close behind. Joel arrived with his wife and three kids, and soon the yard was filled with cheerful supporters laying out a spread of donuts, bagels, and fruit on the old front door resting on sawhorses. The aroma of fresh-brewed coffee and the sound of new friendships forming permeated the air.

Neighbors trickled out of their houses to join the festive atmosphere. Faith Church youth had passed out flyers inviting the neighborhood to a blessing of the house. He'd prayed that no one would come with picket signs and that Wolf wouldn't make a repeat performance. So far, so good.

From his position near the donuts, he watched volunteers who'd worked on the house greet Vanessa with hugs. Her shy smile brightened as Annie and Steph hurried through the crowded yard to join her. During a walk last week, she'd tried to hide her tears when she told him about meeting the girls for coffee. Dealing with the daily issues in life had prevented her from having girlfriends. Real girlfriends, she'd stressed, who talked about dating, clothes, food, and life. Now she had two.

Mike and Joel joined their conversation. Vanessa's smile seemed genuine as she and Joel shook hands. Moments later the small group burst into laughter at something Mike said, and Kurt let the grin in his heart fill his face.

He glanced at his watch, climbed up on the porch and shaded his eyes to look out over a sea of faces. Smiles reflected back at him. While the crowd was smaller than at the initial meeting, the yard was still full and the mood far more upbeat.

He cupped his hands around his mouth. "Good morning, everyone!"

A smattering of people shouted a greeting in return. Several waved from the back.

"Wow. I can't thank you enough for coming out for this. God has blessed us with a perfect morning to start the ministry of River House. This blows my mind."

"Amen!" Mike called out from the crowd.

"I'm just...I'm amazed at God's goodness and the job He's set in front of us. It'll take all of us to run this ministry. Everybody is important, every gift is necessary—tutoring, teaching, praying, leading a small group, and especially just hanging out with the kids. God has unbelievable plans for this community, and I hope you're as jazzed as I am to be part of it."

The response was whoops and cheers.

"You rock, Wagner," came the same male voice that had encouraged him at that first service at Faith Church, and again Kurt laughed.

"Thanks, Johnson. Okay, let's get this prayer meetin' started. We'll pray here as a group, then we're gonna form a circle around the outside of the house while some of you guys pray inside. I'll start the prayer in the circle and squeeze the hand of the person next to me. Everyone will have a chance to pray out loud or you can just squeeze the hand of the next person if you want to pray silently. When it gets all the way around, I'll raise my hands to start a prayer wave. Then we'll be done and everybody can get a tour of the house."

He led them in prayer, asking for God's blessing on this fledgling ministry, on the volunteers and the kids. He prayed for River House to be a blessing to the neighborhood, that new friendships would be born and old friendships cemented. He asked for courage and strength in the face of any adversity that might come and closed with a benediction over them all.

The crowd scattered. Faith Church youth had signed up to pray for specific rooms inside while everyone else formed a circle outside. Kurt had hoped there'd be at least a few people on each side of the house, figuring they'd just shout at each other to signal when they were done. Instead, people stood shoulder to shoulder all the way around. Faces he knew, faces he would get to know. All here to bless River House.

Before joining the circle, he made a quick search for Vanessa. Finding her in the side yard, he grasped her hand and pulled her with him to the front where he whispered that she didn't have to pray. She smiled in response.

He started the circle prayer aloud and then squeezed her hand. She stood quietly, eyes closed, head bowed, her expression serious. After a moment he saw her squeeze the hand of the child beside her. With her small hand snug in his, he thanked God for the miracle of her friendship and turned his attention to the prayers encircling River House.

Twenty minutes later when the last few in the circle had prayed, the next-door neighbor Vanessa had introduced him to earlier squeezed his hand.

Yes! Thank you, Lord!

He raised his hand that clasped Vanessa's, keeping it high as she raised her other hand. In a scene that sent a rush of tears up his throat, each set of clasped hands lifted in a wave around the circle.

Within moments, the entire circle stood with hands raised, faces lifted, smiles wide. Then someone sent up a shout and the yard filled with cheering, laughter, and whistles. Flying high, Kurt wrapped Vanessa in a hug. God was far more creative than he'd ever given Him credit for. This was just the beginning of a wild, amazing ride. As they headed toward the house, he glanced across the street and thought he saw a curtain move. Perhaps Elwood Hauge would be part of the ride.

The next afternoon, Vanessa dragged her old picnic basket to the front door and rang the bell before returning to the taxi for a carton of soda. After all the walking she'd done with Kurt over the past two months, she'd graduated to using only one cane. One day she was going to throw that one away as well.

Kurt held the basket in one hand and the door open with the other. "You came back!"

She laughed as she passed him. Her heart had done a funny wiggle at his welcoming expression. "My calendar isn't exactly overflowing with activity."

"Hey, wait a minute." He followed her into the kitchen. "Does that mean you *wouldn't* have come back if you got a better offer?"

Setting the carton on the counter with a thump, she grinned. "This is the best offer in town. I wouldn't have missed it. Although," she looked around the empty kitchen, "I have an awful lot of food for just the two of us."

He sighed. "Yeah. No visitors so far. I know it's gonna take some time, but I was hoping at least a *few* would show up today."

She loaded the soda into the refrigerator, raising her voice over the clanking cans. "No teenager in the world wants to be the first one. They'll come."

"I know. God will send 'em when the time is right. In the meantime, I'm starved."

With a simple dinner of sandwiches and chips, they settled in the Gathering Place on unmatched but comfortable old couches. She admired the work he'd completed that afternoon. The room pulsed with anticipation, smelling of fresh paint and filled with sunshine.

Three walls had their first coat of sea foam green, a relaxing color that brought out the sheen of the dark woodwork. Sam had insisted on retaining as much of the old house's character as possible, including the mahogany that framed the archways and the coving around the ceiling.

With the wall removed between the dining room and living room, the Gathering Place was open and inviting. The expanded kitchen with its large island had drawn oohs and aahs from people during yesterday's open house. New maple cupboards brightened the room and the picture window by the table offered an inviting view into the garden. The basement had been reconfigured to allow for repair and woodworking projects. Kurt had acted like a child at a birthday party when he'd received the donation of several pieces of power equipment.

In some ways it didn't resemble her childhood home at all, yet it still felt like home. It was enough to be somewhere between the old and the new, the pain of loss and the energy of possibilities.

She turned her attention back to the walls. "You work fast. The room looks great. It was a good idea to leave some of the interior work for the kids to do."

"I want to put bookshelves over there," he gestured toward the corner with his half-eaten turkey sandwich, "and then maybe get a used keyboard to go over there. I'm glad the piano fit in the room next to my office."

"Music was huge in our house." An image of Matt and his buddies strutting like rock stars flashed through her mind, and she forced the bite of apple past the knot in her throat. "It was Matt's favorite thing in the world. And Angie was always practicing some new dance step, or singing the latest song."

"I think music speaks to everybody," he said, then added with a wink, "and so does some friendly competition. The ping-pong table should be here on Monday. And we're getting a couple of computers from the church to put in the tutoring room next to my office."

When the doorbell rang a short time later, they looked at each other wide-eyed before Kurt scrambled off the couch. He led two young men into the room where they stood in awkward silence, hands in their pockets, shoulders hunched, looking ready to bolt back out the door.

Vanessa's heart went out to them. "Hi guys. I'm Vanessa."

The dark-haired boy gave a wary smile. He was a slightly taller version of Kurt. "I'm Razzie. This is Burger."

Burger looked several years older. Sandy brown hair hung over part of his face as he looked from Kurt to Vanessa and nodded.

"You guys hungry?" Kurt asked.

They followed him into the kitchen, returning with paper plates sagging under huge turkey and cheese sandwiches, a pile of barbeque chips and several of the chocolate chip cookies Vanessa had baked. As they wolfed down the food, Kurt drew them out with questions and jokes. Soon they were relaxed and talking easily. When Razzie and Kurt shared a laugh, their dimpled profiles were almost identical.

"Hey, do you guys wanna help me paint?" Kurt asked. "I haven't had time to get this room done."

The boys looked at each other in silence. Razzie asked his friend if he'd ever painted anything before.

Burger shook his head. "Nah. Unless you count graffiti as painting."

Razzie laughed, then sobered and looked at Kurt. "Not that we do that or anything."

"'Course not," Kurt chuckled. "C'mon, I'll show you what to do."

An hour later, the living room walls were finished and the hall to the kitchen had its first coat. The trio moved into the family room at the back of the house. Listening to Kurt joke with the boys, Vanessa smiled to herself. It had taken little time for him to connect with them. They laughed and talked as if they'd known him all their lives.

Kurt had found his calling.

20

Following the second worship service on Sunday, Kurt hurried back to the house, ready to paint and eager to meet the kids Razzie said he would bring. With his iPod cranked up, he laid out the drop cloths, poured Desert Sand into the pan and took up a roller, singing harmony to one of his favorite songs.

The family room gleamed under a second coat before a group of five showed up at three o'clock. The new boys Razzie led into the house were quiet, watchful, and eager for food.

Kurt welcomed them to River House, greeting Pauly with a slap on the back. "Thanks for helping me get the discount, man."

Pauly beamed and stood a little taller. Kurt exchanged a fist bump with Razzie and led the guys into the kitchen where they downed a dozen sandwiches and two bags of chips while Kurt shared his vision for the house. As the food disappeared, the boys opened up. Their language was coarse, their stories painful.

"Yeah, my cousin went to the federal joint last year." The boy's Hispanic accent was as thick as his black hair. "He won't get out for like five years." He looked sideways at the boy next to him. "When's your brother gettin' out?"

"Next month. He says he ain't never goin' back." He shrugged, pushing broken chips around the plate with a dark, slender finger. "That's what he said last time."

Kurt's heart ached for him. "Don't give up on your brother. I said the same thing when I got out, and it's been over three years."

Five pairs of eyes locked on him. Razzie frowned. "*You* were in the joint?"

"A little over two years. I meant what I said," he told the tall black teen who continued staring at him. "Life is so good out here but to stay on this side of the fence, I have to make the right choices every day. If your brother works hard, he can do it too."

He pushed his stool back and got to his feet. "Anybody wanna see the power tools?"

Heading down to the workroom, Kurt prayed silently for wisdom to meet them where they were and for them to come face-to-face with Jesus at River House. After explaining his idea for the bookshelf and how to use the power saw, he held out safety glasses.

Razzie crossed his arms and shook his head sharply. "I'm not wearin' those. Huh-uh."

Kurt shrugged. "Then you can't use the equipment."

"Are you serious, man?" He looked from the glasses to the saw, then to Kurt. The other boys watched in silence. With another glance at the saw, he released an exasperated sigh and snatched the glasses. "Whatever."

Kurt hid a smile as he handed glasses to the other boys. For a moment the group just looked at each other. Then the ripping started.

"What a goon, Smithy."

"You look like my gramps."

"Yeah, well, you should keep yours on. You look smarter. Maybe they'll give you brains."

When the teasing slowed, they turned their attention to learning how to use the saw. Kurt demonstrated simple cuts then stood nearby giving explicit instructions and applauding their attempts.

The wide-eyed amazement on their faces and the puff to their chests when they actually cut something rewarded Kurt for all the effort it took to make this house a reality. Deep in his bones he knew that his whole life had been leading to this moment.

By the following Friday, the bookshelves sat proudly in the Gathering Place, and the house had a stream of a dozen "regulars." Kurt enlisted their help to create house rules, including one that stated no one was allowed near the power equipment without Kurt or another adult in attendance.

"Don't forget the safety glasses," Kurt said, as Razzie wrote the rules on poster paper. When the boy shot him a frown, he shot back a wink. Razzie's smirk made his heart sing.

These kids were so like himself at that age that he could only shake his head and remind them yet again to watch their language, treat each other with respect, and take care of River House. So far it seemed to be working.

Three weeks after River House opened, Kurt sat slumped at Vanessa's kitchen table. She watched him rub his eyes then try to focus on the newspaper. He was about to land face down on it.

"Kurt, come with me."

He started at her command, looking up through blurry eyes. "Hmm?"

She tugged him to his feet and led him into the living room. "Lie down." When his eyes widened, she blushed. "You were almost asleep at the table. You need a nap more than you need dinner."

"You needa nap too?" His slurred words held a note of hope.

"Oh, for Pete's sake. Just lie down and rest."

With a dramatic sigh, he flopped onto the couch. She spread a blanket over him and he gave a sweet, sleepy smile, reaching a hand out to her. Warmth swept through her as his fingers curled around hers.

"Thanks, Nessa." He sighed, his eyelids sliding closed. "You're the...best..."

She stood for a moment looking down at him, a smile still curving his mouth. His grasp loosened and she slowly drew her hand away. Her heart fluttered like a wild bird as she wrestled with the temptation to brush the hair from his forehead. His breathing slowed to even, measured breaths.

With a tiny smile, she crossed the living room and pulled out a counted cross-stitch pattern she'd started last week. Snuggled in the chair next to the window, she tried to stay focused on the sewing while watching Kurt sleep. When she pricked her finger for the third time, she realized she hadn't made much progress on the pattern.

He wore so many hats—fundraiser, chief of police, principal architect, and on-demand friend to the neighbors as well as to the House kids. She'd known he would do his work well, but as she watched him field calls and requests, spend focused time with the teens, and make future plans for the ministry, her admiration grew. It was a little disconcerting. A lot, actually.

When she'd stopped by the House three days ago, he'd had a phone at each ear and three kids in his office. The smile never left his face.

"Sure," he told the person on the phone. "Let me have you talk to Vanessa. She can answer those questions for you."

Her eyes went wide. What questions? She didn't know anything. He held the phone out to her, an eyebrow raised in challenge. His grin sent her heart into a silly pirouette.

She'd accepted the phone and talked with the concerned mother for twenty minutes about the neighborhood, Kurt, and the woman's teenage daughter who needed a place to hang out while mom was at work. When they hung up, she'd felt a rush of satisfaction.

Pulling her focus to the present, she set the fabric aside and ran a hand over Merton where he snoozed in her lap. Kurt's persistent friendship had broken through her defenses and pulled her from the brink of giving up, showing her there was still light and hope in the world. And his laughter touched her heart in ways that sometimes made it hard to breathe. He teased and encouraged and taught and listened. She'd never known anyone like him. It filled her with unfamiliar comfort and energy.

He turned on his side away from her and she moved her gaze to the window, releasing a sad little breath. She was the kid sister he'd never had. His disabled kid sister. He would never be interested in her once she got up the nerve to tell him who she really was and what had actually happened with the kids.

Setting Merton on the floor, she went into the kitchen to make a cup of tea, brushing impatiently at her cheeks. Of course he'd be kind if—when—he found out. He would never hurt her deliberately. But he deserved someone…better. Someone without a disability, who shared the same faith. Like Ashley.

She stood at the sink, staring out the window. The accident had taken more than the kids; it had taken her future family as well. There wasn't a man in Minnesota who would find her attractive enough to marry. The thought sliced into her heart and she pressed a fist against her chest. Her past was a memory, the future was empty. All she had was the present moment.

"Hey."

She turned with a start. He stood in the doorway, rubbing his eyes. Hair tousled, shirt rumpled, he looked like a man who worked too many hours. "Hey."

"Sorry. I didn't mean to pass out on you."

"You needed it." She pulled a root beer from the fridge and handed it to him. "Kurt, you can't keep this up. You're going to get sick."

"I know." He dropped into a chair. "I don't mean to put in so many hours. I just love the time with the kids. But there's so much other stuff that I never expected. And other churches want to talk to me about what we're doing, which just blows my mind. I could work a hundred hours a week and still not get it all done.

"But," he added with a smile that didn't lift his drooping eyes, "I'm not complaining. I can't wait to get out of bed every day to see what God has planned. It'll all work out, once I get a routine going."

Join him.

The whisper of an idea sent a jolt through her. She finished making her tea before settling across from him. "What would help you the most at this point?"

"Three days of solid sleep."

"After that."

He propped his chin in his hand and stared out the window for a long moment. "I can't believe I'm saying this but…I sure could use an assistant."

Her breath caught. "To do what?"

"Answer the phone, set up the tutoring schedule, send out requests for funding. Be the go-to person so I can focus more on the kids. Like you did on the phone the other day."

Her heart picked up speed. She could do those things. At least until he had enough money to pay someone he wanted to hire. "I could do that."

His dark eyes jumped from the window to bore into hers for a long, silent minute, and she wanted to snatch the words back. *Forget I said it. Stupid idea.* She dropped her gaze and played with the string of the tea bag.

"But there's no money to pay you."

She shrugged. "I don't need money right now. I only have a few bills, and I'm living here pretty cheaply. I'd like to pay you back a little for everything you've done for me." Pursing her lips, she hesitated, not wanting to force herself into his life any more than she already was. "I could just do it until you have enough money to hire someone."

His brow lowered. "Are you sure, Vanessa? Because I will totally take you up on it. And then you'd be stuck with me."

His warning released the clench of her jaw and she relaxed. "I'm sure, but you need to be too. You can probably find a better qualified volunteer, somebody in the church who could actually talk to the kids about faith."

He sat up straight, eyes wide. "Better qualified? You've been in on River House from the start. And talking to the kids about your questions and concerns would make them more comfortable asking their own. Nobody has all the answers, Nessa."

He leaned forward with an eagerness that made her thankful she'd listened to the voice. "How many hours are you thinking?"

She lifted her shoulders. "Whatever makes the most sense. I have lots of free time."

"Wow." He jumped to his feet and paced the kitchen, running his hands through his unruly hair. "This is so cool! Okay, well...how about coming in every day at, like, ten? We could get some of the paperwork stuff done before the kids start showing up around lunch. Then you could be there until, I dunno, whenever you want to leave, and we'll see how that works."

"Sounds like a good plan." A tingle danced along her arms. She was going back to work after all these long months.

Kurt dropped back into his chair and stuck out his hand. "Welcome to the River House staff, Miss Jordan."

She took his hand with a laugh. "Thank you, Mr. Wagner. I'm happy to join the team."

"Not half as happy as me." His fingers remained warm and secure around hers. "Thanks, Nessa."

"You're welcome, Boss."

It was his turn to laugh. "Now *that's* a scary thought. Me in charge."

"God first," she said, wondering even as she spoke where the words came from. "You second."

He tipped his head, his eyes narrowing. "God first," he echoed, slowly releasing her fingers. "Thanks for the reminder."

She stirred her tea. This was going to be interesting.

21

Pulling into the driveway at River House Monday morning, Kurt saw the sheet of paper, a stark contrast against the green front door where it was wedged. Juggling his Bible, several notebooks, a computer bag and the box of nails he'd bought on the way over, he pulled the wrinkled paper out and stuck it in his mouth before letting himself into the house.

He paused in the entryway, inhaling deeply. *Man, I love opening the House up for the day.* Anticipation always bubbled up as he opened the curtains and started his iPod. He prayed that the contemporary Christian music was edgy enough to appeal to the teens and that the truth of the lyrics would seep into their hearts.

Stuffing the paper into his back pocket, he headed downstairs. He put the nails away and straightened the workroom from last night's project, smiling at the memory of Razzie and Pauly arguing over the correct angle of a cut.

"Pauly, you are dumber than a fox at math." Razzie had stood, hands on hips, glaring at the other boy through the safety glasses.

Kurt had kept his focus on the wood he was staining, glancing sideways at where the boys faced off over the table they'd designed.

Pauly stood straighter. "Am not. You got the angle wrong, Razz. Ask Kurt."

In the silence that followed, Kurt felt Razzie's reluctance. The boy had become a natural leader. The other boys looked up to his strength and gritty determination, while the girls adored his dark good looks and the heart he hid behind the swagger.

"Fine. Wagner, you wanna show Knucklehead here the right angle?"

"Sure." He'd finished staining the end of the board then set the brush aside and shot Razzie a warning glance. "*Pauly*," he said with emphasis, "let's see what you've got figured. Then we'll look at Razz's idea."

Together they had come up with an answer that satisfied both boys. When Razzie lightly punched Pauly's shoulder after they made the last cut, Kurt lifted a silent prayer of thanks. Building relationships was what this was about. Building tables was secondary.

Blinking away the memory, he unfolded the note. Bold, black letters shouted, "Yor a marked man Wagoner."

Wolf's face leaped to mind and he dropped onto a nearby stool, staring at the smudged printing. Why would he be a marked man? What had he ever done to Wolf—aside from spend two years in jail for delivering his drugs?

Lord, if this is supposed to be a joke, it's not funny. Watch over this house. Don't let my stupid choices affect these kids. Keep us safe.

Anger flared in his chest and he shredded the paper, crumpling the pieces before throwing them into the trash can.

"Kurt?" Vanessa's voice floated down the stairs.

He sucked in a cleansing breath before responding. "Be right up." Jaw set, he headed toward the stairs, praying that God would protect them. And that Wolf would lose interest. He always had if it didn't profit him somehow.

"Good morning," he said, smiling up at where she waited. Vanessa had arrived for her first official shift. Marked or not, it was going to be a good day.

Life at River House fell into a comfortable routine. Vanessa brought in a small coffeemaker she found at a garage sale so they could enjoy a morning cup while talking over plans for the day. She loved being part of River House, getting to know the kids, taking some of the pressure off Kurt. He seemed thrilled at her knack for fundraising. Her enthusiasm for it kept him smiling. And she liked making him smile.

He brought in an old, gray metal desk for her, setting it by the far wall of the Gathering Place. It allowed for an adult to be available out front, whether it was her or another volunteer answering the busy phone. His office was just around the corner. She liked being close enough to chat while they worked.

Tiffani and Brooke came every day after their summer school classes. Vanessa's heart went out to the pregnant teen who grew increasingly uncomfortable as her due date approached. Tiffani remained cheerful and upbeat even as she waddled through her classes and spent late afternoons with a tutor at River House.

Two weeks into Vanessa's new job, Brooke dashed in and threw herself into a chair next to the desk, gasping for breath. "Tiff...went to...the hospital a while ago."

Vanessa pulled a bottle of water from the small fridge behind her desk and handed it to the red-faced girl. "She's in labor?"

Brooke nodded as she gulped down half the bottle. "Her water broke during our math class." She looked pleased that she knew that important information, then frowned. "What does that mean, anyway?"

Before Vanessa could reply, the phone rang. "River House. This is Vanessa."

"Van, it's Tiffani. I'm at the hospital."

"Hi, sweetie. Brooke just told me. Have you had the baby yet?"

"No." The girl's voice was shaky and tearful. "This is so hard. And they said it could be hours. Could you...would you maybe..."

"Of course I'll come. Which hospital?"

"Fairview—oooh, here it comes again. Ow. Owwww."

Vanessa clutched the phone as the girl whimpered through a contraction. She was relieved to hear a woman's voice in the background.

Finally Tiffani came back on, breathless. "Sorry. They just really hurt."

She sounded so young. She *was* so young. "Is that your mom with you?"

"No, it's the nurse. My mom's still mad that I got pregnant so she won't come to the hospital."

Vanessa winced. *What a sad mess.* "I'll be there as fast as I can, okay? Listen to what the nurse tells you to do. She'll help you through this."

She called for a cab then found Kurt in the family room playing a video game with Razzie and several boys. He sent her off with a prayer and a squeeze of her hand. "Thanks, Nessa. You're doing amazing ministry with all of the girls, but especially with Tiffani."

In the cab with Brooke chattering beside her, his words rang in her head. *She* was doing ministry? Wasn't that something people did who actually believed in God? She was just trying to walk beside the kids and share daily life with them.

Relieved to find that Tiffani's mother Wendy had arrived after all, Vanessa introduced herself, then hugged Tiffani. Brooke stayed in the delivery room for an hour, but her friend's tearful efforts to get through each contraction made her sidle toward the door. She promised to return in the morning and slipped out of the room.

Vanessa and Wendy spent the long hours chatting and encouraging the laboring teen. Shortly after midnight, a tiny baby girl entered the world with a shock of dark hair and a solid cry.

The nurse told Tiffani she could have an hour with the baby if she wanted. When the girl shrugged, pain flickered across Wendy's face. The women took turns holding the newborn, exclaiming over her dark lashes and perfect fingernails. The tumult in Vanessa's chest swung between awe and anger. The miracle in her arms deserved so much more than this.

Tears burned into her heart as Tiffani calmly handed the pink bundle to the Child Protection social worker. Wendy looked away, brushing a finger under her eyes. Vanessa chatted with her quietly while Tiffani was settled in for the night. After sharing a silent hug with Wendy, she glanced at the childlike face of the girl asleep in the bed and left the room.

The cab she had called was waiting at the curb. She desperately needed to process the evening's events with Kurt but the red numbers on the dashboard clock read 2:15. Maybe if she sat outside Mike's house for a moment, she could find some of the peace she always felt in Kurt's presence. She gave the address, then settled back and closed her eyes.

What seemed like only a minute later, the taxi stopped. "Is this the right house, lady?"

She opened her eyes and looked at the dark two-story. Right house, wrong time. "Yes, but I'm...this isn't..." Darkness hid the pink filling her face. "It's the address I gave you. It's just not my—" The vibration in her pocket made her squeak. She pulled her phone out and smiled before answering. "What are you doing up?"

"What are you doing in a cab outside our house?"

"How did you know I'm here?"

"Why don't you come in so we can get all these questions answered?"

Her sigh was deep. "You don't have to be up just because I am."

"But I am and you need to talk so you'd better come in. I'm thinking the cab driver might not want to sit there all night. Besides, it'll cost a fortune."

Settled across the kitchen table from Kurt, she sipped coffee and related the events of the birth while Mike snored loudly overhead. When tears spilled over, she swept them away and shook her head. "I don't know why I'm crying. It was amazing to be part of something like that."

Kurt reached across the table for her hand. "You witnessed the most powerful event on earth, but it didn't follow God's plan. That baby should be sleeping with her mother right now, not in foster care. And that's a sad thing. It's best for the baby in the long run, but it's not the way God planned it."

She frowned. "So where was God when she got pregnant? Why didn't He stop this from happening?" *Where was He the night of the accident?*

He was quiet for a minute, studying her fingers resting in his. "There's a price that comes with the gift of free will, Nessa. God gave us guidelines for living a good life, spelled out in the Bible, and the *choice* of living within them or not. If we do, life goes a lot better for us. Not perfect, of course, but we have the assurance He's walking with us every step, helping us get through each day.

"But when we choose to follow our own path," he continued, "He lets natural consequences happen. And sometimes those consequences affect innocent people."

His dark eyes held hers, unwavering. "But Nessa, that's never the end of the story. He can still bring good out of bad. He offers His grace in the midst of our mess and helps make things right. In Tiffani's case, a couple somewhere will have an answer to their prayer about infertility."

Unable to look away from his peaceful expression, she tried to absorb his words, to grasp some of the confidence that radiated from him. It still didn't explain why her family was gone. She slid her hand from his and dropped back in her chair. "I don't get it. If He's who you say He is, why doesn't He have more control over us? Why just let us mess everything up? People do such terrible, hurtful things."

He nodded. "It goes back to free will. He wants us to look to Him because *we* want to, not because He wants us to. It's about having a relationship with Him, not being controlled by Him."

"So He lets people make bad choices and innocent people suffer." Tears knotted her throat. "How does that help those of us on the receiving end?"

Her bitter words didn't seem to bother him. "I wish I could tell you why the kids are gone. Why our moms are gone. What I do know is that He's there in the good and the bad. He was with me in my cell. He's with you as you work through your grief." His expression altered, a shy quirk lifting a corner of his mouth. "He brought us together when we both needed a friend."

The truth of that statement made her blink. Where would she be if Kurt hadn't pushed her from the path of the car? If he hadn't been in the garden? It was a chilling thought.

Yet it all seemed too simple, too neat. "But how do you know those things are true?" she persisted.

"It's not something I just woke up one day believing. It's come over time, learning life lessons the hard way, searching for answers to questions just like this. And when nothing makes sense, I go back to the Bible."

"And there's your answer in black and white." Doubt seeped through the words.

He grinned. "I wish. Usually it comes through a story I read or a psalm that asks the same questions I'm asking now. Sometimes I have to wait for the answer."

"But what if we need it right now? What if the waiting is killing us?" The old pain surfaced.

"He's there in the waiting too. I know that's hard to understand. At least, for me it is. But when we look back at where we've been, at how things happened at just the right time, we realize the waiting was necessary. Maybe even part of the plan."

She held his gaze for a long moment, then looked out the window. The eastern sky had faded from the deep black of night to a dawning blue. She turned wide eyes to him. "What time is it?"

He answered with a smile. "Five-thirty."

"No way. Kurt, I'm so sorry! I can't believe I kept you up all night. I wasn't going to wake you up at all."

He chuckled. "I think it was a God thing that I got up for a glass of water and looked out the window. This has been a great conversation."

She had the sudden, silly urge to laugh. "It really has."

"Man, I learn something new about you every day."

"That I ask a lot of questions?"

"Yup. Really good, tough questions. I've had easier discussions, that's for sure. You're a deep thinker, Miss Jordan."

Heat filled her face. "I don't know about that, but seeing that darling baby being born and then given away…" She shook her head, her heavy heart tinged with a strange joy. "I'm so glad I was there."

"I can't wait for when my kids are born."

Her eyebrows jumped up. "You want a family?"

"Oh, yeah. A bunch. Girls and boys. You?"

"I don't know about a bunch, but a handful would be nice."

When Kurt offered to drive her home, she assured him an early morning walk sounded perfect. At the door she paused to look up at him. "Thank you."

He cocked his head.

"For asking me in at 2 a.m. For sitting here all night answering questions. For letting me be honest with how I feel and what I think."

He pulled her into a gentle hug. "You're welcome. I'm glad you're honest with me. It makes me work harder to put my thoughts into words, which isn't easy for me."

She rested against him, safe and protected, then forced herself to pull back. "I'd say we're even. I'll see you in a few hours."

"You need some sleep. Just go in when you're ready."

"My boss is a real tyrant. I'd better not be late."

He sent her off with a laugh and she started down the sidewalk, so energized it felt almost as if she could dance. She reveled in the peacefulness of the morning, breathing in its freshness, pine trees, and dewy grass.

At the corner she leaned on the cane and rose on the toes of her good leg, lifting her right leg behind her in a move as familiar as breathing. To be balanced in an arabesque on this beautiful morning seemed fitting.

Yes, it felt almost as if she could dance.

22

When the battered clock on the bookshelf managed an uneven pattern of seven chimes, Vanessa watched Kurt drop into his usual place on the couch. It was time for the Wednesday evening worship service in the Gathering Place. The casual service was complete with music from his iPod, time for prayer requests, and a message based on a particular piece of Scripture. Participation had grown from two kids to five to twelve in the first month.

Each night after a brief message on how faith intersected with the everyday struggles of life, Kurt invited them into discussion. At first, they were hesitant to participate, but now active debate kept the conversation lively. Vanessa loved the openness that fueled these midweek sessions. Kurt had done a great job of encouraging the kids to express their questions, doubts, and disagreements in a respectful way.

His messages seemed determined to take root in her heart. His stories, his honesty about the past and what God had done in his life, and the questions the kids wrestled with had chipped away at the ice around her heart. Letting go of the anger was frightening—it had kept her afloat after the accident. To move beyond it meant moving away from pain and into hope—letting go of her family, stepping into the new life growing up around her.

This new message about being created in God's image seemed to strike a chord with the kids, and a vigorous discussion about what God's image might be followed. While Vanessa had always listened to the worship time from her desk, she decided to sit with the two girls new to River House.

As the animated debate bounced around them, the heavyset girl on her right pressed back into the cushions, arms folded tight across her ample chest.

"But if God is perfect," Tiffani said, "then doesn't that mean only the perfect people look like Him?"

"Yeah, what about people who are ugly or fat or stupid? They ain't in God's image." The boy's remark was met with awkward laughter and jostling among several younger teens.

"Whoa, wait a minute." Kurt jumped into the fray. "You guys are taking this way off base here. Don't you see? This is what society has done. We judge each other by whether or not we look like the airbrushed people in the magazines and movies."

"How else would we judge somebody?" a girl asked.

"How about by who they are as a person?" he countered. "How they treat other people, what they do to help make life better for everybody. Why base it on something superficial like how they look?"

He leaned forward, his tattered brown leather Bible between his hands. His gaze moved from one young face to the next, a frown tugging at his brow. The room was silent, every teen focused on him.

When his eyes held hers, Vanessa pulled her right leg under the left. They would definitely judge her on the superficial if they knew what she was hiding.

"Okay, how about this," Kurt said. "What if you meet a guy at school who looks pretty rough. He falls asleep in class and doesn't have a lot of friends, so you decide he's a loser and not worth knowing.

"But the truth is he can't sleep because his parents fight every night and he tries to keep his little brother from freaking out. And then he has to be at work at 5 a.m. to open the bagel shop because the money he makes is what the family uses for groceries. But you decided that he's not worth getting to know because he isn't dressed the greatest or his hair's a mess. You just passed on someone who could have been one of your best friends."

The room was silent. Kids shifted in their chairs, gnawed their fingernails, twirled long hair, looking anywhere but at Kurt. Natalie, the new girl beside Vanessa, pressed farther back into the cushions.

"Would any of you consider being friends with someone who was missing an arm or a leg?" Vanessa was astounded to hear her own voice fill the silence. Her heart leaped into triple time. *Why did I say that?*

"That'd be too weird," Pauly mumbled. Razzie elbowed him.

"Do you know anyone like that, Pauly?" she asked.

"Well, no, but…it would be, like, gross. I wouldn't know what to say. I'd, like, worry about saying somethin' stupid."

She tried to breathe over the frantic pounding in her chest. *What am I doing?* "Why would you have to treat them any different than how you treat Razzie?"

Guffaws broke out around the room and she rolled her eyes, catching Kurt's wink. "Okay, *better* than you treat Razz? Do you think someone with a disability is more fragile or more easily offended?"

"Well, yeah. Maybe. I mean, I'd hate bein' like that and they gotta hate it, too."

In slow motion, her stomach roiling, Vanessa leaned forward and grasped her pant leg. This was going to change everything, but she couldn't seem to stop herself. She pulled the material above her knee.

There was an audible gasp when the kids saw her bionic leg, made of metal and looking something from a sci-fi movie.

"What the—? Whoa. Did you know about that?" came whispered remarks.

Terrified of Kurt's reaction, she looked at Pauly who stared at her leg, his face white. "Pauly, I'm not showing you this to make you feel bad. I just want you—all of you—to know that there are so many layers to who people are, layers that make us act a certain way and affect how we make decisions and what we think of ourselves."

Natalie was no longer trying to disappear into the cushions. She had leaned forward to see what Vanessa was doing and now stared at her, mouth open. "But you're so pretty," she said, then her round cheeks flushed bright red. "Wait. I mean, you still are…"

Vanessa reached for her hand, smiling gently. "Thanks, hon." She turned her attention back to the group, away from Kurt. "I lost my leg in a car accident just this past winter. But did that change who I am *inside*? If you were my friend before, would you still be my friend now? Would you have chosen not to come to River House if you knew a so-called handicapped person was here?"

The intensity of their focus jumbled her thoughts. What made her think this was the right time for the big unveiling? It was going to change everything with Kurt.

Tell your story.

The nudge made her nauseous. But the flood of panic was immediately calmed by a warmth that enveloped her heart and filled her with courage. Drawing a shaky breath, she told them of life before her mother's cancer diagnosis and how it changed when she died. She talked about Angie and Matt, and the short time she'd been able to raise them. Describing the accident was no less painful this time, but the words came more easily, the tears not quite as scalding.

"I'm not so sure about being made in God's physical image." She quirked an eyebrow as she looked at Pauly. "That would mean He's also missing a leg. Maybe it's not so much how we look on the outside but who we are on the inside, like Kurt said. What I do know is that every single one of us is special.

"Some of us are white, some black, Hispanic, Asian, mixed. So if we're truly made in God's image, God must be kind of like a kaleidoscope. I think that's a pretty cool image."

There was a murmur of laughter. Many wore thoughtful expressions. A few girls wiped away tears. No one spoke.

"Wow," Kurt said finally. His voice pulled her gaze toward him for the first time. His face was pale, his eyes narrowed. She squirmed and looked down at her hands. "Vanessa, I think you're on for next week's lesson."

"Yeah!" several of the girls squealed.

"Good idea," Razzie agreed.

Heart still pounding, Vanessa shook her head. "Thanks, but I think I'll just stay in the crowd and listen."

Kurt's dark eyes rested on her another moment. She wanted to leap into an explanation, to apologize for not telling him. She picked at lint on her pants.

"Okay." He slapped his hands on his thighs. "Well, I have a feeling this is going to be an ongoing discussion. Stay tuned for part two next week. Now, how about we close in prayer and then grab something to eat?"

The amen was barely out of his mouth before the boys climbed over each other in a race to the kitchen while the girls clustered together on the couches. Still trembling, Vanessa went to her desk to shut down her computer. She needed air. She needed—

The shuffling of feet behind her stopped her breath. She was afraid to face him, to see the anger in his eyes. *What did I do?*

"Vanessa?"

The female voice allowed her to breathe and she turned. Natalie stood by the desk, tears on her round cheeks. "Hi, hon."

"Could we talk?" the girl whispered.

"You bet. Let's go into one of the meeting rooms."

As they settled in mismatched armchairs, Natalie's story tumbled out. Heavy even as a child, the teasing and rejection of junior high had sent her deeper into eating. Now in high school, the teasing had stopped, mainly because she'd become invisible.

Life at home with a frazzled, working single mother and two skinny younger sisters was no picnic. There was little attention and what she got was negative and insulting. She'd started cutting to cope with the shame and pain.

"But listening to your story," she said, wiping her face with the tissue Vanessa handed her, "makes me want to find a way to be happy, the way you are even after everything you've been through. I don't want to be the sad, silent fat girl anymore. I want to live. Like you."

Vanessa wrapped her arms around the sobbing girl, murmuring words of encouragement, stunned that her story had affected her so deeply. She hadn't thought about being happy—it still seemed a distant, unreachable concept. She just moved through each day tearful with memories, learning to be content.

They shared more of their stories, finding laughter amidst the sadness. Vanessa sent her home with Jenny's card and told her to say Kurt and Vanessa sent her.

Hearing Kurt's voice in the kitchen, Vanessa quietly gathered her purse and jacket and slipped out the front door. The evening air cooled her cheeks and allowed her to finally draw a full breath. Her leg throbbed, making her limp more pronounced as she hurried home.

Merton greeted her at the front door. She scooped him up and buried her face in his fur. "Oh, Mertie. What was I thinking? Why didn't I find a way to tell him before tonight?"

She put food in his bowl then wandered restlessly from room to room. Finally exhausted, she crawled into bed. Into the long, silent hours of the night, she tossed and turned, imagining every possible scenario. Kurt angry, firing her from her work at the House. Kurt relaxed and accepting of her deception, understanding her need for self-preservation. Kurt looking at her with pity instead of friendship. No matter how much she hoped he wouldn't mind, she knew he would.

Through gritty eyes, she watched the first rays of sunlight creep into her room.

23

Kurt drove aimlessly for several hours before finally going home, relieved to find Mike had gone to bed. He couldn't put words to his clashing emotions. His world had tipped sideways and he couldn't figure out which way was up. Why had she kept something like that from him? And why pick *that* way to tell him—in front of everyone? He'd been so blown away, he couldn't speak. He still couldn't.

He stared blindly out into the silent neighborhood, seeing her pull up her pant leg, seeing metal where he'd expected skin. Had he sat there like an idiot with his mouth open? Did he look as stunned as the kids? If she'd kept something that big a secret, what else was she hiding?

These past months of friendship seemed like a joke now. Embarrassment and anger jockeyed for the top of the pile of emotions filling his chest. He'd befriended her because she'd seemed lost and alone. She talked so little about the accident, he'd assumed it was just too painful. He hadn't expected her "injury" to actually be an amputation.

He paced long into the night, thoughts and memories tangling in his mind. There was that guy in prison called Hook, who'd lost his forearm in a knife fight. He boasted he could do everything everyone else did—smoke a cigarette with the claw, tie a knot, write with both "hands." Once he got used to it, Kurt had been fascinated by how it worked.

But the idea of sweet, fragile Vanessa missing a leg was a whole different ballgame. The memory of knocking her down at their first meeting made his face flame. *How many other stupid things have I said or done?*

He started another pot of coffee. Maybe it wasn't even her...disability that got to him so much as the in-your-face lying. She'd lied about who she was. Or at least she hadn't told him everything, which was just as bad.

Slumping into the kitchen chair, he dropped his head into his hands. Her revelation had sent him into a tailspin. He needed to talk this out, to make sense of the ugly questions clouding his mind, and he knew who would help.

Jenny settled back in the chair, her calm gaze resting on him as she waited.

Kurt squirmed. "You know I hate it when you do that."

She smiled.

He huffed and tapped his foot to the ticking of the desk clock. Muffled sounds drifted through the closed door—a woman's laugh, a ringing phone. "She lied to me."

"Did she?"

"Well, she didn't tell the whole truth."

"About?"

"About what happened to her. Did you know she lost her leg in the accident?"

Her expression remained neutral and anger flared in his chest. Of course she did. "Why'd she tell you and not me?"

"Do you think she felt safe enough to bring up something like that?"

His eyebrows shot up. "Why wouldn't she?"

"I don't know that she didn't. It's just something to think about."

With another huff, he jumped to his feet and wandered the room. He'd spent hours here working through his past. Now these were issues that would affect his future. Would he ever get life figured out?

He picked up a small, gray rock with a cross carved in it and let it rest on his palm. "I just don't understand why she didn't tell me. Why did I find out the same time everyone else did?"

"You'll have to ask her that."

"Yeah, right. I sound like a two-year-old saying it to you. I'm not going to go whining to her about it."

"That's how issues get resolved."

He glanced sideways at her. "By whining?"

She smiled. "By talking about them instead of stewing over them."

He returned the rock to the bookshelf. "I was so stunned when she showed us her...the...thing."

"It's called a prosthesis."

"I know."

"It might help if you look at that particular issue first."

"What, that she has a fake leg?"

Jenny nodded and sipped her water.

He returned to the couch. "Yeah. So how do I do that?"

"Perhaps by saying it out loud."

She's missing part of her leg. The friend he thought he knew had been hiding a huge secret. *She doesn't have two legs.* He rubbed his face with both hands. "If she'd just told me up front, I wouldn't have said such stupid things to her."

"So this is about you feeling stupid."

"No. Sorta. Well, that's not the main issue." He dropped his head back against the couch. "If I'd known, I wouldn't have said those things."

"How well do you think you know Vanessa?"

"If you'd asked me two days ago, I'd have said pretty good." He lifted his head to frown at her. "Now I feel like I don't know her at all."

"Would she want you to treat her differently because of her leg?"

He snorted. "No. She'd probably hit me with one of her canes if I did."

"So spending time feeling bad about making comments that you couldn't have known might be hurtful—"

"—is a waste of time," he concluded. "I know. It just...everything feels different now."

"How so?"

He picked at the ragged hem on his jeans. "I can't get past her not telling me. It's like this big secret I wasn't supposed to know but she was forced into revealing."

"Was she?"

"Forced? Well...no. I suppose not." She was the most private person he'd ever met. And the most independent. "I don't think anyone could make her do anything."

"So she made a choice."

"Yeah."

"Why do you think she chose that place and time to do it?"

His mind wandered back to the events before her revelation. She'd taken a special interest in the new girls that day. The larger girl had constantly adjusted her oversized T-shirt and played with her hair. The other was definitely Goth with baggy black clothes, dyed-black hair, chains jingling.

Vanessa had quickly gotten them talking and laughing. She always seemed drawn to the underdogs, those who didn't fit in—even at River House where no one was cookie-cutter style.

"Kurt?"

He blinked and crashed back to the present. "Sorry. What was the question?"

"Why do you think she revealed her secret at that particular time?"

"Because she thought it would help the kids who were struggling with self-image." That made sense. "She did it to show them she understood."

"Do you think she was worried about your reaction?"

He lifted a shoulder. "Maybe. Since she hadn't gotten around to telling me before that, I suppose she was."

"But she did it anyway."

"Okay, okay. I get it." He frowned. "Now I can add brave to her amazing list. But that doesn't explain why she didn't bother telling me personally."

"That's something you'll have to ask her." More muffled laughter from the other room. "How do you feel about her having lost part of her leg?"

He shrugged. "I've been too bent out of shape about her lying—" He held up a hand. "Not lying, just not being completely honest. That's what's bugged me the most."

"Have you been completely open and honest with her?"

"Yes. Well...about what?"

"About your past."

Heat crawled up his neck. "All she has to do is ask."

She looked at him from under lowered brows. "Really."

"I've got an awful long story to tell..." The weak excuse trailed off. The clock ticked. His foot resumed its tapping.

Jenny drained her bottle and set it on the coffee table. "Kurt, you've got a lot to think about. Could I suggest something?"

"Since I'm struggling here, that'd be good."

"Take a day, two at the most, and pray."

"About?"

"What you've learned about Vanessa. What God wants you to do about it. How you can best help her. And where this will take your relationship. Seems to me you have two options."

"And they are...?"

"Close the door on your friendship with her, using this as an excuse to walk away. Or work through your feelings, and then go to her and clear the air. Whatever you decide, don't leave her hanging. Be honest with her. I'm sure she's in limbo right now, wondering what you're going to do now that you know."

It had been almost twenty-four hours since Vanessa dropped her bomb. She hadn't come in to work and he hadn't gone looking for her. He was missing her big time. "Okay. Well, thanks for letting me drop in so early like this. I knew you'd help me sort through the junk banging around in my head."

They got to their feet and hugged.

"Happy to be your sounding board."

"I don't pay you enough."

"You don't pay me at all." She followed him out of the office.

"So I was right."

With a laugh, she stopped beside the reception counter. "My door's always open, my friend."

He winked. "Mine too, Jen."

He paused on the front step. But was his door open for Vanessa?

24

Pounding silence filled the next two days. Vanessa sat in her kitchen, aimlessly dunking the tea bag in her mug. Tears burned as she replayed the shock on his face. Then anger flared at his God who'd decided yet again to rip something good out of her life.

Her reflections turned bitter and anger spilled into a cleaning frenzy as she tried to outrun the thoughts that poked at her from every angle. She rearranged the furniture, washed windows, and vacuumed while Merton hid from her wrath, his glowing eyes following her movements.

"So that's all it took, Mert?" she vented as she jerked the vacuum around the living room on Friday evening. "He finds out I'm...I'm not...I'm like this, and he just walks away?" She paused to glare up at the ceiling, addressing the voice. "I *knew* this would happen. Well, that's it. I'm not letting anybody else near me. If I can't trust Kurt to handle the truth, I'm done."

Despair washed over the anger, making her legs wobble as she dusted for the third time. She'd lost Kurt's trust and friendship, and she was out of a job. Volunteer or not, it had given her a reason to get up every morning. Now she was back where she started, angry and alone.

Early the next morning she let herself into River House one last time. Through another sleepless night, she'd come to the realization that her time at the House was done. If Kurt wasn't comfortable around her, the kids wouldn't be either. He was willing to let her walk out of his life so she would.

She wandered the first floor, memories of her family jumbling with new memories of Tiffani, Razz, Natalie. Kurt. She'd hoped to have many more years within these walls creating new relationships, building friendships.

In Kurt's office, she set the envelope containing a short note on his keyboard. Sticky notes with phone numbers, questions, and Scripture references were plastered everywhere, with photos pinned haphazardly to a corkboard Brooke had made for him. She looked at the photos, pausing on the one in the center—the two of them eating ice cream. The picture blurred and she turned away. Taking the beach ball from his chair, she smiled absently at the memory of getting beaned by an errant beach or nerf ball at her desk.

The fun was over. She wasn't going to beg for her job back. Or for Kurt to still be her friend. She would just—

"So you did come back."

With a squeak, the ball flew from her hands as she spun around, slapping a hand to her chest. "Oh, my gosh, Kurt. You scared me."

Obviously she hadn't heard the floor creak when he entered his office. Her eyes were wide, her hand trembling. "Sorry."

He wasn't, actually. He'd been right in thinking she might try to slip in and out without seeing him. Folding his arms, he leaned against the door frame. There were dark circles under her eyes. Her sweet mouth tugged downward at the corners. "What're you doing here so early on a Saturday?"

She shrugged, studying her fingernails. "Just...leaving a few notes for people."

"I see." His eyes went to the envelope on his keyboard. The half-filled box on her desk told the whole story. Jenny's words rang in his head and he pulled in a breath. *Here goes.* "Vanessa, we need to talk."

Nodding, she seemed to shrink into herself, shoulders slumped. This was not the vibrant young woman of just days ago.

He moved into the room to face her across his small meeting table. "First, I need to apologize."

Her head snapped up, eyes narrowing. "For what?"

"For not following you home Wednesday night. I didn't even know you'd left until like an hour later. I should have gone right to your place to have this discussion."

Her gaze dropped back to her clenched hands and she lifted one shoulder.

"But I didn't because..." He bit his lip. *Total honesty, Wagner.* "Because I was mad."

She flinched.

"And hurt. And really confused. I didn't get why you never told me about your leg. I thought you trusted me. I thought we were friends."

Blue eyes shiny with tears lifted to his. When she started to speak, he held up a hand. "I wasn't upset because you don't have a leg, Nessa. I was mad because you never told me. It felt like you'd kept this big secret because you didn't trust me. And I wondered what else you hadn't told me."

Now that they were face-to-face, the truth was hard to admit. He'd been an idiot about the whole thing. "I haven't handled this very good." He forced himself to hold her gaze. "I'm sorry I was such a jerk."

Her mouth opened and closed. "You're not a jerk."

"Oh, yeah. I am. I needed a time-out."

The corners of her mouth twitched as her frown eased.

"And after I got over myself, I realized you probably thought I was mad about your leg. I was just hurt because I thought we were better friends than that."

"We are."

He nodded. "I know that now. You wouldn't have shown everyone your leg in front of me if you didn't trust me. I'm a little slow but I get it. What really matters is you. Us." Warmth slid up his neck and he crammed his hands into his pockets. "Our friendship."

They stood looking at each other in silence, his heart pounding, her fingers twisting into white-knuckled knots.

"Is it my turn now?" she asked.

"Sure, if you want."

"I'm sorry I didn't tell you." The words poured out, as if they'd built for days. "When we first met, it didn't matter because I didn't think we'd ever see each other again. But when you kept coming back and we got to know each other, I couldn't figure out how to bring it up." She looked away. "I was afraid I'd...it would...you'd never come back. And...I couldn't face that."

He sighed at the admission. "You forget I've been in the joint. Your leg is nothing compared to some of those guys."

"I should have found a way to tell you earlier. I'm sorry I did it that way."

"It was a pretty big shock, but I just played like I already knew about it when the kids asked later."

Her face clouded. "Were they—"

"Surprised? Yes. Freaked out? Not at all. They're mainly curious. Then when you didn't come back the last two days, they thought you were mad at them, that they didn't say the right things, stuff like that."

"Oh, no." She shook her head. "I never thought of that. How stupid of me."

"I just said you weren't feeling good and that I'd check on you." He took a step around the table. The guilt and hurt that had kept him from sleeping the last few nights had faded. He drew in a deep breath. "Will you come back to work? Please?"

Tears filled her eyes. "If you aren't too mad at me," she whispered.

"Aw, Nessa." He moved closer and wrapped his arms around her. He was getting used to hugging her. "I'm not mad at anyone but myself. I was such an idiot about the whole thing." When she pressed closer, he tightened his arms and ignored the goofy dance in his chest.

"Maybe we could start over." Her suggestion was muffled.

He leaned back and grinned down into her smiling face. The cloud had lifted, easing the lines from her forehead, the frown from her eyes. She was so darn pretty. "Hi. I'm Kurt. I'm an ex-con and occasionally an idiot."

She giggled. "I'm Vanessa. I'm a former dancer who's missing part of her leg."

"I see. Well, I happen to have an opening for someone missing part of their leg. Someone who likes kids who are a step or two from ordinary. Someone who can work with my weird hours, and help me keep my head on straight, and who—"

"Will always tell the truth."

Even as they shared a laugh, something pinched deep inside. He was asking her for honesty but all of his cards weren't on the table. He gave her a squeeze and released her. He'd better find a way to do that soon. It was only fair.

25

The boys of River House had a new mascot—Vanessa Jordan. It was amusing to watch their attitudes change from nonchalance to protective concern. They were quick to offer assistance, treating her like a treasured big sister. The girls brought their friends to hang out with her, sharing their questions and issues, their highs and lows of daily life.

Thanks to Vanessa's openness, the atmosphere of the House had altered, the trust level going a notch deeper. Kurt told Joel as much when they met for an afternoon run two weeks later.

"River House has already become what I'd dreamed it might be someday." The easy pace allowed him to let the words flow. Joel ran beside him smiling and silent.

"It's so cool. Kids are talking about all the stuff going on in their lives. I saw a couple of them praying together with a volunteer the other day after the Al-Anon meeting. It blew my mind."

They zigzagged around a young couple pushing a stroller. "That surprised you?" Joel asked.

"Not that it's happening. Just that it's happening so soon."

"What do you think is causing it?"

"Vanessa." He swiped his forehead with the back of his hand. "She's amazing, Joel. Really. Who'd have thought the girl who seemed like she'd blow away in a big wind would turn out to be the strongest person in the house?

"She's got this way of…I don't know. Getting right to the point. Like everything she's been through makes her cut to the chase." He chuckled. "I can tell you she doesn't let anyone get away with anything. Especially me."

"People have a way of surprising us, don't they?"

"Yeah." Kurt looked at the path winding ahead of them. "Yeah, they sure do."

Vanessa was becoming the person he'd glimpsed months ago buried beneath the grief and sadness—smart, feisty, and brave.

"You should hear her in our Wednesday night discussions. She asks some really hard questions that make the kids think with their heart, their head, *and* their gut. Nobody can settle for easy answers or hide from the hard stuff when she's there, including her."

They rounded the second curve of the lake. "You were concerned about how mad she's been at God," Joel said. "Do you see that changing?"

Memories from the last few weeks floated to mind. She'd peppered him with questions after last week's discussion. Her hand flew over the paper as she scribbled notes while he talked. He'd been stunned that she wrote down what he said.

"Yeah, being at the House with the kids is changing her. I think the questions are her way of figuring out who and what He is." He gave a short laugh. "I can tell you, all her questions are making me dig a lot deeper when I get ready for the weekly message. And it's sure making me explain what I believe more clearly."

"Staying one step ahead of your group can be hard work." Joel laughed and slapped him on the back. "That's what keeps us on our toes. Welcome to the club, my friend."

Kurt joined his laughter. Life at River House was sometimes overwhelming, never boring, and always the first thing on his mind when he awoke. It was easily his favorite place to be.

Kurt pulled into the driveway Saturday morning and slammed the car to a stop as he stared at the House. The front was splattered with eggs, wild black graffiti scrawled across the garage. Garbage was strewn across the yard. He sat wide-eyed, unable to move or think, struggling against the rising urge to strike out at something, to race back to the 'hood and beat an explanation out of Wolf.

The spray paint declared he was next. "Why? What did I do to deserve this after all this time?" He pounded the steering wheel. "What do you want?!"

Eyes squeezed shut, he prayed for answers and for help, for protection over the kids and the volunteers who staffed the House. And for control over the anger that was choking him, that threatened to ruin everything he'd worked so hard to change.

He called Joel to discuss a repair plan, then he called Mike and Vanessa. Within the hour, word had spread through the House grapevine. Neighbors streamed from their homes armed with garbage bags and work gloves, and River House kids arrived looking like they'd just rolled out of bed.

Razzie stared at the house in disbelief. "What the h—"

"Hey." Kurt cut him off. "Watch your language, Razz. I know what you're thinking but let's keep it clean."

Razzie turned disbelieving eyes to him. "Are you serious? How can you do that with this—" He waved an arm at the damaged house.

Kurt set his hands firmly on the boy's shoulders. "Because there are little kids around. We can fix this. It's a pain but nobody's hurt so we just gotta buckle down and clean it up. And be thankful for how the neighbors have responded. We've built a solid reputation here. Let's not blow it, okay?"

Razzie stared back at him, frowning darkly. "Okay," he said through clenched teeth. "But I'm gonna find out who did this."

"I know who did it but we aren't gonna do anything about it." When Razzie started to protest, Kurt squeezed his shoulders. "I know it sounds crazy, but we need to show the neighborhood how God wants us to respond to this kind of stuff. And that's not by cranking it up a notch. We're going to clean up, pray over the house some more, and move on."

He held the boy's gaze. "I need you to help me. You're one of the leaders here, Razz. The other kids will follow your lead. Please."

Razzie was silent for a long moment, his breathing fast and shallow, arms stiff at his sides. Finally he nodded. "Whatever. It's weird but we'll do it your way. For now."

"Cool. Thanks, man. Let's get to work."

Vanessa arrived a few minutes later, sharing a tortured glance with Kurt as she pushed up her sleeves and pulled on work gloves. By midafternoon the yard was clean, the garage door repainted, and most of the egg stains washed from the front of the house. It would need a new coat of paint, which Sam promised to get done within the week.

Kurt gathered the kids in the front yard, two dozen in all, and sat in their midst to talk about what it meant to forgive, how necessary it was and how difficult unless God led them through it. And he prayed. He was surprised when Razzie's voice joined him in a terse prayer, followed by Ashley, then Pauly.

When Vanessa's voice followed Pauly's, Kurt's eyes flew open. She sat between Razzie and Natalie, holding their hands, head down.

"And please keep River House safe for all the kids coming here. Give Kurt strength and courage, and the wisdom he needs to continue being a great leader. I'm thankful he's such a good friend to the neighborhood."

Since arriving at the house that morning, God had provided him with an unearthly calm and words of encouragement to share with the kids. But hearing Vanessa's sweet prayer set that calm teetering on the edge of collapse. He let her words sink into his heart, relaxing into the realization that all was well, regardless of the graffiti on the house. God was in control.

Heads lifted and Kurt smiled. "From your lips to God's ears. Man, you guys are amazing. Now, I don't know about you but I'm starving. Let's eat."

Amidst a mad dash to the house, Kurt caught Vanessa's hand and held tight.

26

Kurt jogged up the front steps of his old house and rang the doorbell. Whistling tunelessly, he waited. When she didn't answer, he pushed the bell again, concern poking at him. She'd always been home when he'd stopped by, no matter what time of day or night.

He cupped his hands and looked in the window. Merton sat in a shaft of sunlight, but there was no sign of Vanessa. Why hadn't he thought to ask for a spare key for emergencies? He dropped onto the front step and settled against the wrought iron railing to wait.

An hour later he was giving serious thought to calling the police when a taxi slid to the curb. Seeing Vanessa's blonde head in the backseat, he hurried down the steps. As she paid the driver, he opened the door and reached in to help her out. She ignored his offer. "What are you doing here?"

He stepped back. "Well, hello to you too. Where've you been?"

"Out, obviously."

With her hair pulled into a messy ponytail, dressed in sweatpants and an over-sized T-shirt, she looked more like a homeless person than the Vanessa he knew. Keys jangling, she leaned heavily on both canes as she labored up the front walk. She hadn't used two canes for months.

"By yourself?"

"Do you see anyone else?"

He stopped short. "Vanessa, come on. I was worried when you weren't here."

She struggled up the steps and jammed her key into the lock then paused to frown up at him. Eyebrows pinched together, her pale skin made her look ill. "I just had some things to do. And yes, I was alone."

A sharp sigh escaped as she pushed the door open. "I don't mean to be rude, but I'm too tired to visit today. I really need to lie down for a bit."

Kurt looked down at her, confusion tangling with hurt. "Do you want to tell me what happened?"

"Nothing 'happened.' I had an appointment." Defeat flickered across her face before she lifted her chin and set her shoulders. "I'm fine. I just need to be alone."

"Okay. Fine." His childish response pricked his conscience but he continued, heaping on sarcasm. "Don't let me keep you. After all, why should it matter that maybe I was worried?"

She went into the house without a backward glance, and he wheeled around and jogged down the steps before she could shut the door in his face. Stomping back to his car, he kicked at a rock, missed, and went back to kick it again. It twanged against the bumper of his car then shot out into the street.

"Well, that was a wasted afternoon." He started the car and pulled away from the curb with an unintentional but satisfying squeal.

Throughout the rest of the day he swung between wondering where she had been and reminding himself she didn't owe him an explanation.

The next day his thoughts bounced back and forth, making it impossible to concentrate. Vanessa stayed out of the House, attending appointments with several kids at the high school, meeting with a community panel, running errands. Her absence during the Wednesday evening worship screamed at him. He stumbled through his message and wrapped up early.

Her chair remained empty Thursday morning. He snapped at Mike over nothing and cancelled his lunch date with Ashley to brood alone in his office. Another day would be shot if he didn't have it out with her. If she wanted to quit, she'd have to tell him to his face.

He wasn't surprised when he arrived at her house mid-afternoon and she wasn't home. Something weird was going on, but before he let her bail on their work together, he wanted to know what it was. He plopped onto the front step, settled against the railing and folded his arms to wait. Again.

When she climbed out of the taxi a short time later, he was slow to move down the steps. She stood on the sidewalk looking up at him, dark circles under her eyes, shoulders drooping. The light that had been steadily growing in her was gone.

His frustration evaporated in the face of her defeat. A surge of protectiveness swept over him, and he asked gently, "Now will you tell me what's going on?" The sudden urge to wrap her in his arms made him shove his hands into his back pockets.

She opened her mouth but nothing came out. Instead, she headed toward the steps, her limp more pronounced than usual. He followed her into the house, noting her lack of response to Merton's welcome.

In the kitchen, she moved toward the stove. He put his hands on her thin shoulders and directed her to the table. "Sit."

Without protest, she lowered onto the chair. The slump to her posture made Kurt pause as he filled the kettle. A thousand questions pounded but he bit his tongue and let her sit quietly. He made her tea and took a can of root beer from the refrigerator before settling across from her. And he waited.

She played with the tea bag for a long silent moment. When she finally lifted her gaze, a sheen of tears glistened. "I can't do it."

He raised his eyebrows.

"I've been going to physical therapy," she admitted, so softly he had to lean closer. "Three times a week. To maybe—someday—walk without these stupid canes. But I can't."

Relief rushed through him. This wasn't on his list of potential issues. "You can't walk without the canes?"

"No. It hurts too much." Her sigh was deep and long. "I just want to walk normally again," she whispered, closing her eyes.

Kurt reached across the table to cover her hand with his. He had no experience with amputees. Maybe it wasn't a reasonable goal for the short-term. Maybe it would take many months of therapy.

She was slow to look at him, eyebrows slanting upwards in apology. "I wanted to surprise you. So we could walk to River House faster. Maybe even walk around the whole lake."

"You're doing this for me?" He couldn't help smiling as the anger and fear of the past few days melted. "Nessa, I don't care how fast we walk or if we make it all the way to Canada." He squeezed her hand. "I just like being with you."

There. He'd said it.

Her gaze clung to his for a long minute before a partial smile lit her face. The aura of sadness lifted, letting color seep back into her cheeks. "Really?"

"Really." He released her hand and leaned back. "I'm not much of a talker but with you—" He shrugged, his insides racing around like a kid with his first crush. "It's just easy to talk about stuff. You don't let me get away with anything either."

The sweet sound of her giggle warmed him straight through. "So I don't care how you walk. I'm just glad that you walk with *me*. Okay?"

The lines on her forehead disappeared. "Okay. But...I still want to keep working at it."

"Good. That's good. Do you want me to come with you next time? Maybe just to cheer you on or something?"

Her eyes widened. "Would you?"

"Sure. When's your next appointment?"

Saturday afternoon, Kurt sat off to the side of a large exercise room at the clinic. Beth, the physical therapist, had the bearing of a cheerful drill sergeant—short, stocky, ready to work and happy to be there. From where she stood on the treadmill, Vanessa listened with a focused expression, nodding then looking skeptical.

Beth held a remote control in one hand, clipboard in the other. She finished talking and the machine started at a slow pace. Kurt could see

Vanessa's white-knuckled grip on the black handles from where he sat twenty feet away. An old song from Three Dog Night played in the background. He tapped his foot to its pulsing beat, praying for her to succeed.

The speed increased and her limp became more pronounced. The occasional wince made Kurt's leg ache in sympathy.

"It's hurting again."

"It's going to be sore," Beth acknowledged in a calm tone. "Remember, we're toughening up the site for the new prosthesis. Let's try going at three this time."

"No! I can't!"

Kurt had never heard panic in her voice. The angry, stubborn young woman he was used to had transformed into a frightened, frustrated girl ready to give up. He went around Beth to stand near the treadmill.

"Hey, you can do this."

"No, I can't." Frowning fiercely, bent slightly forward, her grasp remained tight around the handles. Her gait was uneven, most of her weight landing on her left leg. Step, thump. Step, thump. "Neither could you if you were missing a leg."

He grinned. That was more like the Vanessa he knew. "This is hard work, Nessa. Remember your goal."

A sharp breath sent her bangs fluttering. "My goal is to go home. I just have to accept that this is who I am. You said you don't care how fast we walk."

"Oh, no. You're not using me as an excuse to quit." He moved closer and stood directly in front of her. "Vanessa, look at me. I have a question for you."

Her eyes locked on his and for a moment he wavered. "What happened when your mom died?"

She blinked in surprise. "Our lives fell apart."

"I know. But what did you do?"

"I cried myself to sleep every night. What's your point?"

Help me do this, Lord. "But what did you do about the kids being so young?"

Her limp became more pronounced and his heart ached with the pain he was dragging her through. "Well, I..."

"Did you go to court?"

Fire flared in her eyes and her back straightened. "I had to. If I hadn't, they would have ended up in foster care. You know that."

"But that wouldn't have been so bad, would it?"

She looked ready to step off the treadmill and smack him. "Of course it would."

"Why?"

"*Why?*" She leaned forward. "Because we were family. There was no way I was going to let them go to foster care. They were my responsibility."

"But you were only twenty-one."

"I promised my mom I would take care of them." Tears filled her eyes as she glared at him. "I promised I wouldn't let us get split up. We went to court so I could become their legal guardian."

She released the handles with a snort. "The county social worker dropped in at the strangest times. I know they had to be sure the kids would be okay, but still—"

"And the kids wanted to stay with you?"

She looked at him like he was crazy. "Of course."

He moved closer. "Were they happy?"

"Yes." Her gaze drifted, the lines around her mouth softening. "Angie danced at the studio. She was such a wonderful dancer, so natural. And she played the flute in band." The smile deepened. "She was in Math Club too, which amazed me because I hated math."

"Did she have friends?"

"A million. She was so pretty and outgoing. And she was smart and gifted, and yet she had the biggest heart."

"Just like her big sister."

Her gaze swung back to his. "I was none of those things. I was stubborn and hard to get along with. I had a few friends but not like she did. I danced but not with the natural grace she had."

Kurt's heart plunged. She still couldn't see that she was just as wonderful as the sister she idolized. "What about Matt? Tell me more about him."

Her frown eased. She seemed unaware of the slight increase in the speed of the treadmill. Beth had moved off to the side, holding the remote in one hand and writing furiously on her clipboard, a corner of her mouth tilted up. Kurt took that as approval.

"Matt was...Matt. Tall, dark, and handsome even at sixteen. The band was his life. They practiced at our house every weekend." Her laugh was short, full of pain. "He was thrilled to have gotten his license, although I was too afraid to let him drive much."

"Who taught him to drive?"

"Me. We had a few scares and some good laughs. I was glad he caught on quickly. But that was Matt. He caught on quickly to everything."

Her gait had evened out. Step, step, step, step.

He needed to push her a little further, make her see the big picture. "Did they ever get in trouble?"

"Well...nothing major. Just stupid stuff, like detention for handing homework in late."

"Did they do drugs or go out partying on the weekends? Were they ever arrested?"

She was walking hard now, back straight, arms swinging. Fists clenched. Sweat trickled down in front of her ears as she stared at him. "How can you even ask that?"

"Because I want you to say it out loud."

"Say *what* out loud?"

He couldn't push her anymore. "What great kids they were. What a great job you did." He paused. "How special you are."

Her gait faltered and she stumbled then caught herself, confusion clouding her face. "But the kids are...gone. I screwed up."

"The person driving the other car screwed up. You were just in the wrong place at the wrong time. You'd done everything right. No, it's more than that." He set his hands on the treadmill, holding her gaze. "You've done things people twice your age wouldn't even try. And now you're walking normally on an artificial leg when other people would have given up."

Her eyes widened and she looked down at her feet, grasping for the handles as she watched the even steps shared by both legs. Beth slowed the speed slightly, grinning and bouncing on her toes.

Vanessa raised her head to stare at Kurt, open-mouthed. "I'm walking," she said. "I'm walking normally."

The disbelief in her voice choked him. "Yeah. And I'm not sure how since you said you couldn't." Then he turned and left the room, eyes burning. *Thank you, Lord.*

27

The front door burst open and a rowdy group of teens tumbled into River House, shattering the calm of a Thursday afternoon. Full of news of the day and plans for the weekend, their laughter charged the atmosphere with youthful energy. They decimated the snacks donated by Faith Church and half of the chocolate chip cookies Vanessa was baking, sharing highs and lows of their day around the kitchen island.

Kurt settled on the old blue couch in the Gathering Place, calendar and notebook in hand, and called the planning committee together. The group, minus Razzie, sprawled around the room to map out the rest of the month, licking melted chocolate off their fingers.

"Tiff, did you figure out how you want to run the bake sale?" Kurt asked.

Her face lit up. "Yes. My mom and I actually had a conversation without arguing. She gave me a couple of cool ideas—said she did bake sales when she was my age. Natalie and I are writing them all down."

"Glad you and your mom are getting along. Can you get that information to Vanessa by the weekend?" When she nodded, he made a check on his list then turned to Pauly. "What about the ping-pong tournament?"

An hour later, as the meeting concluded, the front door opened and Razzie strode in. The case he was carrying made Kurt's stomach clench.

"Hey, Razz. You missed the meeting," Pauly said. "Whatcha got?"

"A machine gun." He lightly smacked the back of Pauly's head. "What's it look like?"

"Since when do you play guitar?"

Razzie set the battered case on its end and leaned on it. "Since we have a master guitar player right here at River House to teach me."

An excited buzz filled the room as the kids guessed who it might be. Kurt kept his eyes on the calendar, tapping his pencil. His heart had screeched to a stop when Razzie walked in. Now it raced double time.

Razzie put an end to their wild speculations by jumping up on the couch. "Okay, listen up! This person was an original member of NightVision."

The kids stared at each other, mouths open. Kurt closed his eyes. The logo he'd designed for the band danced through his mind, mocking him. The pencil snapped in half. Feet itching to bolt from the house, he glanced at Razzie bouncing on the couch cushions. There was no way to stop the revelation without raising more questions. He shuddered, waiting for his failures to be broadcast to the group.

"C'mon, Razz. You're makin' this up," Pauly challenged. "There ain't nobody around here that played with NightVision. They'd have to be crazy good."

Razzie struck a pose, one foot on the armrest, milking the moment. Then he swung his arm and pointed. "It's River House's own Kurt Wagner, original lead singer and guitarist with NightVision."

In the shocked silence, Kurt struggled to breathe, the broken end of the pencil digging into his palm. Then chaos broke out as the girls squealed and the boys leaped to their feet. In the excitement, they let loose with excited four-letter words, bringing Kurt's head up in a snap.

"Hey! Watch the language."

"Oh, yeah. Sorry. Is it true? You were in NightVision?" Pauly's high-pitched voice grated.

Kurt's gaze slid to Razzie, whose face glowed with awed anticipation. "Where did you hear something like that?"

The boy leaped off the couch and landed with a solid thud in front of him. "I got my sources."

"Maybe your source is full of—" Pauly glanced at Kurt. "Maybe it ain't true."

"Oh, it's true." He pulled a folded piece of yellow paper from his jacket and waved it at Kurt. "I got proof."

Kurt's heart tumbled to his shoes.

Spinning to face the other kids, Razzie unfolded the paper. "It's a flyer for a concert tour kickoff party. Our very own boss is right in front." He turned the creased paper around and they jostled each other to see it, then whooped and danced around the room.

"Whoa! NightVision! Lead singer for the greatest band ever. Woot, woot, woot!"

Their voices were more painful than a badly tuned guitar. Kurt clenched his jaw.

"What's going on?" Vanessa stood in the kitchen doorway, green oven mitts in hand.

Tiffani raced across the room to pull her into the chaos. "We have a star right here at River House!"

Vanessa took in the wild scene then smiled at the girl. "You're all stars in my opinion."

"Not like this." Tiffani pointed at Kurt. "Right there. Our very own rock star."

Vanessa's narrowed eyes met Kurt's. He gave a tiny shake of his head, pleading silently for her to leave it alone.

She turned her attention back to Tiffani. "Hon, the cookies are burning—"

The girl grabbed her wrist. "No, listen! Razzie found out Kurt was the lead singer in NightVision back when they first started. Can you believe it? NightVision!"

"Where in the world did you hear something like that?" she asked Razzie.

"I got sources," he said. "Ask *him*."

Several of the girls were singing one of the band's hits, arms slung around each other's necks as they swayed. A song Kurt had written.

Lips pressed together to keep his emotions in check, he got slowly to his feet, feeling old and tired and very sad. The kids went silent, mouths open as they waited for him to speak.

"Okay. I'm gonna say this once and then we're not gonna talk about it again. Ever. I played with them before they were famous. We knew each other in high school. I wasn't good enough to go on tour so they found someone else. I haven't played since then. That's it."

"You gotta be kidding." Razzie flung his hands in the air. "They said you were beyond good enough. They said you were gonna be the next Primo. There are tons of people who think you should be playing with them right now. They said—"

"Stop!" Kurt turned on him, throwing his papers which scattered across the room. He clenched his fists. Razzie stepped back, eyes wide.

"I *wasn't* good enough, Razz." His words were cold and sharp, like the pain in his heart.

"But they were saying—"

"They're wrong, damn it!" The room went silent. "Just leave it alone!"

Spinning on his heel, he slammed out the door and hurled himself into his car. Rage propelled his short drive home and once inside, he flung himself onto the couch and buried his face in the crook of his arm, his eyes shut against the excruciating burn in his chest.

The dream was over; he'd seen to that with his trademark drinking and brawling. There was no one to blame but himself, and he did that steadily for the first five years. It had taken months of working with Jenny before he could forgive himself and move on. But even now, when one of the band's well-known songs came on the radio, he wrestled back a swell of guilt and abandonment.

He finally drifted into a restless sleep haunted with memories. Writing tunes with Corey late into the night. Jamming with the band in the basement. Driving to a gig in Danny's decrepit van. And pouring out his music onstage, drenched in sweat, beloved guitar in hand.

A bell rang and the images faded. He lay still a moment, trying to go back. The doorbell rang again. Staggering to his feet, he looked at his watch and wondered what day it was. Vanessa stood frowning on the front step in the fading sunlight. He ran his hands through his hair. "Hey."

"Hi. When you didn't come back, I got worried."

"Yeah. Sorry."

He didn't invite her in and she didn't ask. She just looked at him steadily through the screen door. "Nessa, I can't talk about it."

"You don't have to. I just wanted to be sure you were okay. I'll see you tomorrow."

He watched her walk away, frozen between the desire to slam the door on her questions and the sudden need to be with her. "Nessa, wait." He pulled the door shut behind him and met her in the driveway. "Do you have time for a walk?"

"Sure."

"You're okay without the canes?"

She smiled. "Try me."

They walked in silence for several blocks.

"We started the band in high school. When I went to the joint, they went on tour." There. He'd said it out loud. It wasn't the whole story but it was the truth.

Her deep sigh felt like warm, gentle hands cradling his aching heart.

"And you haven't played since?"

Kurt slowed and faced her. "Not in seven years and two months. Give or take a few days."

In the quiet, the impression on his heart was clear. *It's time to be honest.*

He could stop hiding from the past and tell her the whole sorry story. Or he could stuff the memories down and hope they stayed there.

Lord, help.

He met her eyes squarely and stepped off the cliff. "But that's not the whole story."

28

Heart pounding double time, he unlocked the door of his past. "Joel and Jenny are the only ones who know the whole story. I've wanted to tell Mike but I couldn't figure out how to bring it up. There's never a good time to blurt out, 'Hey, I screwed up the biggest opportunity of my life. And I've got more of a record than you know about.'"

"Kind of like me trying to talk about my leg," she said. "Or lack thereof."

The breath that was locked in his chest released and they walked the rest of the way to the park in silence. Her patience allowed him the space to wander back in time. "It started when I was fourteen, when my stepdad gave me my first electric guitar."

"What kind? Stratocaster? Rickenbacker?"

When his eyebrows lifted, she grinned. "Once Matt started playing, we devoured every guitar magazine and stalked every music store in the Twin Cities. We talked frets, capos, amps, and strings. I know far more about guitars than I ever wanted to know."

He smiled. "A 1965 Gibson Firebird. Electric blue." He'd never forget it. Even now he could feel the strings under his calloused fingers. "A classic. It played like...well, I was sure I'd be the next Eric Clapton."

"Not Elvis?"

"No way. We had dreams—big dreams. Much bigger than Elvis."

"Ooo."

The teasing in her voice made him smile. "Okay, smarty. You want to hear this or not?"

She sobered. "Definitely."

For the next hour as they roamed the park, he found the courage to remember. An angry fourteen-year-old with years of abuse behind him, he'd poured his excess energy into mastering the new guitar. Being part of something—no, being the leader of something—meant the world to him.

"We started the band in tenth grade. I wasn't good at school. I hated math, I stunk at writing papers, and I had a bad attitude. Being in the band was the one thing I was good at. Man, I loved playing with those guys."

Music was the release he needed and songwriting came effortlessly. Yet even creating music couldn't erase the pain in his heart and the anger that simmered just below the surface. They'd played at least one high school party every weekend, eventually playing at college frat parties where booze was plentiful. To fit in with the older guys, they were soon drinking themselves into oblivion after every gig.

Vanessa settled beside him atop a picnic table. "So what happened to make them go on without you?"

He sat still for a long moment. "I was arrested. The first of several times." Elbows stabbing the tops of his thighs, he stared at the ground. Boozing had led to brawling, picking fights with anyone and everyone. The festering anger poured out in a torrent one night.

"One stupid night of drinking changed everything." He could hear the taunts, smell the liquor-laced evening air. His fingers curled into fists and he felt the impact of his knuckles against breaking skin. It could have been yesterday.

"Kurt?"

He blinked at her quiet voice and turned toward her.

"You don't have to tell me any more if you don't want."

Swallowing the regret, he looked away. "You should know who you work with."

"I do. A man with a big heart and an amazing faith who does a great job herding a bunch of crazy kids. A man who misses playing his guitar and writing music and who invited me to join him in a job that perfectly suits who I am.

"Whatever happened back then made you who you are today,"

she said. "I'm sure it was a terrible time, but it made you strong and compassionate."

He pushed off the picnic table and moved a few feet away, arms crossed tightly. He'd obviously done a great job creating a façade to be admired. *What a joke.*

"I'm sorry." Her voice was close by. "I wasn't being flip."

He turned and met her earnest gaze. "I know."

"We don't have to talk about this anymore. I just wanted you to know that..." She hesitated before putting a gentle hand on his arm. "...it doesn't matter what you did back then. I don't know that Kurt. I just know *you*. And I'm glad that I do."

Her gentle words made his eyes sting. His gaze roamed over her face, pausing on her mouth. His heart skipped a beat and he turned away, plunging back into the swirling memories.

"I drank a lot in high school. Drank myself right out of a high school diploma. Too much partying, too little studying." He snorted. "Okay, no studying. But I got my GED while I was in prison."

"That's good," she said.

"Yeah. So...I guess I was a mean drunk. No, I *am* a mean drunk. I've had to work really hard to learn how to express anger the right way, how to feel it and know what to do with it. I used to just let it out at whoever or whatever was in my path, especially when I was on a binge.

"I was never drunk when we were writing music. It was easy to be focused on that. But when there was a lull in the action, I'd have a beer in my hand and a couple under the belt."

She stood quietly, those blue eyes steady on him. He tucked a loose strand of hair behind her ear. The rest of his story was going to change her opinion of him. "I hate that I have to tell you this."

"You don't," she assured him.

"Yeah, I do. It's time you knew everything." He turned away, stuffing his hands into his pockets. "Anyway, a mean drunk is a fighting drunk. I was in plenty of fights along with my so-called buddies. One night we were out cruising, looking for trouble, and we found it. Another group of idiots like us.

"We met outside a bar, everybody pretty smashed. One thing led to another and I was hauled off to jail. When the guy died, the charge changed from battery to manslaughter."

He was afraid to look at her. Shame seared through him. "My lawyer argued self-defense since the guy had pulled a knife. There were so many people in the fight, it was hard to tell who did what. But I know I threw that last punch. At least, that's what I remember before I blacked out."

He'd never get over it. He didn't deserve to get over it. "Since they couldn't prove it was actually me who did it, I went to the workhouse for a year on the battery charges instead of manslaughter. The fight happened a few days after we'd signed a contract to start touring so they got a new lead guitar player and they left. My mom..."

He looked up at the darkening sky, blinking quickly. "My mom had had a heart attack two years earlier. When I was in the workhouse, she had a massive one and died before my sentence was done."

"Oh, Kurt." Her sigh was deep. "I'm so sorry."

"Me too." The memory closed icy fingers around his throat. Scotty's despair, the sadness in their stepdad's eyes, white roses on a fresh grave. All because of him. "I wasn't out very long when I got picked up in the drug bust and ended up in prison. At least she didn't live long enough to see me hit rock bottom."

Silence stretched between them. She tugged gently at his sleeve. "Come sit with me again."

He kept space between them as they sat back down. How could any one person screw up so many times in so few years? *What a loser.*

"It all makes sense now," she said. "When I talked about the guilt I felt over the kids' death, you understood it so well. Now I see why."

"Yeah, but you didn't cause the accident. My mom died because of how badly I screwed up."

She sat up straighter. "I need to tell you the rest of *my* story, since we're having a truth fest. You told me I had no control over the accident, that it wasn't my fault they died. But that's not true. It *was* my fault. I hadn't been getting enough sleep. I'd had a long week. I should have told them no to running the errand, but..."

"I was mad at them, tired of how hard everything was. I wasn't paying attention to my driving. If I hadn't been yelling at them, maybe I'd have seen the guy and not turned in front of him."

She climbed off the picnic table and faced him, tears in her eyes. "Over these past months, I've realized I can't change any of it. There's no purpose in spending the rest of my life wondering what-if. It's thanks to you I've come this far."

Her small hands settled over his. "As for you, whether you were in jail at the time or a stellar college student, she still would have died."

He gritted his teeth, unable to look away from the compassion in her gaze. "It's not the same—"

"It *is* the same," she insisted, her fingers tightening, "because life is out of our control. You had a drinking problem. You got involved in a mess that ended in a terrible way. I was raising teens on my own when I was barely out of the teens myself. We were both in way over our heads."

"That makes sense for your situation, but it's just an excuse for mine."

"Kurt, we were doing the best we could with what life had thrown at us. Punishing ourselves for the rest of our lives won't bring anyone back, including our families."

Her gentle voice, edged with a decisiveness he'd never heard in her, poured soothing warmth over him. Finally he lifted his head and gave a slow nod. "I'll think about it."

Her expression softened and she squeezed his hands before settling close beside him. "You need to ask God to show you the truth of that sad time."

He blinked. "Okay. I'll do that. Thanks, Nessa." He put an arm around her shoulders. "I've never had a friend like you."

Pink flooded her cheeks. She smiled shyly and rested her head against his shoulder. "Ditto."

They snuggled together, watching the fading rays of sunlight kindle the autumn glory of the trees around them, flaunting their colors against the dusky sky. An occasional leaf swirled to the ground.

Vanessa sat up slightly, a thoughtful frown tugging at her brow. "Kurt, I know this is going to sound strange but...I have the strongest feeling you need to start playing again. There's something you need to be doing with your music."

Hope struggled to rise against his attempt to squash it. No, he had a different life now. He pulled his arm away and shook his head.

"There's no way, Vanessa," he said firmly. "I don't have time. I've got too many other things to focus on. And...I don't need reminders of the mess I made of everything. It's better to just not play at all."

"You put something on the wall at River House that you aren't living up to yourself."

His mind flashed to the words he'd inscribed over the front door: "Serve our mighty God with everything you've got." *Ouch.*

"There's a whole big piece of you that you aren't acknowledging," she continued. "I think God is calling you back to it. Or maybe forward with it."

He sat very still as her words settled over him. Hope banged against his ribs, filling his heart with long-forgotten music. Was that possible? The music would be completely different now, thankfulness for what God had done, praise for His goodness and mercy—

No. He shook the thoughts away. Reviving the dream wasn't worth the risk that it might all fall apart again. He looked into eyes shining with encouragement. "Nessa, I just don't see it happening."

When she started to speak, he held up a hand in weary defense. "I promise I'll spend time praying about it. I'd appreciate it if you'd pray for me, too."

She nodded, her lips twitching as if she were trying not to smile.

The corners of his mouth lifted in response. "You should be in sales. You're the most persistent person I know." Her giggle lightened the heaviness of the discussion. "Thanks for forcing this conversation and helping me face the past. I'm glad you know the whole story."

"I'm glad we both shared our stories."

They sat for another moment looking at each other with growing smiles. His fingers twitched with the need to touch her pink, flawless cheeks. His gaze moved to her smiling mouth then back to her eyes, his heart doing the goofy twirl he was growing accustomed to when she was around.

"So." He cleared his throat and climbed off the table, holding out a hand. "How about I treat you to dinner?"

Her eyes lit up. "Sounds wonderful."

As they started back toward his place, he kept a firm hold of her hand. In just a few hours, his world had gone from rocked off its foundation to settled on a whole new plane.

Life was sure not predictable anymore. And he was just fine with that—as long as he had her beside him.

She was jealous! The realization brought an intense flush to Vanessa's face as she pretended to read the magazine article in front of her. Just a few feet away, Ashley and Kurt laughed and chatted on the couch. Vanessa clenched her jaw to keep her emotions in check, giving herself a mental slap.

Just because he'd held her hand on the way back from the park three nights ago and took her to dinner and spent the rest of the evening sitting on the front step with her laughing and eating ice cream—that didn't give her license to think of him any differently than before.

But when he kissed her forehead as they'd said goodnight, her insides had gone into a pirouette that hadn't stopped. She'd found it impossible to fall asleep that night and she'd been smiling ever since. Until Ashley showed up at the House today and monopolized Kurt's attention.

What is wrong with you? He'd be so embarrassed to know how totally off the wall you've gotten.

He was her big brother, her friend and confidant. She was his little sister. Being jealous was ridiculous. Useless. Painful.

Propping her forehead in her hand, she tried to focus on the words, randomly underlining a sentence here and there. Ashley's giggle grated on her, making her teeth hurt. It felt like she was eavesdropping on their date.

"Oops. Sorry, Vanessa," Ashley said. "We're being so noisy and you're trying to read."

She looked up and met the girl's apologetic expression. Forcing a smile, she shook her head. "You're not bothering me at all."

They were bothering her all right. It bothered her that Ashley had

Kurt's attention in a way she never would. It bothered her that Ashley was funny and bouncy and full of life. And whole. And perfect.

And it bothered her that she *liked* Ashley. The whole thing was becoming unbearable. She needed something to do. Run errands. Rake the front yard. Walk a dog, any dog.

The front door swung open and Mike's large presence filled the room. *Thank goodness!* He stood for a moment, looking around the nearly empty Gathering Place. "So, where is everybody?"

"There's ping-pong going on in the garage," Ashley told him, "and a group downstairs working with Ryan on building a table. And a few of the girls are trying on new makeup in the ladies' room."

Mike approached Vanessa's desk. "Good. It felt like a morgue when I came in. What's my favorite munchkin up to?"

"Just catching up on some articles I've been meaning to read."

"I was hoping we could get working on the CleanSweep Project. Game?"

She tried to keep relief from her voice as she stood. "Definitely!"

They'd created the Fall CleanSweep Project from their desire to connect Faith and River House kids. Thrilled with the idea of serving the neighbors and bringing the kids together, she and Mike had developed a plan that would offer free lawn service and yard cleanup to the blocks surrounding the House.

Mike glanced at Ashley and Kurt relaxed on the couch, legs stretched out, feet almost touching. "How about we go somewhere so we don't bother those two? That way we'll have room to spread out."

"Good idea." Vanessa scooped random folders together, grabbed a few pens, then pulled her purse from the drawer. The water drops on Mike's shirt reminded her that the morning rain had continued into the late afternoon. "I'll get my jacket and we can go."

"Vanessa, will you be back for the service tonight?" Kurt asked.

She glanced over her shoulder and encountered his frown. "Not sure. Do you need me for anything?"

Mike helped her into her jacket as she waited for Kurt's answer.

Their gazes held across the room for a moment, and her heart knocked against her ribs several times before he shrugged. "I suppose not. I know the girls like it when you're around."

"With Ashley here, they won't even know I'm gone." Neither would he.

The redhead grinned. "They'll be disappointed, but I'll try my best to fill your fabulous shoes, Van."

Vanessa gave her a smile, hoping it didn't look like the grimace it felt inside, then turned her gaze to Kurt's. Creases had formed across his forehead. He seemed annoyed as he looked at her, biting the inside of his cheek.

Well, if he could sit chatting with Ashley like they were the only two people in the world, she could certainly go off with Mike to do some actual work. Kurt was the director. It wouldn't kill him to answer the phone for the evening. She was just the volunteer assistant. A jealous, petty volunteer. Maybe she should quit.

"I'll be in by ten tomorrow," she said before looking up at Mike and forcing a toothy smile. "I'm ready if you are."

"Then we're outta here." He held the door open for her and followed her out before adding, "I'm hungry for pizza so maybe we can head over to Millie's Cafe."

"You're always hungry," she returned with a laugh as the front door slammed shut behind them.

Settled at Millie's with pizza and salad, they started their discussion with a prayer for guidance and wisdom. Mike's cheerful presence and booming laugh and their excitement about the project soon distracted her from thoughts of Kurt and Ashley. She took copious notes as they brainstormed ideas. Finally they dug into outlining what the cleanup project would look like, agreeing to create a task force of kids from both the church and River House.

When Mike dropped her at home hours later, she was happy to realize she'd stayed focused on the planning the whole time. She had dear friends in the people at River House, including Kurt and Ashley, so to want something that couldn't happen was a waste of energy.

She made a cup of chamomile tea and settled at the computer. There was work to be done before next week's initial task force meeting, so she would do what she'd always done—focus on reality and get the job done.

She indulged in one last moment of wistfulness before pulling the pages of notes toward her and placing her fingers on the keyboard. *Life is what it is.*

It took all his self-control to keep from firing a hundred questions at Vanessa when she arrived at River House promptly at ten the next morning. Stretched out on the couch, pretending to read, Kurt gave her exactly three minutes to hang up her jacket and walk to her desk before the words were out of his mouth. "So he took you out for pizza afterwards?"

She looked up from the papers in her hand with a vague expression. "Sorry, what?"

"You and Mike. Pizza last night?"

"Oh. Yeah, we did. He was starving. Boy, that man can eat. I had a salad and he had a whole pizza."

He gave a short laugh. "Yeah. Quite a guy."

She settled at her desk and booted up the computer, humming softly.

His grip tightened on the leadership magazine. "So, do you guys have plans for the weekend?"

Her head came up and she frowned. "Me and Mike? Plans for what?"

He shrugged. "Just…plans. You know. To do stuff."

She leaned back in her chair, tilting her head as she chewed a fingernail. "Well…we were thinking we need to write up an invitation for the kids we want on the CleanSweep task force."

"Over dinner?"

A frown building in her eyes, she looked like someone under cross-examination. "I don't know. We hadn't really talked about it."

"But you'd go if he asked." *Stop asking questions, you goon.*

She blinked several times as she looked back at him, shoulders lifted in a bewildered shrug. "Well, I guess. If we ended up meeting when it was time to eat. Why? Isn't that okay?"

Kurt gave himself a swift mental kick. What bright answer did he have for that? "Of course." *Not.* "Just forget I brought it up."

"Kurt—"

"Never mind," he snapped, jumping to his feet and throwing the magazine to the floor. "I'm gonna check the mail."

Letting the screen door slam behind him, he stomped down the porch steps. *Lord, I don't know what to do with these feelings. They're getting stronger instead of going away. Fix it so I can just be her friend. I'm such a moron around her.*

He yanked open the mailbox, startled to find the door had broken off in his hand. For a fleeting moment he was tempted to chuck it into the street. He closed his eyes and pulled in a long, slow breath, praying for calm. Maybe he should go for a run so he wouldn't have to stay in the house with her any longer than necessary.

As the tension ebbed, his thoughts settled. He collected the mail, then let his feet lead him back into the house. She stood at the counter behind her desk, shuffling papers.

He set the mail and metal door on the desk. "Sorry for being an idiot. Again."

She shrugged one shoulder, keeping her back to him, and he knew. He'd made her cry. He moved around the desk to stand beside her. "Vanessa..."

Her head turned away and she wiped at her cheek.

"Hey, c'mere." He turned her gently to face him and lifted her chin. Tears sparkled in those eyes that made his heart do such weird gymnastics. He sighed. "I'm such a jerk."

She nodded, the corners of her mouth turned down. With a gentle touch he wiped the wetness from her cheek. Her skin was even softer than he'd imagined, warm under his finger. The delicate aroma of her perfume wrapped around him. Their eyes met and he realized she was holding her breath too. Unable to stop, he lowered his head and kissed her.

The contact was electric and amazing. When her arms went up around his neck a delirious moment later, he pulled her closer, a thrill running down to his toes. That she was kissing him back with abandon sent his heart into a crazy tremor. He shouldn't have kissed her but now he couldn't stop. Didn't want to. Ever.

Excitement rang in his ears. He tightened his arms as the room spun around them. When she finally drew back, he realized she'd been standing on her toes. The thought made him grin and a joyful smile broke across her face, sending his hopes soaring.

"I think the phone was ringing," she said, breathless.

"Was it? I thought it was just bells ringing in my head."

She giggled. "Then I heard the same bells."

They looked at each other in smiling silence. Now that she was finally in his arms, he wasn't ever going to let go. She was a perfect fit within his embrace, the perfect balance in his life.

"You're so pretty," he said, watching the color deepen across her cheeks. "I've thought that from the day we met in the garden. And I think I've wanted to kiss you since then."

Her eyebrows lifted. "You have amazing self-control."

He threw back his head with a laugh that burst from his heart. It felt like he could laugh for the rest of his life. "Oh, trust me. It's been a major struggle."

She leaned back against his arms and cocked her head. "What were you waiting for?"

"I thought you and Mike were...should...."

"Mike? He's the big brother I never had." Her eyes narrowed. "So that's what all the questions were about."

Heat filled his face. "Yeah. Sneaky, huh?"

"Not exactly, but very sweet. I've only looked at *you* all this time.

I thought you and Ashley would probably...at some point..."

"No way. I told you that before. She's like a kid sister."

"I guess we were both wrong."

He slowly shook his head. "But...you deserve someone—"

"Like you." Where her hands rested against his chest, she tapped a finger. "In here is the biggest heart I've ever known." She reached up shyly to rest her finger against his temple. "And in here is the most creative thinker I've ever met. And..."

The whisper of a touch burned his lips and his heart throbbed with joy.

"Out of here come the sweetest words of encouragement I've ever heard. You are the nicest, kindest man I've ever known. And your brown eyes make my heart do silly things."

He'd never heard words like that directed at him. Unable to respond, he took her face in his shaking hands and leaned down to draw her into a kiss filled with meaning and desire and joy. His heart danced with thanks and—

The crashing of glass was not supposed to be part of the moment.

30

The brick landed with a thud on the hardwood floor amidst the shattered glass of the front window. Kurt's arms spread instinctively and he pushed Vanessa back against the counter, waiting for another flying object.

Tires squealed and he glimpsed a black car pulling away from the curb. Heart still pounding, he released his breath and dropped his arms. He didn't have to look at the paper secured with a rubber band around the brick to know what it said.

"Kurt?" Her voice was filled with fear.

He pressed a reassuring kiss to her temple before crossing the room, crunching over glass. Shards littered the couch beneath the picture window and the old coffee table. He shuddered. If someone had been sitting there...

Yanking the band off the brick, he uncurled the paper. The short note was scribbled with black marker: "watch yor back wagnor. we are."

"What does that mean?" Vanessa leaned lightly against him, frowning at the paper.

Lord, protect this house and these kids. And this beautiful girl. It's not their fault my past is such a mess. Show me what to do.

With a deep sigh, he pulled her against him in a one-arm embrace. Her arms went around him quickly. He'd just captured her heart and already his past was putting her in danger. Defeat was cold in his chest. Couldn't he catch a break? Just once?

"It's nothing, Nessa," he assured her. "Just...Wolf, I assume."

"I'll call the police."

"No." He tightened his arm around her shoulders. "It's not worth it. I told the neighbors we wouldn't have the police here because of the kids' behavior—"

Her body tensed. "You think one of the kids is part of this?"

"Definitely not. But if we call the police, the neighbors are going to blame the kids, and I don't want that attitude surrounding the House. I'm going to call Sam to get it fixed and we'll just forget the whole thing, okay?"

She pulled away to face him, hands on her hips. "I can't forget this! Someone is threatening you. That's not okay at all."

Her wide-legged stance and incredulous expression drew a weak smile from him. "You're right. It's not okay. And it kills me that my past is hurting you and River House. But there's something else at work here too, Vanessa. This kind of stuff is gonna happen when we try to share the light of the Gospel with a world that prefers the darkness."

He set the brick down and wrapped her snugly in his arms, resting his cheek against her hair. "This just tells me we have to keep doing what we're doing. The world needs to know His grace."

She looked at him with serious eyes. "I need that grace."

His heart jumped at her admission, and a corner of his mouth lifted as he ran his fingers across her cheek. "We all do, Nessa."

"I don't want anything to happen to you."

"Me neither." He pressed a kiss to her forehead. *There's too much to lose now.*

Vanessa's world now sparkled with energy and excitement. She couldn't wait to get to River House each morning, impatient to be with Kurt and spend time with the kids. She posted pictures of her family on her desk, ready to share her story whenever she thought it might help. It was surprising to realize that the more she told it, the more alive her family seemed.

Mid-September brought Kurt's birthday into view. The kids buzzed with excitement as they planned his surprise party. When several shared they'd never had their own party, Vanessa created a poster noting each teen's birthday in bright colors so the day wouldn't pass unnoticed. Seeing their smiles when they saw their names warmed her heart.

On Thursday at three o'clock, a heavy pounding on the front door brought Kurt racing out of his office. Vanessa followed, wearing the grin she'd struggled all day to hide. A young man from the local bakery waited on the porch, holding a large white cake box tied with red ribbon. Behind him, a girl from the party store clutched a dozen balloons in vibrant colors. Another, from The Java Depot, held two coffee cartons and a stack of cups. All three stood silently smiling.

He pushed open the screen door. "Can I help—?"

"Surprise!" A shout went up from the front yard. "Happy Birthday!"

When he stood frozen in place, Vanessa gently pushed him onto the porch so the delivery people could move past them. And so he could see just how many people had turned out to celebrate with him. A rousing birthday song rose up from the crowd.

He turned a stunned expression toward her. "You knew about this?"

"Maybe a little."

"This is amazing!" He swung her into a hug which drew wolf whistles from the kids in the yard.

She squeezed his waist. "I can't believe they pulled it off."

People surged onto the porch with hugs, backslaps and birthday wishes, and Vanessa slipped into the house to help the neighbor ladies arrange the potluck. The brightly decorated sheet cake sat proudly in the middle of the kitchen table, surrounded by an array of appetizers, beverages, and cheerful birthday plates and napkins. Tiffani and Natalie tied balloons to fixtures all around the first floor.

With the party in full swing, Vanessa took countless pictures. The laughter and well wishes from neighbors brought happy tears to her eyes. To see how the neighborhood had accepted River House—and Kurt—thrilled her beyond words.

Joel and the staff from Faith Church arrived with more balloons.

Vanessa watched Kurt and his pastor friend share a laugh before he beckoned her over. Joel greeted her with a friendly hug, inquiring about her work at the House. When Kurt was drawn away a moment later, she and Joel continued chatting.

Smile lines seemed permanently etched at the corners of his eyes. He listened with interest as she shared stories about the kids at River House. She could see why Kurt enjoyed spending time with him. There was nothing about him that set her nerves on edge like the church people who had visited her after the accident. He was calm, friendly. Surprisingly nice. Before he headed back to the church, she took a picture of him and Kurt deep in conversation. It was one of her favorite shots.

Even Elwood and Priscilla stopped by. Kurt greeted them with an enthusiastic handshake before directing them to the nicest old chairs in the Gathering Place and retrieving cake and coffee for them. Elwood's cautious expression faded as Kurt chatted with them. Vanessa added a photo of their conversation to the assortment she'd taken.

Three hours later, Kurt sat in the Gathering Place surrounded by crumpled wrapping paper and grinning youth, opening the last of his gifts. Face flushed, sweaty hair pushed to the side, he was still smiling. Then he opened the box from Razzie and the smile froze. "Oh, wow. This is…wow."

Vanessa looked toward Razzie who had sat up from his usual slouching position, his eyes fastened on Kurt.

"Razz, this is—" When he lifted his gaze, Vanessa's heart melted at the tears in his eyes. "Thanks, man."

"Yeah. Glad you like it." Flopping back against the couch, Razzie's nonchalant reply didn't hide the smile in his voice.

The kids gathered around Kurt to see what the box held. He handed it to Pauly, pushed off his chair and moved across the room, hand extended. When Razzie grasped it, Kurt pulled him to his feet and into a hug.

With a laugh, Tiffani wiped a tear from her cheek and handed the box to Vanessa. "What a cool gift."

Vanessa studied the framed photograph. She'd taken the picture of Razzie and Kurt during a late afternoon picnic at the lake. With sunshine sparkling off the water behind them, the candid shot showed the two of them shaking hands and sharing a laugh after a wild Frisbee game.

The saying engraved below the photograph was something Kurt said often of Razz. She ran her finger across the words. "Brothers from a different mother."

Kurt and Vanessa carried the last of the birthday loot into Mike's kitchen. Depositing a bag of cards and gifts on the table, he turned and swept her into a hug. "How did you pull that off?" he demanded.

"I honestly don't know. There were so many times someone said something about the party, but you never seemed to catch on."

"I didn't think they were talking about *me*." He'd never had a surprise party. "Thanks, Nessa. I can't tell you what this afternoon meant to me."

Her response to his kiss was the perfect end to a perfect day. When he finally pulled back, she was breathless and smiling.

"Wow. Okay." Cheeks flushed, she untangled herself from his arms. "There's one more surprise."

"That kiss was all the surprise I can handle after today."

Her blush deepened as she tugged him into the living room and told him to sit, then went upstairs. On her way down, she ordered him to close his eyes. Paper rustled as she approached.

"Okay, you can look."

At his feet sat a guitar case, poorly disguised with colorful birthday paper and yards of curling ribbon. His heart froze in his chest. *Oh, no.* "No way, Vanessa."

"It's not polite to argue about a gift before you even open it," she scolded with a smile from her perch on the arm of the couch. Hands clasped in her lap, her face glowed.

Dread made it hard to tear the paper off. He shook his head.

"Vanessa, you can't do this." *I can't do this.*

"It needs to be played, Kurt. And you need to play. I think the two of you were made for each other."

This is a gift from the heart. The words were almost audible.

Even the thought of letting music back into his life made him nauseous. He unlocked the case. The wood finish gleamed in the soft lamp light. He ran his fingers across the strings, surprised to find his hand shaking. He didn't have this reaction around alcohol; he could pass up a beer, but he couldn't pass up this guitar without touching it. His Gibson had been an appendage for years—he'd practically slept with it in his hands. A part of him had died when he sold it, and he'd sworn he'd never touch another guitar.

Vanessa sat silently watching. When he frowned at her, she smiled back. There was no hint of doubt in her blue eyes.

It is a gift from the heart.

He carefully lifted the guitar, a black Fender acoustic with the dreadnought shape and built-in electronics. He soaked in every detail—the smell of the spruce and mahogany wood, the solid feel of it in his hands. Matt had taken good care of it.

"It's a beauty, Vanessa." He ran his hands over it reverently.

"Play something?"

He looked up in surprise. Did he even remember how? "Nah."

"Just something simple? I miss the sound of music in the house. I loved having the guys practice in the basement." She looked away for a moment then back at him, her jaw set. "Music has amazing healing qualities and I think we both need that."

Unseen hands seemed to lift him to his feet where he stood on wobbling legs clutching the instrument. The old longing swept over him in waves; sweat beaded on his forehead. He slid the strap over his head. It felt good. Man, it felt *great*.

Not sure if he should laugh or cry, he closed his eyes. It was achingly familiar...as if he'd come home. His fingers moved to the frets and he strummed once; the bold acoustic sound rang straight into his heart. He strummed again and adjusted the tuning.

The first song that came to mind was one he'd written with Corey. A smile lifted the corner of his mouth. He could see his old friend across the kitchen table, writing furiously as first the melody then the lyrics came to them. They'd written and rewritten through the night. It was one of the best songs the band ever played. They still performed it on the road, and Kurt still got royalties for it.

He sang quietly, staring out the picture window, then segued into another. He'd thought the music had dried up long ago, but the truth was clear—it had only gone into hiding. How had he lived all these years without music? How could he go forward without it?

When he finished, he let the final chord ring then turned to meet her smiling, tearful gaze.

"Thank you," she whispered. "That was beautiful."

He nodded, surprised by the wetness on his cheeks. He slipped the strap over his head and wiped his face on his sleeve. "No," he said quietly, setting the guitar back in the case. He dropped onto the couch. "Thank *you*. But there's just no way I can take it."

"Kurt, I want you to have Matt's guitar."

"It's too important to give away, sweetheart." He held her gaze for a long moment. "It's really cool that you'd even consider it."

Lips pursed, she frowned. "It's doing no one any good locked up in storage. It needs a life, it needs to be played." She folded her arms. "If I thought Matt would be playing it in heaven, I'd have figured out a way to send it with him. But now it just gathers dust and that hurts. It makes his death that much harder."

This is a gift for your heart. The impression grew insistent.

For my heart? Why? Why now? He sat very still. "I don't...I can't..." A shaky grin broke across his face as he looked at her. Then he drew a centering breath and sat up straight, running both hands through his hair. "Okay. Wow. This is so...unexpected."

She smiled, face glowing. "Not for me."

"I don't know how to thank you for this, Nessa."

"Just play for God," she whispered. "That's all the thanks I would ever want."

With the wild birthday bash behind them, life at River House had resumed its normal, crazy routine. Kurt's heart had been singing nonstop since he accepted Matt's guitar. Now that his background was out in the open, he couldn't wait to bring music into the House as a permanent part of the ministry. He'd been anxious for his famous friend to help him do that.

"Peter, my man!" Kurt greeted his friend with a backslapping hug and turned to the redhead. "And the ever-lovely Kiera. How was the honeymoon?"

She returned his hug before glancing at Peter, cheeks pink. "Absolutely perfect."

Peter took her hand. "Couldn't have been better. We're having a little trouble coming back to reality."

They exchanged a glowing smile and Kurt glanced across the room. Did he look like that when Vanessa was nearby? "Come on in, you guys. I want you to meet someone. Nessa, these are good friends of mine, the recently married Peter and Kiera Theisen. This beautiful lady is Vanessa Jordan."

He joined her behind the desk and put an arm around her shoulders. "River House wouldn't exist without her."

Vanessa shook their hands, congratulating them on their marriage. As she questioned Kiera about the wedding, Kurt turned back to Peter. "Thanks for coming by. I want to bounce some ideas off you."

Peter nodded, looking around the Gathering Place with interest. "When you told me about getting this off the ground, I couldn't wait to get involved. How about a tour while we talk?"

Leaving the girls to their own chatty tour, Kurt led him through the house. Having recently left his mega-celebrity life, Peter was the perfect partner to help establish music in the ministry. His former-spokesmodel wife would be a great addition to the ongoing body image discussion.

They exchanged ideas about piano lessons, teaching songwriting and music production, and sharing open conversation with the kids about the reality of fame.

"I'd love to lead some discussion about the music industry," Peter said as they returned to the Gathering Place. "Everybody gets so focused on the celebrity part, they don't consider there may be a cost to it. I don't want to stop anyone from chasing their dream, but I'll share what my journey was like so they can at least pursue it with their eyes open."

"That's exactly what I want them to hear." They settled on the couch. "If they see what you went through, it'll have more impact than just me being a talking head."

"You had your own brush with fame," Peter pointed out as the women came down the stairs.

Kurt shrugged. "And I blew that opportunity right out of the water."

Vanessa set her hand on his shoulder from where she stood behind him. "Look at the impact that's had on all the kids, Kurt. Now that they know your story, they're sharing more about their dreams and thinking about how important it is to make good choices."

He tried to focus on the warmth of her fingers rather than the bitterness of what he'd lost. "Yeah, that's true."

Kiera sat beside Peter. "Vanessa was telling me about all the talks around self-esteem and body image. It sounds like you've had amazing discussions."

"Kiera offered to bring her *One of Me* program here for a few Wednesday evenings," Vanessa added. "Isn't that fabulous? I'm so excited."

"Thanks, Kiera." The couple sitting across from him was a reminder of God's goodness. Their own struggles had nearly demolished their relationship. "I'm really glad you guys want to be part of River House."

"However we can." Peter put his arm around his wife. "Our schedules are crazy but we'll give this ministry priority."

Kurt glanced up at Vanessa, smiling at her wink. Life was so good now there wasn't room for the regrets of his past.

The following Saturday morning, thirty-six youth from Faith Church and River House assembled on the front lawn for the CleanSweep Project. Sunshine sparkled through leaves of red, gold, and brown. The cracking voices of the boys mixed with ear-splitting squeals from the girls. Blonde hair in a high ponytail, Vanessa stood in the middle of the throng and checked names off her list.

"If you weren't holding that clipboard," Kurt said as he joined her, "I wouldn't be able to pick you out of the kids."

She glanced up and wrinkled her nose. "People tell me I'll appreciate it when I'm older, but right now looking so young has its disadvantages. Like people not taking me seriously when I knock on their door this morning."

"With your powers of persuasion, no one will be able to say no to having their yards cleaned up."

She shot him a grateful smile before turning away to answer a question shouted from a group of boys.

Kurt called for attention and the noise dwindled as young faces turned toward him. "Man, this turnout is unbelievable!" A cheer went up and it was another minute before they were quiet again. "You've got your assigned side of the street, and by now you should know who your team captain is. Vanessa, Mike, Ashley, and I will be heading out ahead of you to get permission from each homeowner to clean up their yard. Make sure you ask before tossing *anything* away."

"We know," one of the boys said. "One man's junk—"

"—is another man's treasure," the girl next to him finished. He gave her a good-natured shove.

"Right. We're here today to clean up the neighborhood in whose name?"

"Jesus!"

Kurt laughed and pumped his fist. "Yes! We're His ambassadors so watch your language, watch your behavior. Take breaks to visit with people. Play with the kids. We want these people to know Jesus lives in our neighborhood, right?"

Another cheer erupted. Vanessa's laughing gaze met his and he shook his head in wonder. "Okay, grab the hand of somebody nearby and let's pray."

He reached for Vanessa's and closed his eyes. "Father...wow. We praise you for this glorious morning. We're here to be your hands and feet, to be your heart in this neighborhood." He swallowed past the tears clogging his throat. "Touch the hearts of these people through our work. Keep us free from injury, help us make new friends. And thanks for this opportunity. We pray all this in the holy name of your Son, Jesus. And all the saints said..."

"Amen!" Cheers and laughter filled the air as they broke into teams and assembled near the adult they were assigned to.

Kurt looked down at Vanessa. "Ready?"

She squeezed his hand. "Let's do it!"

Her smile made his heart lurch and it took all his self-control not to clean-sweep her into a kiss right in front of everyone.

The morning sped by as the neighborhood opened surprised arms to the energetic youth. Few homes declined the offer and soon nearly every yard for blocks was filled with the sounds of cheerful work being done. Laughter mingled with conversation; the sound of mowers and trimmers echoed between buildings.

Just after a break for lunch, a black sedan roared around the corner. Teens and neighbors scrambled out of its wild path. Rap music pulsed from inside as bags of garbage were emptied out the windows.

A couple of boys chased after the car despite Mike's order not to.

Tires squealing, the driver revved the engine and sped away, leaving a stunned group in its exhaust.

Hearing the commotion, Kurt raced around the house in time to see the car go by. The sight of the familiar sedan was a punch to his gut as he took in the garbage-strewn street. The windshields of parked cars were splattered with slop. Shredded paper swirled in the wake of the car.

As the car squealed around the far corner, Kurt stood very still, pushing back against trembling fury. People stood in groups, bewildered expressions on every face. At least no one appeared to be hurt.

Razzie raced up to Kurt, his young face red and sweaty. "I'm going after them."

Kurt grabbed his arm. "Razz, no. You don't need to be in the middle of this."

"Hello? We *are* the middle of this, Wagner. Anybody messing with River House has to answer to me. And all these guys."

Pauly and several other boys filled in behind him, brows dropped in fierce expressions, jaws clenched. Kurt had seen enough brawls to recognize the start of one. *Help me stop this, Lord.*

"Guys, I want to go after them too, but we can't. That's not going to show this neighborhood the right way to react."

"The right way is with this." Pauly shook his fist. The boys next to him nodded, muttering between themselves.

"That's the *wrong* way, Pauly. That's the way the guys in the car would do it. We need to show everybody how God responds to stuff like this."

Razzie's jaw worked back and forth as he stared at Kurt. "Not this again."

"And again, and again. C'mon, you guys. Jesus was challenged all the time. So were the disciples. They didn't use their fists. They fought with the truth, and the truth is that God's way is through forgiveness."

Vanessa, Mike, and several more youth had joined the group, standing silently behind the boys. Kurt met Vanessa's stricken expression before glancing at Mike. The big man's eyebrows were lowered, the muscles of his jaw twitching, but he nodded firmly.

"We're out here doing God's work," Kurt said. "This is good work, you guys. Let's not mess it up by showing the neighborhood we're bigger idiots than the people in that car."

"Right," Mike said. "We've got more houses to get to. We don't have time to chase those clowns. Let's get back to work. I've got extra trash bags in the van for cleaning up the street. Who's gonna help me?"

Razzie's expression darkened and he turned away, arms folded. Pauly copied his friend. A couple of the younger boys shrugged and gave reluctant nods, following Mike toward the church van.

Kurt reached to put a hand on Razzie's shoulder but the boy jerked away.

"I'm startin' to think you're nuts, Wagner."

Kurt watched him stalk across the yard and snatch up a rake. He understood Razzie's confusion and anger. When God had called him to lead by example, he hadn't known how hard it would be.

Vanessa touched his hand as she went by. He forced a wink and she smiled. Returning to his work in the backyard, he resolved to focus on that smile.

After the CleanSweep pizza party at River House, Vanessa tied up the garbage bags and carried them to trash cans by the garage. Pausing to enjoy the vibrant sunset, the air still and clear, she folded her arms and released a contented breath.

"You okay?" Kurt's voice came from close behind a few minutes later. He slid his arms around her.

She nodded. Standing in his arms, resting against him was the perfect way to end a wonderful day. "What a day. Even with that hiccup this afternoon."

"Yeah. I guess I should have expected Wolf to show up at some point. But the kids calmed down and worked even harder than they had all morning. God does amazing stuff, doesn't He?"

She turned and set her palms against his chest. "How do you know it was God?"

"How else could this have come together, Nessa?" His voice was gentle, a smile in his dark eyes. "Look at how all the details fell into place. The way we ended up with twice as many kids as we'd planned for but more than enough food donated for lunch. Their attitudes and enthusiasm all day long, even after Wolf's stupid stuff. The way the neighborhood welcomed us."

"How could it *not* be God?" he asked. "I've got three men wanting to meet me for coffee Monday morning to talk 'religion' and life and stuff. That's not my doing, Vanessa. Or yours. That's God using us to do His work."

Tears burned her throat. God had used her planning to touch this neighborhood? The event had certainly surpassed her wildest dreams. "But...how can He use me when I'm not even aware of Him?"

The corners of his mouth lifted and he pushed her bangs out of her eyes with a tender touch. "He's aware of you."

She stood quietly, questions bouncing around her tired brain. "Is he aware of Wolf too? And the trouble he's causing?"

"He is."

She frowned. "But He chooses not to stop it."

"Apparently. But hey, it gives us a chance to exercise our forgiveness muscle. Mine is really pathetic so it needs the practice."

She opened her mouth but no words came out. Exhaustion colored her jumbled thoughts.

"Come on." He put an arm around her shoulders and steered her back to the House. "Now is hardly the time for a deep discussion when you're dead on your feet."

Vanessa stopped at the back door to look up at him. "I don't understand this God of yours, but the one thing I do know is that you're amazing. And I'm so thankful you came into my life."

His dark eyes glistened. "Me, too, Nessa." He hugged her tight. "Me, too."

32

Arriving early the next morning to write up the CleanSweep report, Vanessa stood on the sidewalk, mouth open, breath caught in her throat. Spray paint crisscrossed the front of River House again. The ugly words "Its yor turn to pay" screamed at her in black letters from the garage door. An effigy hung from the tree in the front yard.

Fear hammering against her ribs, her gaze jumped from the broken windows on the lower level to the spray paint to the screen door hanging on one hinge. "What does he want? And why Kurt?"

With shaking fingers, she dialed Kurt's number. He met her report with a sharp exhale. "Are you still outside?"

"Yes."

"Don't go in. Go to the neighbors' and wait for me there."

"But—"

"I mean it, Vanessa. I'll be there in five minutes. Do *not* go inside without me. They probably never got in, but in case they did, I don't want you in there alone."

His words frightened her into agreement. "Okay. I'll wait for you."

Minutes later, Kurt parked at the curb and climbed out, phone to his ear. "Yeah, looks like the same paint. No, I don't think so but we haven't gone in yet. Yeah, that'd be great. Okay, thanks, Sam."

Vanessa left the Hauges' front step and met Kurt in the street, her heart breaking at the pain on his face. They shared a brief hug before going up the walk.

Unlocking the front door, he looked back at her. "Stay out here."

His command was firm. She nodded and watched him move

cautiously from room to room. He took the stairs two at a time to the second level, returning a minute later, then disappeared toward the back of the house. Her heart did triple time while she waited, holding her breath, straining to hear any sounds. When he reappeared, her breath released in a rush.

"Doesn't look like they made it in. Maybe somebody came along and scared them off. I was afraid it might have been you."

She joined him in the middle of the living area, looking out the front window through the paint smear. "I can't imagine they'd have been here this morning. They don't strike me as morning people."

He snorted. "True. Sam's on his way over to check out the damage."

Vanessa hugged him hard. "I'm sad you have to go through this."

His arms closed around her and he rested his chin on her head. "Yeah, well, it's what I get for being an ex-con."

She lifted her head so quickly his teeth banged together. "No, it's not! This is about stupid men who enjoy terrorizing innocent people. Whatever their issue is, it's not your fault, Kurt, and I won't let you talk like that. You're the victim here. This isn't your fault."

He stared at her, a smile lifting the corners of his mouth. She pulled abruptly out of his arms and put her hands on her hips. His smile vanished.

"I'm serious, Kurt. I don't want you talking like that in front of the kids. I don't want you talking like that at all. It sounds like you think you have to pay for your crime for the rest of your life but that's not true. You haven't done anything wrong. We need to call the police."

"No."

"This isn't a high school prank. This is vandalism."

"We're not calling the police, Vanessa. I don't want attention drawn to this."

"Why not?" Why was he being so stubborn about this?

"Because it will all blow over if we ignore it long enough. I know these guys. They'll lose interest eventually."

She threw her hands up. "Eventually? How many times do you want to call Sam to come back and fix their mess?"

"As many times as it takes."

"Oh, that's a good plan. Let's waste time and money while we pretend everything's okay." Fear fueled her sarcasm even as she tried to stop the words. "If you wait long enough, maybe you'll even be *in* the house when they show up and they can beat you up too." Tears spilled over. "Then I'll come in some morning and find you. Or even better, one of the kids will find you—"

He wrapped his arms tightly around her, cutting off the rising hysteria. "Shh. I'm sorry, sweetheart. We can call the police. Don't cry."

Vanessa buried her face against his chest. She wouldn't survive losing him. The strength in his embrace calmed her heart and the tears slowed.

"You're right, Ness. We'll call the police. I won't give up River House without a fight."

That was what she feared. It wouldn't be a fair fight.

That afternoon Kurt walked the streets he'd stalked as an angry teen, determined to find Wolf. Many of the storefronts were boarded up now but the memories were still vivid. JP's Liquors was up ahead on the corner, the old sign still blinking and pointing the way to the front door. Matty's Market was closed. Too bad. He'd liked Matty, the cheerful old lady with wild gray hair. Cline's Check Cashing operation was flourishing. How many people owed Hugh their next paycheck?

Three men lounged outside JP's. Part of the old drinking crowd. He nodded at each one. "Roger. Harley. Doug."

"How long you been out?" Harley asked. He was missing more teeth since Kurt had last seen him.

"Three years. You?"

He released a puff of smoke as he ground out the cigarette. "Got out in April, man."

Kurt nodded. "Good. What're you doin' now?"

Tall and thin with a receding hairline, Harley chuckled. "The usual. Lookin' for a job. Sorta. What about you?"

Kurt's eyes burned from the man's alcohol-ladened breath. "I started a youth house to help kids stay out of the joint. It's going pretty good, actually, although I seem to be on Wolf's bad side. He's causin' some trouble."

The men glanced among themselves, heads bobbing.

"Not good to be on his bad side," Roger commented. "How'd you do that?"

Kurt lifted his shoulders. "No idea. That's why I'm lookin' for him. I thought we could talk and put an end to the stupid stuff goin' on. You guys know where he is?"

"Haven't seen him around lately," Roger said.

"I heard he was outta town at a meetin'," Harley said. The men snickered.

"Yeah, I bet." Kurt turned to the third man. "Doug, how've you been?"

The short man with the scarred complexion shrugged. "Okay. Got laid off my job last month so I'm looking for something. You hiring at your youth house?"

"I wish I was." Doug had been an actual friend years ago, the other two only drinking acquaintances. "Right now I'm the only one getting a paycheck and it's not much. Are you getting unemployment?"

"Yeah. At least I can put food on the table. Got three kids now."

Kurt smiled at his obvious pride. "Good for you. Still with Mary?"

"Yup. She's a keeper."

"Cool. You know where Wolf's hanging out lately?"

Doug dropped his eyes and shrugged. "Nah. I'm tryin' to stay out of trouble."

"Good plan. I'm sure Mary appreciates it." Kurt handed a business card to each man. "Gimme a call if you find out where he's at these days. And if you see him, tell him to show his face so we can talk. He knows where to find me."

Sunlight glinted off Doug's bald head as he studied the card. "I mighta heard somethin' when Wolf got out this spring."

The other men froze, expressionless.

"About me?" Kurt asked.

"Maybe." Doug lifted one shoulder. "Just that Wolf wanted to collect on some old debts." His eyes darted up then back down. "Like maybe he was blaming certain people for his bein' in the joint so long."

"Ah." That explained a lot.

"You should watch your back," Harley said.

Kurt spun toward him, fists clenched. "You involved in this, Harley?"

He stepped back, hands lifted. "No way. I'm just sayin'."

It was good to know his tough guy reputation was still intact. He took a wide stance, folded his arms and narrowed his eyes. "I'd hate to think you have something to do with the stuff going on at River House."

"Blame Wolf for whatever you're dealin' with, not me. I'm just sayin' he's not somebody I'd want breathin' down my neck."

He kept his gaze on Harley for a long moment, then looked at the other two. "I'm getting real tired of his games. Next time you see him, tell him to grow a backbone and come by for a visit. I'll be happy to chat."

He spun on his heel and stalked away. Game on. Wolf would now know Kurt was looking for him. He could only pray it would flush the man out of hiding.

Kurt set the guitar case on the floor then let his duffel bounce on the bed. The last bout of vandalism and the information from Doug had cemented his decision to move into River House. He couldn't possibly sleep peacefully at Mike's when on any given night the House might be under attack again.

"Wagner, you're like a girl. You got too many coats, man." Razzie's voice floated up the stairs.

Kurt chuckled. "Just being a good Minnesotan with a coat for every season," he shot back.

The front door slammed, followed by several items thumping onto the floor.

"Where do you want these boxes?" Pauly called.

"Be right down." He was grateful for the boys' help getting his stuff moved in one trip. He looked around Matt's old room and nodded. "Welcome home, Wagner. God, protect this place." Then he went down to join the boys.

Vanessa reread Kurt's draft of his Wednesday night message, puzzling over the third point. As she jotted a note in the margin, the front door blasted open and her pen squiggled off the page.

Mike charged into the house, his expression grim. "Grab your jacket, Vanessa. We have to go."

She stared at him in surprise. "Go where?"

"Just grab your jacket, kid."

The steamroller made a rumbling noise in the back of her mind. "What's wrong?"

"Kurt's been in an accident. He's at the hospital."

Spots danced before her eyes. This couldn't be happening. Not Kurt. "No…"

Mike reached into the front closet for her coat, then moved to the desk, holding out a hand. "Come on, Van. Let's go!"

"Is he—?"

"Munchkin, I don't *know* how he is. That's what we're going to find out." He pulled her up, tightening his fingers when she swayed. "Are you okay?"

She forced herself to draw a deep breath. She needed to be there for Kurt. She couldn't let him die alone. Not like Angie and Matt. Wrapping a stranglehold around the fear, she snatched her purse from the drawer. "Let's go."

Mike kept a white-knuckled grip on the steering wheel as they dodged through rush-hour traffic. Neither spoke. Then they were out of the car, Vanessa racing across the parking lot behind Mike. Inside, they hurried through the corridors, following the signs to the emergency room.

At the desk, Mike questioned the woman. Vanessa stood beside him, clutching the counter as a cold tremble crept up her spine. It was too familiar—the antiseptic smell, the muted voices, the growing hysteria. *I can't do this again. I can't. God, help.*

Mike's voice came from far away. "Vanessa? They said he's doing okay. Come on, they'll show us where he is."

"I..." She shook her head. The spots were back. *He's fine. He's doing fine. Get a grip.* "I can't."

A large hand grasped her elbow, propelling her to a chair. He dropped next to her and took her hands. "Vanessa, we can go back to see him." His voice was firm, his words slow and measured. "He's *okay*, munchkin."

She forced her gaze up. His face came into focus and she blinked quickly. "You go," she croaked. "I'll wait..."

"Are *you* all right?"

The concern in his voice sliced through the panic and she sucked in a sharp breath. "Yes." She cleared her throat. "You go see him first."

He squeezed her hands and got to his feet. "I'll find him and then come get you. You'll wait here?"

She nodded. She couldn't get to her feet if she had to. When he moved away, she leaned back in the chair and pulled her good leg up, wrapping her arms around her knee. The shaking continued and she rested her forehead on her knee, unable to stop the tears. And she prayed.

Kurt opened his eyes when he heard Mike's voice in the hallway. His head ached, as did his left arm that the nurse had just finished wrapping. And his left leg. He felt like someone had pushed him down the stairs.

"Well, there you are. In one piece," Mike said as he came into view. "And with some additional packaging, I see." He stopped beside the bed and looked down with a relieved smile, arms folded. "How are you?"

Kurt gave a slow nod, careful not to jar his head. "Not bad, considering."

"You gave us quite a scare, buddy."

"You and me both. I didn't see it coming, that's for sure."

Mike pulled a chair next to the bed. "What happened?"

He shrugged then winced. "I dunno. I think someone ran a stop sign. They came outta nowhere. Good thing they weren't going all that fast. I'm glad the loaner I'm driving has side airbags. It's a God thing I had to bring mine in for new tires."

Mike gave a short laugh. "Funny how He works things out. When the hospital called, we didn't know what kind of shape you were in."

"What did they say?"

"Just that you'd been hit and were unconscious."

He rested his head back against the pillow. "Not for long." He sighed. "Too bad I'm left-handed."

"Lucky for you there's Vanessa to open your mail." He slapped his forehead. "Vanessa! I told her I'd find you and then go give her a report."

Kurt's eyes flew open and he sat up abruptly then stopped as everything went momentarily dark. "Vanessa's here? You brought her *here*?"

Mike blinked. "She's in the waiting room. She wouldn't come in with me so I said— What are you doing?"

Kurt carefully swung his legs over the side of the bed and slid to his feet. He paused to let the room stop spinning, swallowing against the rising nausea. "I've got to get out there."

"Kurt! Sit down before you pass out." Mike jumped to his feet. "I'll go get her."

A woman's voice gave a firm order. "Sir, you need to get back in bed."

Kurt wobbled, then drew a deep breath and straightened to face the nurse. "I need to see someone."

"Sir, please—"

"Get me a wheelchair or get out of my way," he said through

clenched teeth. "I need to get to Vanessa."

"Okay, okay," Mike agreed. "We'll get you a chair." He looked at the nurse.

She left the room with a frown, returning moments later with a wheelchair. With a firm hand, she helped Kurt lower himself into the chair. Mike followed them out of the room and down the hall.

As the large doors swung open, Kurt spotted Vanessa immediately, knee drawn up, head down. He put his feet down to stop the chair. "Let me walk over there."

Pushing himself to his feet, he paused to get his balance then limped toward her. "Hey."

She lifted a tear-streaked face.

His heart squeezed. "I'm sorry. I didn't mean for you to come. I'm fine. Really."

Her gaze ran over him before she drew a shaky breath and lowered her foot to the floor, eyes locked on his. He sank into the chair next to her and pulled her against him with his right arm. "I'm sorry, sweetheart," he whispered as she leaned into him. She trembled and he tightened his arm, resting his cheek against her hair.

When she finally drew a shuddering breath and sat up, she still clutched the front of his shirt. "You're really okay?"

"Really." He brushed a tear from her cheek. "A little rest for my arm and I'll be good as new." He shook his head. "It didn't occur to me Mike would bring you here."

She gave a weak shrug and attempted a smile. "But at least now I can see you. It would have been worse waiting at the House."

He reached for her hand, entwining their fingers. "I have to go back in to sign something so I can go home. Will you come back with me?"

She looked toward the doors where Mike and the nurse waited. When her gaze swung back to his, he read the fear. "You don't have to," he assured her.

"No, it's...I can do it." She stood as the nurse wheeled the chair over to them. Kurt settled in and reached for her hand again, squeezing her cold fingers.

Back in the bed, he released a sigh. He was bruised and battered, but a swift and complete recovery was expected. He assured her he'd be in good hands with Mike staying at the House over the weekend. "Especially," he added with a cheerful wink, "if a certain blonde brings me her famous cookies."

He was rewarded with a growing smile. He was fine...this time. That smile gave him a reason to fight back.

Kurt's color returned as he rested in the ER and drank two glasses of apple juice, and he was soon talking about his message for Wednesday. Joel joined them, his frown relaxing as Kurt assured him he would be back to normal within a few days.

The conversation turned to upcoming events at Faith, and a strange prodding pushed Vanessa out of her chair. Promising to return in a bit, she left the cubicle and walked toward the circular desk in the center of the emergency room.

The calm was a stark contrast from what she remembered of that January night. Heart pounding, she blinked against the glare of the overhead lights, memories wrapping around her like a tourniquet.

Turning in a circle, she could see the frantic activity of that dark night. Men and women in blue scrubs moved quickly in what seemed like choreographed dance steps. Attention had focused on the forms lying so still in neighboring cubicles. A deep voice asked a question; several people jumped into action. A woman's voice gave direction, people moved again. The room crackled with urgency.

Though she'd seen everything through a haze of pain, she'd known what was happening. She could hear their words over the high-pitched beeping. "We're losing her! C'mon, darlin'. Stay with us. Get her intubated *now*!"

From where she had lain on her gurney, nurses and doctors

working on her as well, she could see the unmoving sole of Angie's tennis shoe, blood on the hem of her jeans.

It was still so clear—voices, running feet, sharp commands. Then deathly quiet. She remembered fighting against the staff working on her, straining to reach Angie, calling for Matt...

The muted squeak of shoes on the tiled floor pulled her to the present and she blinked hard. With shaking fingers she rubbed her forehead, forcing back the searing pain. Somehow she'd survived without them, one excruciating day at a time.

"Can I help you?" a nurse asked.

"No. I..." The tears receded and she dropped her hand. Offering a wobbling smile, she added, "No, thanks. I'm okay."

And she was. She stood taller as the nurse walked away. Each day the realization became a little clearer. She'd done what she feared most—faced the memories of that night—and she was still standing.

Before returning to Kurt, she detoured through the automatic doors, leaving the sterile hospital air to step into the sweet aroma of life. She stood for a moment on the sidewalk, face lifted to the afternoon sun. The thought came to her without bidding. The grace of God.

Yes—by the grace of God—she was going to be fine.

Vanessa snuggled against Kurt on the couch after they'd locked the House up for the night. Since the car accident, she'd watched him slide from cheerful and energetic to serious and introspective. She looked up at him and let her suspicion move out of the shadows. "You don't believe it was an accident, do you?"

He went still. "What makes you say that?"

"It's just too big a coincidence after the other stuff. And you're so serious now."

He stared at the flames dancing in the fireplace. "Maybe if it hadn't been a hit and run it'd be easier to believe it was an accident." His arm tightened around her shoulders and he pressed a kiss to her temple. "I just keep thinking, what if you'd been in the car with me? What if it was you that got hurt? I couldn't stand that."

"But I can't stand that it was *you*. I don't understand. What does he have against you?"

"I went back to the old neighborhood last week to try to get him to meet with me, but nobody would tell me where he was. Someone said he's got a score to settle about the drug bust. I can tell you one thing. I'm gonna be a lot more careful when I drive through intersections from now on."

Only partly reassured, she sank back against his shoulder and rested in the comfort of his arms, content in the moment.

He sat up and faced her. "Nessa, there's one good thing that came from the accident." He took her hands and met her gaze with a tentative smile. "I knew it before but now I know it in my bones." He put a hand to her cheek. "You're the most beautiful girl I've ever known. And I have fallen for you big-time."

The warmth that filled her came from a place deep inside she'd thought was cold and dead. "It took the accident to make you realize that?"

He chuckled. "Only to cement it in my life. I've known it for a long time." He took her face in his hands, smiling at her in awe. "I love you, Vanessa Jordan."

Tears filled her eyes. "I love you too," came the whisper before he leaned in for a kiss that shouted their joy to the heavens.

"Earth to Vanessa. Man, has she got her head in the clouds or what?"

Razzie's teasing pulled her attention from the letter she was supposed to be working on. She looked up and forced her eyes to focus. "Sorry, Razz. What did you say?"

He shook his head slowly from where he lounged on the couch. "You got it bad."

"I've got what bad?"

Razzie looked at Tiffani, stretched across the other couch. "She's got it bad for Wagner, don't she?"

The girl giggled. "I think so."

Vanessa looked between them, pushing back against the heat that inched up her neck. Razzie's teasing was merciless. "Razz, do I bug you about your private life?"

"Not so far." He texted without looking at his phone. "Ain't you curious?"

"*Aren't* I curious. And that's not the point. I don't ask because it's not my business."

Tiffani tossed a pillow at him from the other couch. "In other words, butt out of her love life."

His wide-eyed expression stopped short of innocence. "What love life? Oh, you mean the one with Wagner we're not supposed to know about? *That* one?"

"Exactly." Tiffani giggled. "The one where he brought her flowers yesterday. Her favorite pink roses. Even though they aren't dating."

Razzie winked at Tiffani. "That's what I do when I don't like a girl. I bring her flowers and take her out to eat. And hold her hand when nobody's lookin'."

Vanessa turned back to her computer. "You guys are impossible."

"What's wrong with telling us you like him?" Tiffani asked.

"Yeah," Razzie said, "if you like the guy, even though he's old and kind of a geek, why don't you just admit it? We think he's okay so you shouldn't be embarrassed."

"I'm not embarrassed."

"So you *do* like him."

Now she was embarrassed. "Razz, someday there's going to be a girl you really, really like and we're going to tease you to death about it. Then you'll see how it feels."

"Oh, so you 'really, *really*' like him. That's even better than just sorta likin' him." He swung his feet to the floor and faced her across the room. "But what don't make sense to me is how come a guy like him gets a girl like you?"

"I've been wondering the same thing." Kurt's voice came from behind her.

She spun her chair around. Arms folded, he leaned against the wall. She was no match for the smile in those dark eyes. In the electric silence, she glanced at Razzie and tried to look nonchalant. "Kurt is not a geek and you know it."

"Matter of opinion," he shrugged. "My question stands."

Kurt's presence scrambled her thoughts. "What question?"

"He wants you to explain how a drop-dead gorgeous, talented, smart, funny girl could fall for a useless old ex-con geek," Kurt said.

"Ooo," Razzie said. "Nice description of Van. Five points for Wagner."

His compliment was charming, but his description of himself wasn't. "You believe that about yourself?"

"The ex-con part anyway."

"You tell me not to define myself as disabled first, but you still define yourself as an ex-con instead of all the fabulous attributes that make up who you really are."

"Whoa, ten points for Van," Razzie said.

Vanessa stood. "I didn't fall for a useless, old ex-con geek. I fell for a man with a huge heart, an amazingly creative brain, and a love for crazy kids like those two."

"Another five points for Vanessa," Tiffani chirped.

The corners of Kurt's mouth twitched. "Okay, fine. I take back the useless and ex-con parts, but according to Razz, I'm definitely a geek."

"Five points to Wagner for stating the obvious," Razzie said.

Kurt moved to stand before Vanessa. She fought back the urge to fling herself into his arms.

"But you are still drop-dead gorgeous and a million other words I can't think of right now."

"Twenty points for Kurt," Tiffani sighed.

"Kiss her, you geek!" came Razzie's exasperated whisper.

Kurt's smile deepened and her knees wobbled. She loved his smile.

He tapped her nose and mouthed, "Later." His office door closed with a quiet click.

Vanessa didn't realize she was still staring after him until Razzie's teasing voice cut in. "You can sit down now, Van."

Pressing her lips together to keep from giggling, she dropped into her chair. Razzie was slouched on the couch, hands behind his head, smirking. Tiffani sighed dramatically, a dreamy smile on her face. Vanessa laughed inside. It was exactly how she felt.

Razzie looked at Tiffani and nodded toward the back of the house. "I'm done with this soap opera. Wanna play some ping-pong?"

They disappeared down the hall, leaving Vanessa alone to enjoy the warmth sweeping all the way down to her five wiggling toes. Smart and funny? Drop-dead gorgeous?

She turned back to the computer, a glow in her heart.

Someone was pounding...and yelling. Kurt struggled against the darkness. Where was Vanessa? Something was wrong. More pounding. Frantic voices. He needed to find her. She was in trouble. He could taste it.

Through the fog in his mind, he forced his eyes open. They instantly filled with tears as the night air stung. He rubbed them hard, then coughed as thick air settled over him.

Get up.

Now? Disoriented, stuck halfway out of the dream, he forced his mind to clear. *Vanessa's okay. She's home in bed, just like I am here at River House.*

The pounding became more insistent. Straining to figure out where the noise was coming from, he pushed up on his elbows. The moonlight pouring through the window drifted in strange swirls.

Pulling in a breath, he immediately regretted it. The air scorched his throat, right down into his lungs, and he sat up abruptly, gagging. *Smoke!* He tumbled to the floor, coughing so violently he nearly vomited.

Help...he needed help. Nessa would get help. Crawling on shaking limbs, he aimed for the door. Where was his phone? Wait. On the bedside table. He turned back, coughing and wiping his eyes, then stopped to rest his forehead against the floor where there seemed to be air.

Go.

Pulling his T-shirt over his nose, he reached a hand toward the bedside table and knocked the phone off. Eyes closed against the stinging air, he felt blindly around the floor.

God, don't let my screwups ruin everything we've worked for. These kids need you.

His fingers closed around the phone, and he pushed what he hoped was Vanessa's speed dial. As he turned for the door, the pounding continued, followed by crashing glass. A faint siren grew louder. *She already called for help. God bless her.* He stuffed the phone into his pocket and crawled forward.

The stairs were straight ahead. Weren't they? If he could get downstairs, he could find the door. He moved with blind determination, gagging, burning eyes squeezed shut. Then the world dropped away as he lost contact with the floor and fell, tumbling into darkness.

Vanessa startled awake when the phone rang and fumbled for it on the bedside table. Who was calling at 3 a.m.? Kurt's number on the screen brought her to full awareness. She answered with a sleepy smile. "Hi."

No reply, only a deep, hacking cough. She sat up, pushing the hair from her face. "Kurt?"

He was grunting, like he was working hard at something. In the distance she could hear muffled pounding. Her heart jumped to her throat as she clutched the phone. "Kurt? It's Vanessa. Do you need help?"

The line went dead, leaving her paralyzed. What had just happened? She reached for the bionic leg, fingers shaking as she struggled to fasten it properly. Pulling on yesterday's clothes, she slid her phone into the pocket of her sweatpants and rushed out the door. Running and hopping down the dark street, she prayed aloud in gasping breaths for Kurt, for the House. Did God only answer prayer in daylight hours?

She yanked her phone out and dialed Mike's number. "Come on. *Come on!*"

"Yeah?" came his groggy voice.

"Something's wrong with Kurt! Come to the House," she panted.

"What? Vanessa?"

"Hurry! He called and sounded sick but then he hung up. Oh! There goes a police car. Mike, please! Call Joel. Meet me at River House."

She hung up before he could respond.

Lungs burning, she darted between two parked cars then pulled up short as another police car sped past, lights flashing but no siren. *Wait!* She stumbled after it. Rounding the corner, the sight stopped her heart. Flashing red lights, the rumble of fire engines, people everywhere, all silhouetted against bright lights shining on River House. Smoke created an eerie backdrop. The house was on fire!

Kurt! He'd called from inside. She continued a frantic run-hop down the middle of the street. *God, if you're there, please let him be okay. Please. Oh God, please.*

When she darted around a police officer, he caught her arm. She fought against him, hysteria surging. "Kurt's in there! We have to get him out!"

"Miss, nobody gets closer than this. They've gone in to look for people."

Straining against his grip, tears flooded down her face; the acrid air burned her throat. "He called from inside! We have to find him."

Strong hands held her back. "They're in there right now. Who called you?"

"Kurt Wagner. He's living here. I work with him. We work with kids—" She went still, grasping the officer's shirt as several firefighters emerged through the shattered front door, Kurt's limp body between them. The struggling returned in earnest. "Oh, dear God! Is he dead? Let me go!"

"Miss, you can help him by staying out of the way. Let the paramedics do their work." His voice was calm and firm. "Are there any other people inside?"

"I don't think so. He was staying here to protect it. I don't know."

She stood frozen, watching the paramedics scurry around Kurt's body where they'd laid him in the grass. They put an oxygen mask on his face and hooked lines of fluids to his arms, then loaded him onto a gurney and into the waiting ambulance. He hadn't moved.

"Van, come with me."

She turned to stare up into Mike's face. His words came down a long tunnel, echoing against the chaos around them.

"They're taking him away," she cried. Kurt was going to die and she couldn't do anything about it. Mike's mouth moved but she couldn't hear the words.

He reached for her arm and pulled her to his car. Moments later they sat in the reception area of the ER. Waiting in silence. An inner chill shook her as she stared at the swinging doors that separated her from Kurt. *What's happening? Why won't they talk to us?* She folded her arms across the ache to be with him.

Mike shifted restlessly in the chair and paced the room. Within the hour Joel and Ashley had joined them, then Razzie, Pauly, and several other boys.

"We need to pray." Joel's voice broke the silence, and the group clustered together. Hands joined and heads bowed while he and Mike prayed for Kurt, for the House and the ministry. After the prayer, Mike kept hold of Vanessa's hand.

As the agonizing second hour passed, she rested against his solid shoulder, eyes still glued to the door. *Don't let him die. Please don't let him die.*

Into the third hour, as the world outside the silent room began to lighten, a doctor emerged and everyone scrambled from where they were sprawled around the room.

"Are you waiting for Kurt Wagner?"

Vanessa's nod was jerky. "Can we see him? How is he?"

"Is anyone here family?"

"We are," came several voices.

"He's being treated for smoke inhalation, a broken arm and a concussion. Apparently the tumble down the stairs did the most damage. However, on the flip side, it seems falling down the stairs removed him from the worst of the smoke. They'll be moving him to a room in another hour or so. One or two of you can see him once he's settled, but he's going to be in and out for a few days so give him time to recover."

Vanessa sagged against Mike, grateful for his arm that held her up. Joel shook the doctor's hand then turned to the group. "We can thank God his injuries are as minor as they are. It could have been a lot worse."

They decided Mike and Vanessa would stay with Kurt and call the message tree as soon as he awoke. Joel and Ashley would return to the House to assess the damage. The boys were to go home until they heard otherwise. A House meeting was set for three o'clock at Faith, where they would share the information they'd gathered.

An endless hour later, Vanessa flew into the hospital room and rushed to Kurt's still form. His eyes were closed, his pale face bruised, but he was breathing. A plastic tube ran from his mouth down into a bag of blackish fluid hanging on the side of his bed.

A nurse checked his IV, the monitors beeping quietly at the head of his bed. She paused next to Vanessa and touched her arm gently. "He's going to be fine. These are all treatments to keep him comfortable and help his lungs start to heal."

"Can he hear us?"

The woman nodded. "He'll stay sedated until tomorrow, but he'll be awake off and on. You can talk to him, honey. I'm sure he'll be glad to hear your voice."

Vanessa bent down to Kurt. "Hi. It's me," she said softly. "Mike and I are here. You gave us quite a scare but...the doctor said...you'll be fine." Tears choked her words and she brushed the hair from his forehead with shaking fingers, willing him to open his eyes. The stench of smoke burned her nose. "You'll be okay," she whispered.

"Hey, pal." Mike pulled a chair to the bedside and settled into it, then put his large hand on Kurt's shoulder. His gruff voice was thick with emotion. "These hospital visits gotta stop. I'm gettin' too old for this stuff."

He closed his eyes and pinched the bridge of his nose. Then he looked at Kurt's battered face. "You got River House up and running, Wagner, so you'd better wake up and get back to work. There are a lot of kids counting on you."

They took turns talking quietly to him over the next few hours, telling silly stories about the kids, talking about plans for the next few weeks. The nurse moved in and out of the room, checking his vitals, changing the bag, assuring them he was doing fine.

While Mike dozed, Vanessa alternated between sitting and standing at the bedside, clutching Kurt's hand. She wouldn't relax until she was looking into his brown eyes again, hearing his voice, sharing a smile.

As the noon hour approached, Mike left the room to call the phone tree. Vanessa had settled in a chair beside the bed, still holding Kurt's hand, her head resting on her arms. The tiny squeeze on her fingers brought her head up with a start. His bloodshot eyes were fixed on her.

"Hey." She forced a smile that quivered. *Thank you, God!*

He tried to speak then his eyes narrowed.

"There's a tube in your throat to help you breathe. We'll talk later. You just need to rest."

He held her gaze then blinked slowly and drifted back to sleep.

When Mike returned a moment later, she met him at the door. "He woke up!"

His eyes widened and jumped to Kurt's face. "He did?"

"Only for a minute, but he was awake."

Mike hugged her tight, laughter in his voice. "He is such a tough guy."

"As he keeps having to prove," came the muffled response. She leaned back to frown up at him. "When will this end, Mike?"

He shook his head, his gaze running back to the bed. "I wish I knew, munchkin. We just have to keep praying for God's protection and for a way to end this whole crazy mess."

Vanessa returned to Kurt's side and took his hand. *Please, God. Put an end to this now. He can't take anymore. None of us can.*

36

On her way home, Vanessa had the cab driver drop her off at River House. She stood on the sidewalk and stared in disbelief. Black grime arched over broken windows like angry eyebrows. The front door had lost its battle with a battering ram, and police tape crisscrossed the shattered wood. The yard was trampled, the wet grass coated with soot. Stale smoke tainted the autumn air.

What kind of person tries to ruin a ministry designed to help people? Whatever Wolf's issue, he'd just ramped up the stakes. Had he meant to kill Kurt or just scare him? She shivered. His game had come too close to being deadly.

"Makes no sense." Elwood Hauge stood beside her on the sidewalk, bowtie askew, frowning at the house.

"Not to me, either."

He cleared his throat, his focus on the building. "How's the director doing?"

"He's got a broken arm and a concussion, but he's alive." She managed a smile. "We're so thankful he's alive. I wish I knew who called the fire department so quickly. They saved his life."

Elwood looked down at his feet, hands behind his back, and tottered side-to-side.

"Mr. Hauge?" She cocked her head. "Was it you?"

He scratched the back of his head. "I don't know that I was the first."

"Oh, Mr. Hauge." She threw her arms around him. "Thank you!"

He patted her back awkwardly until she released him. "Can't have houses burning down around here. It's bad for our property values."

She nodded, unable to hide her smile. "That's true. I'm sure we'll have River House fixed up in no time so it won't affect a thing."

"Good, good. Well." He sidled away. "Glad to hear the director is going to be okay. Pretty frightening event for him, I'm sure."

"Thank you, Mr. Hauge. Give your wife a hug for me, please."

Vanessa watched him go, her heart dancing. Elwood Hauge had saved Kurt's life. She couldn't wait to tell him.

Three o'clock at Faith Church and the sanctuary overflowed with concerned neighbors, volunteers, and youth from both the church and River House. Vanessa looked around the beautiful room with interest. It hadn't been as difficult as she'd feared to come here; all she cared about right now was Kurt's recovery and keeping the ministry going. It was good to be here, among friends, in the place Kurt loved.

If God wanted to strike her down for daring to enter church after months of bitterness, He'd have to do it with all these people watching. As she looked up at the wooden cross, tears rose in her throat. *Why?* was all her heart could whisper. *Why Kurt?*

An unexpected calm enfolded her, soothing her chaotic mind, calling her to be still. She closed her eyes and breathed deeply, slowly. Kurt was going to recover. He would no doubt thank God, not Mr. Hauge, for that. She was thankful regardless of who got the credit.

Joel stepped to the front of the sanctuary and the room quieted. He led them in prayer for Kurt's swift recovery and for the ministry of River House, then outlined the initial findings of the police and fire department. His pronouncement that it was being treated as arson brought an audible gasp from the crowd. He concluded with a prayer for resolution to the issue behind the attacks.

Vanessa, Mike, and Ashley joined him for the question-and-answer time. The kids wondered when they could visit Kurt and where they would meet while the house was being repaired. Adults asked what needed to be done, what the estimated costs were, and when a volunteer schedule would be set up.

Vanessa's heart soared at the impromptu testimonials springing up around the room and the concern expressed about Kurt's condition. He'd made such a deep impression in so short a time.

Razzie stood and faced the crowd. "We gotta make sure we keep River House safe. We all need it. Wagner's been helping me make some decisions about my future and what I wanna do when I graduate."

"You gonna graduate, Razz?" Pauly asked from a few rows back.

He stood a little taller. "Yeah. I figure I've put in this much time, I might as well get somethin' out of it. Wagner helped me get my schedule straight so I can finish next summer. I'll be the first in my family to graduate."

Mike rose from his stool next to Vanessa and started clapping, a wide grin on his face. Within moments the entire crowd was on its feet, applauding the bold statement of the young man now seen as a leader at the House.

Face flushed, Razzie's dark eyes moved to Vanessa. She winked and he grinned. Then Joel called for attention once again to say the River House website would have updated information every day.

Sharing hugs and words of encouragement with the kids that pressed around her, Vanessa repeated her promise to be part of the Wednesday night study that would be held at Faith until the repair work was completed and Kurt was ready to return. She would do whatever it took to keep River House running for him.

After eating a light dinner at Kurt's bedside while he slept, Vanessa left Joel with him and returned to the church. Throughout the afternoon meeting, she'd felt a deep pull to come back. It had been a frightening thought at first. Being here in the safety of a crowd was fine, but the idea of being alone had weighed on her while she sat with Kurt.

She moved soundlessly toward the front of the empty room, her eyes on the cross. She'd been angry and sad for so long. Mistrustful. Accusing. *What am I doing here?*

The sanctuary was silent, as if the world held its breath awaiting the confrontation. Muscles tensed, she waited for the lightning bolt to strike her down for her unbelief, her rage, for the sheer audacity to confront Him. Each step brought her closer to the cross and closer to tears.

"I must be crazy." Her whisper was magnified in the silence.

She stepped into the second pew, needing the protection of the seat in front of her, and waited. Finally she addressed the silent cross.

"Umm...it's me. Vanessa. I know you might not want to talk to me, but I have a few questions for you. If that's okay."

She leaned against the front pew, the wood under her palms cool and solid. "Can you tell me where you were the night the kids died? Were you too busy to stop the accident? Didn't they matter to you?"

She was surprised to realize there was no anger. Only sadness and a strange, wild longing that made her legs tremble.

"Why didn't you step in to protect them? If you really are God, you could have. But then...you saved Kurt from the fire, and I'm grateful for that." She lifted her hands in confusion. "Why some people and not others? How do you choose who lives and who dies? Why everyone in *my* family?"

She wrapped her arms around herself, against the sorrow that weighed like a stone. "I miss them so much," she whispered. "I have so many questions and doubts. But Kurt doesn't doubt you." She shook her head slightly. "I don't know how to trust the way he does. How can I when everything seems random?

"He believes completely in who you are and what you can do. I think...I'd like to feel that way. I'm tired of the anger and the grief. But how do I let it go?"

She sank down onto the cushion, hands limp in her lap. "You have to know how hard it's been to figure out life without Mom or the kids. Or my leg. If you're who Kurt says you are, you *must* know. But now…these months with him have given me something I never thought I'd have again. Hope."

Tears slipped down her cheeks and she lifted her eyes to the cross again. "I needed to ask these questions out loud so you know I'm still wondering about them, but I also…I want to thank you. For saving Kurt and River House.

"I'm probably crossing the line, but I remember Kurt saying we can come to you with all our questions and needs. Could you help us put River House back together? Maybe if you have some angels that aren't real busy, they could protect it, so we don't have to go through this again?"

She drew a deep breath. "And…if you're not too mad at me, could you maybe help me go forward? I don't know how to let go of the guilt. I'm sorry for all the things I've said. And for how I messed up and caused the accident. Kurt said you forgive us when we're sorry, and I want you to know that I am. I really am."

Warmth touched the top of her head and gently flowed down her neck and over her shoulders like fragrant oil, loosening the muscles that had held tight since the fire. The sense of calm returned. It was reassuring. Loving. The way she'd felt so long ago surrounded by her mother and the kids. Now she was alone—and yet she wasn't.

She lowered to her side on the cushion as tears of release fell, relaxing under what felt like a comforter that covered her from head to toe. In the sweet silence, she knew. Kurt would be okay and River House would be restored. Matt and Angie were loved; her mother was loved. She was loved and even forgiven. Without hearing a single word, she was sure of all of it, deep in her bones.

A smile touched her face as she closed her eyes. "Thank you," she whispered.

37

His head ached, an awful smell scratched his nose and throat. Kurt forced his eyes open, squinting against the overhead lights, and stared at the white ceiling tiles as he waited for his mind to clear. His right arm was weighted down. Warmth surrounded his left hand and he carefully turned his head that direction. Vanessa was holding his hand between hers, her eyes closed. He squeezed with what little strength he had and her eyes flew open.

Her beautiful face filled with joyful relief. "Hi."

His response was a croak and he closed his eyes against the fire that seared his throat. She adjusted the bed to sit him up slightly and held out a glass with a straw poking up. Fumbling with the plastic thing over his nose and mouth, he pulled it under his chin so he could drink. The first swallow of cool water was excruciating but a sudden, frantic thirst made him pull in more until the small glass was empty.

The exertion squeezed the air from his lungs, and he coughed violently. Pain shot through his head with each spasm. Finally he dropped back against the pillows, sweat running down his neck. Vanessa repositioned the mask and he gratefully drew in the clear air.

"Thanks." The word was muffled. His eyes traveled around the room then found Vanessa's. "I'm in the hospital again?"

"Afraid so."

He frowned, his mind in a jumble. When the doctor had removed that tube from his throat—was it this morning? what day was it?—he still hadn't understood what had happened. He remembered a nightmare. It was dark, he couldn't find Vanessa, couldn't breathe.

His eyes widened and he pulled the mask away. "River House?"

he wheezed.

She nodded. "There isn't as much damage as we first thought, but the important thing is they got you out alive."

Kurt closed his eyes, his heartbeat ramping up. Wolf was actually trying to kill him. What if other people had been in the house?

"I remember I couldn't breathe. It was dark...but not completely...more like gray." He opened his eyes to frown at her. "I tried to call you but then there were sirens so I figured you already knew I was in trouble."

Another coughing jag made his head pound. He drank eagerly from the glass Vanessa had refilled, then sank back against the pillows.

She settled into the chair, her small hands closing around his. "How do you feel?"

"Worse than last time." He wrinkled his nose. "I must stink somethin' awful. Sorry."

"I wouldn't care if you smelled like a sewer. I was so scared when they brought you out. Hey, I have to tell you this. You'll love it. When I stopped by the house after the fire, Mr. Hauge came out to ask how you were."

Kurt raised his eyebrows.

Vanessa giggled. "Wait. It gets better. So I told him and then said I wished I knew who had called 9-1-1 because they saved your life. Guess who it was?"

He frowned. "Not—"

"Yup." Her eyes sparkled. "Isn't that the best? I'd say you've already won him over. Who would've thought?"

"Not me," he admitted, then sighed. "I miss all the action."

"That's because you *are* the action."

He brushed his fingertips against her cheek. "What I remember most was needing to get to you. That was the worst part...not knowing where you were."

"I'm here now and I'm not going anywhere."

Her shining assurance calmed the chaos in his mind. There was so much to think about, but for now he would rest in her promise.

"It's not going to sit well with the kids," Joel said.

"I know." Kurt sat across from him at The Java Depot, steaming mugs in front of them. In the downtime that two weeks of recovery had forced on him, he'd come to an agonizing conclusion. As long as he stayed at River House, everyone was in danger. The only way to stop the threats against the House was to separate himself from the ministry. He couldn't live with the guilt if anything happened to the kids or the neighbors. Or Vanessa.

"I'm in the process of writing letters to try to explain it." He frowned. "Even Vanessa, Mike, and Ashley think we can stand together and fight this thing."

Joel had understood his dilemma, prayed over it with him, and now supported his decision. Kurt was grateful for his wise counsel and enduring friendship. "Since Wolf won't meet with me, I have only one choice."

There was pained understanding on his mentor's face. "Have you got a destination in mind?"

"Not really." Kurt swirled the coffee in his cup. "I figure I'll wander the country a bit, make sure I'm not being followed. I'll find some place to settle down in a few weeks."

"I've got friends in Oklahoma, New Mexico, and Oregon who are willing to help, so just say the word and I'll let them know you're on the way," Joel offered.

He nodded his thanks. But after these months of threats, he wasn't about to endanger Joel's friends as well. Maybe in a few months, when he was sure Wolf wasn't going to hound him for the rest of his life. Until then, he was on his own.

To be of such little help during the weeks of repair work was beyond frustrating. Kurt retrieved the requested tools, supervised work that needed no supervision, and spent hours on the phone with the insurance company, the city and the police department. The final ruling of arson only cemented his decision.

The local fire restoration company was efficient and caring as they cleaned the house. Walls were scrubbed clean and painted, carpet pulled up and replaced, every window washed or replaced, ceilings repaired. Hordes of kids swarmed in to help dig through waterlogged items.

Kurt sat with them as they sorted and cleaned, talking about faith in times of trial. His own had nose-dived since the fire but he would not let that happen to these kids who were so new to theirs. So he talked and listened, encouraged and applauded. And deep inside, his heart cried out against the unfairness of it all.

He spent extra time with Razzie whenever he could, playing guitar and video games. They talked and joked, prayed together, and gave each other grief the way only brothers could. Kurt tried to imprint their time together deep in his heart.

At the end of the third week, as repair work neared completion and winter's first dusting of snow fell over the city, Vanessa handed him a mug of cocoa and settled next to him on the couch. They looked around the repainted Gathering Place with satisfaction.

"Nessa, I'd never have believed all this work could be done so quickly."

She smiled. "It helps to have contractors as members of Faith and so many kids and adults to help. I think we've almost doubled the number of kids involved in River House now."

He forced a smile in return, rejoicing with a sad heart. The near-destruction of River House had been his doing. The reconstruction was hers. River House was on solid ground now. Himself, not so much.

"You've been awfully quiet." Her observation cut into his thoughts.

"Have I? Just tired, I guess. You should be too. You've been a one-woman renovation crew."

Her face shone with a contentment that had become her constant expression lately. It made her even more beautiful. "It's been amazing to see what God's done to restore River House."

He lifted an eyebrow. "So you're giving God the credit, even though you've done all the work?"

She shook her head. "I had nothing to do with all the amazing people who rallied around the House. It wasn't me who asked people to send money anonymously. And it sure wasn't me who brought the kids of River House and Faith together to get the house cleaned up."

She set her cocoa on the table and leaned against him. "Watching you start River House from scratch was incredible. Seeing you grow closer to God through every issue was the best way to learn who He is and what He can do."

Kurt put an arm around her and rested his chin on top of her head. "That's so cool, sweetheart."

After a moment she twisted to look up at him. "I thought you'd be more excited about this, about me changing my mind about God."

"I am."

She studied him, blue eyes filled with concern. "The fire changed you. You're so quiet and sad now." Her eyebrows pinched upward as she placed her hand over his heart. "How can I help you?"

Her gentle words hung between them. She'd become his better half, his encourager, his best friend. It might possibly kill him to leave her behind.

He sat up, leaning his elbows on his knees. After a moment, he looked sideways at her and forced the lie out. "I'm okay. It'll just take some time to regroup. Honest."

Doubt filled her face but she didn't push for more. He was glad. He couldn't explain what was about to happen. The less she knew, the safer she'd be.

She offered a half-smile. "I'm here whenever you want to talk."

"I know. C'mere." He pulled her against him and pressed a kiss to her temple. He'd never forget the fragrance of her hair. God could have River House and its growing ministry. He would carry the love of this beautiful woman in his heart and pray for her forgiveness if they ever crossed paths again.

Vanessa slipped her hand into his as they entered Faith Church the following afternoon. Kurt's fingers tightened convulsively. There wasn't another hand in the world that would fit his this perfectly. He looked around the foyer and frowned. Its emptiness was a stark contrast to the crowded parking lot.

"Didn't Mike's email say the planning meeting starts at 2:00?"

"It did. Let's just go wait in the sanctuary. The cars must be for a different event."

"I guess. Just seems weird that we're the first ones here."

Vanessa pulled open the door to the sanctuary and waited for him to enter first. The excitement on her face made him pause, but before he could ask there was an explosion of noise from the large room and he jumped.

Applause filled the air, whistles and cheers adding to the racket. He stood paralyzed, looking from one smiling face to another. Two colorful balloon bouquets waved from the front of the room. A sign strung along the stage declared, "River House Rocks!"

When Vanessa prodded him forward, he reached for her hand and continued down the aisle, waving his new, smaller cast at them to stop the ruckus and sit down. Vanessa laughed at the cheerful comments thrown from the celebratory crowd, wiping tears from the corners of her eyes. She stopped at the front pew and urged him forward.

At the podium, Joel greeted him with a hug. As the applause continued, the pastor said quietly, "You can still change your mind, but if you believe this is what you need to do, I'm behind you 100 percent."

Kurt met his gaze and nodded once. "Thanks."

Joel motioned for the crowd to be seated. "I think we pulled off the surprise quite nicely, don't you?"

The kids whooped and cheered.

"I want to thank all of you for the hard work, money, and prayers offered as we restored River House. It's amazing to think that just a month ago we were faced with the daunting task of putting the house back in order after the fire, yet now we're celebrating God's work among us once again.

"We've seen God's hand in so many ways since this idea first left the ground. From the enemy trying to stop us by vandalizing the house to new friendships that are thriving. Kids who didn't know Jesus now call Him their best friend and Savior. Adults who didn't know they had a talent for working with teens are now among the most reliable volunteers. So let's take a minute to thank our mighty God for what He's done and what He'll do in the coming months and years."

The lump that had grown steadily in Kurt's throat as Joel talked made breathing nearly impossible. He closed his eyes and focused on taking slow, deep breaths, letting Joel's prayer wash over him.

"And all the saints said..." Joel finished, then laughed when the audience roared "Amen!"

"I'm thinking we also need to thank Kurt for the work he's been doing even as he's recovered from the smoke."

The kids were on their feet whistling and clapping as Kurt replaced Joel at the mic. He gestured for them to stop. "Aw, cut that out."

"You rock, Wagner!"

He laughed. "What would I do without you, Johnson?" His gaze ran around the crowded sanctuary. Having expected a small gathering, he was at a loss. How could he explain his decision to so many people? *Help, Lord.*

"I never imagined when I went in for my review with Joel last spring that this was the journey we'd be on together come fall. I can't thank you enough for getting behind the River House project, for believing in the dream and being so faithful to God's call.

"There's no way it would've gotten off the ground without all of you. It definitely takes a village to run something like this, to reach so many kids with the Gospel. To change lives. And believe me, lives are being changed every day."

Applause answered him and he looked at Vanessa. Her smile sparkled with love and pride. His mouth went dry.

"I've been really honored to be part of starting something like River House. It's been the coolest opportunity and I know I can't make you understand what it's meant to me. And will for the rest of my life. Which brings me to this."

Vanessa's smile faded. He moved his gaze away from her and tightened his fingers on the edge of the podium.

"The vandalism and threats over the past few months have been killing me. And then the fire almost *did* kill me. At first I thought they'd lose interest and pick on someone else, but now we see that the stakes are a lot higher and the blood they want is mine, for whatever reason.

"So what that tells me is that for the safety of these great kids and cool volunteers, for the sake of the neighborhood and for the River House ministry to continue..." He paused before forcing the words out. "I have to step out of my position, out of the way. I'm leaving Minnesota. Today."

The stunned silence was louder than the welcoming cheers. The faces looking back at him were wide-eyed, frowning, open-mouthed. Then their response rose like a tidal wave—loud and angry, roaring with confusion and shock. Several of the boys sprang to their feet and shouted back at him.

Razzie stared at him, pained confusion on his face. Leaving him without a goodbye was almost as hard as leaving Vanessa. *Help him understand. Please.*

Kurt lifted his hand. They were slow to quiet. "Okay, wait a minute. Let me explain."

"This doesn't rock, Wagner!"

Kurt dipped his head. "I know, Johnson. Just hear me out." *God, give me the right words.* "The dream of River House has been on my heart for years, and to see it come true was amazing. Really, really amazing. *But*," he added with emphasis, "to see it destroyed would kill me. And as long as I'm a target for revenge, the House and everybody who's part of it is in danger. I can't allow that. I *won't*."

"You can't leave! River House exists because of you," a girl's tearful voice called out.

"River House almost burned to the ground because of me," he said. "What if that happened when there were other people in the house? What if someone had died? River House doesn't exist because of me. It exists because of God and His plan for this community. I'm just a worker in the kingdom."

"So you're gonna walk away, just like that?" Pauly stood in the third row, pointing at Kurt with an angry jab. "You're chicken."

"This isn't about being chicken, Pauly." He leaned forward. "It's about knowing what needs to be done and not letting my ego get in the way. Do I want to walk away? Of course not!" His voice rose. "But if I don't, River House is goin' down. Look, if they weren't afraid to try burning it down, they're gonna try other ways and someone else is going to get hurt. That's not happening on my watch."

"So we hire security." The boys around Pauly murmured their agreement.

"With what money? And for how long? I'm not using ministry money for that when my leaving can solve the problem immediately."

"Who's gonna run it instead of you?"

"We don't want anyone but you."

"I'll quit coming if you leave."

Kurt ran a hand through his hair as shouted comments rained down on him, pummeling his heart. This wasn't going the way he'd planned. How else could he make them understand the danger they were in? *God, where are you!*

"Okay, listen. Listen to me."

"Why should we?" Razzie rose slowly to his feet. The betrayal in his eyes stabbed Kurt's heart. "What kind of leader turns tail and runs? If you wanna leave so bad just go, but don't give us some story about protecting the house. If you were worried about us, you wouldn't run away. You'd stay and fight for us. *With* us."

He moved forward to face Kurt across the podium. The microphone amplified the hurt in his words. "I believed in you. We all did. I thought you were the real thing. I thought you believed all that stuff you were saying about God. But you're not gonna let God be God and watch over River House."

He shook his head. "Man, I thought you were the coolest. I was so stupid. What a waste."

Kurt's eyes burned as he watched Razzie stalk out of the sanctuary. The sudden hush pressed down on him and for a moment he couldn't breathe. *God? Isn't this what you want? I don't know what to do.*

An icy silence seeped into his bones. He had never felt so alone...drained...abandoned. God wasn't answering anymore. He was on his own.

He lifted his head and met Vanessa's distraught expression. "I'm sure this does sound like I'm running away," he said, "but I've been praying nonstop since I woke up in the hospital. God has great plans for River House. For me to stay because that's the way it's been is stupid and dangerous. Dangerous for every single one of you.

"This isn't a game, people! It's not a TV show. This is real, hardcore stuff that we can't control. If I get out of the way, they'll follow me and leave River House alone. They don't care about the ministry, they're just aiming for me."

His gaze ran from one beloved face to another. Some were angry, others looked confused and frightened. River House youth sat among Faith youth; neighbors and volunteers and church people sat side by side. The dream was displayed before him in living, breathing, angry color.

Joel stood beside him and put a hand on his shoulder. The warmth of his friendship infused a last burst of strength. "River House will go on with Pastor Joel's guidance and great leadership in Mike and

Ashley and Vanessa. I know you'll work together to keep the House going strong because God is the foundation. It's not about me, it's about Him. Keep your focus. Keep the faith. And keep changing lives. I'll be watching."

His footsteps echoed in the silence of the room as he followed Razzie's path down the aisle.

"River House," he heard Joel say, "is all of us. God may have started this work through Kurt, but it has taken all of us to make it happen. I understand his decision because I understand how dangerous these people are. He didn't make this decision lightly and while I don't like it any more than you do, I agree with his actions. It's up to us to pray him through this dark time."

As the front door closed behind him, Kurt pulled Joel's words deep into his heart. He would need all their prayers as he went forward with this. Unable to draw a full breath, he got into his car and pulled away with a squeal of tires, glimpsing Vanessa in the rearview mirror as she dashed from the church. If he stopped, he'd break down for sure. He had to leave all of it behind—his life here, his dreams for River House, and Vanessa. It was the price he'd pay to keep her safe.

He glanced down at the dirty, crumpled sheet of paper on the seat beside him that he'd found in his mailbox three days ago.

"Yor pretty litle girlfren is next."

Vanessa slumped on her front step, staring blindly across the street. He was gone. No goodbye, no final hug. No warning. She wanted desperately to be angry but a numbing chill blotted out everything else.

Leaning her head against the wrought iron railing, she released a trembling sigh and closed her eyes. She'd known something was wrong. No matter how much she'd encouraged him, he had continued to pull away. He'd put up a good front for the kids, but she had seen the defeat in his eyes.

A black sedan rumbled to a stop at the curb, facing the wrong way, and three men climbed out. Chains swinging from ragged jeans, their dirty bandanas, metal-toe boots and unshaven faces should have sent her running. A warning bell went off in her mind; she ignored it. These people had ruined Kurt's life. And hers as well.

"Well, boys. Look at this purty li'l thing," the tallest one drawled, stopping in front of her. He wore a black leather vest over his bare chest. A faded dragon tattoo crawled up his bicep. The aroma of stale cigarette smoke stung her nose. "Tiny, I'm thinkin' this is the girlfriend Wolf was talkin' about."

Vanessa met his gaze without flinching. Fire burned in her stomach, seeping into her veins, tightening the muscles in her jaw. Bitterness overrode common sense as she stared him down.

"Where's your weasel of a boyfriend, darlin'?"

Teeth clenched, she could barely speak. "If you're talking about Kurt, he left the state yesterday. Your so-called leader can be satisfied he did what he set out to do." Her hands curled into fists as she glared at the vile man before her. "I hope he rots in hell."

The men exchanged grins, jostling each other. The short man, Tiny, rubbed his hands together in front of his bulging belly, making the fingerless leather gloves squeak. "Ooo. She's a feisty one, Spike."

"He left you here all alone?" Spike settled into a wide-legged stance, hooking his fingers into his belt loops as he grinned down at her. A front tooth was missing. Sunlight glinted off his earring. "Not much of a man, I'd say. I'd be happy to show you what a real man is like."

Bile rose in Vanessa's throat as a blistering rage filled her chest. With a screech, she leaped to her feet and shoved him as hard as she could, toppling him backwards off the sidewalk where he landed on his back on the grass.

"How dare you?" she shrieked. "You wouldn't know a real man if he kicked you in the head." Seething, she kicked at him repeatedly as he rolled away, covering his head from her hysterical outburst. "Wolf can't even fight his own battle and you call him a leader? You're pathetic!"

Tiny grabbed her arms and yanked her back, while the fat man pulled the target of her attack out of the way. Fury fueling her frenzy, she continued kicking. Car doors slammed nearby.

"Don't touch me!" She twisted and wrenched one arm away. Another kick connected with Tiny's shin. "Let go, you—"

He grunted but kept hold of her arm in a crushing grip.

Spike approached with a scowl. "You don't know who you're messin' with, b—"

"Hey!" A man's voice sliced between them. Two young men ran full speed toward the group, one blonde and one Asian.

Shoved aside, Vanessa fell to the ground as the three men set themselves for a fight. The other men, while well-muscled and obviously fit, seemed to be at a serious disadvantage as they faced the trio.

"This ain't your problem, boys," Spike said. "Just a little domestic squabble. You can run along."

The young men stood side by side. The dark-haired man motioned at Vanessa with a flick of his wrist and she scrambled behind him. "Sorry, *boys*," he replied. "We can't do that. The lady is under our protection."

She blinked. *What?*

"Nice try. She belongs with the scumbag that lived here. Or did until he ran away with his tail between his legs."

Vanessa took a step forward. The young man stuck out an arm and she held her ground, glaring defiantly past him. She'd never felt such hatred in her life.

"Why don't you gentlemen move along." The blond spoke with a smooth, firm Southern drawl. "You don't have any business with her."

Spike strolled toward them, chains rattling. "I think we'll jus' take her with us. We know someone who would love to...meet...her."

Vanessa's fury morphed into quaking nausea. If these two men hadn't arrived when they did... The young men took a step forward and the trio leaped into action, fists swinging.

Vanessa dashed toward a dark blue car in the street, searching for her phone. *I just had it—* She looked toward the house and saw it on the front step. She could try to get to it, or maybe just run to the neighbor's for help.

Horror kept her rooted in place while she prayed fervently for the outnumbered younger men. They were light and quick on their feet, fighting with a finesse the others lacked. Their punches were well-timed and accurate. Tiny hit the ground a moment later.

Spike reached into his pocket and a knife blade caught the sunlight. The two young men stood side by side, arms tensed, feet planted. They were barely out of breath while sweat poured off the red faces of the trio.

"You shoulda minded your own business," Spike snarled, starting toward them.

The Asian man spun in a blur of movement, kicking the knife from Spike's hand and catching his chin with a right fist that sent him to the ground. The blond was moving as well, his foot connecting with the fat man's stomach. The man folded over with an "oof" and staggered backward onto his rear.

In the silence that followed, Spike got to his feet, glaring at her protectors as he yanked the crooked bandana from his bald head. "The hell with this. I'm not wasting my time on you punks or that whore." He looked at Vanessa and raised his voice. "You tell Wagner if he steps foot back in Minnesota, we'll find him and finish him off."

He snatched up his knife before they stalked across the yard to their car, squealing away from the curb in a spray of gravel. Her heroes brushed themselves off and approached with smug expressions.

"What just happened?" Adrenaline drained out of her, leaving her shaken.

The Asian man grinned. "We had an opportunity to be knights in shining armor."

The blond looked at their black T-shirts and jeans and shrugged. "Or black armor, anyway. I'm Keith. He's Chen."

"I'm Vanessa. But I have a feeling you already know that."

Chen nodded. "Kurt told us all about you."

"You've seen him?" She hurried around the car to face them, the last of her apprehension gone.

Keith shook his head. "Not since he hired us."

"For what?"

"To protect you."

She stared back at him.

"Get used to seeing us," Chen said with a smile. "We're your shadow for the next month or two. Our job is to protect you for as long as necessary, until Kurt decides the threat is over and calls us off."

She tried to blink sense into the chaos in her mind. "I don't get any of this."

"Here." Chen pulled something from his back pocket and reached a fist toward her. "Kurt said this would show you we're legit."

He dropped an earring onto her palm. The one she'd lost in Kurt's car last month. Closing her fingers around the tiny piece of jewelry, she bit her lip to keep the tears back.

"We met Kurt a couple years ago when we did a personal safety class at the church," Keith explained. "We own a security and personal protection agency."

Chen added, "He called two weeks ago saying he needed to leave town and he wanted to make sure you were safe while he's gone."

Fingers of dismay wrapped around her throat. "Two weeks ago?"

"It wasn't an easy decision for him to make, Vanessa. He spent a lot of time praying about it. He was really worried about leaving you behind."

The words brought no comfort. She looked away from the sympathy in his eyes. So she was safe but alone. Again. *God, where are you in this mess?* What good was life now without Kurt? What good was anything anymore?

Still unsettled the following afternoon, Vanessa set out on a walk. When she found herself at Faith Church, she drifted into the sanctuary and dropped onto the back pew. She sat in silence, unmoving. The steamroller rumbled in the background, a nearly forgotten sound from the early days of grief, but she had no strength to fight it.

The patterns of sunlight on the front walls had shifted to the right and started to fade when she felt a presence beside her.

"Vanessa?" Joel sat down, his bearded face solemn as he looked at her. "How are you?"

How was she? Kurt had taken her heart with him and now there was only futility. She had no idea how to cope with that. She held his gaze for a long moment before giving a small shrug.

"Jackie and I would like you to stay with us for a few days. The kids would love it too. I don't think you should be alone. Would you come at least for the weekend?"

She met the kindness in his eyes. Even at his house she would be alone. She would always be alone. "Okay."

He drove her home where she collected a few things and set out extra food and water for Merton. When they pulled into the Barten driveway, Keith pulled up to the curb in the car she'd hidden behind during the fight. He gave her a nod and settled back in the front seat.

Jackie Barten met them at the door, a tall, willowy woman with brown hair that brushed her shoulders. She hugged Vanessa for a long moment before showing her to the guest room where she left her to rest with a promise to call her for dinner. Vanessa thanked her, climbed onto the embroidered quilt and closed her eyes.

39

Vanessa woke to find the bedside lamp lit and a plate on the table with a wrapped sandwich, chips and an apple. *Such dear people.* She managed two bites of the sandwich before sliding back under the blanket someone had put over her. She slept through the night and through the entire next day, a deep, dreamless sleep where she floated in suspended silence.

Come back.

The words reached through the darkness, gently calling her to wake. Morning sunlight streamed through the window and she lay still for a moment, waiting, wondering if she had imagined it.

Come back.

From where? To what? Kurt's abrupt departure had left a gaping wound. The months of joy they'd shared had filled her life with radiant promise. But the light was gone now, leaving her once again in the dark.

She felt protected here, safe enough to face the confusion and raw pain that had left her stumbling blindly in this nightmare. Rubbing her eyes, she realized she'd been crying in her sleep.

God had called her back to life. She stared up at the sunlight splashed across the ceiling, her battered heart beating steadily. There was more for her to do—kids that needed help, a man she loved with all her heart who needed prayer. She wouldn't give up hope that he would come home. He *had* to come home. She couldn't consider a future void of his love. She would stand before God with that request day after day after day until Kurt returned.

And she'd have a few choice words for him before holding him tightly for the rest of her life.

In the private bath, she showered and dressed, then left the quiet haven to face the world. Joel was reading the newspaper at the kitchen table. Jackie stood at the sink. They greeted her with welcoming smiles.

"Can I get you something to eat, honey?" Jackie offered. "How about some toast and juice?"

Vanessa's stomach gurgled. "That would be great. Thanks."

Joel set the paper aside and motioned to a chair across from him. The compassion in his eyes was a physical touch, wrapping warmth around her bruised heart. "That was quite a sleep."

"I only sleep that long when I'm sick."

Jackie set a small glass of orange juice before her and touched her shoulder. "Your heart is, hon."

Blinking against a stab of pain in her chest, Vanessa sipped the juice.

Joel was quiet for a moment. "Do you understand why he couldn't tell you?"

"No."

He leaned his elbows on the table. "Wolf is out for revenge. Kurt found out enough to know it had to do with their time in prison. He and River House and you were all targets—that much he knew for sure. He received a note last week singling you out in the threats."

She dropped back in her chair. Keith and Chen had left out that piece of news. "Why didn't he tell me? At least let me be part of the decision. I'm not a child."

"Would you have agreed to his leaving?"

"Well...no. Maybe." She rolled her eyes. "I don't know. Maybe I would have gone with him."

"What would that have done to the kids at the house, both of you disappearing like that?"

"If he'd stayed, Keith and Chen could protect him—"

"He can't live like that, Vanessa."

No, he couldn't. She rubbed her forehead. *So now he lives a life on the run? Alone?* "But why didn't he at least let me know ahead of time?"

"He wrestled greatly with that. In the end, he believed this was safest for you. He can live with your anger as long as you're alive."

Jackie set a plate with two slices of buttered cinnamon toast before her and ran a gentle hand over her head before returning to the counter. The simple gesture made Vanessa's heart sigh. Oh, how she needed a mom right now.

Enticed by the aroma, she finished both pieces in a few bites.

"Pray about it, Vanessa," he urged. "Take your feelings and questions to God and let Him help you deal with them."

She wanted to understand. She wanted to wake up and find this was a dream.

"If He'd prevented this, I wouldn't *have* these feelings." She frowned. "Why didn't He? Is He determined to push me past what I can handle? Because I can't handle this, losing another person I love."

"If we could handle all the hard things in life ourselves, we wouldn't need God."

"So He sends bad things our way to make us need Him?"

"Not at all. He may allow bad things to happen but He doesn't cause them. When stuff like this happens, He longs for us to lean on Him for strength and answers. And He wants that more than anything right now, for you to turn to Him with your doubts and sadness."

"Kurt said..." The amazing late-night conversation after Tiffani gave birth played in her head. "He said that God can make something good out of things that have gone wrong. But what good can possibly come from this?"

"I'd like to give you a black-and-white answer," Joel said, "but I don't know how this will turn out. What I do know is that someday we'll look back and see His hand in this situation. Because He's always at work in our lives, Vanessa. Every minute."

She looked at Joel and Jackie and tried to make sense of the conversation. How would she ever see God at work in this mess? "It'd be nice if He'd show His face once in a while."

Joel smiled. "He does, but it may look like someone in our lives who gives us hope, a hand up, or a hug when we need it most."

She sat quietly for a long moment. God looked like people? Like Joel and Jackie? Like Kurt?

The doorbell rang and Joel excused himself. Jackie refilled Vanessa's glass and sat down across from her. "It breaks my heart to see you hurting like this, honey."

Vanessa managed a smile at her compassionate gaze. Perhaps God did show His face in the amazing people around her.

"There's my favorite munchkin," came Mike's booming voice.

Relief lifted her out of the chair. Another connection to Kurt.

With Ashley close behind, Mike carefully set down a large white box and enveloped Vanessa in a bear hug. He looked down at her with a serious expression. "You okay?"

"I will be. You?"

"Same." He stepped out of the way to allow the girls to hug then cleared his throat. "So are you wondering why we come bearing gifts?"

Vanessa looked at the box then at the black trash bag Ashley had dragged in. "Actually I wasn't. Those are for me? How did you even know I was here?"

"Mr. Wagner told me if I don't keep track of where you are every minute, he'll hunt me down." He grinned crookedly and added, "Jackie called us yesterday."

Vanessa frowned up at him. "I appreciate his concern but I'm not helpless."

"Trust me, we all know that. Anyway, we bring a gift for you from Mr. Wagner himself."

Hope burst alive in her chest. "You've seen him?"

He sighed. "No. He had this all arranged before the fire."

"Oh."

Ashley offered an encouraging smile. "It's a surprise he's been working on for a while. Since September, actually."

"Honey, why don't you open it?" Jackie suggested. "That might answer your questions."

Vanessa looked over at the smiles of her hosts then lowered to the floor beside the box. As she lifted the lid, a contented sigh drifted up from inside and she pulled back in surprise.

"It won't bite," Joel assured her.

Mike added with a laugh, "While it's sleeping, anyway."

She peeked over the edge and caught her breath. A puppy lay asleep in a pile of shredded newspaper. With curly golden hair, a tiny black nose and dainty paws, it looked like a toy. "Ohhh. That is the cutest thing I've ever seen."

"She's nine weeks old," Joel said. "She's a yorkiepoo. Part Yorkie, part poodle. I guess she won't get bigger than about six pounds, she won't shed, and I hear they have great personalities."

Mike reached in and gently lifted the limp puppy, setting it in her arms. With another deep sigh, it snuggled against her neck. Vanessa's heart melted at the sound, the smell, the softness of the fur.

"Oh, my..." The magnitude of the gift set her heart racing. Could she bear to open her heart to another being she'd have to say goodbye to someday?

Jackie handed her a white envelope. "This is also from Kurt."

Vanessa stared at the familiar handwriting, desperately needing a connection with him. Cradling the puppy, she got carefully to her feet. "You are the dearest people in the world," she told them. "You've become my family and I just...I can't thank you enough for the precious gift of your love and friendship. And for bringing me *this* precious gift."

"We love you too, hon," Ashley said. "And the fact that Kurt planned this weeks ago, even before the fire, tells you how he feels." She dragged the black bag closer and reached in. "She's supposedly already trained to use a potty sheet in the house. Here are a bunch of those. They should keep her from messing on the floor. And here's a little kennel."

"There's puppy food and a collar and a leash," Jackie added, which Ashley pulled out for display.

"And a pooper scooper," Mike added, "although it's a pretty small one."

"That's because you grew up with huge retrievers, so your idea of a scooper is a full-sized shovel." Joel winked at Vanessa.

She smiled and buried her nose in the golden fur, inhaling the sweet puppy smell.

"What are you going to name her?" Mike asked.

"Maybe she should get to know her a little before she comes up with a name," Jackie interjected.

Vanessa shook her head. "No, I know just the name for her. Grace. Because that's what you've all shown me. I think she's proof that God doesn't forget us, even in the hardest times."

"Little Gracie," Ashley said. "It's perfect! Can I hold her?"

As they passed the puppy around, the smile on Vanessa's face wriggled down into her soul, and she breathed a silent prayer of thanks.

Late that evening, Gracie asleep in her kennel in a corner of the guest room, Vanessa climbed into bed and slid beneath the covers, Kurt's letter in hand. Throughout the afternoon as she and the Barten children played with the puppy, she had kept Kurt's letter within reach, but she'd wanted to be alone when she read it. She ran a finger lightly across her name on the envelope. Finally she pulled out the paper and unfolded it.

Dear Nessa,

I can't tell you how sorry I am for the way things turned out. I had such cool dreams for us and the House. This isn't how I ever thought things would go.

When you said you'd work at River House, I knew for sure you believed in me, in what God was calling me to do. And I knew right then you were going to mean a lot to me. I just couldn't have guessed how much.

I've never known a girl like you. You're beautiful and smart and you make me laugh. And you've never been afraid to get in my face for a reality check. I need that. Nobody was more surprised than me when we got together. And nobody could have been happier. I know God has great plans for you, Ness. After everything you've gone through, He has good things in store. So don't be mad at Him because I'm gone. Be glad for everything we had.

I need you to keep River House going, okay? You and Mike and Ash will do a great job. I hope maybe someday you can forgive me for not telling you I was leaving. I think Wolf will leave everyone alone now that I'm gone. But just in case, you've got a great safety net in Chen and Keith and Mike.

You have so much to offer everybody, even the tough guys. I've seen how much they respect you and trust you. They don't trust easily so the work you've done with them has been a God thing.

Have a good life, Vanessa. No, have a GREAT life. You deserve it. You really changed mine and I will never, ever forget you. Maybe, if we ever see each other again, you'll be able to forgive me.

Just remember how much I love you. I'll be praying for you every day.

Love, Kurt

She studied his handwriting for a long moment, then carefully folded the sheet and slid it back into the envelope. She set it on the bedside table and reached a trembling hand to shut off the light. Then she laid her head on the pillow, wrapped her arms around the knot in her stomach, and let the tears out.

40

In three days of aimless driving, Kurt had slept a total of twelve hours. He needed to close his eyes and shut out the thoughts that taunted him, reminding him of every stupid decision he'd made and every loss he'd endured.

"Just a little farther from Minnesota and then I'll stop. Somewhere."

The road ahead remained blurry, no matter how many times he blinked and rubbed his eyes. The last can of root beer from the gas station was flat. Maybe he'd have a real beer next time he stopped.

He cracked open the window to let the cold air whistle in. Another hour and then he would crash at a motel in...whatever town he happened upon. Where was he, anyway?

The whine of a siren sounded close, like it came from his trunk. He glanced in the rearview mirror and did a double take. *Oh, man! Now what?* The police officer was motioning for him to pull over. Waiting for him to approach, Kurt lowered the window. The winter air slapped him awake.

"Hello, sir." The voice was distinctly female in its firm tone, and he looked up in surprise. She stood a step back from the window, sunglasses and brown highway patrol hat accentuating her serious features.

"Hello, officer."

"Do you know why I pulled you over?"

"No, sir. Ma'am."

"In the past two miles you changed lanes twelve times without signaling. Have you been drinking, sir?"

He straightened. Thinking about it didn't count. "Not a drop, ma'am."

"Could I see your license and registration, please."

Kurt reached for his wallet. He had tossed it in the car at the last gas station, on the floor maybe. "It's here somewhere. I threw it in when I got gas. Just a minute." Fast food wrappers, soda cans, and candy wrappers were tossed aside as he groped through the junk. "I know it's in here..."

"Step out of the car, sir. Now."

Lord, help. It was all his exhausted brain could muster. He reached to unhook his seatbelt and realized he hadn't hooked it after his last stop. *Great.* The officer waited, unsmiling, as he unfolded himself from the cramped sitting position.

"Put your hands on the car. Are you carrying a weapon?"

His fingers recoiled from the arctic shock of the metal. "No, ma'am. I don't own one."

"What's your name?"

"Kurt Wagner."

He shivered as she patted him down. Icy fear squeezed the breath out of his chest as the familiar smell of prison wafted over him. This was it. He was going back to jail for being stupid.

"Please come with me, sir." She led him to the squad car and opened the back door. He slid in and the clanking of the cell door closed out the world.

She climbed in the front seat and asked for his date of birth and address. As she typed at her computer, Kurt studied her stern profile. A blonde braid hung just past her shoulders, and he caught the glint of tiny earrings when she turned her head.

The static sounds and voices from the police radio added to the surreal moment, and he dropped his head back against the seat. *Wasn't walking away from everything I care about enough? You need to lock me up too?*

"Where are you headed, Mr. Wagner?"

Though her tone was polite, he had the impression he'd better answer correctly. But he had no answer. He didn't even know where he was. He lifted his head to look at her. "Seattle." *Seattle?*

"What business do you have there?"

"My brother and his family live there. I'm going…I just left…" He released a short breath and rubbed the back of his neck. "It's a long story but I just left a job in Minnesota. I'm headed to Washington to figure out what to do next." *Brilliant.*

Her leather jacket squeaked as she turned to look at him through the bars that separated them. She'd removed her sunglasses and hat. Vanessa flashed before him. This woman had blue eyes, but not the same breathtaking blue. Her hair wasn't head-turning blonde. And there was no spark of joy lighting her face.

"Looks like you've stayed out of trouble since your jail time."

"Yes, ma'am."

"I don't smell alcohol on you. Can you explain why you were driving so erratically?"

"I'm tired. I haven't slept much since I left. I'm planning to stop at the next motel I find. I'm sorry. I should have stopped sooner."

"Sleepiness causes as many accidents as alcohol, are you aware of that?"

"I can see that now."

She turned back to look at the computer screen. "How do you intend to pay for the motel room without your wallet?"

Good question. "I'm sure it's in the car somewhere. I had it at the gas station in…" Wherever he'd just been.

"Do I have your permission to check your car for you? I'm not doing a drug search, but you understand that if I find something, it changes everything?"

"I do. Go ahead. There's nothing but garbage in there." He lifted his shoulders, cringing at the mess. "Sorry."

The slightest smile touched her mouth before she got out of the car. He watched her search the front seat then the back. A moment later she returned, his wallet in hand. Relief flooded through him so quickly he thought he needed a restroom. *Thank you, God.*

"May I pull out your license, Mr. Wagner?"

"Sure."

She typed on the computer, wrote something in her pad of papers, then climbed out and opened the back door. When he stood, she looked him in the eye. She was a tall one. "There's a motel three miles up the highway, at the edge of town. I suggest you stop there for at least twenty-four hours. They have a good restaurant as well."

"I'll do that. Thank you."

She held out the wallet. "This is your only warning. If I have to stop you again, Mr. Wagner, I won't be as nice."

He shook his head. "You won't have to. I really need to crash so I'll be off the road for a day or two."

Her smile changed her demeanor. Vanessa's laughter floated between them. "Good idea. I'm happy to escort you to the hotel."

Tempted to protest, he held his tongue and hurried to his car. Careful to stay at the speed limit, he found the motel within minutes. As he turned onto the exit she continued past, and he released a long breath. Crisis averted. Barely.

The hotel room was neat and sterile. Standard paisley bedspread, tan walls, fake brown woodwork. No character, no life. Like him.

He hung the Do Not Disturb sign on the door, then tossed his duffel bag on the floor and clicked on the TV. The 5:30 news told him he was in Billings, Montana. He went to the window and stared out at the distant hills. He'd never been in Billings. He'd never been in Montana, for that matter. Too bad he didn't have the energy to sightsee.

In the bathroom he splashed cold water on his face and leaned his hands on the sink. A scruffy, exhausted man stared back at him from the oval mirror. Dark circles under puffy eyes, hair sticking out every which way, life beaten out of him. He'd seen that man before—in a cracked prison mirror.

Where was the excited, faith-filled leader of River House? He shook his head. That man didn't exist anymore. The fire of faith that had burned in him since that pivotal moment on his knees in the cell had been extinguished with the River House fire. His future lay in the ashes. He had tasted success and joy and best of all, love. With all of it gone, his grasp on faith and hope was tenuous and fading.

Muttering an oath, he turned away from the reflection and sprawled across the bed, letting the smooth voice of the news anchor wash over him. As his eyes fluttered closed, he welcomed an escape from the memories and voices that had haunted him since he drove away from Faith.

Wednesday evening's worship time, the first held in the House since the fire, centered on sacrifice. Vanessa and Mike led the discussion, determined to help the kids understand what had gone into Kurt's decision, the heartbreak involved in sacrifice, and the joy to be found in giving oneself for others.

"Every day we make choices," Mike said. "What to eat for breakfast, what to wear, if we're going to school or not. Sometimes the choices are harder because of the potential for pain, whether it's ours or someone else's. How to break up with someone. Telling someone they're drinking too much and you're worried about them."

"What if," Vanessa said, "some kid was bullying a friend of yours? Would you stand up for them?"

"'Course," Pauly said. "There was this guy who kept, like, pickin' on my little brother's friend because he talks funny. So I got in the guy's face and told him what I'd do if he did it again."

"Did he stop?" Tiffani asked.

"Nah. So I found him down at the park and..." He glanced at Vanessa. "And did what I said I'd do. Then he stopped."

"What if the guy always had three big friends with him," she said, "so there's no way you could do what you need to do without getting yourself beat up?"

"Well, I could prob'ly take 'em all on," he blustered. "I'm fast and I've got a freakin' fast right."

Subdued laughter made him flop back against the couch, frowning darkly.

"You probably could," Mike said, "but it might not be the best choice. What if you found a way to get their attention away from the little kids? Give them something else to focus on so they quit bugging your brother's friend."

"Then hopefully nobody would get hurt and the bullying would stop," Natalie said.

The room was quiet.

"So you're saying," Tiffani said slowly, eyes narrowed, "that's what Kurt did, right? He left to get their attention off River House."

Vanessa met her gaze and nodded. "He's tough enough to take on Wolf, but since Wolf stayed in hiding, this was the next best option. He loves you guys." Tears crawled up her throat. "He loves River House. All that mattered was keeping everyone safe."

"Will he come back?"

Vanessa and Mike exchanged a glance. "When he thinks it's safe enough," Mike said. "Which may be a while. In the meantime, we pull together and keep things going. Right?"

"Yeah," Pauly said quietly. "We can do that."

After closing the House for the night, Vanessa sank onto the couch and looked at Mike, sprawled on the other couch. "That was hard."

Mike nodded. "But I think God was working in their hearts to help them understand."

She rested her head back, running her fingers lightly over Grace's curly fur. "So many of them have already had such hard losses in their lives. Losing Kurt just compounds everything. Hopefully sharing stories about him helped them see it in a different light.

"I wish Razz had been here to hear it," she added. The boy's absence accentuated the hole left from Kurt's departure.

The shock and pain on Razzie's face at Kurt's announcement had stayed with her. Would he just slip back into his old life? Give up his dreams, his future? In that moment, she knew what she had to do. It was what Kurt would do. And Kurt would do what Jesus did—find the lost and bring them home.

It took three days to track Razzie to a part of town she'd never been in. And hoped to never visit again. She was glad Keith and Chen were waiting just feet away in the car. Shivering, hands deep in her jacket pockets, she waited for Razzie to look up from the crowd he huddled with. A cloud of smoke hung over them in the frigid air.

When he glanced over, his dark eyes, so much like Kurt's, went wide. He spoke to the man next to him, then slunk toward her like a child caught being naughty, his ragged jeans dragging on the sidewalk. Her heart warmed when he stopped before her. She'd missed him.

"What do you want?" Eyes down and shoulders hunched, he fiddled with his cigarette.

"Hello to you too. I want you to come back to River House."

"That ain't happenin', so you can just go." He returned to his friends, keeping his back to her.

Vanessa stood her ground, her eyes never leaving him as she burrowed in her jacket against the wind. She wasn't leaving until he agreed. The guys jostled Razzie with comments, then looked at her with gazes that made her recoil inside.

When the taller one started toward her, Razzie shoved him with a snarl that drew laughter from the others. Then he strode toward her, grabbed her arm, and dragged her away from them.

"How stupid are you coming here?" he demanded, releasing her with a curse. "This ain't no place for you, Vanessa. Go home."

She didn't flinch. "I can't."

"Why not?"

"Because God sent me here to find you and bring you back to River House. I'm not leaving until you agree."

"Well, then, you're gonna be standing here all alone 'cuz I ain't comin' back. Why should I? It's all just stupid."

"Because Kurt loves you, Razz." She saw him wince before he turned away.

"Like hell he does. He left, remember? Just walked away from the whole thing. When you care about somebody, you don't walk out on 'em."

"In most cases, that's true. But Kurt was putting us all in danger by staying. He loves us enough to walk away from his dream because it's what's best for *us*."

Razzie glanced sideways at her. "You talk to him lately?"

She shook her head. "No. I haven't seen him since the meeting at Faith. I didn't know he was leaving either, Razz. It was a shock to me too."

"Then why would you think he gives a rip about you? He walked out on you too." He dragged on the cigarette and then tossed it into the street, releasing the smoke in staccato puffs.

She waited for him to turn his angry gaze toward her. "As hard as it is to understand, I know he did it to keep us safe. I *know* it. I watched him struggle to make River House a reality. He'd do anything to keep it alive. He already has."

A half-smile touched her face. "He was so thrilled that first day you and Burger showed up," she said softly.

His shoulders dropped a fraction as the edge to his expression softened. "Yeah. He acted like a little kid, showing us around the house and teaching us to paint."

"You, of all the kids, are the most special to him, Razz."

His dark head lifted and he stared up at the sky, blinking rapidly. His Adam's apple slid up and down, and a wisp of air released into the cold as he sighed. "Then he shouldn't have left. We coulda handled Wolf together."

"You know that's not how he works. His faith is who he is. Fighting back wasn't the answer. Not long term, anyway."

He faced her, jamming his hands in his pockets. "So what is?"

The angst in his voice made her eyes burn. She grasped the sleeve of his battered jacket. "The answer is to keep River House going, make it stronger, reach more kids. He entrusted it to us but we have to do it together. Razzie, don't let everything he went through be in vain."

He closed his eyes and shrugged. "You don't need me to run it," he said, sounding young and sad and hurt.

"We do. Without you, it'll just be a bunch of adults trying to do something for kids who don't care. With you there, they listen. They want to be involved. They care because *you* care. So yeah, we do need you. And I think you need us."

She pulled an envelope from her pocket and held it out to him. "He wrote each of us a letter before he left. This is yours. I don't know what it says, but take time to read it, Razzie— really read it. Then please come back soon. We'll be waiting for you."

Rising up on her toes, she pressed a kiss to his cold cheek and returned to the car. She was glad for the quiet presence of Keith and Chen, a comforting reminder that Kurt still cared.

At home, she settled in the chair by the living room window. With Gracie snuggled on her lap and Merton at her feet, she prayed for Kurt and Razzie, for Mike and Ashley and the House ministry. And for her broken heart.

42

The Sunshine Motel in south Seattle could hardly be called homey, but it was neat, clean, and anonymous. Until he figured out what he was going to do, that was all he needed. A microwave helped.

It took two days to find the courage to drive by Scott's new house in a picturesque neighborhood on the north side. He returned to his motel room in a deep funk. Their lives had turned out completely different. Scotty was obviously thriving in his CPA career. All those nights struggling through finance and accounting in college had paid off for him, his pretty wife Hayley, and their little girl, Lily.

He flopped on the bed and stared at the ceiling. So what was the point of his life now? He couldn't just waltz back into Scott's life and be the wise older brother. Scott hardly needed his counsel or his influence.

He needed to get a job. But who would hire an ex-con, ex-ministry leader with an impressive talent for messing up every golden opportunity presented to him? What had been the point of following God these past years, anyway? Where had it gotten him? Right here in a cheap motel room with no future, no hope, and a growing desire for a drink.

The biting questions were relentless, leaving a bitter taste. With an oath, he rolled off the bed and pulled another soda from the mini fridge, then dropped onto the chair at the small table. He couldn't even have a lousy beer without putting another nail in his coffin.

Maybe that wasn't such a bad idea. He retrieved his wallet from the dresser. Twenty bucks. That would buy a case or two. Walt's Liquors was right down the block. Good ol' Walt could fix him up in no time.

Memories flashed in a staccato pattern—fights, hangovers, prison. He dropped the wallet like it was scorching. He might not have anything to live for, but at least he was free. That first beer was guaranteed to send him back to the joint.

He pressed the heels of his hands against his temples and paced the small room. His skin itched as he wrestled with the need to drink and the desire to stay on the path. He should find an AA meeting. He knew better than to go this alone. And he was more alone than he'd ever been.

His eyes jumped around the room, skimming over his meager possessions before landing on the guitar case in the corner. Corey still occasionally emailed from the road to see what Kurt was up to or share news of when NightVision would be in Minnesota. Kurt never responded. He had nothing to say to a group of guys living the jet-set life of megastars.

It's time.

The words were a clear impression on his heart, the meaning less so. Time for what, a beer? A decision? Starting a new life or just ending this one?

He reached for the photo on the bedside table, a bittersweet smile touching his heart as he looked at Vanessa's beautiful face. He ached to touch her, hear her laughter, feel her arms around him.

Time to let her go? He'd done that when he left the church. Without her, his life was a blank canvas. But the decision was his. He could leave it blank or he could paint something on it. The portrait of his life might be dark and gritty, but experience had shown him that life's darkest moments could make the best songs.

Setting the picture carefully back in its place by the bed, he retrieved his guitar and started painting on the canvas.

Four days later, Kurt had completed five songs. He was excited by the fresh wind of creativity and a sense of accomplishment that was familiar, personal. Something he hadn't felt in years.

Now he needed to hear his songs in the daylight, outside the confines of the cramped motel room. He'd learned years ago that what sounded amazing at 4 a.m. could be laughable in the light of day. But sometimes it was magical.

He stuck the loose sheets of paper into his guitar case and checked the mirror on his way to the door. Dark stubble on his face, hair in wild disarray, he looked more like a mad scientist than an energized songwriter. Jamming a baseball cap on his head, he headed out into the gray November light.

The neighborhood park was deserted on a Tuesday afternoon and he settled on a picnic table near the small lake. Using rocks to keep the papers in place, he started the first song. Self-conscious, he sang quietly at first. The second time through, the music flowed through his veins and out his fingers. It was strange hearing how his voice had developed character over the past few silent years.

The final chords rang up into the bare trees overhead and he sat content, looking out over the sparkling water. He still had it in him.

"Did you write that?"

A teenage girl stood beside the picnic table. Curly brown hair stuck out from under her knit cap. A bike lay on its side behind her.

"Yeah, I did. Whadya think?"

"Not bad. I liked the second one best. What's it called?"

"I haven't got a title for any of them yet. Any suggestions?"

She perched on the picnic table and leaned her elbows on her knees in deep thought. "Crisis of Faith."

Her words were cold water in his face. "That's what you'd call it?"

She looked at him with a steady gaze that brought Vanessa to mind. "Isn't that what it's about?"

He considered the lyrics. "I guess you're right. I hadn't thought about it."

"Are you a Christian?"

"Well, I..." He hesitated. Was he? "I used to be. I suppose I still am. I've been on a rough road lately."

The girl nodded. "Me too. Maybe that's why I liked that one. It kinda describes me." She reached for his guitar. "Can I play one for you?"

"Sure."

She handled the guitar with ease. Her song echoed his with similar questions, fears and doubt. But hers had an upbeat tone that his was lacking.

"You're good."

"I know." She shrugged. "Not sure what it does for me, though. I'm stuck here with no way to get to Nashville where I could maybe have a future."

He understood her longing. He extended his hand. "I'm Kurt."

She shook it firmly. "Lorene."

"How old are you?"

"Sixteen. You?"

"Twenty-eight."

"So how come you're here and not in Nashville? You're good too."

The blunt praise warmed his heart. "Thanks. I have a brother here. I'm just visiting for a while."

She handed him the guitar and climbed off the table. "Well, when you get to Nashville, remember me back here, will ya?"

"Sure will. But in the meantime, don't give up the dream. I have a feeling you'll be famous long before me."

She slid her backpack on and waved as she rode off. Kurt watched her go, a smile touching his mouth.

Somehow that spunky teen with the dream in her eyes had given him the affirmation he needed to move ahead with his music. Returning his guitar to its case, he studied the song sheets on his way back to the car. There was a key change in the third song that didn't feel right.

43

Kurt sat in his car at the end of the block. He'd watched Scott's family for three days. Today he'd either summon the courage to ring the doorbell or leave town. Lurking on the fringes of his kid brother's life was pathetic.

A brown Volvo turned the far corner and Kurt slid down. It pulled into Scott's driveway and the family climbed out. Scott headed for the mailbox at the end of the driveway while a very pregnant Hayley took their toddler into the house. *It's now or never, Wagner.*

He swung out of the car, straightening his shirt and smoothing his hair as he walked on rubber legs toward Scott. His heart pounded so hard he thought he might have to stop and throw up in the neighbor's shrub. Giving himself a mental shake, he quickened his steps.

Scott glanced toward him as he thumbed through the mail, then stopped short. His gaze swung back and he stared.

Kurt stood a few feet away, the corners of his mouth lifting in response to the smile of welcome on his brother's face. Man, it was good to see him. Tall and lanky, with their mother's eyes.

"It's about time," Scott said, closing the gap and throwing his arms around Kurt. They stood locked together for a long minute.

Scott finally released him enough to lean back. "I was running out of excuses for Hayley whenever she asked when you were coming."

Kurt took a step back to look him up and down. "I heard my kid brother was doing okay out here, but I figured I'd better come out and see if the rumors were true."

"I'm doing a lot better now that you're here." He put an arm around Kurt's shoulders. "Come on. This will probably send Hayley into early labor but she has got to see you. And you haven't seen Lily since she was born. She's the cutest little kid."

Hayley released a delighted scream and waddled across the kitchen to hug Kurt hard. While Scott went to find Lily, Hayley showered Kurt with questions, hugs interspersed. Her happy chatter relieved the last of his reservations. Scott reappeared with their daughter who shyly hid her face against her daddy's neck, drawing a laugh from the adults.

Kurt felt like royalty all afternoon as they fed him, shared family photos, gave him a tour of the new house. He happily played peek-a-boo with Lily. Their joy at seeing him was gratifying and humbling.

After dinner the men settled in the living room, sodas in hand, while Hayley gave Lily a bath. When his brother leveled his gaze on him, Kurt squirmed. He'd been able to deflect most of the questions, but now he'd have to 'fess up.

"So tell me what's really going on."

Kurt studied the bubbles in his glass and wondered how much he could share without breaking down. Vanessa's face swam before him and he closed his eyes briefly.

"Are you in trouble?"

He flinched. That Scott even thought to ask was humiliating. "Not anymore. Not since leaving Minnesota." When Scott's eyebrows lifted, Kurt raised a hand to reassure him. "And I'm sure it didn't follow me out here. To be honest, I don't even know why I was in trouble. It just sorta found me."

Scott settled back into his chair. "I've got all night. Let's hear it."

An hour later, Hayley wiped her eyes where she sat beside her husband as Kurt finished his story. He was glad he'd held it together through the telling. Lately he seemed to cry over almost anything—TV commercials, kids playing, the sight of a church.

"She's beautiful, Kurt," Hayley declared, fingering the tattered photo. "I want to meet her someday."

Her declaration pinched his heart. "If you ever make it back to Minnesota, I'll give you her address."

Scott folded his arms, studying his brother. "You aren't going back?"

"Not at this point."

"Not even for Vanessa?" Hayley's wide eyes sent a twinge of guilt through him. She handed him the photo. "You know she's waiting for you."

"I left her a letter and tried to make it clear that she should go on with her life. I don't know if I'll ever be able to go back. It's too dangerous." He looked at the picture before returning it to its place next to his heart. "Maybe someday...in the meantime, I'll find a place to stay—"

"You'll stay right here," she said firmly. "Don't you dare think about going anywhere else. He can stay in the room downstairs, don't you think, Scott?"

Before he could answer, Kurt spoke up. "Thanks, Hayl. I appreciate the thought, but I'd be more comfortable in my own place."

Her eyebrows pinched upwards. "You'll stay here in Seattle though, right?"

"Yeah. I'd like to hang around here for a while, if you guys don't mind."

"Christmas is only six weeks away and the baby is due in four, so you *have* to stay for those big events."

He chuckled, exchanging a wink with Scott. "I wouldn't dream of missing my nephew's arrival."

Hayley punched Scott's shoulder, and he lifted his hands in defense. "He's always been a good guesser."

Kurt laughed and got to his feet. This amazing day had been an answer to a prayer he hadn't dared utter. "Thanks for dinner, Hayley. It was the best meal I've had in a long time."

"You're welcome." She hugged him. "You're always welcome here, Kurt. I can't tell you how happy we are to see you again."

The men exchanged a warm, back-slapping hug. "See you Saturday?"

Kurt nodded. "We'll get the cupboard doors fixed and then we can work on that bookshelf for Lily."

Back in his motel room, Kurt collapsed on the bed with a happy sigh. Why had he waited so long? Seeing his kid brother was exactly what he'd needed. Until he could finally go home to Vanessa, he'd keep painting on the canvas. It didn't look quite so blank now.

A few days later, Kurt stopped by the small music store in the nearby strip mall for new strings. The owner, Sherm, was a gregarious man with a shiny bald head and a deep laugh. They chatted for almost twenty minutes before he had to answer the phone. Waiting at the counter, Kurt smiled at a teenage girl who was admiring a guitar hanging on the wall.

When Sherm returned, Kurt had convinced the girl and her father to buy a slightly less expensive guitar that still had a solid sound and to sign up for the guitar lessons advertised in a flyer on the counter. She left the store with a sparkling smile, clutching the guitar case to her chest.

Sherm looked at Kurt, eyebrows raised. "How'd you do that?"

"Do what?"

"They've been coming in here for three months but I haven't been able to sell them anything. Now you talk them into a decent guitar in ten minutes."

Kurt grinned and lifted his shoulders. "I know guitars?"

"Obviously. Do you happen to need a job? I could use you on my sales floor. It doesn't pay a whole lot, but I can give you a discount on equipment and supplies. And I'm a fun guy to work with."

The air left his chest in a whoosh. Maybe God hadn't forgotten about him after all. The test would be full disclosure. "I actually could use a job, but I need to put everything on the table. I'm a convicted felon, out almost four years. Been sober and on solid ground ever since. Until recently I was running a ministry to keep kids off the street. I hope to get back to it someday."

Sherm folded his arms and nodded. "Thanks for telling me. I appreciate the honesty. I've been sober for about twenty. I'm willing to give it a try if you are. No funny business and we'll be good."

Kurt stuck out his hand. "No funny business."

Over the weekend, he moved into a cheap furnished apartment two miles from Scott's neighborhood. When he wasn't working at the store, he was writing music or fixing things around the house. His brother had the brains of the family but no clue how to build or repair anything. Kurt was glad to have a way to pay back their generosity and warmth, still stunned that Scott continued to enjoy spending time with him.

Sunday night after exchanging emails with Joel and reading Chen's daily report, Kurt lay in bed, indecision scrambling his thoughts. The longing for River House, for the life he'd loved, and especially for Vanessa was intense. He hadn't contacted her since he'd left. Maybe she thought he didn't care anymore. It was killing him to think that. Maybe if they just talked for a couple minutes…

He gritted his teeth. "No! It's not all about you, Wagner." He'd told her to move on and he'd meant it. Wolf was an idiot but he wasn't stupid. Kurt knew Wolf had tracked him online as River House was created. And he was sure Wolf was still watching, waiting to see if he'd return to Minnesota. Chen said all was quiet now, but that didn't mean all was forgotten.

With a grunt, he pushed out of bed and settled at the kitchen table to log onto his computer. The Facebook comments from River House kids tied him in knots. But responding would only open a door that had to stay shut. They needed to focus on life without him.

Vanessa's page made his heart leap. Cheek to cheek with the puppy, her blue eyes smiled back at him, tinged with sadness. When he had planned his surprise, he'd been so excited to see her reaction. Thanks to Wolf, he might never actually see the puppy in person.

She sent emails every few days, telling him what Grace was up to, what the kids were doing. How much she missed him and prayed for him. Itching to respond, he pressed his fists against his forehead and prayed for strength. What if he couldn't return?

"Don't wait for me, Nessa," he whispered fiercely. "There are a million guys just waiting for a chance with you. You deserve so much more than I can give you."

A few days before Thanksgiving, Kurt thanked the last customers and locked the door behind them while Sherm closed out the register. They worked in companionable silence putting the store in order.

"Hey, Sherm. Mind if I stay to do some recording in the studio?"

"Stay all night." He shrugged then lifted his head and grinned. "Just make sure you're awake for your shift tomorrow."

Kurt laughed. "I won't be here that late. I just wanna hear what this new song sounds like."

"Knock yourself out."

Half an hour later, Kurt set up in the recording studio at the back of the store. Sherm was an accomplished musician and an enthusiastic mentor to local budding artists. He'd launched the careers of several nationally known artists from this small studio and music store.

Kurt settled on the stool and arranged the music on the stand, then played through the new song, grimacing at several chords. He made the adjustments and played it again.

The rush of being alone in the studio sent him to his feet. He played like he was on stage, singing for the audience in his head. These songs were definitely better than what he'd written long ago, with one distinct difference. His faith was now the foundation of every song. The newest expressed his endless gratitude about rediscovering the joy of music and family.

He danced around the recording room, playing hard, singing strong, thoroughly immersed in the music. It was complete and utter delight to be singing for God, as Vanessa had requested when she'd given him Matt's guitar.

Finally spent, he wiped his forehead with his sleeve, set his guitar in the stand and started toward the control room to shut down the equipment. Seeing Sherm's bald head where he sat at the mixing board on the other side of the glass brought him up short.

Embarrassed by the free-flowing show he'd put on, Kurt shook his head with a laugh. "I thought you left."

"Forgot my billfold. And I'm glad I did." The chair protested as the heavy-set man leaned back. He studied Kurt through narrowed eyes. "I would never have guessed you had that in you."

Heat filled Kurt's face and he shrugged. "I can get a little crazy when no one's lookin'."

"Crazy good, man. Professional-level good. Why aren't you performing for a living?"

Kurt dropped into the other chair. "It's a long story."

"Give it to me."

Letting himself into the apartment an hour later, a tired smile crossed Kurt's face. Sherm's unbridled enthusiasm for his songs and his promise to share several of them, including "Crisis of Faith," with a producer friend had been an amazing way to end an ordinary day. Even if the conversation went nowhere, Kurt was buoyed by Sherm's praise and encouragement.

Maybe Vanessa had been right, maybe God really was leading him back to music, this time as a way to share his slowly rekindling faith. He'd never be famous, but he could be Kurt Wagner, faithful singer. That would be enough.

"Razz!" Pauly shouted a greeting.

Vanessa's head lifted. Standing in the entryway, hands in his pockets, Razzie gave her a shy smile before responding to his friend. "Hey, Pauly."

"Razzie's back!" reverberated through the house, and soon the Gathering Place was filled with excited chatter. Kids crowded around, guys slapping him on the back, girls hugging him, high-pitched squeals filling the air. It was a welcome for royalty.

Vanessa wrapped him in a warm embrace. "Welcome home," she whispered.

He gave her an awkward pat. "Thanks. I dunno how long I'm staying. I just wanted to make sure you weren't lettin' the place fall apart."

She grinned. "We appreciate that. Don't run off too soon, okay?"

Indecision flitted across his young face before he shrugged. "We'll see."

In the days that followed, Vanessa realized this was not the wisecracking young man who had teased her and Kurt mercilessly. This Razzie was serious, an intensity in his dark eyes she hadn't seen before.

When he told her he was trying to find Wolf, she begged him not to get into trouble with the volatile man. "Razz, promise you won't mess with him." She couldn't bear the thought of Wolf turning his erratic, explosive attention on the boy. And with Kurt gone, the threats had stopped. There was no point in stirring things up.

Razzie assured her he was being careful, that his detective work was on the down low. "I'm just tryin' to find out what his problem is."

Her fingers curled around his forearm as they stood in Kurt's office. "It's hard enough with Kurt gone. If something happened to you—"

"Nothin's gonna happen, Van." He hugged her. "I'll be careful. Until Wagner gets back, somebody's gotta watch out for you."

A few nights later as Vanessa updated the River House Facebook page, Razzie's quiet statement at the close of yesterday's Bible Study floated to mind. "Life's not what you expect. Get over it and move on." There was such pain in the words, but also wisdom beyond his seventeen years. The kind born of adversity and struggle and sorrow.

"Oh, Kurt," she sighed. "Razzie needs you so much. Please hear his heart."

She opened Facebook, hoping Kurt still checked his page, although not a word had been changed since he left. His silence magnified her loneliness. Finishing the River House update, she sent a message begging him to call Razz, to touch base and hopefully touch his broken heart. And as she slid into bed, she prayed for them to connect enough to heal both their wounded souls.

Razzie hung around River House the rest of the week. Vanessa watched Joel step into Kurt's role with the boy, taking him to lunch, checking in with him daily. She was thrilled when Razzie decided to start an evening study for the guys, to share what he learned from Joel.

He spoke openly about his new friend Jesus, calling Him the "coolest guy to hang with." He was quick to relate some of the talks he'd had with Kurt over the summer, encouraging and challenging the other kids to be more and expect more out of life.

That Friday the door blew open and he strode into the House with a broad smile. Vanessa couldn't help grinning at his youthful enthusiasm.

"Looks like you got some good news," she observed.

Energy radiated through the sparkle in his dark eyes and the bounce in his feet. "A couple of good things. First, I got that job I applied for. The one at the restaurant?"

"Razzie, that's great!"

He laughed nervously. "I never had a real job before. I hope I don't mess it up."

"You'll do great. You're a hard worker. When do you start?"

"Monday." He rubbed his neck. "I kinda need some new clothes. Black pants and a white shirt. And black shoes."

He'd never asked for money. Or anything else. Vanessa was delighted to help him. "Let me get you one of the gift cards—"

"No, I don't need money. Well I do, but...I was thinkin'...would you maybe go with me? I don't know how to buy nice clothes and I don't think my mom would pick out the right stuff."

The uncertain boy was still there, crouched behind the wall he'd erected around his heart. "I'd love to. How about Sunday afternoon? We could run over to Kohl's."

"That'd be great. Thanks."

"So what other good news do you have?"

The big smile reappeared. "Wagner called last night."

"He did?" Vanessa's heart skipped a beat as she stared at him, relief and hurt colliding. So he *did* read her messages. She pushed a smile to her face. "That's great!"

"Yeah. I was really surprised. When he cut off his cell phone, I figured he didn't want to talk to us anymore. But now he's got a new one and he just wanted to check in, see how I'm doing."

The old pain rushed out of hiding and knocked her breath away. She kept the smile plastered on, nodding as he relayed the conversation. Talking to her occasionally would hardly jeopardize her safety. Obviously he thought it would. Or maybe he didn't care anymore. Maybe—

"He asked how you're doing," Razzie said.

She blinked. "You told him I'm fine, I assume."

"I told him you're hurting big time."

"Razz!"

His eyebrows shot up. "What? You are. He needs to know that."

"No, he doesn't. He made a huge sacrifice leaving here. We don't need to make him feel worse."

Confusion darkened his face. "But you don't want him to think you just forgot about him."

A knot formed in her throat. "He knows I miss him. But I don't want him worrying about me. Will you be talking to him again?"

"Yeah. He said I could call him."

"Good. I want you to tell him we're all doing fine. Okay? Promise you'll do that?"

He held her gaze for a long, frowning moment. "I think it's wrong but okay."

"It's not a lie, Razz. I *am* doing fine. We all miss him like crazy, but God is holding us up, helping us move forward."

He blew out a breath that sent his long bangs fluttering upward. "Yeah, but still…"

The front door opened, letting in a stream of kids and cold air, and their quiet moment evaporated. As activity filled the house, Vanessa returned to her work, thankful Kurt had reached out to Razzie. That the boy desperately needed the contact had been obvious. That Kurt didn't see her own need was equally obvious.

That night she sent a simple message. "Thanks."

Vanessa awoke Thanksgiving Day with such a large lump in her throat, she thought she was sick. As the significance of the day broke through the fog of sleep, burning tears spilled out and she turned her face back to the pillow. She had dreaded this first Thanksgiving without the kids, never dreaming it would also be without Kurt. What was the point of getting up? She didn't want to face the day. Right now she didn't want to face life.

A whine from the kitchen made her sigh. She would feed Gracie and let her out, then they would both go back to bed. Joel and Jackie would understand when she called to say she was going to skip the festivities. Grace gave a sharp bark and Vanessa slid out of bed and into sweat pants and a tattered gray hoodie, wiping her eyes on the sleeve.

The puppy's cheerful face gazed up from the kennel, her little rear end wagging furiously. Vanessa couldn't help the smile that touched her mouth in response. Out in the cold, gray morning, she shivered as she urged Grace to do her business. Back inside, she fed the animals then stood at the counter, looking out at the fresh layer of snow on the lawn.

The teakettle's sharp whistle matched the stab in her chest, and she stood for a long moment pushing back against the despair. When she opened her eyes, her gaze landed on the pumpkin pie recipe she had set out last night. She'd promised to bring two pies and a pan of bars for dessert. The Bartens had gone out of their way to be kind and supportive. She had no right to spoil the holiday for them.

She pulled out the pie plates and got busy.

45

The sharp ring of the phone broke into her dream. Vanessa's hand snuck out from under the covers to stop the noise, pulling the phone back under the comforter. "Hello."

"Vanessa, this is Elwood Hauge. You need to come to the house right away. There's been a shooting."

She bolted upright. "What? Who?"

"Come now. Please hurry. There are police everywhere. They need you." The tremble in his voice slapped her awake.

"I'm coming right now. I'll be right there." She struggled to pull on the bionic leg and fumbled for her clothes. *This can't be real.* The call was a nightmare echo of Kurt's cry for help the night of the fire. Her panic mounted. *Kurt.* What if he'd had slipped back into town to confront Wolf and it had gone horribly wrong?

"Please, God. Don't let it be Kurt," she begged as she raced out the front door.

Moments later she faced a scene eerily similar to that terrible night, minus the smoke. Blinding lights on police cars, people huddled together against the harsh wind. Ambulances waited at the curb, doors wide open.

"No, no, no." The words matched her steps as she ran the last half-block. Three bodies lay on the ground, paramedics working intently on two of them.

She stopped beside a police officer, grasping his sleeve as she gasped for breath. "I work here. What happened?"

"We're trying to figure that out, ma'am. What's your name?"

"Vanessa Jordan." When one of the paramedics moved to the

side, she saw the boy's pale face in the floodlights. Her hand went to her mouth. "Razzie! Oh, God, no. No!"

When she started toward him, the officer restrained her. "Please, ma'am. Stay back here."

Another set of paramedics worked on a figure not far from Razzie. The third body, a large man, was sprawled on his back farther along the sidewalk, arms spread wide. Two police officers squatted beside him, writing in their notepads. Another stood over them taking pictures of the body.

Ashley darted up, dark eyes wide. "A neighbor called me. What happened?"

"I don't know. I can see Razzie. There are two other guys. I can't tell... Oh, no! It's Burger." The man on his back was too big to be Kurt. She wobbled under nauseating relief. The shadows from the light made it hard to focus but the profile was vaguely familiar.

Razzie was being loaded into one ambulance, Burger into the other.

"We have to follow them. I need to be there."

The officer stopped her again. "Miss, we need to get some information first. You called the boy Razzie? Do you know his full name?"

"Brian Razidon. He's going to be eighteen next month. And he's going to finish high school this summer. He promised." Tears burned paths down her cold cheeks. "He said he would stay away from Wolf, that he'd be careful."

"Who is Wolf?"

Her gaze went to the body on the sidewalk. "A terrible man. He's caused so much trouble for Kurt and River House. Razzie said he wouldn't get into trouble. Please, I need to get to the hospital."

"I'll stay and answer questions," Ashley said. "Maybe Mr. Hauge will take you to the hospital. I'll be there as fast as I can. And I'll call their families."

This time in the ER, she was the one at the desk asking questions, standing alone in the waiting area. Only her. She paced the waiting area, watching the wall clock as it ticked off each minute from 1:30 to 2:15.

"Miss Jordan?"

She spun around. A doctor stood just behind her. "How is he?"

"Are you his family?"

"I'm a good friend. Ashley is calling his family. How is he?"

When he indicated for her to sit, she shook her head. "Please!"

He pursed his lips. "I'm sorry. He didn't make it."

She stared at him blankly. *What?* No. This wasn't happening. She needed to wake up. She blinked hard to ward off his words.

"The bullets hit several organs." The words bounced off the walls, reverberating in her mind. She struggled again to focus. "There was too much internal damage, and he'd lost too much blood by the time help arrived. I'm very sorry."

Sorry. The end of another young life and all there was to say was "sorry."

"I don't...this doesn't..." She put a shaking hand to her forehead. No. *No!* "Can I see him?"

"They're cleaning him up right now. I'll have the nurse come get you in a minute." He pressed her arm briefly and left the room.

She looked up at the ceiling, hands lifted in question. "Why? Why didn't you stop it!? What's the point of this?"

A grim-faced nurse led her down a long, silent hall to a room at the far end. Razzie lay on his back, his young face calm and gray. A pale blue sheet was pulled up over his chest. Vanessa stood for a moment at the foot of the bed before glancing at the nurse and nodding. The woman pulled the door closed behind her.

Vanessa approached slowly, willing him to open his eyes and tell her it was all a joke. She brushed the dark hair from his cold forehead with shaking fingers. "Razzie, you promised..."

Sinking into a chair beside the bed, she reached for his hand. It was cold, stiff. She prayed for him, for the kids who would be devastated, for Kurt. She prayed for River House and for God to lead them through the grief. She prayed through endless tears until a hand settled on her shoulder. It was the nurse. Behind her stood a sobbing woman with Razzie's dark coloring.

For the next hour, Vanessa stayed with Mrs. Razidon, telling stories of Razzie's work at River House, his teasing, his love for Kurt and Kurt's for him. When she finally left the woman at his bedside, she went to the circular desk to learn that Burger was alive and under arrest for Razzie's death. Burger's gun had taken his friend's life.

She walked out into the lobby and into Joel's waiting arms.

Emotions ran deep and strong at River House that day. Between heavy silences, anger would explode from one of the boys, followed by tearful questions from the girls. Disbelief hung over the house as kids huddled at a makeshift memorial in the yard. The mound continued to grow with flowers, handmade signs, stuffed animals, and blue balloons.

Vanessa hugged, consoled, encouraged, and talked with every teen who came through the door. Her determination to help them through their sorrow kept her moving all day from one kid to another, one hug to the next. Ashley handed her another box of tissues and reminded her to eat, her own eyes puffy and red. Vanessa obediently took several bites of a dry sandwich before returning to the grief-stricken teens.

Mike hung with the kids, answered the phone, and accepted donations from the stunned neighbors to pay for the funeral of a boy who had been an unlikely friend to the community.

River House stayed open through the night. Pauly, Tiffani, and others crashed on the couches and the floor. Restless and unable to close her eyes without seeing the grisly murder scene, Vanessa turned on her computer.

An email from Razzie, sent just hours before the shooting, popped up. She stared at his words with disbelieving eyes. After reading it several times, she closed herself in Kurt's office, laid her head on her arms and sobbed.

"No way." Mike's whisper sliced into the silence. He read the email a second time and his large frame deflated. "He set them up."

Vanessa had woken him where he slept in the family room. She'd needed someone to read the email and tell her she was crazy, that it didn't say what she thought. Mike did the opposite, staring at her in disbelief. He motioned to her and they closed themselves in Kurt's office.

She slumped into a chair and rubbed her aching temples. "He promised he wouldn't do anything stupid. He *promised*."

The room pulsed with anguish. Mike met her gaze. "He didn't think it was stupid. He needed to clear Kurt. He thought if he could take Wolf out, Kurt could come home."

Exhaustion made it hard to put the pieces together. "But Wolf knew Kurt left the state."

"Sounds like Razzie put the word out that Kurt was back. Apparently he lured Wolf to River House. He was wearing that gray hoodie Kurt gave him. He looks so much like Kurt, especially in the dark, Wolf probably couldn't tell the difference.

"So," he finished with a deep sigh, "whether he died in the attempt or went to prison, he was deliberate in his actions. He actually laid down his life for Kurt."

Arms folded across her stomach, Vanessa leaned forward and began to rock. "How can we tell him?"

"I don't know, munchkin."

She pushed to her feet and paced the room, pausing at the window to stare at the flowers mounded on the spot where Razzie was shot. The world felt tenuous, unsafe. And so unworthy of the sacrifices made by Kurt and Razzie. The twisted mind of one man had ruined so many lives and threatened the ministry of River House.

"You okay, kid?"

The gentle words floated into her muddled thoughts. She was slow to look at him. "I have to be. We all have to be. For the kids' sake."

He trudged across the room to stand before her; his large hands settled on her shoulders. "Have you slept yet?"

She shrugged. "Every time I close my eyes...I'll sleep later."

"We both need to crash for a while. Ashley said she'd be here by 9:30, so when she gets here, you go home."

When she started to protest, he held up a hand. "I'll go once Joel gets here. Neither of us will do the kids any good if we're falling apart. Deal?"

She held his serious gaze, wanting to offer assurance that she would be okay. Would she? She nodded. "Deal."

46

Kurt answered his cell phone on the second ring as he put the finishing touches to his newest song. "Hey, Joel. Good to hear from you."

"Kurt, I wish I were calling just to say hi, but I have some bad news. I wanted to be sure you heard it from me before you saw it online somewhere."

He straightened, heart in his throat. "Vanessa."

"She's fine. It's…Razzie."

Joel's voice held a tone Kurt had never heard. His fingers tightened around the phone.

"He died early yesterday morning after a shooting."

"What?" Kurt's heart squeezed. Not Razzie. Not the kid with so much potential, so much life ahead of him. His other little brother.

Not Razz. Please, God. Let it be a mistake. Please…

"It's going to be really painful, but I want you to hear me on this. Razzie's actions are not a reflection on you, your past or because of your decision to leave town. This isn't your responsibility, although I know you're going to think it is. It's about the choices Razzie made, and what he thought he needed to do."

Kurt held his breath, trying to prepare himself. When Joel finished, he realized nothing could have prepared him. He managed a few words before hanging up, then sat motionless in the chair, staring out the window until daylight faded from the apartment.

Razzie was dead because of him. Every stupid choice he'd ever made led to this. His screwed-up life had killed Razzie as sure as if he'd held the gun himself.

He paced the small living room, bombarded by finger-pointing accusations that raced through his head. There wasn't a foul name on the planet he didn't call himself, not an ugly or scathing thought that didn't play across his heart.

The pages of the new song mocked him from the table. Who was he kidding? With an oath, he threw the papers across the room, stomping on them, shredding them. His songs were garbage. He could pretend he had answers, that God was *the* answer, but one look at his life and everyone would see he knew nothing.

Aching rage filled his heart and he cleared the rest of the table with a single swipe, then dumped it on its side. Songwriting was a joke. Life was a joke.

There was no sleep that night, no peace for his broken heart. By noon the next day he'd returned from the liquor store and finished half of the first bottle of whiskey. He had no reason to stay sober now. He could never redeem his past, never erase the sacrifice Razzie made for him. And he couldn't face a future that was guaranteed to hurt one more person he loved.

Vanessa was lost to him, and better off for it. Joel had more important things to do than continue to drag him out of the mire of his life. Mike and Ashley were busy running River House. Scott and Hayley were raising their perfect family while living in the perfect house and having perfect friends. He was a blight on Scott's future.

"So here's to me. World's biggest loser." He forced down another mouthful of the foul tasting liquid. And the world went a shade grayer.

The memorial service for Razzie was held at Faith Church. People lined up down the block waiting to get in—River House neighbors and Faith members, kids who knew him and kids who had only heard about him.

Tiffani brought a huge bouquet of balloons in Razzie's favorite blue. Several of the boys came in black leather jackets similar to Razzie's. Pauly stood at the foot of the casket the entire evening as if to protect his idol from any last threats.

News had spread on the grapevine that Razzie died protecting Kurt's name, killed by his own friend but only after shooting Wolf. Razzie's courage was lifted high by River House kids as the story unfolded in the crowded room. Vanessa heard snippets as she moved among them.

"Pauly said the whole thing is on video. Razzie set up a camera for proof."

"Whoa. Great idea. He was really thinkin'."

A few more hugs and Vanessa heard another piece of the story between two boys who were regulars at River House.

"Wolf thought Kurt ratted him out during the drug bust and that's why he was in the joint longer than everyone else. An' when he said somethin' about hurting Vanessa, that's when Razz shot him. Got him with one shot."

"I heard it was Burger that was the rat," the other boy added. "And that made Razz so mad he shot him too."

"Yeah," the first boy said, shaking his head sadly, "but Burger got off the last couple of shots. Razz should've beat it outta there. Then he wouldn't be dead."

Vanessa squeezed her eyes shut against a stab of guilt. To know that Razzie had been protecting her as well as Kurt made his death that much more difficult. If only she had known what he was planning, maybe—

"Van?"

She turned. Tiffani waited with wide, tear-filled eyes. They hugged for a long moment. Vanessa offered another tissue when the girl finally let go.

"Do you think it's true?" Tiffani hiccupped.

"What, hon?"

"That Razzie pretended to be Kurt to get Wolf to face him?"

She brushed Tiffani's dark hair back from her wet cheek and nodded. "It seems that was his plan. He couldn't stand Kurt being away and he wanted to put an end to the whole thing."

Tiffani drew a shaky breath, her forehead creased in confusion. "But didn't he know he might get shot? Why would he do that?"

Vanessa sighed, praying for words to comfort her. To comfort them both. "Razzie was willing to do what he thought he had to, to get to the truth, but he went about it the wrong way. Violence isn't the way to fix things. That's why Kurt didn't fight back. He wanted to live his life and deal with problems the way he knew Jesus would want him to."

The service ran nearly two hours as person after person stood to share a story about how Razzie had impacted them. Razzie's mother and younger brother sat in the front row, sandwiched between River House staff. Neither spoke during the service, often moved to tears by the stories. Directly behind them sat Elwood and Priscilla Hauge, pale and silent.

Vanessa was the last to go to the podium, praying for strength and dry eyes. She stood for a moment, looking from one familiar, tearful face to the next. He had touched so many people.

"Razzie was such a cool guy." There was a smattering of applause in response. "He was, to me, the epitome of a diamond in the rough. But we were starting to see a lot more of the diamond. He didn't want anyone to know how smart he was. He had a tough guy image to uphold.

"From the first time he came to River House, he continued to grow in his faith. He loved Jesus with his whole heart." She released a shaky breath and looked at his mother. "He was so important to all of us, but especially to Kurt. He told me he wanted to be like Kurt when he got older, working with kids, making a difference in people's lives. I don't think either of them understood the impact they had on each other."

Turning her gaze to the casket covered with white carnations, balloons waving gently above, she managed a crooked smile. "Heaven isn't the same now that Brian Razidon is there. Save a place for us, Razz. We'll see you soon."

Kurt covered his eyes from the blinding sunlight, turning his head away. His stomach churned, its vile contents rising up in a wave that sent him staggering for the bathroom. Afterwards he sat slumped beside the toilet, head on his arm. Man, he hadn't been this sick in a long time. It had to be the flu. He was shaking so hard he could barely sit up.

Needing to rinse his mouth, he pushed himself to his feet and wobbled out of the bathroom, a hand over his eyes to block the light.

"Looking for another drink?" A voice stopped him before he reached the kitchen.

The words were angry, accusing, and Kurt stood still, squinting toward the living room. "What?"

Scott unfolded himself from the couch and crossed the room to loom over him. The anger vibrating from him made Kurt feel small and shriveled. "I must have the flu. I can't remember the last time I felt like this."

"It was the last time you were drunk."

His icy tone made Kurt blink in confusion. "What are you...?" The words dwindled as a memory took shape. Sitting on the floor with a bottle in his hand. *But I don't drink anymore.*

Scott grabbed his shoulders in a biting grip, giving him a shake. "What is wrong with you? You can't drink, Kurt. Ever. But here you are, hung over like some homeless bum, your apartment trashed, and you want me to buy that you have the flu? How stupid do you think I am?"

Kurt pushed him away and lurched toward where the kitchen table had been. It was lying on its side, the chairs tipped over as well. It took a moment for his trembling grasp to get one upright then he fell into it and dropped his head into his hands. Another memory flashed past. A phone call. Tears.

"Why would you go on a binge like this?"

Eyes closed, Kurt shook his head. "I don't drink, Scott. I'm sorry you think I'm such a los—" The word brought yet another memory to mind. Hoisting a toast to someone. *World's biggest loser.* The words reverberated through his jumbled brain.

His head lifted and he opened his eyes fully for the first time since waking. The room was a mess. Papers everywhere, stuff knocked to the floor, furniture overturned. It looked like there'd been a brawl. He frowned at Scott. "What happened to my apartment?"

Scott glared back at him in disgust. "You tell me. When you didn't answer your phone, I got worried. This is what I saw when I got here."

Kurt let his gaze roam the room, trying to force the memories to the surface. There'd been a phone call. Joel. Something about Vanessa? No, not Nessa. Something was wrong with Razz.

The truth slammed into his gut and he dropped his head back into his hands. Razzie was dead and it was his fault. His attempt to drink himself to death hadn't worked.

"I'm ready when you are," Scott said.

He couldn't say the words aloud. It was his fault the boy he loved almost as much as Scott was dead. He had killed him. This was the worst of all of his screwups.

No, he couldn't say it out loud. Scott would just have to think he fell off the wagon. He hadn't fallen—he'd jumped. "I decided to have a party."

"Try again."

Blazing fury pushed him to his feet. He didn't have to answer to anyone. It was his stupid life. "You know what, Scott? I don't have to make excuses for what I do in my own apartment. If you don't like it, go back to your perfect world and leave me alone. I don't remember inviting you here anyway."

Scott blinked.

Kurt pushed over the stab of regret. "I'm sure Hayley needs you for something, so why don't you run along and be a good husband and daddy. I don't need you." *I can screw up what's left of my life just fine on my own.*

"I'm thinking you do."

"Well, you're wrong. Maybe you get all the answers right at your job, pal, but you don't have all the answers for my life. So get out of here. I have things to do."

"Like drink yourself to death?"

Kurt shrugged and brushed past him. "That's one option. I have a lot of 'em."

"Maybe I don't want you to kill yourself." Through the angry words, he sounded young and scared. "Maybe your dying would be hard on Hayley and Lily. God knows why, but it might even be hard on *me*. So maybe you should just grow up and realize that."

The guilt was paralyzing, suffocating, and Kurt spun around, shoving Scott with both hands. His brother crashed back against the wall but didn't fall.

Kurt staggered sideways, flinging an arm toward the door. "Maybe you should get out! I don't need your self-righteous little presence. Go find someone else to guilt. Now get out!"

Scott stared at him, eyes wide. Kurt struggled to stay upright, desperate to hold onto the anger and not let the despair send him to his knees. After what seemed like forever, Scott turned and stalked from the apartment, and Kurt dropped against the wall, sliding down to the floor.

He had now successfully driven away everyone who mattered in his life. He could die in peace. Alone and as wasted as he wanted to be.

47

Vanessa found it impossible to focus. Every ounce of joy had been sucked from life. Joel mentioned he'd talked to Kurt the day after the shooting but hadn't been able to reach him in the week since. Knowing he would blame himself for Razzie's death, she was afraid to consider what that grief and guilt would do to him. So she prayed for his broken heart—in half-sentences, in muddled thoughts, often without words.

The atmosphere around River House was somber, conversations subdued, attention spans shorter than usual. In the midst of his own sadness, Mike was working as hard as he could to keep the kids engaged and talking. He looked exhausted.

Chen and Keith stopped by the House on Saturday to say goodbye. In the weeks they had shadowed her, she'd come to rely on their steady presence. There were no words to express her gratitude for their vigilance and friendship. Saying goodbye to them was like losing another connection with Kurt.

Her restless heart knew only one refuge.

That evening, she stood alone in the silence of the sanctuary at Faith Church. Turning on the stage lights and a few periphery lights, she settled in the second pew and waited. For what, she didn't know.

In the stillness, she could hear Joel's passionate voice preaching words of truth and youthful voices lifted in praise. She heard the whisper of prayers, the laughter of greetings and the joy of friends in conversation. Surrounding her, lifting her, she heard the very life of the church.

She'd stood here alone after the fire looking for answers, surprised when her broken heart began to mend that very night. And as she'd stood here beside Kurt on Sunday evenings, she'd slowly released her anger, accepting life for what it was. Through him, she'd learned to laugh again, to love with abandon. Working with the kids had given her purpose and meaning. But her life had splintered into a million pieces the moment he walked out of her life.

Shedding her coat, she wandered toward the front. The old boombox used for rehearsal sat at the edge of the stage. She pressed the CD button and the voices of a trio filled the sanctuary, singing a song she'd never heard. The music stirred something deep within, filling her, calling her to the cross. She stood at the steps, head back as she looked up at it, and a soothing warmth poured over her, quieting the inner battle.

The song ended and she hit Play again. This time she walked up the steps, pausing to remove her boots. In the middle of the stage, she lifted her arms. The words of forgiveness and encouragement flowed through her, rising straight up through her heart and out her fingertips.

Using her bionic leg to propel her, she spun lightly on her toes with arms spread wide. Dancing beneath the cross, she released the sorrow and fear that had held her captive for weeks. The fog lifted and cleared. Understanding flooded her soul. God loved her with a passion beyond comprehension. He'd cried with her when the kids died and held her as she grieved. He had protected Kurt through every attack. And dear Razzie was done being the swaggering tough guy and could now just hang with Jesus the way he'd wanted.

Her empty heart now overflowed with thankfulness for the love she'd experienced, tempered by sadness for what was gone and uncertainty for the future. But He would be there too. She stretched toward Him, thrilling at the joy that surged through her veins, amazed at how her legs moved without conscious thought.

She twirled around the stage then held an arabesque, lifting her gaze to the cross. As the song ended she sank to the floor, overwhelmed and exhausted. Indescribable peace stole over her and she rested her forehead on her knee as she slowly relaxed, breathless.

She and Kurt were not alone. They were still connected over the weeks and miles that separated them, by a God who knew the desires of their hearts and fanned the tiny flame of hope that kept them moving forward.

It was enough.

The banging set Kurt's head pounding and he pulled the pillow over his face. When it continued, he pushed off the couch and stumbled to the door. "Stop pounding!"

Scott and Sherm waited in the hall. Kurt rolled his eyes and turned away, swallowing against the turmoil in his stomach. *Great.* Another fight, with his boss watching this time.

"Sherm called, wondering why you missed work," Scott said.

"I'm a little under the weather. But come in anyway and have a seat. Can I get you a drink?" He was only half kidding. The cold silence was like a slap upside the head. "It was a joke."

"Uh-huh."

He plopped onto a dining room chair as Scott cleared off the couch. Sherm settled next to Scott and the room grew quiet.

"Joel called last night," Scott said. "I know about your friend Razzie. I'm really sorry, Kutty."

The childhood nickname burned into Kurt's heart. He gave a stiff nod and looked away, tapping his foot.

"Now that I know the whole story, the drinking makes sense. It's stupid, but it makes sense."

"Yeah. I do stupid well."

"You also do compassion well. And you live your faith well. Joel knew you'd blame yourself for what Razzie did. I'm not surprised, either. You've always cared for other people more than yourself."

The unexpected words blew warmth across his frozen heart and stung his eyes. He didn't do anything well that he could see. Actually, he could still drink pretty good. Clenching his shaking hands, he ran his tongue over his fuzzy teeth. A drink would be good at this point. Didn't even have to be liquor. Anything to wash the foul taste from his mouth.

Sherm spoke up. "I thought hearing my story might help with what you're going through."

Kurt shrugged. It couldn't come close to the guilt and loss that were his constant companions.

"I killed my best friend."

Okay, that's close.

"Accidentally, but that didn't matter. Since we'd been drinking beforehand, and I already had two DWIs on my record, I spent the next six years in prison.

"I'd gone through treatment two times before the accident but I didn't have my heart in it. My wife stood by me through the treatments, but she'd had enough when I went to prison." He sighed. "I couldn't blame her. She stuck around a lot longer than I would have.

"I was in a jazz ensemble that was pretty well known around here. Prison changed that. I lost my job in the ensemble, my wife left with our two kids, my best friend was dead. I'd pretty much destroyed every good thing in my life."

Kurt sat very still. *This better have a good ending or I'm gonna open another bottle.*

"When I was in the joint, I hooked up with Prison Fellowship. Jesus changed my life from the inside out. He made a new man out of the sorry mess I'd become. It wasn't easy, but I started working on making better decisions, thinking about the people around me instead of just what I needed or wanted. Life got better when I got Jesus-focused instead of me-focused."

A smile broke across Sherm's round face and something stirred inside Kurt.

"Since getting out twelve years ago, I've gotten married and have three great step-kids. I started the music store and have been doing my best to make amends to my family and the community. That's why I started the studio, to help other musicians make their dreams come true. And I spend time talking to guys like you, who are guys like me.

"I know you know Jesus, Kurt. I'm here to remind you that

nothing will ever matter as much as Him, no matter how low your life goes. It's all about Him. He knows what you're going through and He cares."

Kurt looked around the disheveled room that mirrored the chaos in his heart. He knew there could be redemption like Sherm's. He just didn't know if he could make that uphill climb. It would be so hard and the inevitable fall so horrendous.

"What plans do you have now?" Sherm asked.

"None at the moment."

"I'd like to spend some time with you this week. And I think attending a few AA meetings would be a good idea."

There was a long silence as Kurt rubbed a hand over his face. He had nothing else to do. And certainly nothing left to lose.

Sherm stayed glued to Kurt's side in the hours and days that followed. They attended AA meetings every evening, walked the neighborhood, played hoops at the deserted park. And talked. With each passing hour, Kurt was able to share another piece of his childhood, another brick that had built the wall around his heart.

At the coffee shop late the third evening, he sighed and picked at the styrofoam cup. "I don't remember ever having a real conversation with my dad. He'd come home from work and expect it to be perfectly quiet while he read the paper. We never talked at dinner."

He stared into the distant memories. "I could never understand what my mom saw in him. She was so—just so much better than him in every way. He was a jerk."

The story continued into the next day. The first time his dad backhanded him after some innocuous comment was the start of war as far as Kurt was concerned. He would do whatever was necessary to keep his dad's anger away from his mom and little brother. He learned to be quick on his feet and took perverse pleasure in making the old man work to catch him.

"The day my dad left home for good was the happiest day of my twelve-year-old life," he said as they cooled down after one-on-one basketball on Wednesday.

"I'll bet the tension level went down a few thousand notches."

"Yup. My mom had to get a job, which I know was hard on her. But she started looking better, healthier. And happier." He could hear his mother's laughter across the years. He wiped the sweat from his face with the bottom of his T-shirt. "I'd never seen her happy before that.

"When she started dating Don, I was pretty mad. I didn't see why we needed a man around. *I* was the man of the house. But he was really nice to her. He started hanging around playing catch with Scotty, doing stuff with both of us that my dad never did."

"So he was a good guy?"

"Yeah. She was beautiful on their wedding day." He could still see her that sunny spring afternoon. Cheeks pink, radiant in a light blue dress with flowers in her hair, she'd smiled all day. "She was so happy. They all were—Don, my mom, Scotty. I tried to be, but at that point I'd forgotten how. So I just tried not to be a jerk. It was my wedding present to her," he added with a half-smile. "It was the best a nearly fourteen-year-old could do."

Don had borne the brunt of Kurt's anger and disillusionment. Giving Kurt the guitar when he turned fourteen was a peace offering that Kurt grabbed onto like a drowning boy. Playing gave him a sense of accomplishment and pride.

He'd rediscovered those feelings while building River House, and again recently when writing songs. And then Razzie's death had blown it all out of the water. It had been raining pieces of his heart for the past week and he was tired.

By Friday evening, his story had come full circle. There was nothing left to share. Seated across from him at a diner, Sherm looked at him over a plate heaped with French fries, his gaze serious.

"Your friend Razzie's death was the last straw. You held it together through a childhood of abuse, a stint in prison, starting a new life, building a youth ministry, falling in love, and having your life threatened. You were smart enough to make a move to protect the people you love. Those aren't the actions of a loser, Kurt."

Kurt concentrated on his chocolate shake, forcing the ice cream past the lump in his throat. He hadn't thought of it that way.

"As a young kid you had the presence of mind to watch out for your kid brother and your mom. You had the inner strength even then to stand up to an out-of-control adult. Man, you are one amazing person. Can't you see that?"

He pressed his lips together and met Sherm's gaze. He'd been so used to thinking of himself as a loser, he didn't know there was another option. He shook his head.

"That doesn't surprise me." Sherm leaned back against the booth, a crease between his eyes. "I'll be praying for God to help you see the solid, dependable person you became, despite all the ugly stuff life threw at you. You have a really amazing story."

He grinned and folded his arms. "I can't imagine what you're going to accomplish in the next thirty years because you've already done some pretty powerful stuff, and you're just getting warmed up."

Kurt couldn't stop the answering grin that started in his heart and forced its way out. After a week of reliving his story, he was starting to see what Sherm meant. Yes, he'd screwed some things up, but he'd also done some good, thanks to God. And wasn't God in the business of taking broken, messed-up lives and making them whole? Wasn't that the message he longed to share with every teen who came through the door of River House?

It's time.

The words came back to him with a start. Maybe it was time. To go forward with a new attitude, accept Razzie's sacrifice and find a way to make it count. Time to stop acting like a loser and be the man God was calling him to be.

"Kurt, my boy!" Kurt held the cell phone away from his ear as Sherm's hearty voice returned his greeting the next day. "Good to hear from you. Feeling better?"

"Yeah, lots. I just wanted to say thanks." It had been a long week. Jumping off the wagon was a lot easier than climbing back on. But with God's help, he was on with both feet now.

"My friend, it was an honor spending time with you. So, we didn't talk about your schedule. Coming in this weekend?"

"I'll be there tomorrow. What time do you want me?"

"Noon would be good. Oh, and we'll have to find time to talk about what my friend Mark had to say about your songs. He called last night."

Kurt's stomach flipped over. He should never have put his music out there for someone else to judge. "Why don't you just tell me now? Let's get it over with."

"You sure you want to hear it over the phone?"

"Beats waiting. Give it to me straight."

The pause was deafening. "Okay. Well, the way I see it, you've got two choices. One is to stay here in Seattle and work with me on producing your debut record. The other is to go back to Minneapolis and work with Mark Simmons at Simmons Music Production. The offer is wide open at both places."

Kurt blinked several times and shivered.

"Well, how about that. I actually shocked you into silence." Sherm chuckled. "I'm thinkin' this is a pretty good dilemma to be in, picking between the two."

"He liked my stuff?"

"Liked it? He called before he finished listening to the third song. And Mark Simmons has a solid reputation for producing only great stuff, so you can take his opinion to the bank. You can't go wrong working with him and SMP.

"On the other hand, you wouldn't go wrong working with me either. We'd be partners in producing the CD exactly the way you want, hands-on learning for you. 'Course, you'd get some of that at SMP as well, but I'm funnier than Mark."

Kurt smiled at Sherm's unbridled enthusiasm. "He liked my stuff," he repeated, finding it difficult to process. "You both like my stuff."

"You better change that attitude, pal. You've got major talent but if you don't believe in yourself, nobody else will. There's good reason the two of us want to produce it. You've got amazing potential and this album will jump-start the career you want."

Reality cracked through the dam of disbelief, and panic washed over him. "But I need more songs. You only sent him three. How many should be on the album?"

"Twelve, if we can pull it off. Think you've got nine more up your sleeve?"

"I'll look up both sleeves and under my hat too." Thank God he'd only had one long weekend of drinking. *If you hadn't sobered me up, Lord, I'd be blowing this opportunity just like before.*

"Good. Get your hind end back to the table and finish what you're working on, pronto. And take some time kicking your options around. We'll talk when you come in tomorrow."

"Okay." There was a stunned smile in the word.

He spent the next few days holed up in the apartment, working hard on the new tunes rolling around his head. And he prayed.

The chance to start his career with Mark Simmons was not

something to pass up lightly. He could have a CD produced at the same place his friend Peter had recorded his top-of-the-chart hits. Yet going back to Minneapolis meant facing his demons, revisiting everything that had brought him amazing highs and devastating lows. His stomach clenched. *Maybe they blame me for Razzie's death.*

Staying in Seattle would give him the opportunity for more hands-on involvement in producing the CD. And he was beyond grateful for everything Sherm had done for him. Staying near Scott and his growing family would be amazing.

In the end, there was no contest.

Minneapolis meant Vanessa, the woman who held his heart. He could only pray she hadn't given up on him.

At the Bartens' urging, Vanessa moved into the guest room for the few days leading up to Christmas. The children adored Gracie, who had doubled in size and personality, and they loved snuggling as Vanessa read to them each night. Their warm bodies and hugs were balm to her heart.

Christmas morning was a riot of gift opening. The noisy, loving chaos was completely different from the quiet holiday she had shared with Angie and Matt, but she reveled in the action with few tears and lots of laughter.

In the afternoon, she asked Joel to drive her to River House in case any kids showed up. What she didn't say was that she needed to be where she felt closest to her family. And to Kurt.

Parked in the driveway, Joel raised an eyebrow. "You're sure you want to be alone?"

She nodded. "I expect a few of the kids will wander over at some point." She touched his arm and smiled. "I'm okay. Really. I'll see you in a few hours."

Inside the quiet house, Vanessa set Gracie down, turned on lights and plugged in the Christmas tree before going to the kitchen to make tea. Christmas music drifting from her iPod, she wandered the main floor, pausing before the twinkling lights of the tree. She closed her eyes and drew the memories close. Razzie's teasing voice, Tiffani's grins as they bantered with her about Kurt. The sweet scent of the cookies she'd been baking and the kids' excitement when the news had exploded about Kurt's musical past. And Kurt's whispered assurances of love as he held her...

Gracie's whine at the back door jerked her from the past. She let her in and watched her dash upstairs to curl up on Kurt's bed, then she continued her rounds, sipping the peppermint tea. In the days before Christmas, the House had been filled with energy and excitement. The low-cost gift exchange had been a hit. She'd been amazed at the ingenuity of every gift and the appreciation expressed as each was opened.

She paused before Razzie's photograph on the wall, the one Mike had taken the day Razz gave his life to Christ. The light in the teen's face still touched her deeply.

Emptiness enveloped her as she stepped into Kurt's office. With Wolf dead, she had hoped he'd come rushing home, but still no call, no email. Nothing. Had he truly forgotten her so quickly?

Setting her mug on his desk, she stared out the window at bare branches silhouetted against a winter sky. Tears burned paths down her cheeks and she dropped her head, crying silently. How she missed her family. How she ached for Kurt. *Please bring him home.*

Hearing the muffled sound of the front door, she clamped down on the tears, wiping her face. Joel had probably come back to check on her. Footsteps approached and she pulled in a steadying breath that stuck in her throat when she saw the reflection in the window.

She turned in slow motion.

"Hi." His dark eyes locked onto hers, an uncertain tinge to his shy smile. "Remember me?"

49

Vanessa stared at him for a long silent moment, eyes wide, her expression unreadable. At least she hadn't thrown something at him or run screaming from the room. Since getting off the plane an hour ago, he'd thought of nothing but seeing her again. Paralyzing fear had almost kept him from following Joel's directive to find her here.

He was unable to breathe as he waited for her to say something. Anything. How was it possible she was even more beautiful than when he'd left?

Her eyes narrowed. "Are you real?"

"I am."

She blinked quickly, shaking her head slightly. "How did you know?"

He moved closer. "Know what?"

"How much I needed you tonight. I asked God to bring you home and here you are, just when I thought I couldn't be alone one more minute."

Relieved joy knotted his throat. He shoved his hands into his pockets to keep from sweeping her into his arms. "I needed to see you so bad, but I wasn't sure—"

Her stunned expression was as real as the smile filling her face. Wrapped in pulsing silence, they looked at each other. Finally he shook his head. "Only God knows how much I've missed you."

"It can't be more than I've missed you. To see that you're okay... I was so afraid Wolf would follow you across the country."

The sound of her voice made his heart tremble. "He lost interest when I left the state. I hoped he would lose interest in everything."

"You know about Razzie."

"Yeah." Grief punched the air from his lungs.

"It's not your fault, Kurt. It was his decision. No one blames you, you know," she added softly.

No one? His eyes stung as he managed a nod. "That's good to know."

A shadow crossed her face, tugging the corners of her sweet mouth down. "So all this time...why didn't you call? Or answer my emails? You talked to Razz and Joel and Mike, but never to me."

Here we go. Help, Lord. "I didn't think Wolf would follow me if I left town, but I wasn't so sure he'd leave you alone. The last note I got was threatening *you*. That's why I hired Keith and Chen. And made sure Mike kept an eye on you all the time."

Her frown deepened. "That's nice and comforting, but it doesn't explain why you wouldn't at least talk to me. In all this time, no calls? No response to any of my posts? Did you think he was tracking your phone or your email?"

They stood facing each other, the future hanging unspoken between them. *Jesus, give me the right words. I can't lose her again.*

"I carried your picture with me everywhere. I put it on the nightstand by my bed. I can't tell you how many times I started an email or dialed your number but I always stopped myself. It wasn't fair to hold onto you." He released a short breath and turned away, shaking his head. "You weren't mine to keep."

Her silence was louder than if she'd shouted at him. He closed his eyes, waiting.

"I don't understand."

He turned his head. She looked at him in classic Vanessa style—focused, expectant. She looked angry and hurt and so beautiful. "Nessa, I didn't know if I'd ever be able to come back. It wasn't fair to keep you waiting for something that might not happen. I wanted you to be free to move on with your life."

She pursed her lips, slowly shaking her head. "*You* don't

understand."

He raised his eyebrows.

"When you left, you *took* my heart. There was nothing left to give to someone else even if I'd wanted to someday."

He took a step toward her then stopped, blood pulsing in his temples.

"When I fell for you," she said softly, "it was hard and complete and for good. If you never came back, I just..." She shrugged and looked away. "I just figured I was on my own."

He closed the distance between them to grasp her shoulders. "Vanessa, you will never be alone again. If you can forgive me, I'll spend the rest of my life making this up to you."

Her brow slowly relaxed as they studied each other. Finally she rolled her eyes. "Kurt Wagner, I want to be mad at you. I want you to know how much this has hurt." Her tone softened as she relaxed in his grip. "But...I understand the sacrifice you made. I know you gave it all up for me."

She set trembling fingers against his cheek. "You are the bravest, strongest, kindest man I've ever known. And if you think for one second I'm going to let you go again—"

Kurt pulled her into the kiss he'd gone to sleep every night dreaming of—full of life, love and commitment. Joy, deep and powerful, sent a shock through his body and his heart shouted its thanks to the heavens. It was over—the agony of waiting and praying and hoping. By God's grace, he was home.

A short time later they nestled on the couch, sharing stories of the past weeks, hands clasped, heads together. Gracie had settled contentedly in the crook of Kurt's arm after giving his face a thorough bath. His delighted laughter sent happiness dancing across Vanessa's skin.

Christmas had burst into color. Beautiful carols floated from the kitchen. The tree glowed in glorious abandon, its tiny lights winking at her as if sharing in her joy. And Kurt held her hand between his. Tightly.

"Hey, you won't believe this." He sat up and faced her. "Sherm, the owner of the music store I was telling you about? He's friends with Mark Simmons, the guy who owns Simmons Music Production here in the Twin Cities."

"That's where Peter had his CD done, right?"

"Yup. And now I'll have mine produced there too."

Vanessa stared at him, fingertips pressed to her mouth. "You're making a CD? Right here?"

His smile went ear to ear and she threw her arms around him, tears flooding her cheeks. *Thank you for answering his prayer. For filling his world with music again.*

"I'm thrilled for you, Kurt. And so excited to see where this leads you."

"Us. Wherever it leads me, you'll be right there with me." He brushed her bangs to the side. "I don't ever want to be apart from you again, sweetheart."

"I don't either. While you were gone, there were times when I felt so lonely. But then something incredible happened. I was alone at Faith one evening just...sitting. Waiting. I didn't even know what I was there for. I turned on the CD player and the most amazing song came on. And...I danced. For God."

His eyes widened. "Danced? Like, for real danced?"

"For real." The memory still thrilled her. "Not exactly the way I used to, but I danced."

Leaping to his feet, he pulled her up and swung her around. "Vanessa can dance! Woo hoo!" When he finally set her down, they were laughing and breathless.

"Wow!" Kurt said. "God has given us back what we love most—each other, River House, and our music." His expression brightened. "It's something we can do together!"

She frowned. "How?"

"Have you heard of worship dance? It's an actual ministry. A way to worship through music and movement."

Her heart thumped so hard she pressed a trembling hand over it. *I can do that! I could even teach the kids.* His music. Her dance.

"Nessa? What's wrong?"

As she looked into his beloved face, a rainbow of joy and gratitude burst within. "Nothing," she assured him. "I'm just trying to soak it all in. This morning I had no clue what tomorrow would look like. Now I see it filled with everything I thought I'd lost."

Heavy footsteps on the porch sent Gracie flying off the couch, barking excitedly. The front door burst open and Mike barged in with Ashley close behind, followed by Joel, Jackie and their children. Kurt laughed at the tears on his face as he hugged each one.

Word spread quickly of Kurt's return and within an hour, Pauly, Tiffani, Natalie, and others filled River House with laughter and excited conversation. More than a few tears flowed as they shared memories of Razzie. Vanessa's heart swelled as she watched Kurt with the kids he loved.

But even as he chatted with the ever-growing group, he was never more than a few steps from her. He kept hold of her hand, whispered in her ear, or just looked at her with a silly grin when they had a moment alone. She was sure her feet hadn't touched the floor since that first kiss in his office.

The impromptu party went on long into the evening as more people arrived to welcome him home. The Hauges stopped by to see what the commotion was about. Elwood's eyes went wide when Kurt appeared before him and for once, Vanessa noted with smiling satisfaction, Elwood Hauge was speechless.

Kurt gave him a hug and pressed a gentle kiss to Mrs. Hauge's cheek before they left. There was childlike joy on Kurt's face as he waved to them. When he turned to her a moment later and gathered her in his arms, that same joy tingled through her. She leaned into his embrace, legs trembling under his smile.

Standing in the Gathering Place, amidst the people they loved the most, he held her gaze, cocking his head. "You know what I hear?"

She smiled. "Noise?"

"The sound of God's grace in our lives. All these people, this House, our future together. It's God's love pouring over us."

The awe in his voice brought a fresh rush of tears up her throat. It took several attempts before she could respond. "I've never thought to listen for grace, but you're right. This is what it sounds like."

His grin deepened, a spark of mischief on his face. "And I hear one voice in particular."

She raised her eyebrows, toes curling in her Christmas socks.

"Razzie's. Want to know what he's saying?"

She shivered and nodded.

"Kiss her, you geek."

And he did.

Four years later

Standing alone in the cemetery in the quiet shade of a maple, Vanessa traced her fingers across the headstones and smiled.

"Hi guys, it's me. I haven't been here for a while, but I'm sure you understand." She folded her arms over her extended stomach. "Life is so busy with a toddler. Angelique is two and a half now, and she's the spitting image of you, Angie. She's full of dynamite, and she dances and sings through the whole day."

She chuckled, shaking her head. "And she's as feisty as you too. When she doesn't want to do something, look out. She stomps her foot like you did. I have to work hard not to laugh sometimes. Other times, not so much.

"The baby is due any day." She ran a hand over her stomach. "It's a boy this time." Her gaze ran to Matt's image carved in the marble. "I'm sure he'll have the same music running through him that you and his father have. We've decided to call him Matthew Scott." She smiled. "I know you'd have loved that."

As she wandered to the next headstone, her smile turned bittersweet. "Mom, I miss you so much. When Angel was born, all I could think was how thrilled you and her other grandma would have been. I know you're rejoicing in heaven, but I just—" Tears threatened and she blinked hard. "I wish you were here to help me do this mommy thing. I'm glad you taught me so well, but sometimes I wish we could just sit and have tea together…and talk. I could use some reassurance."

She drew a steadying breath. "Anyway, it's good to be home now after all the traveling we've done the past few years. You should hear Kurt's music—it's fabulous. We couldn't believe how the worship and dance ministry took off.

"I've been working at River House and the Children's Hospital. We started a new program for kids called RazzleDazzle, using music and dance to help them deal with surgery and traumatic injuries. It's been so well received—people call from hospitals across the country wanting to learn how to do it."

She wrapped her arms around herself and smiled. "And you'd be proud of Kurt, Mom. He finished his degree at seminary last winter, the same time I finished mine—finally. He's amazing, and I think I fall deeper in love with him every day. I know he's exactly the kind of man you hoped I would find."

"Mama!"

Vanessa turned to see their tiny, white-haired daughter racing across the grass, Kurt and Grace close behind. Vanessa bent to hoist her into her arms. Chubby arms wrapped around her neck, and Vanessa breathed in her sweet innocence.

"Hi, baby girl. Did you have a good nap?"

"Mm-hmm." She leaned back and put her hands on Vanessa's cheeks, her expression serious. "You sad, Mama?"

"Why would I be sad, honey?"

"'Cause—cause—Daddy said you might be an'—an'—we should he'p you," she said solemnly.

Vanessa's gaze met Kurt's as he came up beside them, and they shared a wink. Turning back to Angelique, she shook her head. "No, I'm not sad, honey, but thank you for coming to check on me. I'm never sad when you and Daddy and Gracie are around."

"I'm hungry," Angel declared.

Her parents laughed. "Well then, we'd better go have a cracker since it will be a while before supper." Vanessa let her gaze run back to the headstones. "I'll come back after the baby is born," she said softly.

Kurt reached for Angelique, then put a gentle arm around

Vanessa. "Ready to go?"

She reveled in the love and encouragement in his dark eyes. With a firm nod, she smiled. "Yes."

Angel slipped out of Kurt's arms to dance down the path as Grace bounded ahead to lead them home.

The Lord is faithful to all His promises and loving toward all He has made. The Lord upholds all those who fall and lifts up all who are bowed down.

Psalm 145:13b–14

Gratitude Beyond Words

As always, one of the most amazing parts of my writing journey has been encountering the people God put in my life along the way. Here are just a few who have helped make this second book possible.

Thank You to...

Mike, my husband extraordinaire. Thanks for decades of laughs and great memories.

Camry and Nate, Aaron and Rosanna – What a blessing to be inspired by such godly, caring young adults.

"Special K" and "Eb" – Being Gramma just continues to be a hoot! You're my favorite munchkins.

Brenda Anderson – God's smiling instrument of peace and encouragement, and extraordinary patience.

My family – Constant in reassurance, love and support.

My girlfriends – The most wonderful BFFs ever. On to New York!

Nina Engen – An amazing editor and even more amazing friend.

Noelle Epp – An inspiring and creative graphic designer.

My readers – For sharing sweet notes of praise and encouragement, and spreading the word. You rock!

And to...

All of the wonderful, talented writerly people God has put in my life. Critique partners, retreat buddies, chapter-mates, brainstormers, chocolate lovers, dedicated servants of Christ. What a joy to create alongside every one of you!

Thank you, Sweet Jesus, for the privilege of serving you through writing.

About the Author

Stacy Monson writes stories that show an extraordinary God at work in ordinary life. Dance of Grace is her second novel in the Chain of Lakes series; Shattered Image released in April 2015. A member of ACFW (American Christian Fiction Writers), Stacy is the current secretary and past president of MN-N.I.C.E., as well as the area coordinator for ACFW in Minnesota. Residing in the Twin Cities, she is the wife of a juggling, unicycling physical education teacher, mom to two amazing kids and two wonderful in-law kids, and very proud grandma.

For more information visit www.stacymonson.com.

Made in the USA
San Bernardino, CA
11 October 2015